A
FRACTURED
REIGN

CROWNED CROWS BOOK III

VERONICA EDEN

A FRACTURED REIGN

Copyright © 2022 Veronica Eden

Photography: Michelle Lancaster | @lanefotograph | www.michellelancaster.com
Model: Josh Culley

AUTHOR'S NOTE

This is the third book in the Crowned Crows series following a gritty brotherhood of antihero bad boys and the feisty heroines that capture their hearts. Each book in the series should be read in order to understand the continuing plot, each book is not intended to be read as a standalone. If you're not a fan of morally bankrupt book boyfriends, steer clear.

This mature new adult romance contains dubious situations, crude language, and intense sexual/violent content that some readers might find triggering or offensive. **Content warning** for themes of past abuse and neglect, dubious consent, suicide, and mentions of past rape and trafficking. Please proceed with caution.

Crowned Crows series:
#1 Crowned Crows of Thorne Point
#2 Loyalty in the Shadows
#3 A Fractured Reign
#4 The Kings of Ruin

Sign up for Veronica's newsletter to receive exclusive content and news about upcoming releases: bit.ly/venewsletter

Follow Veronica on BookBub for new release alerts: bookbub.com/authors/veronica-eden

ABOUT THE BOOK

THE CROWS ARE MORE THAN NIGHTMARES LURKING IN EVERY SHADOW. THEY'RE A BROTHERHOOD. FAMILY. WHEN THREATS CREEP IN, THEY'LL PROTECT WHAT BELONGS TO THEM.

QUINN

Does a wrong make a right?

In my case, it has to.

The Kings gave me no choice, no chance to fold.

I betrayed the guy who believed he was protecting me while I gave his secrets away.

Now we're enemies once more.

My brother and I burned all our bridges. Begging Colton DuPont for his help again is my only option.

The Crows demand a steep price, but to buy our safety I'll do anything.

Even sell my soul to the man who wants me dead.

COLTON

Our unmatched reign is going up in flames.

And I know exactly who our enemy is. *Quinn Walker.*

My queen turned out to be my downfall.

Any danger to my brothers is a threat I won't allow.

Once these flames sputter to ashes and the dust settles, our next hunt begins.

My monster has come out to play, and I won't rest until I get revenge.

Burn me once, shame on you. Burn me twice?

Baby, you better run, because I'm coming for you.

PLAYLIST

Enemy—Imagine Dragons, JID, League of Legends

cut my fingers off—Ethan Bortnick

FEEL NOTHING—The Plot in You

Revenge—Mariah the Scientist

Enemy—Tommee Profitt, Beacon Light, Sam Tinnesz

skeletons—KINGS, Drew Ryn

Never Say Die—Neoni

Chaos Mode—DEZI

Chaos—Like A Storm

REVENGE—$werve, Leftoz

ALL GIRLS ARE THE SAME—RØNIN

Vendetta—UNSECRET, Krigarè

Fed Up—Ghostemane

The Search—NF

Nemesis—Ryllz

Don't Forget(to Forget Me)—CoaastGxd

"Give my your hand out of the depths sown by your sorrow."

Pablo Neruda

SERIES RECAP

PREVIOUSLY IN THE CROWNED CROWS SERIES...

WELCOME to Thorne Point, where darkness rules. In this gritty city on the coast of Maine, everyone who is anyone can be found amongst the city's elite high society, and their heirs populate the prestigious Thorne Point University.

Rumors run rampant throughout the campus about the mafia-esque Crowned Crows—four friends, the richest boys in school, and the ones who run everything on campus. Wren Thorne, the ruthless king of control. Levi Astor, the brooding shadow and lethal fighter. Colton DuPont, the cocky jokester and genius hacker. And Jude Morales, the enigmatic conman. Their reign doesn't stop there, stretching across the city where it's said they own the night.

A transfer student, feisty hacking queen Quinn Walker, and her brother Sampson seek out the Crows and pay their steep price: a secret. Intrigued to find a fellow computer savant with hacking skills on his level and a clever mind that meets his constant flirtation with sharp wit, Colton provides his help, allowing them to take shelter in his apartment. He tests her skills for his own gains and finds she's willing to take on any job he presents her with as long as she's paid for it.

Something else is at work in Thorne Point and the Crowned Crows are the target. They have been unraveling the web of secrets surrounding a secret society called the Kings since the first moment Rowan Hannigan came to them to find her missing brother, followed by Isla Vonn's foiled kidnapping. With each new discovery of how deeply ingrained the Kings are with the city's history, they've pulled back on the bigger picture.

As they gained more answers, they realized nothing is a coincidence in this city. Isla's traumatic past was another piece to the puzzle they've been putting together. None of them are willing to stand for what the Kings represent: monstrous greed and a sickening inclination to use any means to achieve power. With her brooding champion Levi vowing to always protect her, Isla and the crew challenge the Kings at a masquerade ball hiding the Kings true entertainment in a sinister operation known as the Castle.

Following their victory against the Castle, the Crows were poised to strike back against the Kings. They know who their enemies are now that they've crept out from the shadows and they'll fight for control over the city. But Colton's computer system was infiltrated by a mysterious hacker moments before the Nest was consumed in fire, leaving the group in grave peril.

The Crow's Nest Hotel—their home, the symbol of their power—is no more.

TP
U
THORNE POINT UNIVERSITY

CHAPTER ONE
COLTON

Fire and smoke closes in from all sides. It doesn't just choke us out, it blocks mine and Jude's path to escape.

"Fuck!" The frustrated curse costs me, leaving me hacking on a lungful of putrid black smoke.

With a grunt, I adjust Jude's weight, re-securing his arm slung around my burned shoulder. I grit my teeth against the white-hot pain and we hobble in another direction. The others better have gotten out. I can't think about them right now, my stomach churning at the images flashing through my head of my best friends perishing in the flames.

No. *Fuck* no.

Jude grimaces in pain, gesturing for another way to try down a hall that leads to the terrace behind the Crow's Nest Hotel. He tests putting weight on his hurt leg and falters.

Everything was going as fine as it could while racing against time to avoid a fiery demise, but we got separated from our friends when the hallway shit the bed, collapsing on Jude's leg. Burning debris rained on me as I struggled to get him out from under the rubble pinning him, singeing through my hoodie. Hurts like a goddamn bitch, but we have to keep moving. We'll deal with the fallout once we're not in danger of suffocating or burning alive.

"Just—stop. I've got you." I won't let him go until we're out of this crusty century old death trap.

Sweat pours into my stinging eyes and the roar of the blazing inferno surrounding us has my heart pounding a million miles a minute. Or maybe that's the third energy drink I downed before everything went to shit, now converting into pure fear-fueled adrenaline to keep my heart pumping at a cool 200 beats per minute. Roughly. I'm not stopping to check my smartwatch to find out. I'm operating purely on survival mode, and it'll be game fucking over if I make one more wrong move.

My first screw up was thinking I could trust the hacker who infiltrated my system. There's only one person I know with the skill to match mine—Quinn Walker. The girl I let into our lives, the one I was too busy flirting with to disconnect my brain from my dick. I'm livid she gained access to my private network. She better hope she's not in my apartment when I get there, because when I get my hands on her I'll wrap them around her pretty little neck and squeeze until she screa—

Jude halts, holding me back from walking into a hole in the floor.

Right. First we need to get out of the burning building before I plot revenge. Life and death shit.

Focus.

We carefully weave through the deadly flames. The sound roars in my ears. Keep moving. Don't stop. The mantra repeats as we reach the end of the hall.

The Nest has seen better days, but we liked it in its decrepit state. Seeing it decimated by destruction is a shock that doesn't fully register until we burst through a bay window and scrabble over the stone window ledge to get out. Jude grunts in pain, dragging his leg to keep up with the faster pace I set now that we're not navigating Satan's asshole. I don't stop until we stumble down the stone steps to the weed-choked dead grass above the cliffside the hotel sits on, both of us struck by what we escaped.

Holy fuck.

We gape at our haven, the place we built our legacy around, our goddamn *home*. It's gone. The Nest is fucking gone.

A deep, cutting ache lances through my chest.

My mind races now that we're not in imminent danger of succumbing to death right along with the hotel. It runs through what happened in an attempt to make sense of the situation. One minute, we were all together still riding the high of our win against the micro-dick energy secret society working in our goddamn shadows, ripe for our next win when I finally decoded Ethan Hannigan's file on the bastards, and the next—

An explosion.

My fists curl, a caustic, lethal anger spreading through me. For once, I get Levi's inclination for knives. I could use one right about now.

Quinn is a dead hacker walking. My little queen distracted me with the ways she challenges me, countering my flirting with a bite that turned me the fuck on. I was too busy dreaming of all the ways I wanted to play with her tight, sexy little body and make her scream from my tongue, hands, and cock. Was that her plan all along? Because she fucking succeeded in clouding my head from analyzing what's been in front of me this whole time. I never screw up like this—not when it comes to keeping threats at bay from what me and my boys have built.

There's no way she's working alone.

Burn me once, shame on you. Burn me twice? Baby, you better fucking run because I'm coming for you.

"Let's find the others," Jude forces out. "We have to make sure they got out, too."

"Shit, yeah."

Tearing my gaze from the fire, anxiety at the unknown constricts my throat and turns my stomach to a raging acid bath. The Nest was our home, but our friends are more than that. We're all fucking family. If anything happened to them—I slam down on the thought, refusal rocketing through me.

Before the hallway collapsed, we were all heading for the front of the hotel. "They must have gotten out through the ballroom."

Nodding, Jude limps with a stony expression, not complaining about how fast I rush around the side of the property. The flickering light from the burning building illuminates his face, his bronze skin sallow, damp tendrils of hair matted against his forehead. We made it out alive, but the image of the wall collapsing on him and the sound of his yell when the rubble pinned him is seared into my mind. I tighten my grip on my brother, clenching my jaw.

Whoever is responsible for blowing up our Nest is going to pay for this. Not only for taking a swing at us, but for putting my boys and their girls at risk.

A Crow will always remember the enemy, and we show no fucking mercy.

CHAPTER TWO
QUINN

"Let that be the end of their rebellion in Thorne Point."

I hate this guy's nasally voice every time I have to endure his supervision. Right now, it barely registers over the sound of my thundering heart.

"They truly think it's alright to threaten potential legacies?"

The question comes from the other man in the room. He stands by the windows in the dark corporate office overlooking the city. He's new, someone I haven't seen before.

From the first time he tracked me down at Castlebrook College and lured me into the back of his limo, Fitz Mortimer has always been alone when he reaches out to me with a task in exchange for payment. That's the only reason I'm here at all—the money.

I fucked up. Never should have listened to a man with a superior attitude and an unsettling gleam of ambition in his beady eyes.

Each barely controlled breath I drag in without trying to draw attention to my turmoil scrapes my throat raw as I stare at the screen. If I'd known this is why Mortimer wanted me—I didn't, though. I didn't know he wanted me to get close so he could hurt them.

"Even if they spurned the path opened for them, they're the future," the stranger adds.

"Exposing one of our most lucrative ventures is a step further than spurning a path, I'd say," Mortimer answers. "Extreme correction is the only solution."

I fucked up so hard.

"Still, Thorne won't be pleased with his name tied to this since that hotel is part of his family's legacy."

Mortimer scoffs. "A failed part of it. His son used it for his own whims. Thorne would do well to remember that he doesn't hold all the power in this city just because his family dates back to the founders. He can fall just as easily, opening up opportunities for us to advance our positions. Rebellion won't be tolerated. Any threat to our goals is one we cannot ignore."

The pompous men's voices filter in and out behind me. I can't focus on the rest of their conversation, too shaken by shock and horror. It's difficult to breathe. I can't look away from the awful sight before me on the laptop screen.

The hotel succumbs to flames from the explosion in a matter of minutes. The flames burn so fast, eating through the old architecture, collapsing the infamous ballroom where I dressed as Nyx for their themed Halloween party last month.

I drop my hands into my lap, the stiletto points of my manicure digging into my thighs to claw back my hold on my emotions. Don't let them see. They can't know I'm affected.

This is what I get for not asking questions. Do Mortimer's tasks, get the money. Simple. Easy. Fuck, fuck, *fuck*.

God, were they still inside? The admin window still open beside the video feed that I used to access the network says CONNECTION LOST. It drives a spike into my chest. My heart beats hard and a lump lodges in my throat. Did they get out?

Is Colton trapped in there?

Sharp pain drills a hole through my heart. My nostrils flare as I try to control my breathing. I dip my head, my braids falling in my face to hide from my handlers.

I did what Mortimer wanted. I got close enough to Colton DuPont to figure out how to access his system. My jaw clenches to smother the cry of anguish that has threatened to tear free in the last ten minutes when everything went to shit.

"Proceed. Trigger the C4."

The second my finger hit the key to execute the system purge of Colton's local network, Mortimer's order sounded behind me while he hovered to ensure I did exactly as he demanded. He'd muttered what an asset I am to him, that he was glad he'd discovered me. The bastard thanked me for my loyalty, whatever the fuck that was supposed to mean.

My only true loyalty is to my brother, Sampson, and myself.

Colton's cocky grin filters through my mind, making my heart beat harder. It doesn't stop there—something he'd love if he ever knew how much I had to wrangle myself around him—his playful demeanor, the swoop of his messy brown hair over his devious green eyes when he peers at me, and the way his fingers are always drumming on something all surfacing in my memories, amplifying the anguish choking me.

I didn't know. The lump in my throat becomes unbearable and my vision blurs as tears well in my eyes. I bite my lip to keep them from falling. I didn't fucking know they were going to blow up the Crow's Nest Hotel.

Teeth clenching, I crush the memory of his smile and the way his eyes always light up with mischief. We were an almost that was never meant to be. I was only there because of the money. It wasn't real.

We never would have crossed paths otherwise. It's not like he and his buddies would ever have helped me the way they supposedly do favors for others. Not after they caught me making bank at their card games.

For the first time since Mortimer made me that offer when he found me the morning after cleaning up at one of the illicit poker games on campus, regret blooms inside me like a poisonous, deadly plant, taking root in me. My skewed, often-ignored sense of right and wrong flickers to life to underline how badly I screwed up.

Don't let them see. Never show any weaknesses. I won't let anyone know I'm getting emotional over Colton DuPont and his friends. I can't. I have to keep surviving. It's Sammy and me. That's what this has all been for.

A sharp pain slices through my chest. The barbed wire that's meant to protect my heart pricks deeper as I will the burning building on the video feed to show someone getting out safely.

I bite the inside of my lip hard to halt the sting of tears. If I didn't follow the orders I was given, it could be Sammy in that fire. It could be me. This is what the men like Mortimer in this city are capable of. Awful, monstrous acts to achieve their goals.

Colton is nothing to me. A flirtatious fuckboy. Someone I could never have, not if he found out why I was sent to him for help. I will myself to believe it, but it doesn't stop the concern carving a hole in my sternum.

My stomach clenches. Not everything between us was a lie.

It's just another hard-knock lesson my life served up—that I have to fight twice as hard as anyone just for the right to exist, and if I don't then everything will be ripped from me. My inheritance was stolen, my life uprooted by the greed of others.

I press my lips together, typing a key sequence with shaking fingers to change the angle on the building. Bile climbs my throat, my stomach roiling at the devastation I inadvertently had a hand in.

Colton was so proud of that place. I could tell it was more than a party spot the Crows used to flex their power.

And I'm the reason it's gone.

Don't do it, Q. Stay quiet. Head down. Survivors don't ask questions.

"This isn't right. I thought I was just erasing the stolen information."

Shit. My idiot mouth just went and ran itself.

Mortimer and the stranger stop their proud chuckling and back patting.

"What was that, Miss Walker?" Mortimer drawls.

Fuck. Why am I going out on a limb?

"Nothing," I mutter.

"I believe you mean nothing, *sir*."

I hold my breath, clenching my jaw hard enough the dull ache spreads down my neck. He gives a satisfied, egotistical snicker, aware of how much his correction rakes across my nerve endings. My net worth would be more than his if my family's money wasn't stolen. My IQ is also far higher, yet even if I had the wealth taken from me, he'd continue believing he's better than me. Would still look down on me. He's the type of man who enjoys his position of power over me.

"And I do believe I heard an unwarranted opinion from you," he continues in a tone of false concern.

"No." I try to backpedal, hating myself for it.

Survival outweighs pride. Now's not the time to school this motherfucker.

"I don't pay you for your moral compass," he sneers. "You have no idea what we represent."

"My mistake." I swallow the acid flooding my mouth, aware of their stares boring into the back of my skull expectantly. "*Sir*."

The word tastes like disgusting defeat. If my granny could see me now...

If ever there was a time she watched over me after her death put Sammy and me through a life of hell, I hope she looks away now as I bow my head demurely to hide the furious spark in my eyes.

"I'm glad you've realized your error." Leaning over my shoulder and drowning me in the stench of his pungent cologne, he takes the liberty of touching my laptop.

Wrestling back the side of me that wants to chew his hand off for touching the one thing in this world I hold as dearly as my brother is damn near impossible. As I force my skin not to crawl when his chest presses against the back of my head, he pulls up the administrative backend for the security company partnered with Thorne Point University.

"Thorne Point's greatest pride is our future. The legacy of greatness fostered in the students who receive an education at the university—many of whom are descendants of the city's founding families."

My blood runs cold as he clicks into the security feed on campus. The small video on the screen shows my brother at his internship.

Sammy started last week. He was so relieved his application was chosen amongst the hundreds who applied for the position with the school's law department.

The realization slams into me so hard it knocks the wind out of me. My brother wasn't selected based on merit.

"We can take opportunities away as easily as we can present them."

Fuck. The threat is clear: keep my head down or Sammy's future is at risk. They plan to use him to keep me in line.

How did I miss this? I'm the one who keeps us safe. It's my job to think five steps ahead, yet my blindspot was open.

Colton. My gaze flicks to the raging inferno visible at the edge of the new window.

He distracted me. Took my mind off my goals with his joking smiles and the late nights he stayed up with me at his place while I was faking the need to lay low. Faking the need for his help and the protection the Crows offer to those that bribe them with secrets.

"We would hate to see another promising future crushed. You understand, Miss Walker?" I nod, unable to form words. It's taking everything I have to control the rage quaking inside me. "You're such a smart girl."

Fuck his smarmy praise. It's empty, another way for him to say he owns me.

No one fucking owns me.

"Your payment will be wired to your account. I'll contact you the usual way. For now, it's best if you keep a discreet profile." He plants his hands on the desk, forcing me to hunch lower in the cage of his arms to keep him from touching me. "We wouldn't want anyone to connect you to this terrible incident at the old hotel. Though it's always been an eyesore, I'm aware it's a popular party spot for university students."

Another veiled threat to tug tighter on the invisible leash Mortimer believes he holds to control me.

"Got it," I say tonelessly.

He finally steps back and allows me to pack up my gear. I tuck my laptop away and sling the backpack over my shoulder. Keeping my head down, I get the hell out of there while my mind races.

CHAPTER THREE
COLTON

The sight of Levi Astor falling to his knees in defeat, his girlfriend holding him back, is soul-crushing. It reignites my anger at Quinn and whoever the fuck she's working with. Working for, more likely. If I vetted her better, if I never let her in, this wouldn't be happening. Our home wouldn't be on fire, my family's lives at stake.

"Hey!" Jude shouts hoarsely. He limps faster, the two of us hobbling to get to our friends. "Here!"

Rowan whips toward us and releases a broken cry of relief. She sprints across the weeds and gravel, slamming into me like a force of nature. I grunt, letting go of Jude to return her embrace. My throat clogs as I try to soothe her trembling, stroking her back with my own shaking hands. The others rush over in her wake, Isla wrapping her arms around Jude while he leans on Levi for support. Wren crushes Rowan between us, cupping the back of my head.

"I thought we'd lost you," she chokes out in a strained tone that breaks me.

"Can't get rid of me," I joke tightly.

Her laugh is more of a sob. She hugs the life out of me until I groan from the throbbing pain in my shoulder.

"Sorry." Rowan and Wren let go. She flutters her hands over me

"You're hurt?" Rage bleeds into Wren's words.

"The goddamn hall collapsed on us," Jude explains. "A piece of the wall pinned me. He got me out."

"Just a little banged up and burned. I'll be fine. I wasn't leaving him behind." I aim for a smile, unable to get further than an angry grimace while I wiggle my burned, blistering fingers. "Typing will suck. And jerking off. Any volunteers to help?"

Isla punches me in the side, then wraps her arms around me from behind. "Shit. Sorry." She sniffles. "I'm so glad you're both alive."

Levi passes Jude off to Wren and grabs a fistful of my hoodie, butting his head against mine. He doesn't speak, but I get it.

"Aww." I swallow past a thick, painful lump. "You do love me."

"Shut the fuck up, asshole," Levi mutters without letting go. If anything, he holds on tighter.

"They'll pay for this," Wren growls.

He faces the burning hotel. His broad frame is silhouetted by the flames. We have other property, but the Nest is the first symbol of the legacy we've spent the last five years building. It's not just Wren's history, his first success against his screwed up dad. This is our home. The place two of my best friends fell in love with their girls. Where people came to pay us their secrets and kneel at our feet in our shadows.

We became what we are today because of the hotel. Seeing it destroyed is gutting for all of us, especially Wren and me.

This loss is one we'll build back from—a plan to go bigger was already in motion in the last couple of weeks—but our pride takes a hit.

My fists clench. The pain fuels my hatred and fury. We won't show mercy. Not for Quinn once I track her ass down, and not for the bastards responsible for this.

"They really fucked up this time," I say coldly. "Fuck around with us and find out how hard we hit back."

My brothers give me vicious looks in agreement.

Rowan fits herself against Wren's side, twining their fingers together. "We have to show everyone in this city," she says fiercely, as thirsty for revenge as her King Crow is. I love how well she fits in with us. "Anyone connected is going down."

"Do you think it's related to Silas?" Isla's voice quavers. "Because we burned down his sick private club and killed him?"

The gutted old ruins of a tower the four of us are all too familiar with comes to mind. We didn't know when we went out to the sprawling estate outside of the city for the masquerade ball hiding the Castle that it was the same place we were five years ago. The night Pippa betrayed us. The night we burned down that tower. The night that girl died.

"All his friends," I spit. "They want to play eye for an eye. Except I don't believe in eye for an eye. Someone comes for my eye, I'm cutting off their fucking arms and legs."

The gears in my head turn faster now that we're out of immediate danger. I rake a hand through my damp, dirty hair and work my jaw. We had no idea then that our first job would connect to a bigger web of bullshit. For all I know, the tower was part of the Castle, too.

"Before the explosion, what was going on with the computer?" Jude asks.

My fists clench, the sensitive blisters on my hands throbbing with sharp pain. "I was hacked." I blow out a breath at the surprised looks the admission earns me. "It was Quinn. That hacker I've been—helping."

Fuck. Fucking fuck, she lied to me. She didn't need help.

This is my goddamn fault. I exposed us to this threat.

My gaze drops to the dead grass, unable to take it if my friends look at me in disappointment.

The wail of a fire truck's siren cuts through the dull roar of the waves crashing against the cliffside, red lights flickering against the treetops. The emergency responders will reach the top of the hill any minute.

"I need to go to the warehouse," I say. "My apartment might be compromised. Not that I kept anything important on that computer. I finished migrating everything from the Nest to the new setup at the warehouse two days ago."

"Good. Take Jude with you." Wren tears his attention from the hotel to cradle Rowan's face. He gives her a hard kiss. "I'll stay here with Levi to deal with this. Rowan, you and Isla go to our place. We'll pick you up when we're done here and we'll all meet up at the warehouse."

"You know how I feel about you treating me like I'm made of glass," Rowan grumbles, unwilling to let him go. She presses on tiptoe for another kiss and he obliges. "But I want to make sure our house is okay. Enjoy this moment of me doing what you say without a fight."

"I love you," he says against her lips. "If anything had happened to you—"

"Hey. It didn't." She touches his jaw. "We're all okay. We're alive. That's what matters."

Levi and I keep Jude between us as the five of us head for the terrace, Wren hanging behind to meet the emergency responders. The shockwave set off the alarms on half of them. I sigh in relief when my black Mustang is unharmed at the edge of cars lined up outside the hotel's original grand entrance.

The rest of our collection didn't fare as well. Levi and Jude freeze at the sight of their bikes on their sides, surrounded by broken glass from the blown out windows. They must have been parked too close when the explosion happened. A hunk of stone is embedded in the cracked windshield of Wren's prized Aston Martin. The paint on our other rides is chipped and scraped from the debris, some tires going flat with pieces of metal piercing them. At least Levi's SUV looks like it'll drive.

"Goddamn it," Levi mutters.

"You can afford a new motorcycle," Isla says. "Better a bike than your life."

"Or yours," he says gravely, a hint of vengeful psycho creeping out.

Eyes shining, she cups his face between her hands when he steps away from Jude's side, giving him a bright, tearful smile. Our group's little sunbeam can't be snuffed out. "Come back to me."

"Always." He kisses her forehead before capturing her mouth.

I help Jude hobble to my ride. He catches my eye and his throat bobs. He's not one to show his true emotions to anyone but us.

"What's that look for?"

His attention shifts to the Nest. "Take me to Pippa."

I stiffen. "Try again. You asked to go to the hospital, but you said it weird."

"Fuck off." A muscle in his jaw twitches. "I need to see her."

"You hit your head in there?"

"Just do it, you dick."

Groaning, I get behind the wheel. "Your near-death trauma response is skewed as hell, brother."

He glares. "Shut up and drive, or I'll get there myself."

* * *

Standing outside of Pippa's apartment, I side-eye Jude while playing with my tongue piercing out of idle habit. "I don't get why you wanted to come here."

"Yes you do," he mutters. "I just—needed to see her."

"You're a masochist." I shake my head and knock again, not giving a shit if I wake up her neighbors. "I know you're home! Your car's in the parking lot."

The door wrenches open, jerking the chain. Pippa's annoyed face fills the small crack. "What the hell do you—?" She cuts off once she gets a good look at us covered in soot and ash. Her horrified gaze locks on Jude. "Come in. You're an idiot. You should've gone straight to the hospital."

"If you die on her watch, I told you so." It comes out prickly.

My joking doesn't carry its usual lighthearted vibe. I'm too on edge from every possibility running through my head. An unhinged anger claws at my chest from the inside, hungry for brutal revenge. I'm itching to get my phone out to check Quinn's location in the tracking app I built and installed on her phone when she was in my shower.

Jude ignores my barb as we move through the cramped hall to Pippa's living room. Her apartment is even shittier than the last time we were here a few weeks ago to bring her in on our plan to kick the Kings Society in their damn balls. It still stings like salt in the wound to see her, the ex-Wendy to our band of crazy lost boys.

"Put him on the couch." Pippa bangs through her kitchen cabinets. I deposit Jude on the ratty cushions, muttering an apology when he curses in Spanish. Pippa bustles over with a bundle of first aid supplies in her arms, dumping them haphazardly next to him. "You should've at least gone home to your grandmother first. Why are you such a stubborn jackass?"

He snorts, then winces with another grimace. "I can't go home like this. Abue will skin me alive for getting hurt." He rubs at his nose, avoiding her eye. "I don't want to break her heart anymore than I have lately."

My stomach clenches at his honesty. He hasn't been by to see his grandmother much since this shitstorm with the secret society started. It's got to be killing him by now. That incredible woman basically adopted all of us once we befriended him at Thorne Point Academy, more of a mother to each of us than our own flesh and blood.

Not that the rest of us had winning parents—Wren's checked out after his sister's death, Levi's died and stuck him with his evil uncle, and mine... mine cared more about collecting gold stars by bringing up foster kids for a year at a time instead of giving a shit about me. I slam down on that direction of thoughts. Nothing good comes out of thinking of my childhood. The family I've chosen are the ones that matter.

"You're so infuriating." Pippa's voice is strained. She ducks her head, fussing with the first aid stuff.

"As ever," he mutters. "It's a medical condition. No cure."

I roll my eyes. These two drive me to the brink of insanity. I've never met two people that wreak misery on each other every chance they get, yet they're incapable of fully letting go of what they once had together.

Pippa's gaze bounces between Jude's leg and my singed hoodie. "These are serious burns. What happened?"

I cut Jude off. "We didn't come to chat."

He presses his lips together, chin dipping in the slightest inclination to signal to me he gets my distrust. We each understand how the rest of us think. He's got to be concussed to forget we don't know how the fire went down yet. The last time Pippa was involved while we dealt with a fire, things didn't go so hot. He's got the arson charge on his minor record to remind him.

I'm watchful of how she works efficiently to cut away his pant leg to access the injury. Sparing me a brief glance, she tosses some medical supplies at me. I catch them, locking my jaw when I register bandages, alcohol wipes, and antibiotic cream.

"Clean the burn on your shoulder with water," she orders. "Use the alcohol wipe for the cuts."

"I'm fine. Just worry about him, Pipsqueak."

Exhaling harshly, I struggle out of my ruined hoodie, swallowing back a groan as the sore, inflamed skin pulls. I'm panting by the time I have it off. Jude eyes me over Pippa's head while she examines the nasty burned gash above his knee.

"You're lucky the bone didn't break. The cut shouldn't need more than butterfly stitches, and this burn doesn't look like a third-degree." She fits herself between his legs, concentrating on the wound. "It should heal in a few weeks, but you'll need to keep it clean."

"Right back where you belong, baby girl," he croons in a cracked rasp. Her gaze flies up through her lashes. The corner of his mouth curls with a mix of bitterness and heartache. "On your knees."

I turn away from them because I can't. I can't do this right now with those two. My brain is overloaded with eight hundred and forty-two things, at least, and I'm reaching a damn limit. A stray manic thought passes through my brain about an article I read on twin flames at two in the morning while high. For as much as they're in tune, they're doomed to destroy each other.

My shoulder hurts like a bitch the more I think about it, unable to block out the pain receptors with selective thinking any longer. Gritting my teeth, I move to Pippa's bathroom. It's as small as the rest of her crap box apartment. Why the hell does she put up with living here when her family has money?

Tearing the alcohol wipe open with my teeth, I rinse my blistered fingers and dab at the cuts and scrapes on my palms.

I brace against the sink until the unbearable sting of rubbing alcohol eating my scraped hands alive subsides. If my hands hurt this bad, healing my shoulder is going to suck. How long does a burn take to heal? My fingers flex. Fuck, I don't want to get my phone right now to check.

My focus locks on to the first thing to catch my eye—a small teal vibrator sitting in the shower caddy. A laugh punches out of me. My grip tightens on the porcelain, but there's little I can do to wrestle my impulsive urges right now. I'm barely in control. I grab it, run it under the tap, and pocket it.

Dick move to steal a girl's shower vibrator, but I'm in a shitty as fuck mood and I don't want Pippa to have nice things right now.

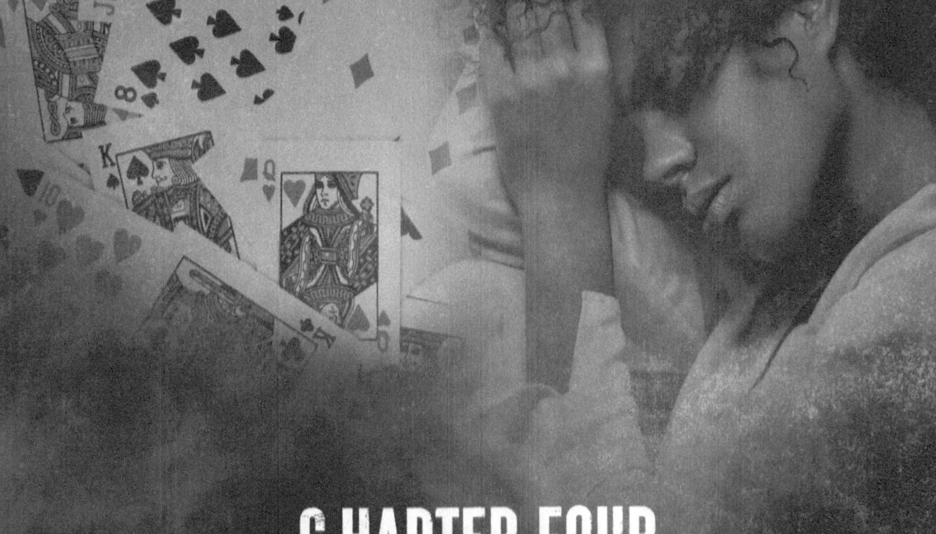

C HAPTER FOUR

QUINN

THE pop of a champagne bottle sounds behind me as I exit Fitz Mortimer's office, followed by his nasally, punchable voice.

"To advancement and our brighter futures. *Carpe regnum.*"

The words snag in my head, but my mind is too muddled to recall where I've heard the phrase. I'm too preoccupied by pressing thoughts about my brother's predicament.

How can I convince Sammy to quit the internship? He doesn't know everything I've been doing. He actually believes I was awarded a full ride to TPU and paid for his exorbitant tuition with my poker winnings from online games. We came to Thorne Point for better opportunities, but what he doesn't know is that I sold my soul to the highest bidder to get here.

It doesn't matter where I make my money. I accepted Mortimer's job because it was easy money, and while I worked to gain access to Colton, he amused himself by testing my hacking skills. He pays better, giving me a grand for every string of corrupted code I debugged for him.

I've stolen, lied, cheated—whatever I needed to do to make it out of the incompetent foster system we were thrust into, reunite with my brother, and work to scrape our way back to the life we were supposed to have. The life mercilessly wrenched from us when Astor Global Holdings bought out the company our grandparents built and bled it dry—then our estate through a loophole that gave them access to *everything*—until there was nothing left.

The hardest lesson I've ever learned is that the world will take, and take, and take from you whether you have anything left to give or not.

No one cared when our granny suffered a massive heart attack and died, leaving Sampson and me orphaned and penniless. No one helped.

Sighing, I rub my forehead. I'll figure something out. I always do.

The long hall to the bank of elevators is lit only by the fluorescent glow emanating from the small lounge area by the elevators. I can't wait the fifty floor descent and the drive to my other apartment—the one I really live at in Thorne Point when I'm not faking damsel in distress locked away in Colton's upscale tower with my brother.

Ducking into an alcove by another office near the one I left, I'm grateful for the shadows providing cover while I whip my backpack off and crouch low. Mortimer doesn't read code. Even hovering over me the whole time, he has no idea I slipped in a command to copy the file open on Colton's screen when I hacked my way in before I wiped everything.

If it was important enough information he wanted it erased, it interested me. I snagged the copy as leverage in case I ever need a bargaining chip.

I wake my laptop from sleep and skim the contents of what I downloaded. My brows lift higher the more I read. Thorne, Astor, Stone, Mortimer—the list of Thorne Point's wealthiest family names goes on. In addition to names there's a brief, confusing paragraph about castles and kingdoms, reading like it was hastily written. At the top of the page, two Latin phrases are defined—*carpe regnum* and *clavis ad regnum*. Seize the kingdom and keys to the kingdom, according to the translated note.

Wait. *Carpe regnum.*

Mortimer said it a minute ago. Tonight's not the first time I've heard it, either.

Colton muttered it to himself one night while I acted like I was ignoring him. He was in the zone, unaware of anything outside his field of focus, tuning out the world around him.

"Shit," I breathe.

What the hell is this? And why did Colton have it?

The elevator dings at the end of the hall, the sound making my heart skip a beat. It's after hours. I've never seen any staff staying late when I'm here. The only other people Mortimer keeps around are his roided up lackeys.

Heavy footsteps echo down the hall with purpose. I freeze, shutting my laptop silently and crouch lower in the shadows. Survival instinct kicks in, honed from eight years of watching my back once I was taken from my nice, normal life and plunged into the harsh reality of the world.

Something's off.

I know I'm right when a tall figure strides past my hiding spot and enters the office I left.

"Where's that computer girl you've kept around?" he grunts brusquely.

Oh shit. I recognize his voice.

Tanner Sosa. He's one of the mercenary goons that lurks around Mortimer's office building after hours—the time I'm usually called in for a task. Ex-special forces with a dishonorable discharge that was covered up under so much bullshit, even I had a hard time hacking my way past red tape and redacted records to find out who the fuck was watching our apartment in Castlebrook before I was paid to get closer to Colton. He never found me at Colton's place downtown while I stayed there.

"We just finished up," Mortimer says. "Why?"

"Mr. Snyder had an analyst combing over what happened at the Castle. He's interested in her. I'm here to detain her."

Stunned silence follows—from the men in the office and me. Detain me? The fuck?

"What does she have to do with it? Her use has run its course after tonight's task. I doubt I'll need to call on her again."

My eyes narrow. A bad feeling settles in my stomach like a jagged rock. Why would some rich, musty white dude send private security after me?

The response is too low for me to hear. It doesn't matter. They're done with me. This is where keeping my head down when I know shit is shady and not asking any questions gets me. My jaw clenches. Easy money is always too good to be true. I know better, and now I'm in the shit for it.

It could be anything. The fact I'm expendable highest on the quick list scrolling through my head, followed by the kidnapping thing I helped Colton crack to protect Isla Vonn that turned out to be a trafficking ring. It was all over the news after some gala outside of the city ended in chaos from rogue fireworks starting a fire. The creepy ass Castle Delivery Co. van was in the background behind the reporter, sending disgusted chills through me.

These are people willing to kill the most prominent heirs in the city over stolen information. They'll do the same to me without a doubt.

"I see." Mortimer sounds unhappy. "Well, she can't be far. She's a flighty one, but she left only a few minutes before you got here."

Tanner's boots echo, coming out into the hall. "I didn't pass her. She could still be on the premises."

My heartbeat stutters. Scarcely breathing, I send Sammy a coded text. *We're out of cereal.* It's our signal to each other that we'll always find each other. The last time I said it to him, he was driven away from the orphanage that allowed us to be separated, leaving me behind. A code I never wanted to pass between us again.

I don't give him enough time to respond before I turn my phone off. Once I get out of this building, my SIM card is coming out, too.

I never should've accepted the offer. Playing poker was far safer than the high stakes game I've gotten my younger brother and me tangled in.

"Check with the security desk downstairs," Mortimer instructs. "If she's already gone, it's not worth your time. She's no one."

"No other elevators were in use," Ex-Sergeant Steroid Dick grunts. "I'll do a sweep on this floor first."

Time to move. The stairs are too risky. My best bet is tricking him to think I went that way, then hauling ass to the elevator to beat him downstairs. I draw a shaky breath and come out of my crouch. This better work.

Tanner pushes into offices. Good. While he's busy checking, I sneak to the end of the hall and prop open the stairwell door. Digging through my bag, I grab something heavy enough to cause an echo. I swallow, gathering my courage. Tossing the small bottle of lotion over the railing, I kick the door stop and back up into the shadows behind a plant.

The distant echo on the steps and the slam of the door draws Tanner out of the office. He flies through the door and starts down the stairwell in pursuit. I wait twenty harrowing seconds before slipping as quietly and quickly as I can to the elevators.

By some miracle, those idiots didn't think to call down to building security to recall the elevator. It's still on this floor. I smash the button to close the doors and scarcely breathe until I reach the garage floor beneath the building.

My Vespa's out. It cracks my heart to leave my baby girl behind. She was the first thing I bought myself with my online poker winnings and we've been together through hell and back. The scooter's pearlescent red is too conspicuous.

I leave the garage on foot just as a city bus pulls up to the stop on the corner. Hurrying over, I pay the fare from the pocket of emergency change on the outside of my backpack. I've never been more thankful for the ingrained habit to always be ready than I am now. Keeping my head down, I head for an open seat close to the back doors and duck down, lifting the hood of my pullover up.

My throat burns with anxiety that refuses to settle four stops in. I switch buses at the next one, ditching my SIM card in a public trashcan and becoming a ghost in the wind.

Every choice I've made has always been to protect us both. Yet all of my choices since coming to Thorne Point clang around in my head as the wrong decisions. I've burned the wrong bridges. The only person I can think of that could help me out of this could be dead right now if he didn't make it out of the fire.

My heart lodges in my throat. I have to believe he's alive, because I'm going to need him.

It's time to sell what's left of my soul again, offering it up to the man that will want me dead once he finds out the truth.

* * *

Five Weeks Ago

A loud crash by the door startles me at four in the morning. I'm awake, playing my third round of online poker. Sleep never comes easily for me while I'm stuck in Colton's apartment. The money is too good to turn down, I remind myself for the millionth time.

What's a little forced cohabitation for a cool half a mil? This payout is bigger than any score I've pulled off on my own. He's only here intermittently, anyway.

Though when he is, he's all over me, constantly up in my business. He's nosy, tactile, and always has a disarming smile locked and loaded. I press my lips together, ignoring the dip in my stomach when I think that he's not so bad to look at or be around. Except I'm not going there.

Sammy's not here tonight. It's another reason I can't sleep. He's working overnight on a research project.

With a tense sigh, I close out of my Queen_Q account—my main account, not the second profile I've used while here to protect my stats from Colton's invasive snooping—and poke my head out of the room I camp out in as my safe zone in the ritzy three bedroom apartment with floor-to-ceiling windows and state of the art appliances.

The open living space is dim, lit only by the LED lights Colton has everywhere, casting the room in a continuous neon glow that shifts from red to blue and back again. The source of the noise isn't immediately obvious. I creep past his display cases packed with expensive games and anime figurines and his custom-built computer setup.

When I spot Colton sprawled across the tile floor, I relax, rolling my eyes. A fruit bowl from the counter that gets restocked when a personal shopper stops by whether he's here or not is spilled around him, his hand clutching the wooden bowl like he grabbed the nearest thing for balance before tripping ass over teakettle to the ground. Idiot.

Twisting my lips, I play with the knot securing my head scarf. I'm seriously debating leaving him there. He's not my problem.

Except this is a good opportunity to get close without having to succumb to seducing him. Heaving a sigh, I crouch beside him. He doesn't move when I poke him hard, only snuffles in his sleep. I keep my guard up while I pat him down for his phone.

When I find it, I curse under my breath. It's as locked down as his computer security is. Damn his over intelligent, paranoid ass. I'm never going to complete my objective if I can't crack him. If I have to stay with him forever, I'll go out of my mind. Why couldn't he be like every other idiot that uses birthdays or important dates rather than difficult multilevel encryption protocols on all his shit. He's so extra and it drives me crazy.

I slip the phone back into his pocket using the edge of my Mario star-themed hoodie blanket after wiping my prints. He hums, making my heart stutter. With his disheveled hair sweeping across his forehead and his full lips parted, he looks—

I slam down on the thought, determined to never admit a weakness. My hand hovers over his head, hesitating before my fingers sift through his messy dark brown hair.

His green eyes fly open. They're bloodshot, darting around until they land on me. He relaxes slightly, still deceptively on guard. "Oh. I hallucinated that I made it to bed. That tracks." He pats the hard floor with a lopsided smile. "Lay down with me. Your tits will make perfect pillows, little queen."

I shove him with a scoff. "You start with that fool shit again, and I'll leave your ass on the floor." He chuckles. It's scratchy, crackling with exhaustion. "Get up. You look five seconds from passing out again."

He plants his hands on the floor. They draw my eye. The long, tattooed fingers, prominent veins, and bony knuckles stir heat low in my stomach. My brain has always turned into a thirsty bitch for hand veins and tattoos, and he has both in spades. His biceps flex, stretching his graphic tee.

Cheeks hot, I tear my gaze away. It's not hard to miss how easy he is on the eyes. The flirtatious, cocky fuckboy charm when he runs game on me only adds to the irresistible effect, but I shut down my attraction with iron force. That's not what I'm here for and I refuse to allow any distractions. Any vulnerabilities in my protective walls.

Colton gets to his feet, leaning heavily on the counter. My hands fly out automatically when he sways, eyes unfocused.

"Whoa. Trippy." He snickers at his wiggling fingers, delirious and past the point of exhaustion. "It's all tingly."

Goddamn it. Emitting a frustrated noise, I step into him. "Come here, dumbass."

I give an inch and he takes five thousand miles, wrapping his arms around my shorter frame like some cliche anime tentacle monster. His nose grazes the top of my head. I stiffen, smothering the traitorous hitch in my breath.

"Mm, you smell good, babe. Makes me want to lick you all over for that sweet taste."

My neck prickles with heat, growing used to the dirty talk he slips into every conversation. I'd cut my tongue out before admitting it, but he does, too. "Just shut up and go to bed."

We shuffle down the hall, but he leans too much of his weight on me, pretending to be asleep. I don't know why, but I give up making it to the master bedroom and divert to my haven instead. His mouth curves in a smirk when I deposit him on my bed. I purse my lips. He knows exactly what he's doing.

"I finally got you in bed," he taunts.

"Just—go to sleep." If I'm lucky, he won't even remember this.

Huffing to psych myself up, I climb into bed with my laptop, sitting on top of the covers with a throw blanket I stole because I don't trust him. I shoot him a glance, then log on to join a new poker game. His breathing evens out and I get into the zone.

"Ante up."

I jump at the gravelly interjection, glaring at him. He's hugging one of my pillows, watching me play.

"Who asked you?" I mutter.

Except he's right. I've got a great hand and my opponent's confidence in bets has been wavering after a strong push at the start of the game.

When I win, he releases a rumble of approval. "Nice. Who taught you to play? You're good."

I hesitate, biting the inside of my cheek. "My grandmother."

The little piece of truth slips out in a strained whisper. I miss her every day. I'll never forget when she sat me down and dealt my first hand after her bridge cub ladies left the estate. I always played in the room while they played cards. She said, "Quinn, baby, it's time you learned the only card game that matters."

His tired smile stretches wider, hooded eyes growing heavier. Within seconds he drifts off into unconsciousness while my heart thumps. I've never told anyone the truth. Usually I lie and say I just picked it up on my own.

Unbelievably, I manage to fall asleep. When I wake up, he's gone. I check the apartment to make sure, finding a note left behind on the main computer screen. I open up the folded paper and crumple the edges in my rigid grip. The security feed screenshot shows us in my bed, angled toward each other. Underneath, he wrote *told you I'd get you into bed ;)*.

"Ante up," I grumble.

Is this his way of showing his hand to let me know he's aware I've been working on cracking admin access on his system? My eyes narrow, enjoying the challenge.

CHAPTER FIVE
COLTON

The remains of the Nest look even worse in the bleak daylight. The turn of the century hotel has been reduced to a few standing walls and rubble. Ashes to ashes, dust to dust for the first symbol of power we showed this city. But the thing about destroying a symbol of power is that it doesn't take out the power we wield. This isn't fucking over because our enemies blew up our Nest.

As angry as I am at Quinn for lying, at myself for falling for it and putting my family in the path of danger because I didn't catch this when it's my goddamn job to analyze the available data, I know the Kings are the ones behind this. How or why she's working for them remains a mystery tugging at the edges of my turbulent mind. Money is a good motivator, and I know she looks for any opportunity to get it between playing cards and the payment I offered to get her help debugging Hannigan's file without her realizing what it was I had her working on.

We haven't gotten the okay from the fire department that it's safe to reenter—a joke because there isn't a building left to enter, the place is decimated. That's not stopping us, though.

We're all picking through the charred stone and ashes. Jude is waiting for us at the warehouse, giving the contractors updated instructions to clear out for the weekend and resume renovations next week. Long enough for us to map out our revenge plan from our new base. We weren't going to completely move there until the club was closer to opening night, but things have changed.

We made the move to do something about the property closer to downtown a couple of weeks ago, when Isla and Levi came back from getting tattoos in the shop next to it. The warehouse is property we bought last year with the vision to go legit with our nightclub as our notorious reputation grew. With Wren and Jude graduating from Thorne Point University, it makes sense to eventually improve our operation, to evolve with the extension of our reach.

A humorless smile tugs at the side of my mouth. Our enemies think of us as punk kids playing around in abandoned buildings. Nah, we're coming back bigger, stronger, unstoppable.

Wren stands at the cliff edge. Rowan is by his side, comforting him. Her head rests against his arm and the wind whips off the ocean below, lifting her auburn hair. The cold air is dry today. Feels like it might snow.

Despite our plan to build bigger, this is a piece of Wren's history. The Crow's Nest Hotel was our first big accomplishment, back when we were dumbasses getting high and drinking up here. This was our spot where we forged the bond of our brotherhood. The birth of our rebellion against the expectations our family names hung over our heads like guillotines.

I kick at a smoldering piece of stone that crumbles. Isla crouches nearby at the edge of what was once the ballroom, her brown hair up in a bun and one of Levi's hoodies drowning her. She sifts through the destruction with gloves on and salvages a piece of the vintage settee that served as our ironic thrones. I frown when she smiles sadly at the frayed, ruined scrap of fabric. Instead of getting ready for the dance performance she's been practicing for tonight's showcase, she's here with us, surviving another harrowing aftermath only a few weeks after we took out the Castle and her rapist.

"What do you think?" She holds up her find. "Keep it? It has sentimental value. You can frame it in the new office."

I rub my fingers together, scouring my mind for a joke. I've got nothing. Standing in the destruction of our Bat Cave leaves me more shaken than I'm willing to admit. More off-kilter than I'm able to control. I can't be the jokester right now, not until I see our enemies eradicated.

All this time we've been dancing toe to toe with this city's secret society and I'm sick of playing this game on their terms.

To smoke out the enemy, you have to light a fire underneath them. It's time to strike some fucking matches. Burn, bitches, burn.

* * *

After Rowan talks me into leaving the cliffside, I return to the warehouse downtown. It has a history as a front for a speakeasy and some of the old secret passages still work. There's also a basement level the blueprints don't have on record. Ultimately, that's what drew us to it. In the last year since we bought it, we've gradually turned it into one of the places we land when we need to lay low, fitting the building with our own personal touches to upgrade it. The place is our Nest 2.0 and the beta period is over.

My new setup is upstairs in the office overlooking the main space. It's been transformed in the last few weeks with three balcony levels designed to look like steel rafters, the bones of the warehouse vibe remaining the same to give our signature atmosphere of hedonism amidst disrepair. No one can spot me through the one-way glass. Much like the doors in our Bat Cave, I installed biometric scanners and custom built the programmed user storage to make it more difficult for a hacker to access remotely to steal the data.

No one is getting in—or out—without one of us. I've built a state of the art security system for the entire building—one I'll be double checking to make sure no one, not even Quinn, will be able to access it this time.

I've skimmed my network backup log three times. I still can't work out how the fuck she did it. When I had her on my setup at my apartment, I was careful about generating two-factor encrypted passwords that weren't my personal logins. I know my systems inside and out and she has me stumped. There's no way she stole one of my logins.

What cuts me worse than her hacking my shit on my watch is that a deranged side of me respects her skill. It's fucked up, but it turns me on to think of her outwitting my firewalls in a wicked game of cat and mouse. If my brothers knew that, they'd kill me. This is my fault. I ignore my racing pulse at the thought of them turning their backs on me and the persistent ache splintering my skull. Goddamn it. I thump a fist on the desk as anger burns in my stomach.

I'd still fuck her. That's the messed up part. Shit, the way I want to bend her over this desk right now and ram into her so she feels how fucking pissed I am with each rough thrust, giving it to her so good she'd feel the imprint of my cock permanently. A good, brutal, dirty as shit hate fuck. That's what I want. Pour everything into her pussy—how twisted she has me, my furious hatred because she tricked me, the fear that has me in a goddamn chokehold my brothers will decide I'm no longer good enough.

I press the heel of my hand to my dick and will it to soften. "Ain't the time, buddy. We'll fuck a pocket pussy and chill out with our VR waifus once the world stops being on fire for five fucking minutes."

Quinn's feisty mouth curled in a smirk and her gorgeous intelligent brown eyes bombarded my mind. My fists ball so tight, the nerves twinge and two of my knuckles crack.

I was into her from the first moment she looked me up and down and called me a fool. Arguing with her late at night in my apartment about the best methods to slip into backdoors and drop Trojans made me want more. I'd thought maybe we could be something when she helped us crack the kidnapping ring for the Castle. My mouth curves bitterly. I'm such an idiot.

The scrap of woven fabric Isla recovered sits at my elbow, the faded red and gold design even more discolored from going through the fire. I play with my tongue piercing, fingertips tapping a random pattern on the desk. On the dual monitors, the corrupted file from Rowan's brother mocks me, the last of my efforts to restore the list of Kings Society members the journalist uncovered before he was caught and killed erased.

Why is it always the most important work that causes someone to ignore their normal protocols? I'm neurotic about my backups, yet I was too hyped about showing the others I'd finally finished the bitch of a debugging project that occupied every waking moment I could spare.

Not that I had much time to execute syncing for my offsite backup before the explosion. Closing my strained eyes, I push my fingers against them. I need sleep. But I can't stop yet. I swig my energy drink—I don't know how many I've had at this point. The last forty-eight hours have left my erratic mind buzzing. Probably enough to be a medical concern considering I was already living off them to finish decrypting the file the first time.

It's the norm for me lately. Hard to believe we've been in this shitstorm for almost three months since Rowan first came to us.

I've always pushed myself hard, my brain never able to settle. I work best in chaos mode. Not only because I prefer to keep my mind busy to stop myself from dwelling on my 3am anxiety thoughts of the past—those fuckers still bleed through at the worst times, anyway—but also to always pull my weight. To show my brothers I've got their back. That I'm useful.

If I'm useful, then I won't be left behind when they decide I'm not worth keeping. The deep-rooted thought hardwired into me that doesn't allow me a moment's rest anytime I fuck up. Bred by the man I hate.

I grit my teeth and throw myself back into my work. The silver lining is I had the idea to install a tracker on her and her brother's phones before I put them up in my apartment downtown where I used to stream. I wasn't completely thinking with my dick when it came to her.

When I open the tracking software I programmed, my eyes narrow. Only one signal pings a cell tower near campus. It's her brother Sampson's phone. I adjust the search parameters to strictly search for her.

Nothing.

A muscle in my cheek twitches and I smirk coldly. "Clever girl. You even found the backup."

I try one more way to find her by accessing her service provider's system. Getting through their firewalls is child's play to me. I regularly spoof the supervisor accounts to slip in and out without detection whenever we need to find someone.

The search gives me a message that pisses me off: *number out of service.*

She removed her SIM card. It doesn't make her impossible to find, but it does up the difficulty level by a solid forty percent.

So we're playing it like that, little queen? Game on.

I picture her husky laugh when I challenge her, the sardonic scoff and flash of her eyes that go right to my dick. Goddamn it, the way her laugh says *yeah? Go ahead and try it* makes me want to haul her against me by her tiny waist and show her I'm not messing around.

Pulling up the login screen for the private network I bounce off VPN to mask the server origin, I become Dolos, my online codename to my recruited minions—hackers I've tested when they showed promise. They help me when I'm tapped out on extra brain space. I put out the order to doxx Quinn and find her ass.

When I find her—and I will, no doubt about it because she can't hide from me—she'll find out what happens when people fuck around with me. The anger fights against my attraction to her, the lust I haven't quite killed off despite what she's done because I get off on a challenge. Fuck. I scrub my face and push her enticing dime body from my mind.

My old man would eat this weakness up. The bastard thrives on fucked up punishment over any action he deems below his high standards. My jaw works and I rub the crown tattoo on the inside of my elbow. Almost every one of my pieces covers a small scar, a memory I want to overwrite. Most were never severe enough to notice, and any that were got quickly taken care of with a bribed plastic surgeon to cover up his sins.

I don't regret taking the brunt of Dad's anger—it was either me or the shiny gold stars they brought home as their good deeds. Foster kids from rough homes, giving them a taste of the high life for six months to a year. Like prized fucking show ponies, my parents paraded the unfortunate flavor of the month around the city to every function, every brunch, every diner party to collect their charitable clout.

But I found a way to beat him. My first win. The moment I understood that strength wasn't only physical. Intelligence could outwit anything and come out on top. The punishments stopped because I learned his secret at twelve.

I should thank him. Without that asshole, my obsession with secrets never would've been born. How I could use them to protect myself and others. How to get them, how to keep them, how to *use* them to my benefit.

Switching screens, I open the database I built for every secret we've collected. Our bank is flush with them. The top entry is the very first taste I got of how important secrets can be, the power I can wield by using them as currency. Once I learned that lesson, I was the one in control and my father never had the leverage or the balls to punish me again.

They stopped taking in foster kids for a while, until Fox Wilder when I was eighteen. I was surprised since it had always been girls when I was younger. At first I worried Dad would start up again, but by then I had the leverage to shield Fox from my dad and I'd grown into a man, not a shrimpy kid he could beat on anymore.

Fox is the only one that stuck for longer than my parents liked to keep them around, the only one my mother actually loved like a real son. More than she did me since she turned a blind eye—not that I was her biological son to begin with. My real birth mother is dead and I have the proof Dad did it to cover up the statutory rape. Because the only thing to bury sins are worse sins.

Maybe Fox was her do over. She never viewed quiet, surly Foxy as a badge of honor amongst her society friends and with the secret I held over Dad's head, he never touched Fox while I protected him as I protected the others.

My lips contort. I should text him, but I know how he gets. If he hears how much deeper this shit has gone after he took his fiancé Maisy back to their home in California, he'd feel like he owed it to us to come back to help as our honorary brother. I can't do that to him. I won't put anyone else I love in danger.

"Tell me you're not misty eyed over cartoons again." Jude and the guys enter.

He's walking with a crutch to keep the weight off his leg, but he's looking better than last night, some of the healthy color of his bronze skin returning. It's a relief to know he'll be okay.

"Fuck off." Clicking out of the window, I kick back in the chair, crossing my ankles on the desk. "Where's my cannoli?"

The joke lacks my usual theatrics, my tone flat.

Wren's lips twitch for a moment before his expression settles back into cutthroat anger. He's been quiet since this morning when we picked through what remained of the hotel. It burns another layer through my stomach lining to see him like this knowing I'm the one that fucked up.

"Anything?" He props a shoulder against the wall.

Sighing, I shake my head. "First we need to track down Quinn Walker."

"Your little pet?" Levi broods in the corner, flipping one of his beloved deadly knives pommel to tip.

A line of tension snaps taut in my shoulders. "She's the hacker that got in before the fire. She's the only one good enough to do it."

"I told you not to let her too close," Levi growls.

"I—didn't see it coming. Her secret was legit. I checked it out to verify it." I pinch the bridge of my nose to avoid my best friends' disappointed gazes. Was her disgust that seemed genuine when she helped us unravel the kidnapping ring for the Castle an act, too? "I checked the tracker I planted on her phone, but it's disabled."

"So we hunt her down on our own," Jude says.

I nod. "I've got my minions scouring for any activity online. It's been radio silent, but her brother's phone pinged the cell towers closest to campus."

"Right." Wren strokes his chin. "We'll start there."

"She did the hack to wipe my system, but there's more to this. Why bother infiltrating my local network if it was inside a building rigged to blow?" Out of the four thousand scenarios that have flitted through my head, her motive remains murky. "I don't see the benefit from her taking us out. Even if protecting her was a lie, what does she gain by removing us from the board? Someone else hates us more that she has to be working for."

"The Kings Society," Wren says. "There's no doubt in my mind this is their doing."

"I want to kill them all." Levi snatches his knife from the air mid-twirl with a deadly scowl that only drops around Isla.

"I do, too, but as much as I'd revel in the violence, a murder spree isn't going to solve this," Wren grits out. "Murder is easy, but it's not power. We need to be smart about countering this."

"Agreed. As badass as it would be to burn the whole city to the ground in the name of revenge, we can do better than that. I want to make them feel the pain of our power so it crushes their spirits." I drop my legs off the desk and pull up the database of secrets I had open before they came in. I turn the monitor so they can see. "Scorched earth the Crows way."

Jude's chin dips, his glinting hazel gaze peering through the dark hair that falls across his forehead. "We'll cash in our secrets."

My grin is manic as I type through the twinge of pain from my blisters. "I have a backup of Hannigan's file from a few days ago. I'll have to redo the last bit to reconstruct the corrupted information, but we'll have our target list." I mime a gun with my hands, taking aim at the wall. "*Pop*. We'll work through it systematically. Pick them off one by one."

Wren strokes his chin, his expression icy and calculating. "We'll make them regret underestimating us once again. This time the lesson will stick." His attention shifts to Levi. "For every one of those assholes. Including my father and your uncle."

Levi's expression promises violence. "Yes."

"I'll call Penn. Levi, you're with him. And you," Wren directs when Jude starts to follow, "get some goddamn rest."

Jude's lips twist wryly. "I'm fine."

Wren gives him a stern expression. "Don't make me hurt you more just to prove how not fine you are."

Jude huffs in amusement and assumes a loose boxing stance, compensating to keep the weight off his leg. "Go ahead and try it. Busted leg or not, I'd never go easy on you in the ring."

Wren smirks, squaring off with him. This is how it is with us. We bust each other's balls and fight, but it's because we love each other like family.

"Spar later. We've got work to do," Levi says gruffly.

Wren nods and watches Jude use the crutch to follow Levi to the door, the flare of amusement gone. "Colt?"

"Right behind you." I gesture to my monitors. "I still want to see if I can make our hunt easier from here and take care of the debugging I have to redo."

They leave first. I squint at the screen. She believes she outwitted me, but she's wrong. This is only the first round that started back at my apartment.

"Let's play a game," I mutter.

I've always thrived on the thrill of the chase. It's fun for me in a deranged way. Those high octane moments just before closing in gets my blood pumping. The artificial high of success when I win is more addictive than any substance I've tried.

And the thing Quinn doesn't realize? I always fucking win.

CHAPTER SIX
QUINN

For four days, I've remained on the move, watching my back. I'm sure I've evaded Tanner Sosa, if he even bothered to keep hunting me after I escaped on the city bus. I haven't stopped long enough to look back. I'm worried as hell if they don't find me, they'll go for Sammy to lure me out. It eats at me every second until I risk going to campus. I've got to see him, to convince him to bail on the internship and lie low—for real this time.

I'll give my brother every dime to my name if he'll take it and leave the city. We were better off back in Castlebrook. Clawing back what was stolen from us isn't worth it if it means we're in danger.

Blending in on Thorne Point University's campus wearing an oversized school hoodie, a beanie, and a caramel-toned wig I bought on my way here and slipped on over my box braids, I remain alert, gaze flicking around my surroundings. It's not my best disguise, but it's not like I had time to see my stylist while on the run to take them out a couple of weeks early to change things up. Next time I need a protective style, I'm listening to her and going for micro braids. If I make it to next time after all this.

It's mid-afternoon, the busiest time on campus between classes. Trust funders and silver-spooned elite students laugh and socialize, milling around the quad without any idea of what's going on in the city after dark. I dip my head to hide my face when I pass by someone from my information systems class, scrolling through the campus' Twitter feed using the school's wifi on the prepaid phone I picked up.

There's not a single tweet or trending hashtag about the fire when usually the feed is buzzing by the end of the week with talk of partying at the illicit spot. I can't find it on any news sites either. Fitz Mortimer gives me the vibe he's the type to brag, the type that would pay to have the local news cycle running the story continuously, but the Crowned Crows wouldn't want it getting out that their abandoned hotel went up in flames. Are they suppressing the story?

Biting my lip, I try not to let the flicker of hope in my chest burn out of control before I know for sure if they made it out of the fire. First I have to take care of my brother, then I can find out if they're alive—if Colton's okay and can help me.

I debate texting Sammy's number from the burner, but if they have anyone with half a brain cell out looking for me, they could be tracking his incoming and outgoing call and message logs. Weaving through the flow of students, I make an effort to get to the Keaton building without making it obvious I'm heading there.

Once I slip through the doors behind a professor and their TA, I keep my head down and take the long way around the marble-tiled main hall that circles the first floor. Sammy's working on the other side of the building. The closer I get, the harder my heart drums. He's going to be okay. He's there. They wouldn't waste time taking him.

I repeat every reassurance to myself.

Hands grab at me when I round the final corner, yanking me against a wall of muscle. My heart stutters violently. Fuck, Sosa found me.

It's empty in the hall, the thick wooden doors closed. The guy drags me into a stairwell, away from my brother. I open my mouth to scream, but the bastard who's got me covers half my face with his gloved hand before I get it out. Motherfuc—I sink my teeth in hard, grinding my jaw to inflict as much pain as possible.

He grunts, but doesn't drop me. His hand presses harder against my face, squeezing. "She fucking bit me."

"Move," someone else orders in a savage tone.

Shit. *Shit.* This can't go down like this. I need to get away, need to get to Sammy. If they take me, there's no one to watch his back and keep him safe. I'll fail the goal I've always put above all else—survive and protect my brother.

Neither of them sound like Fitz Mortimer's roided up shithead I've been evading. They must be working for him.

Sosa's team of retrieval assholes is bold, grabbing me in broad daylight on campus. I'm not going down without a fight, and no way in hell am I letting them keep me. When my captor adjusts his hold and lifts me from the ground, then drags me back into the shadows of the stairwell, I fight back the bolt of panic and focus on struggling without draining my energy.

Drawing a breath to keep my cool, I wait until they're rounding the corner and kick off from the marble support pillar with all my might. Not expecting it after I faked a typical struggle of someone inexperienced, the guy crashes against the wall, head smacking the polished wood molding hard. I have mere seconds to wriggle an arm free and get the taser in my hoodie pocket while he's distracted.

He grumbles, regaining his footing. Whirling us around, he uses his strength and height against me, pinning me to the wall. My mouth is free as he goes for my hands.

"Tell Sosa he's a fucking dick," I sneer.

They're silent for a fraction of a beat, then one mutters, "Who?"

With a vicious growl, I jam the taser against my attacker's side and hit him with a jolt of 50,000 volts. I hope the strangled noise he makes is because the electricity goes right to his groin.

The attacker falls back with a strangled yell, only to be replaced by his accomplice. This one is bigger, more muscular, and aware that I'm not some damsel he can incapacitate so easily. I jerk against the hold he puts me in, barely able to move. Within thirty seconds, he has my mouth taped and my wrists bound by zip ties with ruthlessly efficient movements. This isn't his first rodeo.

Shit.

"Jesus christ!" The first guy recovers once he walks it off. He picks up my weapon while I struggle and clicks the trigger. The high voltage electricity crackles between the tines. "She's got a goddamn taser. A serious one, not the shit they sell to co-eds. Lev—"

"On it."

I struggle harder, survival mode ratcheting into full throttle. It's no use. His fingers pinch something in my neck and my vision goes black.

* * *

The dank basement I'm in when I come to twists my stomach in knots. Is this some black site Sosa has? It looks like a shitty one, considering who pays him.

My mouth isn't covered by tape. I slide my dried lips together, trying to peer past my limited view into the shadows blanketing the large room. No gag means if I scream, there's probably not anyone coming to my rescue. No one who cares if I scream, anyway.

I blow out a breath, taking stock of my body. It doesn't seem like I've been out that long from whatever pressure point the guy exploited. My fingertips don't tingle, but I am splayed in a chair, secured to it by zip ties on my ankles, knees, and wrists. These guys know what they're doing, keeping my mobility extremely limited without cutting off my circulation. The thought isn't comforting.

A scuff echoes through the room, tricking my brain into thinking it's coming from one direction until another sounds in the opposite. Then the unmistakable snick of a switchblade, followed by a chilling raspy laugh.

"Bet acting like boogeymen makes you feel like your dicks are real big, assholes." I scoff, jutting my chin.

"Hardly," a smooth, mercurial voice responds. "Those are simply rumors. But if the dark makes you uncomfortable, we should be more hospitable and turn on the lights, hmm?"

Wait. I recognize that voice. My brain was in panic mode before, reacting to being grabbed unexpectedly. If it's not Sosa, then—

An industrial switch flips and I squint against the blinding floodlights pointed at me. Three tall silhouettes stalk closer. When my eyes adjust, my throat constricts. Wren Thorne's icy glare is pinned on me, his muscular forearms crossed, shirtsleeves rolled up to display his tattoos. Beside him, Levi Astor twirls a knife through his fingers with deadly precision, glaring at me. Flanking Wren's other side, Jude Morales leans on a crutch, though he looks just as formidable as his friends; someone who will fuck my shit up, injured or not.

Well, fuck. It's not Tanner Sosa who captured me, it's the notorious Crowned Crows.

The relief that they're okay, that they made it out of the fire is short lived. This puts an Everest-sized snag in my plan to go to them to offer anything I have in exchange for their help to undo my mistakes. Rumor has it, they make people disappear for far less mild transgressions than what I was involved in.

My fingers curl into my palm and I force my pulse to calm down. "I'm not afraid of shit. Especially not you."

Wren's smirk is hard-edged and cutthroat. Levi cracks his knuckles and Jude cocks his head, those clever golden eyes of his seeing right through me. The only one missing, the one my stomach burns with the need to see alive and well is—

My breath catches at the grind of a door opening, metal against concrete, past the bright lights.

Colton strolls in. The last time I saw him, he was laughing at me for flipping him off when he told me good work. Seeing him unharmed makes my eyes sting as another wave of relief crashes over me. I take him in with a frantic sweep, pulse pounding in my ears.

They part for him, giving up control like this is his game to run. His grin sends chills racing across my skin. It's nothing like the cocky, flirtatious one he used to give me. The one that, no matter how much I resist, makes my heart thump. This smile is sinister. *Manic.*

"Hey, pretty baby."

I flinch. Colton's tone is light, but it's only a mimic of his usual relaxed vibe. Underneath, it's full of the shadows he's been hiding, promising brutal destruction. Promising revenge.

This isn't the Colton I lived with for weeks. I knew he'd hate me, yet I was unprepared to face it. Not ready to lose the easygoing attitude he had toward me once he realized I broke his trust. I need his help and he wants me dead.

His gaze slides over me, the tip of his tongue tracing his full lower lip.

"You brought my monsters out to play. I hope you're ready, because they want to take a big fucking bite out of you."

CHAPTER SEVEN
COLTON

Tʜᴇ sight of Quinn's tempting full lips contorting in a mix of outrage and an undercurrent of uncertainty at my challenging tone sends a thrill into my veins. Or maybe that shot of heat to my dick is because I have her at my mercy.

My gaze drags over her in the harsh light of the construction lamps the contractors' crew left in the warehouse. She looks like she's been through hell, yet we're the ones that walked out of a fucking fire. Her beautiful dark brown complexion is usually smooth and luminous, but her eyes are puffy and bloodshot from fatigue. Doesn't make me want to kiss her any less. In fact, the urge only grows to kiss her hard enough to make her bleed, to leave my damn mark on her the way she's left hers on my mind.

Lie, lie, lie, I remind myself brutally. A better use for her lying mouth would be warming my cock.

I click my tongue in disappointment. "Shouldn't have scrolled Twitter. We figured you'd go to your brother eventually so we were ready, but really, babe? Searching Twitter for the Nest? I pinpointed your burner's IP as soon as you did that. You're smarter than that dead giveaway."

"How—?" She clenches her teeth, unwilling to let her mouth run like she usually does when I prod at her missteps.

The corner of my mouth kicks up higher. "I told you. There's nothing that gets by me." My gaze hardens. "Except you."

She sets her jaw, tearing her gaze from mine. "Are you done gloating?"

Some of the feisty attitude I'm addicted to ebbs, her hairline trigger to fight me reset to the baseline. It's as if she doesn't think she's still in the shit for her part in putting my brothers' lives at risk once she realizes who captured her. Like we're going to cut her loose any minute after we went through the trouble of catching her. I bite back a huff. This isn't enough. I want her to admit I won, after spending every minute since the Nest burned to the ground split between tracking signs of her and working on the corrupt file.

The laugh that rips out of me is this side of psychotic. "Not by a long shot."

Her lips slide together. She won't meet my eye. "What are you going to do with me?"

"Up for debate," Wren cuts in cooly.

"So many options." Jude's fluid tone is infused with danger.

He's walking easier with his leg on the mend, but I haven't stopped reliving the unbearable moment the hall collapsed on us, the memory on permanent loop at the back of my mind. My heart pumps hard, thoughts picking up speed to flash through my head with possible ways this scenario plays out. We need answers more than we need to torment her. She doesn't know that, though.

We all agree she's not the mastermind behind the fire. She's involved with the crusty, micro-dick energy Kings bastards somehow, and we need her to spill the specifics.

"See, you've crossed us, little queen. We don't abide that shit on a regular day. But you've been cozied up with the wrong fuckers." Her shoulders tense the more unhinged my voice gets. I grip the collar of her hoodie and get in her face, slipping the gun tucked in the back of my waistband free and dragging it down her temple. "You're gonna have to give me one good reason why I shouldn't pull the trigger and paint this room with your pretty brain matter."

Quinn freezes, her wide eyes snapping to meet mine. Now the fear bleeds through the cracks in her mask of bravery. She's never seen this side of me. Only the guy who wants to get to know the inside of her pussy—not the one just as deadly as my brothers.

"You're not gonna shoot me," she says after a tense beat.

A crazed laugh tinged with all the anger-induced anxiety I've been constantly battling for days falls from my lips and I dig the muzzle into her cheek. "Timer's racing toward zero. Better cough up a reason before we find out exactly what I'll do."

Quinn's chest heaves and her eyes dart around the room while her jaw works. She's nervous, though fighting to keep her cool. I can see the gears of that clever little mind working to find her way out of this. It's the mark of someone that's faced danger and come out on the other side. A survivor that doesn't allow her fear to win.

I clench my jaw and tighten my hold on her hoodie, slamming down on the admiration that unfurls in my chest. "Tick tock, tick tock, tick tock."

"You need me," she grits out.

"Also debatable," Wren mutters. "Don't be so fucking predictable."

"You do," she insists in a ragged outburst. "Look, I'm not a threat. I'm no one."

"And look where that got the Trojans," Jude says.

My lips twitch. That's exactly what Quinn is. A goddamn virus infecting me before I catch the infiltration.

"Which is it, Walker? We need you—which we don't, because we have me, so we've filled our computer genius hacker quota," I growl. "Or you're no one? Can't be both."

She meets my eye, leaning into the gun I have trained on her, big brown eyes hardening with the confidence that doesn't quite keep her voice from shaking. "It is both. I need help guarding my brother, and you'll do it because I have something you want."

I snort. "That's not how this works, babe. You think you're in the position to ask for my help? You're like the girl who cried wolf."

She bares her teeth, and, shit, it's my favorite look on her—fierce, full of life, fearless. Ready to take down the damn world for getting in her way. A beautiful fighter with nothing left to lose. What a gorgeous liar she is.

"I have a backup of the file you had on your screen right before the guy who paid me to get close to you gave the order to trigger the explosives."

My grip on the gun eases. I have a backup, too, but it's not complete yet. If I was in her shoes, I would've made the same move, swiping a copy for myself. She licks her lips, seizing my hesitation to push what she wants to sell me.

"So I'll give you that, and you'll help me."

I'll help her. Not a plea or a question—a demand already set in stone. The balls on this chick, making claims like that while we've got her restrained.

Her attention shifts to the guys looming past my shoulder before returning to me. I'm her best bet, the path of least resistance. "The file's in my bag, if your boys didn't break the thumb drive when they grabbed me."

"I heard you bit Penn before you tased him." He was bitching about it to Levi while they brought her in through one of the old speakeasy tunnels to the basement level of our warehouse.

She juts her chin. "That's what happens when clowns attack me."

I hold back a tight smirk, not ready to give up on my anger yet. There's no shiny red bow to tie this off neatly. The world is way more fucking complicated than that. "Doesn't seem like you want to play nice. But since you've given over your best leverage…"

"Damn it, asshole." Quinn jerks her wrists against the zip ties. It's useless. "The only thing I want is help protecting my brother! He's got nothing to do with this. I've been cut loose and I don't want them to go after him. I'm no longer working for the people that burned your hotel down, okay? I was told to get rid of leaked information. That's all. I—I didn't know they were going to—"

"Burn us alive in it?" Wren supplies in a frigid tone. "If you're going to play in the dark with the monsters, at least have the stomach to say it."

She shakes her head and a small, exhausted huff leaves her. "I didn't know about Mortimer's plan with the fire. It happened so fast. I was going to come to you guys for help once I realized things were beyond shady as fuck." Her throat works and her words come out hoarse. "If you were alive. But some guy named Snyder sent Mortimer's favorite attack dog after me that night."

My shoulders go rigid. One of the guys mutters behind me, as on edge at that name as I am.

Snyder? Fuck, we haven't heard his name in a long time. Not since the night of our first job five years ago. The burned out tower ruins we stumbled on when we took out the Kings' Castle trafficking ring a few weeks ago springs to mind once again, along with the sight of the dead girl we failed, permanently burned into my brain.

The thought of him coming for Quinn sends ice into my veins. Refusal rockets through me, the innate protective instinct blaring to life, outweighing my anger before I get it under control. Ain't no way. Ain't no fucking way I'll let that sick bastard near her. Liar or not, I won't let him touch her.

Waiting another beat to make her sweat it out, I release her and tuck the gun away, scrubbing my mouth. "It's going to cost you a lot more than giving us the file."

She watches me carefully. "My skills are yours. Let me owe a favor. Anything."

I toy with my tongue ring, glancing at the guys. "I don't think you can afford our price." Sliding my hands in my pockets, I walk into the space between her spread knees, peering down at her. My voice lowers, scraping past my lips in a rough and gritty whisper meant only for her ears. "My price."

Her gaze shifts to my mouth, lips parting. She clamps them shut a fraction of a second later, covering the reaction. I want to see those lush lips stretched around my cock. Part of me is ready to take my dick out right now and make her atone for her lies with her mouth while my brothers watch. Heat tugs into my groin, my cock beginning to get hard at the mental image of making her take every inch until she's not sure if I'll let her breathe or not.

One thing's clear. I'm not ready to give her up yet. Not even close.

Quinn's staying within reach so I can wring every answer out of her and use her to beat the fucking bastards she ran from that want all of us dead.

"You're going to work for me." I turn my back on her to clear the haze of lust from my head and meet my brother's ruthless gazes. They each give me subtle nods to convey they'll follow any choice I make. "Convince me you're loyal to the Crows now, and I'll think about helping protect you and your brother."

Fucking déjà vu. This better not be another trick.

Facing her again, I cross my arms. "But know this. There's no turning back. No backing out. You're in with us as my asset, you feel me?" I wait for her stiff nod. "I want full access. The file only tells us so much. You're going to start by telling us everything you know about the Kings."

"The who?" Her brows furrow in genuine confusion.

"Cute," Jude says. "Did they give you that script?"

"No. There isn't much else to tell. This all started when Fitz Mortimer rolled up to the Castlebrook campus and gave me an offer I couldn't refuse."

"You expect us to believe that you had no idea who was paying you?" Levi's tone is savage. "That he wasn't connected when you helped us figure out the kidnapping threat?"

"What else was there to know beyond the fact he's a rich, narcissistic asshole? It was a job," she pushes out. "I wasn't paid to ask questions. And no, he never mentioned anything about that creepy ass delivery van."

Some of the endless acid razing my insides settles. My gut instincts weren't completely fooled by her lies—she doesn't seem to get she was working for a secret society. Then again, this could be an act, too. She's fooled me once. I'm not making the mistake of taking her at her word ever again.

Narrowing my eyes, I lean down, invading her space once more. "Was that secret you paid me with bullshit, too?" I drag my nose across her cheek, hissing venomously in her ear. "Is everything about you a fucking lie? Your grandma teaching you to play poker?"

A strangled sound gets trapped in her throat, but it brings me no satisfaction. She strains away from me and my lips twitch. Nah, baby. This is how we're playing the game.

Signaling to the guys, I get them to clear the room without giving her an inch of relief from my fury. She's my problem to deal with. I'll get all the answers we want out of her one way or another.

"Are you going to untie me yet?" She lifts her brows, wiggling her fingers. "I'm not into bondage."

Cute. Once it's just the two of us, I grasp her jaw, wrenching her face up to force her to meet my eye. For a moment, her eyes flash with heat and her lips part with a gasp.

"Answer me," I grit out.

Her brows flatten and she grumbles, jerking to get free. I dig my fingers into her skin. All that attitude in such a tiny little thing. Shit, she gets me hot when she fights me.

"Make me," she counters.

A dangerous smirk twists my lips. "Challenge accepted, little queen." My grip on her jaw and throat flexes, letting her know I'm in control of the board. It's my move. Time to test how willing she is to play. "You love to fuck around with games, so you're going to show me right now you'll do anything I say."

"Anything?" The question comes out husky after a beat.

Her throat constricts with a swallow, moving against my hand. I massage the column of her neck.

There's a flare of defiance in her captivating brown eyes, and a hint of something that pulls at my impulses—the unmistakable hint of desire. The same hint I've caught glimpses of all the times I push her buttons dropping dirty lines and making my interest known. She loves this little dance of tension between us as much as I do. If she didn't, she wouldn't have put up with my shit.

Shit, there's no denying I'm still attracted to her. Still three seconds from grabbing her by the throat and taking what I've been craving from her—fucking everything.

Fuck it. Hate sex is still on the table. The others don't have to know that. Part of me tries to excuse the allure as a way to work out my frustrations. I can't fool myself. Being pissed at her while I fuck her will only ratchet up this addiction I have to getting under her skin.

I take her chin. "Open this lying mouth." Her lips tighten in refusal. I lift my brows, coaxing her lower lip with my thumb. "Anything. That's what you said, remember? Show me it's not another lie. Pledge your loyalty to me and prove that you won't stab me in the goddamn back again."

"It wasn't personal," she whispers tightly. "I just needed the money."

My fingers dig into her chin and I squint down at her, waiting her out. If I'm right—and my dick sure as shit hopes I am—she'll do it.

Her burning gaze holds mine. Neither of us are backing down. Then wicked gratification crashes through me as she slowly parts her lips for me. A sensual, silky chuckle rumbles in my throat.

"Wider." Her lashes flutter and she complies. "*Wider*, little liar."

She huffs, but does as I command. Jesus, she's a gorgeous sight like this. I want nothing more than to sit the tip of my cock on that perfect tongue. I stroke the full shape of her lower lip with my thumb, tracing the stretch before pressing my forehead to hers.

"I'd praise you for being a good girl, but we both know you're no good girl," I murmur. "Let's wash those lies out of your mouth."

Gathering saliva on my tongue, I watch the moment what I'm about to do registers in her expression. Her gaze says *fuck you*, yet she keeps her mouth open, eliciting a shot of heat to my dick. *Good girl.* The edge of my mouth curls and I spit into her waiting mouth.

My tone turns rougher as I dole out another order. "Swallow. Every. Drop."

She remains still, breathing thickly. Her lashes flutter again as she closes her eyes, then shuts her mouth. I attention fixates on her throat, watching it flex with her swallow.

With a sharp laugh, I hold her jaw and lick across her lips, flicking them with my tongue piercing in an imitation of how I'd tease her clit until she was crying so pretty for me. The second she gives in, parting her lips and pressing against mine for a kiss with a strangled noise, I draw back just far enough she can't have what she wants.

"If you're going to accept deals with a devil, at least make sure it's one that will let you come when he fucks you over," I croon against her mouth. "I won't do you dirty like that. When I fuck you—and have no doubt, that's where you and I have been heading on a goddamn bullet train—I'll wrench the sweetest pleasure from you with every ounce of my hatred using my cock, my tongue, my fingers..."

Quinn's gaze is molten hot, pupils blown with arousal when I hover my face over hers. She gives a satisfying shudder, her breath hitching. I grin, basking in my victory.

Game fucking on, baby.

My mouth curves wickedly against her cheek. "It'll be the best fucking O of your life, babe. All of that only to make you choke on it as a reminder that I'll never forgive you for fucking lying to me. You played the wrong game, Quinn, and now you'll pay for that mistake."

CHAPTER EIGHT

QUINN

THE wrong game. Don't I fucking know it. And now I'm stuck playing by Colton's rules if I have any hope of surviving, any hope of protecting my brother. For him, I'll do whatever it takes—I'll always find a way for us to make it through.

Even with my survival on the line, Colton still has a way of getting under my skin like no other. I've offered myself. My mind. If he demands my body as payment, too, I'll pay the steep price. It won't be the worst thing I've ever done to get through the shitty hand life dealt me. I ignore the way my heart gives a little flutter of anticipation at the thought.

My cheeks are on fire. They have been since he grabbed my jaw and made me open for him, the heat spreading through my body and settling in my core. I've explored a gateway kink or two that gets me hot, but this one is a shock. I didn't think I'd be into that. It was so dirty, yet it turned me on. I'm not sure if it's the filthy act, or the allure of this darker side of him. Or just *him*—impossible to ignore, impossible to resist.

Either way, I forgot where we were, the fact I was his captive, consumed by his orders delivered in that honeyed, raspy tone and his intoxicating scent drowning me. My thighs rub together, but it does nothing to help the ache of my throbbing clit. Big what the hell at myself.

I can't believe I was going to kiss him after I let him spit in my mouth. Where is my head? After I've held out for so long when it comes to him, I give up that easy? My lips slide together, tingling with the phantom sensation of his skin against mine. Maybe it's because I'm so tired after days of running... or because I was really glad he wasn't dead, even if he hates me.

Jesus, get it together, Q. We don't lose our shit over cocky, unhinged fuckboys.

"Game on," I say as evenly as I can manage. "I can handle whatever mind games you want to throw at me. You won't break me."

His dark chuckle sends a shiver racing down my spine. I tamp down on it, not wanting him to see how he affects me.

"Babe, you really haven't been paying attention. Too busy focused on manipulating your way past my defenses to hack my shit, yeah?" He shakes his head, stepping back to survey me thoughtfully. "We've already started. It began the moment you thought you could trick me. Should I leave you like this for the night? It might help things sink in."

"What the—? Fuck no. Cut this shit off me." I jerk against the zip ties when his expression remains serene, eyes glinting with mischief. "Colton."

The bastard traces his lower lip with the tip of his tongue. "Mm, I love it when you say my name in that pissy tone. Gets my dick so hard, babe."

"Let me up." Instead of undoing the restraints, he takes out his phone and snaps photos of me. "You're such an asshole. All of you."

He smirks, propping a foot on the chair, right between my splayed legs.

I freeze, my pussy still tingling with a simmer of arousal. Is he going to make me do something else just as depraved as swallowing his spit, like rubbing against his shoe? Liquid heat coils in my stomach. Fuck, I hope not. I'm not ready to find out how I'd react to that.

Aware of his piercing stare, I duck my head. The last thing I need is him finding another way to toy with me. All he did before was come at me with flirtatious dirty talk and an obvious interest, but he backed off when I shut him down. I get the sense we're past that now—he's ready to act on what he wants without stopping.

Colton hums and pushes off the chair, sending it scooting back a few inches across the chilly concrete from the force. He moves past the floodlights into the darkness, returning a moment later with my backpack dangling from his nimble fingers. I watch him through my lashes as he rifles through it to remove my laptop, pressing my lips together when he dumps the remaining contents to the floor carelessly. Empty flash drives, a handful of tampons, a beat up deck of cards I've had since I was a kid, and a pocket-sized guide to mythology book that makes my heart clench all scatter at his feet. Fucking dick.

When he finds the thumb drive I stashed in a small inside zipper pocket, he palms it with a dexterous move, flashing me an arrogant look. "We'll start with this."

After ditching my bag, he rummages in a tool box sitting by one of the lamps. At last, he saunters over with a box cutter. Relief shoots through me. He might despise me for my deception, but he's not so cruel he's going to leave me tied up wherever the hell we are. His messy dark brown fringe falls into his eyes when he concentrates on slicing through the zip tie on my wrist.

"What is this place?" I squint past the bright light. "I thought I woke up in a shitty black site."

"Our Nest 2.0. Bigger, better, fully upgraded." He gestures with a flourish of his hand. It's the first time I take stock of the healing blisters on his fingers, my stomach plummeting at the sight of his injuries. "Can't keep us down with a little smoke and ash. That's all you need to know for now."

Guilt rises again. I've kept it at bay in the last four days running circles around the city to keep Sosa busy and away from Sammy.

"There are some ground rules."

He loses the chaotic air. It's replaced by seriousness, and beneath that, the same bone-deep exhaustion I feel right now. The dark circles smudged under his bloodshot eyes give him away. I don't like the niggle of worry that blooms in my chest. It's unwelcome. There's no room for anyone in my heart but my brother.

"You go everywhere I go. I have full access to you twenty-four seven. None of us trust you on your own."

My stomach clenches. He can't mean legit every minute of the day.

What does that mean about when it's time to sleep? Will I be forced to shower while he camps out? If he follows me into the bathroom, I'll drop kick his balls in. The night we did spend together in my bed surfaces in my mind. I still can't believe I fell asleep with him. It won't be happening again if he forces me into his bed.

He slices through the next zip tie and I massage my wrists when he crouches. While he's distracted, I carefully slip my hands into my hoodie pocket, shoulders sagging when I find it empty.

"Looking for your burner? I took it apart already." He gestures with his head. "And the taser—classy—you're not getting that back either, obviously."

I huff. "What about the others?"

"As far as they're concerned, you're still my problem to deal with," he mutters.

"I want to talk to Sammy first. I was on my way to see him." My heart constricts. Shit, it's been four days since I sent him our secret message. "Just let me call him. I'll put it on speaker."

He peers up at me through his fringe. "Prove yourself and maybe you'll earn enough gold stars to score a field trip. Not right now, though." He rakes his long, tattooed fingers through his tousled hair to drag it back from his handsome, boyish face. "Right now you're on lockdown."

I explode from my chair and keep on his ass, working double time to match his long strides with my shorter legs. "You can't keep me from Sammy."

Colton whips around with speed and fluidity that I'd never expect from how languid he always is and pins me against a brick column. He's strong—I know it from his penchant for wrapping his arms around my waist and lifting me in his apartment. His expression is hard and threatening, another flash of the dangerous side he keeps hidden behind his joking.

"Keep testing me, Quinn. Fuck around and find out what I will and won't do."

I swallow thickly, taking a shaky breath. I hate his response, his belief he can boss me around and keep me from my brother, yet that animosity is no match for the electric thrill shooting through me at his roughness. This would never work between us. I knew it before, when I was living a lie to get close enough to do what I was paid to.

Gritting my teeth, I fist his t-shirt and yank hard on the material. "You don't understand—he's my brother. He's all I have in the world."

He leans down, getting in my face, his sharp jawline set in disdain. Something haunting casts shadows in the tightness around his green eyes. "Never underestimate how much I understand the bonds of siblings. I'd die for my best friends. They're my brothers. I might be an only child by blood, but you don't know anything about all the people I consider family."

The fierce, unyielding conviction in his voice makes my heart skip a beat.

Understanding arrows through me, no matter how much I want to fight him on principle. I get it. And I get why those mesmerizing green eyes burn with fury, because I helped Fitz Mortimer put the people he cares about most in this world in danger. If I was in his shoes, I'd be angry as fuck, too.

I have no clue how to handle him like this. He's unpredictable. Volatile. A tripped red wire without a countdown, threatening to explode at any second.

"I won't let this go." My grip tightens on his shirt and I tug again. He narrows his eyes, stepping into me so we're flush, his body pressed against mine to trap me against the brick scraping my back. My pulse drums. "Don't think I'll be easy."

"I don't want easy, little queen," he rasps. "The fact you aren't easy is what I've always liked best about you. Fighting with you is a highlight of my day." His jaw works and he stares at my mouth. "At least it was, little liar. As much as I want to keep doing this with you, we've got work to do."

Colton steps back, dragging a hand down my arm. He locks his long fingers around my wrist and my eyes widen when he hauls me over his shoulder in a swift move that takes me by surprise. My legs kick and he jolts me to resettle my weight, making my braids swing wildly.

"Yo, what the—" The loud, stinging crack of his hand clapping my ass cuts me off.

"No more talking. I'm having enough focus issues as it is, babe."

I gape at the shadowed industrial space he carries me through, automatically scrabbling against his lower back for balance. We leave my bag behind. Frowning, I pinch his side. He grunts, choking back a laugh.

Colton takes me through a dark passage that leads to a wide set of stairs. He takes them without faltering from my added weight, his muscles flexing to keep me balanced. Then we move down a long, narrow hall. Low echoes drift through the wall. My brows furrow until we pop out through a false wall into an alcove. When he slides it back in place, I have trouble locating the seam of the hidden door to the basement, though I only have seconds to scope it out before we're moving through the first floor of a huge warehouse with tiered balconies and big arched windows showing the darkening sky.

My cheeks burn at our audience. The echoes were the others talking, plus Levi Astor's broody double I've seen around the hotel on club nights. He glares at me, turning back to Levi. Isla, Levi's girlfriend, waves at me with a smile less bright than she's given me before and her best friend Rowan tightens her auburn ponytail, sizing me up with a guarded expression. None of them trust me.

Wren crosses his arms when we pass. "Colt…"

"We're going to get Hannigan's file backed up, big guy," he answers. "With the list, we'll be able to figure out our plan of attack and prioritize which secrets will benefit us best."

"Good." Wren's attention flicks to me. "Now that we can focus our efforts, we're heading out tonight to scope out potential targets."

Colton pauses inside the freight elevator, angling to look back at his friends. "We'll get them all."

The hair on my nape tingles at the formidable stances they all take. All of them, even the girls, have a badass, threatening air of *don't fuck with us*. One of them mutters an agreement.

Colton's shoulders are stiff beneath me on the ride up to the top floor. We exit onto the rafter balcony encircling the top of the warehouse and slip through an archway. At the door, there's the distinct sound of a security system granting access before we enter an office with a vintage leather sofa.

I yelp when I'm deposited into a gamer chair, clutching the arm rests. "You could've warned me you were about to drop me, dumbass."

"Nah. I like the little thrill I get when you scream for me."

His words match the old Colton I know, but the tone is all wrong. Something rankled him between being alone together in the basement and here. Perching on the large desk, he boots up the impressive computer system—custom build, top of the line core processor, the best graphics card money can buy. Damn his enviable toys. He has way more security protocols on this one than the one in his apartment.

Pulling the thumb drive from his back pocket, he inserts it in a port on the USB hub below the monitor, fingers tapping an endless erratic pattern until it connects. He ignores the few other files on the drive—random assignments I've copied to it for my classes—and opens the file I skimmed briefly.

The sigh that leaves him slices into my chest. It's full of relief, tinged with his exhaustion. He scrubs his face, the rigid lines of his back relaxing. With another handful of keystrokes and commands, he has copies of the file synced to the local network and two different backup servers, one of them an encrypted FTP.

"Sweet, sweet dopamine." He allows himself another somber moment before he claps, his energetic mood returning. "Okay."

I'm beginning to think he's not the jokey, carefree guy he constantly portrays himself as. My teeth sink into the inside of my cheek to remind myself I'm only here for protection. I don't want to get involved in the weird as hell turf wars of the wealthiest, power hungry in Thorne Point and their psychotic brats.

"We've got recorded video, audio, the list, and—oh." He drums his fingers against his chin, studying me. "I'm getting ahead of myself."

He snaps his fingers, grabbing a chair from the corner and sitting so close his knee brushes my thigh. He braces his forearms on the desk, typing away on his phone. I try to peek at the screen.

Colton smirks, hiding it. "Just putting out an order for my minions to handle. We're gonna be here a while and I don't have time."

My gaze slides to the list on the dual screens. Whatever this is, I don't want it to touch my brother, don't want it to tarnish the future I've fought hard to restore for him. He's a year younger, so I'm the one that took charge after we lost our granny and everything else. Baron Astor's name glares at me from the top of the list.

"Promise me you'll protect my brother." It comes out low and strained.

Colton pauses. He doesn't answer, messing around on his phone. My fists clench. As I gather everything in me to make him agree to my demand, the cell phone slides across the desk, stopping in front of me. A call is in progress to my brother's number, set on speakerphone.

My gaze darts to Colton. He crosses his arms and lifts his brows, leaning back in the chair. "Don't tell him where you are."

"Obviously," I push out in a rush, hunching over the phone. When it connects, my throat constricts. "Sammy?"

"Jesus, Quinn." His ticked off voice crackles over speakerphone. A wet breath punches out of me and I cradle the phone closer. It's my only lifeline to him at the moment. "You had me worried after what you texted. Then radio silence?"

"I know."

It's difficult to get words out. My eyes sting, but I won't let Colton see me cry. It's not his fault I'm in this situation, it's mine. My greed. My mistakes. My choices in the name of survival.

"I contacted your professors to make an excuse that you were sick," Sammy says. "They gave me your last exams and a graded paper back to pass on to you."

People have always mistaken us for twins because we look so similar. I lay a hand over my heart, picturing his wide smile.

"Nerd," I mumble. "I'm sorry for going radio silent. It—"

Colton clears his throat. I nod stiffly, racking my brain for some way to tell him to watch his back.

"I'm fine. False alarm. Just... Don't forget what granny always said, okay? You learn more looking around you than in the classroom, so keep your eyes peeled." Sammy goes quiet for a moment, then hums in agreement. I glance at Colton in my periphery. "I'll see you when I see you, okay? Stay at the apartment downtown instead of spending every minute on campus. Take care of yourself. That internship isn't worth it."

"Yes it is. It's a guaranteed edge, which I'll need. The connections I'm making will get me recruited." He pauses. "You good?"

He recognizes the cageyness riding my tone. I sigh. This is torture.

Colton reaches across me for the wireless keyboard. Within a couple of minutes, he has access to the CCTV security feed on campus, locating my brother outside the Keaton building where most of the undergrad law degree classes are. A strangled noise catches in my throat. Sammy's fine.

My relief is palpable. Colton points to a student seated on a nearby bench and gives me a thumbs up. I meet his eye and he mouths *safe*. I blink to keep the well of tears at bay, snapping my attention back to the feed.

It's going to be okay. They'll guard Sammy from any threat, and in exchange I'll give Colton anything he wants.

"Yeah," I breathe. "I'm good. Promise."

Sammy rubs his nose on the screen. "Aight. Did you ditch your phone? I tried your number, but it said it was out of service."

"It broke." My lips twitch. "If you need me, save this number. Cool?"

"Got it."

Colton mutters something under his breath. It sounds suspiciously like *clever girl*.

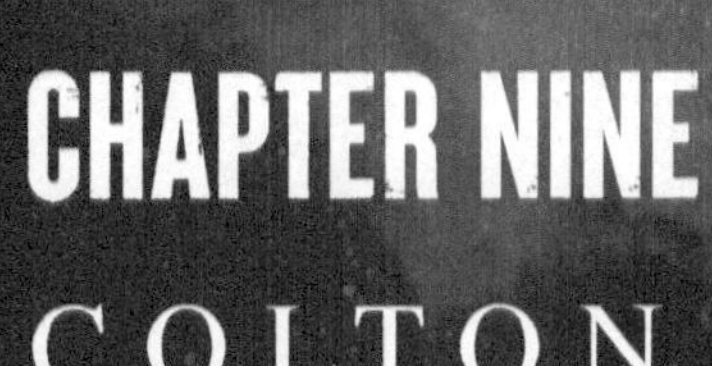

CHAPTER NINE

COLTON

Having the file restored brings me more relief than I anticipate, allowing me to release some of the anxiety I've carried since the first moment I realized I fucked up. With it, I can redeem myself in my brothers' eyes and reaffirm myself as a reliable protector of our most sensitive assets—namely, our flush bank of secrets.

It puts me in a good enough mood for now to allow Quinn to talk to her brother. Maybe it's the rush of chemical reactions in my brain sending the happy signals to ease my stress and my severe lack of sleep catching up with me. She's resourceful and opportunistic, as all good liars are, setting up her future point of contact through my phone to keep in touch.

I give her the universal gesture to wrap it up. She lifts a brow, ignoring me. I prod my cheek with my tongue. It's clear she's reluctant to end the call, but she needs to remember she's not on vacation here.

When I get up and twirl the computer chair around, I brace my hands against the desk on either side of her. Looming over her, I slowly lift my brows. The look she gives me is mutinous. It makes me want to laugh.

I invade her space, keeping my voice low enough the phone's mic won't pick it up. Her brother has no idea I have her right where I've always wanted her. "Time's up."

She holds her damn finger up to make me wait more. I smirk, shaking my head. Reaching past her, I take the phone, hovering my thumb over the end call button.

Her eyes widen and she blurts, "I've gotta go. I'll talk to you later. Text me."

"Yeah, I should get back," Sampson says. "Professor Kirkmund is a stickler about timed breaks."

I hang up before she gets out another goodbye, tossing the phone back on the desk. I level her with a sharp look.

"Was that necessary?" She collapses back in my new gamer chair, arms folded, the oversized sleeves of her hoodie giving her fucking adorable sweater paws—my goddamn kryptonite. "It wasn't hurting anyone."

I ignore her. If I don't, those sweater paws and the combative twist of her lush lips are going to tempt me to further distraction. I've wasted enough time.

Grabbing a tablet and a laptop from the shelf where I'm storing my extra devices, I get everything set up, pulling up the footage from the Kings meeting Wren went to at the Founders Museum.

"So that guy works for you, or whatever?" Quinn prompts. "Because if he's just some random who happened to be in the vicinity and you tricked me—"

"Tricks are your game," I interrupt. "Yes, he's one of our grunts. Levi trained him, so I promise he can handle the task. We haven't been utilizing our full network, but now that we understand who the hell's been screwing with us, we're hitting back twice as hard with everything we've got at our disposal."

My chin jerks as I push the tablet between us and give her the laptop. The Kings have no idea we're more than the four of us.

Something clicks in my mind once I'm set up. "It was you that night."

"What night?"

I gesture to the screen. "The Founders Museum. When we were setting up, you were the one we chased down. Your shit interfered with my equipment."

"Oh. Yeah, I was paid to install a frequency scrambler after hours. I thought you were security and booked it."

Sighing, I press play on the footage.

"Uhh, what in the cult shit?" Quinn mutters when Wren gets to the candlelit lower level and meets the robed society member that almost lost a hand for frisking him.

I snort. "Close. Secret society."

She leans closer to the recording. "Fuck. For real?"

My eyes narrow. Before I put the pieces together about her being the person in the hoodie we chased at the museum, I thought she didn't know the truth. Shouldn't she realize something was off about it all? She disappeared through a secret passage that night when me and Levi were setting up for the summons they planted on Wren during the raid on our fight night.

"I wish I was lying. See the names on the list?" I tap the main monitor with the recovered file. "They're all here. The Kings Society is a greedy, incestuous club of power junkie narcissists obsessed with themselves and their dirty deeds."

I pause, rubbing my fingers together as she scrubs back a few seconds to watch the moment Wren gets to the room with everyone in it. A muscle in my jaw twitches.

"This is who you were working for. Who sent you to spy on us. You seriously didn't put that together?"

There's no point hiding any of it from her when I need her skills on our side. It's not like I'm letting her walk out of here on her own.

She leans an elbow on the desk, playing with the cuffs of her baggy hoodie. "I already said I kept my head down. I was told this file was leaked information. That's all I knew, I swear."

It doesn't sound like the Kings gave her an insider look into club douchebag. Maybe they just utilized her computer skills and considered her expendable. I grit my teeth against that sentiment.

"It was leaked. Technically." I pinch the bridge of my nose. It doesn't take away the sickening discovery of Ethan Hannigan's fateful end, or Rowan's broken voice once we discovered his body. "Rowan's brother is—was—a journalist investigating drug runners and it led to this. These bastards have their thumb in every illegal pie you can think of."

"Kidnapping. Human trafficking," she hisses as the realization of what we revealed to her before connects in one big web of corruption. "Shit."

"Bingo, babe. In Thorne Point, the elite are synonymous with seedy. If there's a line they won't cross, we haven't discovered it yet. Case in point, filicide is on the table by way of blowing up a building with their precious heirs in it. So much for all that legacy crap they shove down our throats before we learn to toddle."

She flicks a wary gaze my way. "It was Fitz Mortimer's order. Him and some other guy I didn't know. I remember them saying something about rebellion and Thorne not holding all the power." Her brows furrow in thought. "I was kind of in shock, but I think they were saying they did it so they could level up."

I stroke my chin, gears turning in my brain. "Infighting. That's good for us. Chaos and disorder leads to distractions."

Distractions mean they won't see us coming when we destroy them with the nooses they've tied themselves. One by one, they'll all fall down. Crash and burn, bitches.

The corner of my mouth lifts. "We need to go through this and the audio to match as many names from the list to these fashion-challenged idiots as we can." I ruffle my hair and slouch against the stiff back of the chair. Mental note, order a second gamer chair because this rickety ass shit ain't cutting it for lumbar support. She's not stealing my good chair. "Some we know. Wren's dad. Levi's uncle."

"Baron Astor," Quinn spits venomously.

My brow lifts. "Mood. Devil incarnate, that one." I eye her from my periphery as I point out the robed members we think match up with them. She glares at the screen, tugging relentlessly on the stretched cuffs of her hoodie. "A few other strong maybes."

"What about the guys in the purple robes and the silver engraved masks?"

"In full cliche fashion, we think they're like the elders in charge. Daddy Thorne defers to this guy in the tacky chair throughout the meeting."

She holds up a finger in my face, whipping to me so hard her braids swing. "Never. Say daddy again."

I smirk. "Bet. I won't be the one saying it, little baby. It'll be you."

She scoffs. "You're so not daddy vibes."

I move without thinking, grabbing her and hauling her from her seat to my lap. My lips brush her ear. "You ain't seen nothing yet. I'd have you begging for daddy's cock so much you'd be crying from how bad you needed it."

She stiffens with a gasp of undeniable arousal—I'm no stranger to what it sounds like when I have a girl hot and bothered—then squirms, jamming her elbow back into my side. I halt it before it connects. My brain catches up with my actions and realization sets in.

Shit. I shove her back to the other chair and rein myself in. This is what happens when she goes off. I follow instinctively, loving the battle of wits between us.

I'm not even into the whole daddy thing, I just reacted to her. When the grasp on my control doesn't feel like it's slipping, I clear my throat.

"Come on, little queen. Hacker versus hacker." I lace my fingers together and crack my knuckles before wiggling my fingers over the wireless keyboard. "Show me what you've got and doxx the crusty bastards. Winner picks dinner."

She gives me that husky, challenging laugh I love. "You're on. I hope you like spicy food."

* * *

I lose track of time as we fall into our tasks. It's late, that's all I'm distantly aware of. Jude and Rowan checked in with texts an hour apart, both of them urging me not to work through the night. None of them plan to come back here, leaving me and Quinn alone at the warehouse.

She makes an inquisitive noise, leaning closer to the laptop screen with her chin propped in her hand. I don't stop typing command lines to access information on Fitz Mortimer. I'm not familiar with him, which means he's got to be a bottom feeder trying to get ahead. My guess is he could be the ass tier of the society, looking to claw his way to the top.

"Whatcha got?"

"Uh—nothing." She quickly clicks out of the window and scratches the tip of her nose. "The firewalls are legit."

I quirk a brow. "Uh huh. That's why you severed the connection, you had full access through."

She hunches her shoulders, covering her mouth with the collar of her pullover. I didn't miss the smooth way she coaxed her way into the financial records she was combing through. Aware of my penetrating gaze drilling into her profile, she shoots to her feet and heads for the door.

"Where do you think you're going? I didn't say you could go anywhere without my permission," I bark.

In response, Quinn flips me off without looking back. She's in for a rude awakening when she reaches the door and finds out she doesn't have any way to open it since her biometric ID isn't encoded into my security system. I fold my hands behind my head and watch as the realization dawns on her. She smooths her clever fingers over the wood, looking for a secret catch that doesn't exist.

She whips around with a furious scowl. "What sick shit is this?"

"It's called security protocols. And, in case you forgot, you're the reason I had to upgrade the shit out of my system."

She huffs, muttering under her breath. "Let me out."

My head jerks with my scoff of disbelief. Even after she admitted to our faces she lied and manipulated us, sold us the fuck out, she still challenges me, choosing fight over flight every time.

I pretend to think about it. "Nope. Your ass is stuck here, remember? Now walk your ass back over here and get back to work."

Folding her arms and squinting at me, she waits a full minute before complying, dragging her feet the entire way. When she drops into the chair, she clenches her jaw.

"You're an asshole."

"I know. You've only told me a hundred times today alone."

Anger reignites, going off like dynamite in my veins. She brought this on herself by lying to me about needing help. About needing my protection. I grit my teeth, annoyed that my need to keep others safe when they can't help themselves was exploited through her deception. It reminds me I can't fucking trust her, can't let my guard down around her again.

I reach across her for the laptop to find out exactly what the hell set her off and she knocks my arm out of the way.

My features twist into a scowl. "If you hadn't lied about everything, we wouldn't be here, Quinn. Own up to your fuck ups and deal with the fallout."

The faster we go back and forth sniping at each other, the more we lean into each other's space. Her warm breath fans my mouth and I squash the urge to claim those lips in a vicious kiss. She needs to learn if she's going to get in my face, there are consequences.

"Admit it. You're only pissed because I beat you," she spits. "You hate that I'm smarter than you. That you never saw me because you were too busy thinking with your dick to take me seriously as a threat. Let me tell you, dumbass, it was *easy*."

I grab her throat with a growl, spurred on by how close to home her words hit in the days after the fire when I realized what went down. We both freeze. My dick throbs, rock hard and straining in my jeans from fighting with her. I can't discern between fighting and flirting with her anymore. The lust blends with my anger at her, creating a potent mix of hatred and desire. I'm going to hate fuck the shit out of her, wreck her throat and pussy with everything I have in me to purge this from my system.

My thumb caresses Quinn's pulse point. "Let's play a game."

Her lips part, eyes flying to mine at my sensual tone. It's the same look she gave me before I ordered her to open her mouth and swallow my spit. She's not backing down. *Good.*

"Get on your knees," I rasp.

She remains still, her breathing growing thicker, pupils blown. Her chest rises and falls against my forearm. She's as turned on by this as I am. I lift a brow.

"No? Giving up so soon? You promised to do anything," I remind her.

It's not that I'll push her to do something she really doesn't want. If she shuts down, I'll stop. I'm not a complete monster, not like my father and the other bastards who think they hold the power in this city. But I'm not above manipulating things in my favor to push her over the edge when it's clearly all she needs to give in to this inescapable pull between us.

It's not going away. We've been speeding toward this from the first moment I caught her counting cards at one of our tables. Everything that's happened in the last four days has only added fuel to fan the flames into a raging inferno.

We're dancing on the line here, living out the alluring, illicit fantasy of who's in control and being forced. The illusion that I'll take her mouth whether she wants me to or not.

I play with my tongue stud, smirking as I grab her hand and press it to my erection. "You started it. Now I expect you to take care of this. How far are you willing to go to atone for your lies?" I squeeze her throat and her breath hitches. She bites her lip, heat flooding her gorgeous big brown eyes. "My dick isn't going to suck itself—I've tried."

The air in the room is warm and crackling with the electric tension sparking between us. She holds my gaze for a beat before rubbing my cock. My eyes hood and I press harder on the back of her hand, grinding against her palm.

Leaning in until her lips almost brush mine, she whispers, "You won't break me."

Then she slides down to the floor like a confident siren straight from my fantasies and I release a deep groan. Fuck, why is everything about this girl so hot? Every time she pisses me off, it gets me hotter.

"We'll see about that," I croon. "Take me out."

The edge of her mouth curls and she goes for my fly. I can read her thoughts all over her face. She believes she's got the edge here, but she has no idea what I'm planning. When she wraps her fingers around my erection and pulls my cock from my briefs, a rough exhale leaves me. I let her think she's running the show for a few moments, enjoying the feel of her fingers jerking me.

Sitting forward, I grab her nape, tugging on her braids so she's forced to look up at me. "I said my cock isn't going to suck itself, little liar."

The confident smirk drops off her face as she stares me down. My grip tightens and she smothers a small cry of pleasure. She folds under the pressure I put on the back of her neck, resting her hands on my thighs as her lips graze my cock. I bite back a curse when she takes me in her mouth and gives a tentative suck. She's testing the water, seeing whether I'm going to ram down her throat.

"Sloppy," I order. "Make a mess, or you're not doing it right."

Quinn forces out a huff through her nose that makes my lips twitch. Even with her mouth full of cock she finds a way to convey her contentious attitude that gets me horny. She takes me deeper, her tongue lighting me up as it drags up the sensitive underside of my length. Pulling off, she flashes me a burning glare and lets her spit drip down from her perfect puckered lips to land on my head, using her tongue to spread it when she swallows me again. Shit, that's good.

There's a vibrator in the desk drawer by my knee. It's the one I stole from Pippa's place. I've been keeping it close since I haven't slowed down in days, pausing only long enough to shower and crash for short periods of time. I'm planning to burn it—because hashtag petty—but this opportunity is too good to pass up and I'm seizing it. I cleaned it so it's fine. Fine, fine, fine. There's no way in hell I'm stopping to go get a different one.

"Take your pants and hoodie off." My fingers thread into her braids and I gather them in my grip to control her pace for a moment, urging her to go fast enough for the slurp of her mouth on my cock to fill the office with the obscene sound. "Mm, fuck, baby. Do it."

Tugging with more force, I make her stop before I get swept away by the rush of heat. Her lips remain parted, shiny with saliva and slightly puffy. I pull on her hoodie, peeling it off for her. She has a vintage Mario Kart shirt on underneath with a cut in the neckline, offering a tempting peek of her tits. My fingers curl around her throat and my gaze bores into hers. She licks her lips and goes for the button on her jeans, working them off.

Christ, the sight of her on her spread knees in a black sports thong and that Mario Kart shirt is the hottest thing I've ever seen, sexier than any of my VR waifu skins or any porn GIF saved to my phone.

Smirking, I draw her back to my cock with a sharp tug on her neck that makes her gasp and arch her spine. My fingers twitch with the need to slide down her back and dip between her legs to find out if her pussy's dripping from this. She falls back into a perfect rhythm, head bobbing while she sucks me.

I reach for the drawer and chuckle wickedly when I click the toy on. She stills at the audible buzz, mouth full of cock. I hold her jaw, applying enough pressure to her throat to challenge her airflow.

"If you stop..." My grip tightens to choke her. Her lashes flutter and her throat convulses against my fingers, vibrating with a hidden moan. "Use this on yourself. You're going to make yourself come while I fuck your face, little liar."

An uneven breath hisses out of her. I trace the vibrator down her hollowed cheek, the vibrations teasing my cock. She snatches it from me, flashing me a dirty look. I smirk, mapping the stretch of her lips with my fingertips instead. My grip squeezes her throat until she forces out a strangled noise and drops a hand between her legs.

Quinn's body shudders from the first moment the toy touches her pussy. She bites back a sound of pleasure, closing her eyes tight. She can hide all she wants, her body tells me everything I want to know. Her chest heaves and her thighs tremble. I thrust shallowly into the wet heat of her mouth, grinning deviously when she inhales sharply, then rolls her hips slowly with a smothered sigh.

Sweet fucking victory.

"I thought you weren't going to break?" I taunt. "Come again, little liar. Keep coming while you choke on me. Soak through your panties and make a fucking mess on the floor."

I don't give her the chance to respond, clamping her nape and forcing her to take me deeper. She sputters and lets her mouth go slack so I can fuck her face. My head hangs and I groan. Noticing she took the vibrator off her clit, I choke her again. Her acrylic nails dig into my leg, sending another jolt of heat to my balls. I don't let up or grant her mercy until she growls and rubs her pussy with the toy.

Shit. I'm not going to last much longer. Her mouth is too good, and it's too hot to watch her shiver from the stimulation she's giving herself.

"Don't swallow when I come," I grit out.

It's not clear if she heard me. She's too consumed by playing with herself, her husky breaths coming in pants, little noises of ecstasy escaping her. Fuck. *Fuck.*

I groan as my balls tighten, fire rocketing through my cock as my orgasm hits. My dick throbs while I shoot my load into her mouth. Taking a ragged breath, I pull free, adjusting my hold to wrench her chin up.

"Open. Show me."

Her eyes are glassy, foggy with lust because she still hasn't stopped using the vibrator. She parts her lips and displays my come on her tongue. I grin, tipping her head back. Leaning down, I spit in her mouth for the second time tonight and pat her cheek. She shudders, another soft noise slipping out of her.

"Now you have permission to swallow." My gaze roams over her, savoring the fire in her eyes when she closes her mouth, gulps my come and spit down, and shows me her tongue once more to prove she did it.

I collapse against the chair, watching Quinn with a hooded gaze as her hips keep circling, chasing the chance to come again. Her lashes flutter and her mouth drops open with another faint moan as it hits, sending her over the edge once more.

Holy shit, that's hot. If I wasn't about to pass out from the lethal combo of a killer orgasm and lack of sleep, I'd haul her up by her tiny waist and drive my cock in her to give her something to scream about while tormenting her clit with the stolen vibrator until she's nothing more than a gorgeous wreck in my lap.

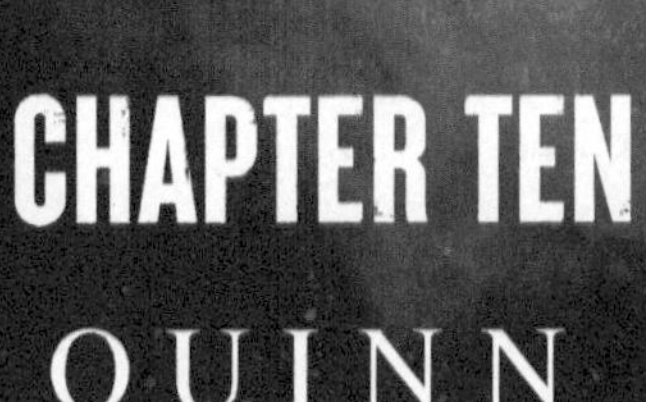

CHAPTER TEN

QUINN

Oн shit. This feels so good. It's exactly what I needed. My clit throbs in time with the vibrations, wave after wave of pleasure crashing through me.

"Time for bed."

Colton's languid words kill the come down of my orgasm, snapping me out of the haze of lust that exploded between us. The filthy desires I succumbed to, allowing him to make me suck him because I wasn't about to admit defeat.

Jesus.

I didn't even think about saying no, a dark, alluring side of me captivated by what he demanded. I drop the vibrator, the buzz loud as it rolls across the floor, bumping against the wheel of his gamer chair. My thighs quiver and my knees ache from how much pressure I put on them rocking against the toy with abandon. My pussy tingles with the phantom sensation.

The way it felt to have my mouth filled, being used while I got pleasure from the vibrator—god, how much I liked it. Heat erupts in my face and mortification rockets through me.

He sighs in satisfaction, tucking his dick away. His legs remain spread on either side of me. "Goddamn, I always knew your mouth would be sinfully perfect." My heart jolts as he grasps my chin and forces my face up again. That confident smirk rakes across my resurfacing pride. "These lips look even better swollen from sucking my cock."

I jerk away with a harsh breath. "That's not happening again. That was—"

"Hot as fuck," he finishes for me.

And, goddamn it, he's not wrong. It was hotter than any kinky thing I've ever tried. I've always been too worried to ever voice the hidden curious desire to explore what it would be like if I couldn't say no. That requires a level of trust I've never granted to any of my quick hookup partners.

Yet I let it happen with Colton of all people? Someone I definitely can't trust? Who hates me? God, I'm messed up.

Selling my soul to him is going to drive me crazy. We're either going to kill each other, or crash together so hard the consequences will be irrevocable. There's no coming back from that once we know what we've been resisting.

I refuse to allow myself to become attached to him—I don't need him, no matter how much he sets my body on fire.

"Whatever." I climb to my feet, legs still shaking from how hard I came using the toy. My cheeks prickle with heat when I realize it's still on, droning against the chair. I snatch it up and kill the power. "Are we going back to your apartment?"

It's sad part of me looks forward to it. The room I stayed in has become synonymous with my safe space to shut the world out, as ridiculous as it is when I was really there to play him.

Colton takes the vibrator from my hands and stuffs it back in the drawer with a weird smile on his face. He laughs, raking his tattooed fingers through his messy dark hair. The sound is tinged with a chaotic air.

My shoulders tense. This fool better not be laughing, because he didn't win. I shove my feet into my jeans and hop to hike them up in two forceful tugs.

He continues snickering under his breath as he backs up our work. Once he's done and everything's powered down, he stands, stretching his long, lithe inked arms overhead, cracking his neck so the crow tattoo ripples. I hate myself because I can't help the way my attention strays to the curve of his bicep and the flex of his shoulder muscles. He's the least built of the four infamous Crows, but his build is exactly what I like—not too much muscle, not too skinny.

Everything about Colton is my type. Which is exactly why I can't allow myself to get swept up in his devious mind games.

I rub the space between my brows and blow out a breath. I need to up my game starting now. Ever since I escaped Mortimer's corporate building downtown, I've existed in a constant state of stress. Getting caught by the same arrogant assholes I had to beg for help has only compounded everything. I was bound to snap at some point.

The only reason I picked the fight that led to the tension shattering between us was because I needed a distraction. It was a tactic to cover my tracks from digging too far into Astor Global Holdings' acquisitions and financial records to look for the money stolen from my family. Colton's system is better than what I've gotten by with on my phone and laptop, giving me the means to access firewalls I've failed to crack time and again.

Astor's name is on the list as one of the people they're planning to go after. If I bide my time, this could work out in my favor, too. I could have the chance to take back what Sammy and I lost. It's a dangerous idea to play Colton twice, especially now that he plans to keep me under his thumb without a moment's respite. I doubt he's joking about twenty-four seven access.

Yet I'm not built to pass up opportunities like this. Learning to survive taught me to seize every chance.

"Come on." He takes me by the elbow. I tear my arm from his grasp and he snorts. "Chill, or I'll leave your ass in the basement all night."

He blocks my view to unlock the door. I squint at his back, following him around the industrial balcony that wraps around the top floor. We pass a bar top with a vintage aesthetic. He draws back a thick crimson velvet curtain that shows a dim, narrow hall lit by Edison bulbs. We go into the third door and I stop in my tracks when he flicks the light on.

It's a bedroom. Weird to have in a warehouse that seems like it's going to be their new nightclub, though it does have secret passages and whatever the hell the basement is supposed to be for.

There's not a lot in it other than the bed—silk sheets, he's so cliche—and a random assortment of his discarded clothes. A drone sits in the corner, plus a VR headset. When he snaps his fingers, LED lights turn on, surrounding the bed. Sound activated. Typical.

Inexplicably, my brain supplies an image of being on my hands and knees while he takes me from behind, the LED changing colors each time he claps my cheeks. My clit pulses, still sensitive from what we did in the office. I slide my thighs together to relieve the ache, berating myself for fantasizing about getting railed by him.

He strips out of his shirt, showing off more of his tattoo collection, then shucks his jeans and faceplants on the bed with a weary groan. I blink, not moving further into the room.

There's only one bed.

Oh hell fucking no.

"No dice. I'm not sleeping in here with you." I fold my arms, regretting leaving my hoodie behind.

Colton rolls to his side, propping his head on his fist. "Suit yourself. I'm going to ride you hard, though. No excuses if you're slacking off. You look like you need the rest as bad as I do, babe."

My lip curls and I click my tongue, gesturing at the bed. "I'm not sharing a bed with you. For real."

A hot rush moves through my chest. This is too much. Too intimate.

The time we did share a bed because he came home punch drunk and well past the point of exhaustion rises to the forefront of my mind, my heart fluttering at the pieces of truth I gave him about myself.

Colton gets up, rifling through a duffle bag sitting on a bench. He shoves a wad of fabric at me. "Here. Relax, goddess of the night." I freeze, fingers clenched in the soft material. He still remembers my Nyx costume from Halloween. He winks. "We're only sleeping in the bed tonight. You can wear this until I get a delivery tomorrow."

He lets go and his t-shirt unfolds. It's a Lord of the Rings shirt that reminds me of the conversation we had in the Thorne Point student union the day I found my *in* by feeding him a fake secret about my parents' being tied to the mob after us—a lie to secure the Crows' protection aka give me access—and schooled him with my hacking skill to access the dean of Castlebrook College's emails. I swallow past the lump in my throat.

"Come to bed," Colton says.

"Not without checking for gross ass stains under a blue light," I counter.

He snorts. "Knock yourself out. There's a mini handheld one somewhere around here. Might've got lost in the move. Next time I jack off, I'll leave you a secret message on your side."

"God, I hate you."

"Same here, baby." His tone doesn't match his words. It's smoky and his gaze drags over me seductively. "Hate you so much."

Oh hell. How am I supposed to survive him? *You won't*, my mind whispers. No. I will. I have to.

Taking a steadying breath, I toe off my Docs and steal the elastic purple skull print laces from one boot to act as a makeshift tie to keep my braids piled on my head. It's far from my usual nightly routine, but it's the best I can do with the hand I'm dealt.

I eye him warily, waiting for him to turn his back before I hastily strip and pull his shirt on. Damn it. It's big on me, hitting mid-thigh, and it smells fucking amazing. *Don't do it, Q.* Ignoring my own warning, I make sure he isn't looking when I lift the collar to my nose and sniff. Jesus, why does he have to smell so great? The woodsy scent with notes of spicy and sweet undertones is irresistible.

Shaking my head, I edge around the opposite side of the bed, rubbing my fingertips together.

"Quit standing over me like a creeper." Colton's voice is muffled by the pillow his face is smashed in. He holds out an arm blindly, grasping at the air. "I can sense you standing there psyching yourself out."

"I'm not psyched out." I slide into bed with stiff movements, facing him. I'm not turning my back on him. "It won't be the first time. We've done this before."

I sound like I'm trying to convince myself. My body doesn't relax and I'm hyper aware of every breath I take. The air is tinged with his scent, though I'm not sure if it's the shirt I'm wearing, or his sheets, or just his proximity.

He cracks his eyes open and traces the curve of his crooked smirk with his thumb, running it back and forth maddeningly along his lip. "I knew you couldn't get me out of your head."

"Psh, you wish," I mutter.

"Don't ruin my post nut good mood by reminding me you're a wicked little trickster." His tone hardens, the languidness evaporating.

I knew it. He's such a hypocrite, luring people into a false sense of security with his easygoing nature, yet he's always hiding what's really underneath—an intelligent, observant guy always on the hunt for vulnerabilities to exploit. The fact we're similar in looking for weaknesses to survive isn't lost on me.

Sleep is going to be impossible. My mind doesn't settle, anxious thoughts creeping up on me. Is Sammy okay? I should steal Colton's phone to check if he texted after his classes. I wait until his breathing evens out, staring at the ceiling counting the minutes.

Once I'm sure he's passed out, I carefully slip out of bed. His phone isn't on his side or in his pants when I check them. Damn it. My attention darts to his pillow. Did he—? Shit, I bet he did anticipate that I'd want it. It's too risky to reach beneath his pillow for it.

Biting my lip, I consider my options. I could go back to the office and get into my accounts, or sneak into the basement to get my laptop and look for the pieces of my dismantled burner. First I have to figure out what sort of security I'm facing.

I pad to the door, halting when it registerers that there's no door handle. No keypad, either. I flick an annoyed look at the lump in the bed. Paranoid control freak. Sighing, I graze my fingers over the door, searching for its secrets.

My eyes widen when I hit a spot that lights up blue, then red, the integration so seamless with the black door that it's easy to miss. Crouching down, I pass my hand over the spot again. It's some kind of scanner. The interface isn't obvious, stumping me. Without it, I don't know how to override it to fool the system. If I had my phone, I could try to connect to it via bluetooth.

I purse my lips to the side as I think this out. Knowing Colton, it's complicated as fuck. The coded puzzles he presents to people he wants to recruit to his network come to mind. I avoided them multiple times in the last few years even though he was persistent about wanting me to join him. Except I wasn't about to let some pretty boy with a huge ego give me orders.

Had I known what I do now, maybe I would've made a different decision. My choices didn't bring me any closer to solving mine and Sammy's problems. It only put us deeper in shit, caught between a war for control of the city between the elite upper class' nasty secret society and Thorne Point's most notorious sons.

A lump of regret and disgust at myself forms in my throat. My tunnel vision made me look past everything shady for the sake of payment when Colton and his friends are the ones I should've sided with. They're the ones standing up to people like Baron Astor to stop them.

Arms slide around my waist and the intoxicating scent of vanilla shot through with a rich, woodsy spice surrounds me. I jump, caught out. Holy shit, I didn't even hear him. How'd he sneak up on me so silently? Angling my head, I glare over my shoulder.

"Nice try, little queen," Colton rasps.

He drags me across the room, lifting me as easily as he always does. I put up a mild fight, because I'm not about to accept this. The rumble of his chuckle vibrates against my back and he hauls me against him once we're in bed again. I pry at his arm locked around my waist, digging my grown out stiletto manicure across his forearm, but it's no use. He only holds me tighter. I huff, trying to ignore how nice it feels to be in his arms.

It's been a long time since someone's just held me. The emotions it triggers are too much for me to handle after I've spent years of foster care hardening myself, training myself not to need anyone like this.

Foster care is rough. It's an eat or be eaten experience. Maybe you luck out with a good placement, but those never last because the bleeding hearts are too worried about helping as many unfortunate souls as they can. The houses you're stuck in the longest are the ones that crush your hopes and leave marks on your soul before you find the strength to build up walls. The ones that have limited food, that don't care if they separate siblings. The caretakers that take liberties and touch you without permission because they believe you're too weak to fight back or have a bribe contact at CPS that doesn't believe your anguished pleas to be moved.

I swallow past the burn in my throat, trying not to break down at the feel of Colton's embrace. Maybe I could've had this with him, if I wasn't too stubborn, too focused on doing things my way. He hates me now, and this is just another punishment to throw in my face.

"Tire yourself out yet?" he taunts in a crackling, gravelly tone. He snorts at the click of my tongue, bringing his lips to my ear. "Sweet dreams. Tomorrow we can go back to hating each other. For now, just sleep."

CHAPTER ELEVEN
COLTON

One of my Dolos minions messages me that he's got my delivery in the morning. I confirm the drop point outside of the warehouse, then shift my gaze to the venomous sleeping beauty beside me.

Quinn's curled into a tight ball, shoulders hunched as if she's got her defenses up even in her sleep. Some of her thick braids have come loose from the way she twisted it up and secured it. The purple skull print elastic looks like the pastel goth laces on her sexy Doc Martens.

My lips twitch with a smirk. Resourceful as always.

I set my phone on the nightstand and roll to my side, pulling her back into my arms. Her ass fits perfectly against my hips, tempting me to grind against her. I press my face into the crook of her neck and breathe in her warm brown skin before it occurs to me I'm being affectionate. Everything she's done slams back into me and my hold on her turns punishing, my arms bands of steel locked around her waist. She releases a soft sound of distress and I let go.

Quinn's not mine to hold.

Sighing, I get up to accept the delivery of supplies I ordered—clothes and toiletries for her since I'm not letting her out of here. I make sure to grab anything she could get a connection with, leaving her locked in the room with the monitoring sensors activated on the custom phone app I built to manage the Nest 2.0's security. I'll receive an alert if she moves from that bed or tries to crack the biometric scanner like I caught her doing in the middle of the night.

For all the fuss she put up, she did sleep. Surprisingly, so did I. Last night's the best rest I've had in weeks. It finally feels like I've kicked the constant twitchy buzz the elevated caffeine of my energy drinks leaves me with when I'm forcing myself to stay awake. I'm not willing to analyze the contributing factors any further than blowing my load in her mouth after she gave me head. Everyone sleeps better after a good orgasm. It's basic science.

On the ground level of the warehouse, I collect the packed duffle bag from the lock box I installed in the back alley. I crouch to check the contents in the chilly morning air, batting away the light flurries early December is trying to dump on New England. I hate Maine winters. Fox and my brothers love the snow, but as fun as our epic snowball fights were growing up, it makes my fingers too cold to type.

I trap the tip of my tongue between my teeth, huffing in mischievous amusement as I check the underwear. Good. The special request I put in is hard to detect on every pair, sewn between the layers and lightweight enough no one would guess these are upgraded. It almost feels like extra stitching.

Rather than the high end toys designed to be worn discreetly, I went with a small flat disk that has a mini vibrating motor embedded in the smooth silicone that syncs to another program I've written for the drones I build. It might not fit as closely to her pussy as other brands of wearable vibrators since this isn't the intended use, but that's fine—I wanted it like this. The switch off is a quiet yet powerful vibration she'll definitely still feel when I control it from my phone. The quarter-sized disk is in every pair I'm providing, and when she's not looking, I'm stealing the hot little sports thong she's got on so she'll always be at my mercy.

I'm a perverted diabolical genius. At least until she figures out what I've done, then opts to go commando. Still a win/win for me either way.

My phone pings with the alert I've been waiting for, informing me of movement in the room. Quinn's up.

A grin stretches my mouth and I pop to my feet, whistling as I head inside. Wren and Jude are in the middle of the dance floor with steaming mugs of Mexican coffee, speaking in low voices. I perk up on my way across the unfinished section of the ground level that'll be the dance floor of our nightclub when renovations are complete. That's Jude's grandmother's special recipe, brewing cinnamon and sugar in with the coffee for a sweet yet spicy flavor. I'd recognize it anywhere after she introduced me to it and it shot to the S-tier of my coffee rankings.

The first thought that pops in my head when I meet Jude's eye is *fuck*. The second is a mental note to get rid of the vibrator I not only stole from the ex he's permanently hung up on, but used in a pinch on the girl that's got me twisted up in knots. I've got to ditch it before he finds it stashed in the office. A nervous chuckle escapes me, and when his eyes sharpen—because he knows me and my tells too damn well—I avoid his attention and change the subject.

"Did you go see Mariela?" I ask. "Please tell me you brought me some of that."

"I did." He doesn't complain when I steal his mug for a sip, groaning in bliss. "She said she lit her Guadalupe candle for me. She had a feeling I needed it."

Religion might not be my bag, but I'm glad she asked for a higher power to watch over him. Maybe she's the reason we made it out of the fire by the skin of our teeth.

I eye him up and down. He's in a loose pair of pants and a university pullover. "No crutch? How'd that go?"

His lips twitch and he lifts a shoulder. "It feels okay to put pressure on now. I played the limp off as a pulled muscle from working out too hard in the gym with Levi." His enigmatic smile falls. "Not sure she bought it, though. She did stare at me pretty hard. I swear, abue can always tell when I'm lying somehow. She stocked me up with food before she was willing to let me leave yesterday."

"It's good you got to see her," Wren says.

I nod. "Is she okay?"

"She misses us, but her place is clean. No bugs, no one watching it. As long as she's safe. That's all I've ever cared about." Jude sighs, his grip on the mug tuning rigid.

It's not the full truth—he cares about more than only his grandmother. Us. Pippa, at one time, was a large part of his heart. Like the rest of us, he wants to keep those he loves safe.

"I'll make it up to her once we finish this and show those bastards we don't know the meaning of mercy," Jude finishes in a low rasp.

Wren and I make dark sounds of agreement.

"I've got the file fully backed up. We worked through the information we had from your first meeting at the museum to achieve more matches. I'm compiling a target list organized by the secrets we have on them."

"Good." Wren's jaw sets. "We start now. Strategize based on who won't make waves. I want them to feel what it's like to realize we're breathing down their necks before they've noticed the knives we sink into their backs."

His blond hair is slicked back, fresh from a shower. The sharp designer suit is his own brand of armor to face the world. For the first time in days, he's looking like he'll survive the loss of the hotel, the cold ruthlessness back in place.

"I'm on it." I clap him on the shoulder in silent support. We've got this.

"I've got a meeting at city hall with the zoning board to speed up the timeline for the proposed Crowned Crow Club." He gestures around us with an arrogant flourish. "Some wheels need greasing."

"I think you mean knee caps need cracking," Rowan corrects. "They'll bow down to you, King Crow. Or else."

"Oh, ow, ow," I howl at the sight of her, clutching my chest. "Ro. You have to warn a guy, babe. Damn, girl, I wasn't ready."

"Stop." Her sly grin matches the big guy's.

"Are you off to slay hearts?" Taking her hand, I give her a wolf whistle and make her twirl to show off the oxblood jumpsuit that's as impeccable as Wren's tailored suit.

Their king and queen power couple vibes are off the charts.

"And taking names," she says.

Wren steps between us, tugging her into his side. He tips her chin up for a kiss, speaking against her mouth. "The only name you'll take is mine. But slay as many hearts as you want, my queen. I'll enjoy watching."

A husky laugh leaves her and she touches his jaw. "Don't ruin my lipstick."

"Do you have any idea how much I want to ruin you all over again, right here so everyone knows you're mine?" he mutters.

She hums, her thumb stroking his chiseled jaw. "Later."

"Aww." I nudge Jude with my elbow. "Mommy and Daddy are flirting."

Jude snorts, hiding it in his coffee while Wren levels us with one of his formidable, icy stares. My phone vibrates with a text. When I check it, I find a message from Levi letting me know he and Isla are fifteen minutes out.

"Lev's on his way," I say. "We're hitting up young master Newmont on campus to smoke his dad out. Turns out nastiness runs in the family—junior's got his daddy's taste for buying unwilling girls. I remember seeing his dad in the front row of that creepy ass auction theater. We're going to nail them all for what went down at the Castle."

The database of secrets we've gathered over the years has every immoral black mark imaginable on it. From illegitimate children to murder of every variety, virginity stealing clubs that prey on young girls served up by their own families, affairs both open and secret to swingers and legendary orgy parties where, *oops*, someone fucked their actual flesh and blood. Even literal skeletons in the wall from a grandparent that bricked a sibling in. No one would want even the tamest of secrets to get out. They'd spell their own ruin with the shadowy deeds and family history.

Then there are the biggest secrets we have on the majority of the high society community—they're all rocking a membership through inheritance or private invitation to a long-standing secret society operating in the city's shadows dating back to the founding of Thorne Point. On top of that, sick pedophiles and human traffickers to cater to their no limits lifestyles.

My teeth clench. I checked twice last night, but neither of my parents are on the list. Doesn't mean they're not members, just that Rowan's brother didn't find them. It doesn't absolve my father of his sins, either. His secrets check multiple boxes—an affair outside of his new marriage with a maid that lied about her age, resulting in a bouncing baby me. He made her disappear after he took me from her. I rub the inside of my ring finger over the royal crown ink that covers a small surgery scar when he almost severed my finger in one of his rages.

I hold the strap of the duffle bag on my shoulder with a white-knuckled death grip. I've dangled my dad's secret about my biological mother and his cover up over his head, but if we're cashing in the others, maybe it's time the world sees Vance DuPont for who he really is.

"I'm going to grab Quinn and the gear I'll need for this job." I bump my fist against Wren's, Rowan's, then Jude's. "Check in with you later."

"Be careful," Jude cautions. "Don't get attached to your asset."

Damn him. He sees too much and knows me too well. I salute him with two fingers. "I know what I'm doing. She understands what's up."

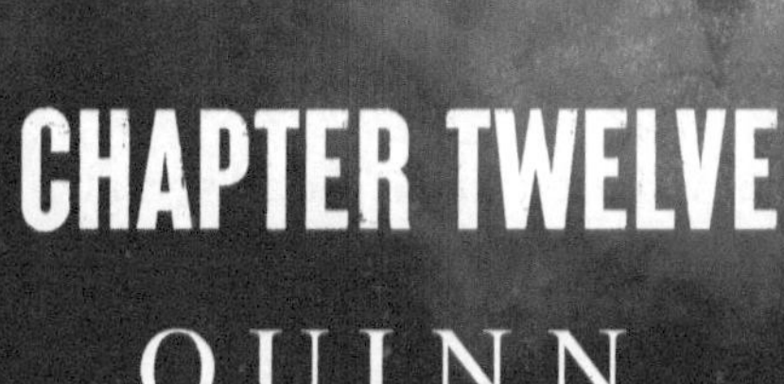

CHAPTER TWELVE

QUINN

After waking alone in bed, Colton didn't return for long enough to annoy me. I was fuming by the time he opened the locked door, pissed he left me trapped in his room. Then he chucked a bag at me to cut off my snarky tirade. Inside, I found clothes, a toothbrush, some silk head wraps, and anything else I could need. Even the brand of lotion I like—which I didn't replace after using the bottle I carry with me as my distraction to escape Sosa. My lips slid together, battling the unwanted bubble of gratitude. Then the jerk smirked and told me I had less than two minutes to get ready before we had to leave, giving me barely enough time to process what I threw on.

Colton doesn't tell me where we're heading when we pile into a brand new black SUV with surly and brooding Levi at the wheel. His sunshine personification girlfriend, Isla, dances in the front passenger seat to the music station she turns on while Colton skims through a class roster on his portable tablet beside me in the second row. Ten minutes into the drive, Levi's lips shift into a ghost of a smile as Isla serenades him on the chorus of the next song using the belt of her fashionable peacoat and he reaches for her hand, threading their fingers together.

It's not until we reach the familiar streets around campus that I catch on. Thorne Point University sprawls across several blocks, nestled at the upscale edge of the city's downtown. The historic buildings dating back to the founding of this place mark the prestige of the students that go to the renowned school. Levi scans his access card at the security gate and pulls on to the cobblestone drive behind a swanky town car and a limousine.

"Which building is the lecture in?" he asks gruffly.

"Mason," Colton answers without looking up from the screen.

"You're going to class?" I curl my fingers in my lap when Levi's dark gaze pins me in the rearview mirror. "I thought things were more...urgent."

"Trust the man with a plan, babe." Colton shoots me cocky finger guns while Levi parks in a lot full of luxury brand cars near the central lecture halls.

"Which would be?" I prompt with a frown when none of them fill me in.

Isla opens her mouth to answer, but Levi turns her by the shoulders to face him, pinning her to the side of the SUV. He cups her cheek and his gaze roams her face. "Are you sure you're okay to do this, princess?"

"For the hundredth time, yes." She leans into his touch with a bright, infectious smile. "I know I have you by my side always. That's all I need. Oh, and Pointy. Our happy, stabby little family."

He huffs when she pats her thigh. "Things shouldn't get so out of hand you need to use your knife. And if they do, I'm here to protect you."

It never made sense to me why a bubbly senator's daughter like her was with him other than the typical appeal of a bad boy until now. The rumors of Levi Astor's borderline knife fetish are rampant throughout campus. Though they seem opposites, I look at their connection in a new light. It's obvious they're attuned to each other and how protective he is over her. I lock down on the pang of longing in my chest. I'm fine on my own.

"Taking on my father and the men that use that awful club is more important," she says seriously, her voice shaking with emotion. "They're not going to do what they did to me to any other young girls."

Levi's gruff response is unintelligible, but it makes her release a soft laugh. The rigid line of his shoulders relaxes marginally and he draws her into his strong arms for a kiss.

Colton's fingers twine around my wrist and he tugs me along. "Catch up with us. I've got his signal pinging off the campus network. He's heading to class."

I peer over my shoulder curiously. They're completely in their own world. Nothing exists to them outside of their kiss.

"I don't like flying blind," I say.

Colton's grip tightens on my wrist. "You know how to clone a phone, right?"

"Yeah. Cake." I scoff. "Excuse you for doubting me."

He flashes me a smirk. "Good. That's your part of the plan. We're going after Maxmillian Newmont VIII. Well, actually we want to nail his dad, but from what I found when I hacked his Insta in the Hamptons this summer, when I was bored out of my skull at the White party, this tool is going down, too. Whole family line is rancid, I bet."

The ferocious conviction in his tone takes me by surprise. "Are they—" I cut off when he squeezes my wrist hard enough to bruise without looking at me. He lets up when I jerk my arm free of his grasp and rub my wrist. "On your list?"

"Yes." He checks his phone, then rummages in the messenger bag he carries, slipping me a fresh, top of the line device. It's the latest model that just released. "Don't get any ideas about swiping this for yourself. No phone privileges. I'm watching you, got it? The lecture is forty minutes, so you'll have plenty of time to work. If you can't pull it off in under ten, then know that I'm better at it than you."

I press my lips together. "Can I see my brother after?" My gaze drifts across campus to the steeple of the Keaton building where the law students have most of their classes. "We're here. I didn't get to see him before you assholes dragged me off. I just want to check on him to make sure that private security guy isn't sniffing around."

"If anyone came within a few hundred feet, I'd know about it. He's fine."

He tows me off the wide path into an arched tunnel that leads to a different section of campus. His thumbs tap his phone screen rapidly, then he shows me Sammy is in the student union playing on his NintendoDS. I clutch the phone like a lifeline to my brother, bringing it close to my face. A couple of guys I recognize from his major are eating with him, plus the one who was around him last night that works for the Crowned Crows. The guy I bit.

Colton plants a hand on the brick beside my head, leaning near enough to send my pulse stuttering. I wish I was immune to him. It didn't matter that I resisted his flirting while I was staying with him—it's been less than twenty-four hours of being forced to remain near him and my resolve has taken critical hits. As fucked up as it is, there's a side of me that wants the man who hates me.

"See? He's making new friends. Remember, little liar," he sing-songs. "Gold stars. Start collecting them. Make me believe you're a loyal asset, or your brother might not be so safe anymore. Until then, you don't have a leg to stand on."

I blow out a breath. "Fine."

"I know you think you're hot shit, little queen. But it's likely the Kings don't actually give a fuck about wasting resources to go after you. They'll have bigger problems to worry about since they failed to take us out. They're going to forget all about you with us picking pieces off the board, so relax and fall in line."

Lifting my attention from the phone, I swallow at his proximity. The vivid memories of his body against mine in bed and the taste of his come flooding my mouth makes my face flame and my stomach flutter. His full lips twitch with a lopsided cocky smile as if he can read the thoughts running through my head.

Shoving against his chest, I clench my teeth. "Step off. You don't have to be in my face all the time."

"Just making sure I watch you closely so no more lies come from these lips."

I tamp down on the urge to shiver when he traces the shape of my mouth with his thumb. Instead, I level him with a fierce glare, pushing my attraction to him deep down so he doesn't know his touch feels good. He chuckles, taking his phone. I roll my lips between my teeth to keep from begging for it back.

His gaze burns into mine. "Stay focused."

The unwavering attention sends another bolt of heat straight to my core. We stare each other down for another beat, neither of us willing to back down or be the first to look away. His infuriating smirk grows. Gritting my teeth, I shove past him, ignoring his cocksure laughter.

When we emerge from the tunnel, Levi and Isla have caught up with us. Levi nods to Colton as he shadowboxes with a devious grin.

"I love the smell of fresh chaos in the morning," Colton crows.

"Say it louder," Levi says sternly. "Let the entire campus know we're up to shit."

"That's any day that ends in *y*. We're always up to shit." Colton nudges him as the four of us fall into step, blending in with the students entering the Mason building.

Isla hooks her arm with mine, shooting me a reassuring smile that catches me off guard. She's the least wary of me out of all of them, her demeanor warming back up to me compared to last night at the warehouse. "I'm glad we get to hang out. It gives us a chance to get to know you better. Don't mind the guys doing what they did to you—they're just like that. Levi sort of held me captive too when he brought me to the Nest."

"I think it's a little different than that." A laugh of disbelief works its way up my throat.

Hang out? Normalizing holding people against their will? We're about to crash a class to pull a more high tech version of a bait and switch on some hapless trust funder. I'm aware that my own idea of normal is skewed from having everything ripped from me and learning to survive in foster care, but these guys play by their own set of rules.

"We're the good guys," she promises. "And I don't get the vibe you're a bad person, so that's that."

I snort. "Thank you?"

Guilt bubbles in my stomach. When I first met them all, she was the first to welcome me. It's been far too long since I've made a genuine friend and I was afraid I threw away the chance by betraying them. The others might not trust me, but she's willing to forgive. I glance at the guys and chew on the inside of my cheek.

"I'm sorry," I whisper to her. "If I'd known, I would've made a different choice."

She shakes her head and pats my arm. "We don't have to dwell on it. We're all okay and you're with us now."

"Isles." Colton twists to face us, walking backwards. "You're our dazzling distraction. Ready to shine, gorgeous?"

Isla gives him energetic spirit fingers. "Roger that."

CHAPTER THIRTEEN

QUINN

WE slip into the lecture hall as if we belong there. Colton's playful behavior sobers when he scopes out the mark. He drapes an arm over my shoulder and flicks his fingers to point him out to me.

Maxmillian Newmont VIII has a helmet of gelled dirty blond hair and flashes an expensive mouthful of veneered teeth. He's all over a classmate who clearly isn't interested in his smarmy demeanor. It doesn't stop the guy from putting his hands on her waist, drifting lower. A scoff of disgust sounds under my breath. I'm not one to get involved, but if he doesn't move his hand, I'll step in and remove it for him.

"Exactly," Colton mutters. "This douchebag's epic downfall caught in the crossfire will be the cherry on top."

"Maxie Newmont, is that you?" Isla coos. "Oh, it's been too long!"

It's almost sad how fast the guy's head whips around at her effervescent tone. His lascivious grin is gross. Levi shoves a hand in his pocket with a dangerous growl. I'd bet anything he's palming a concealed weapon as our target approaches with eyes only for his girlfriend while he's standing right there.

Colton steers me away for a back row seat at the top of the tiered hall, keeping his arm across my shoulder. As Isla chats with the guy, Levi picks out seats directly in front of us and Isla lures the target without making it obvious, turning to chat with him animatedly, then taking a few steps.

"Shoot." Isla waves her phone and steps closer to rub Maxmillian's arm. "I totally thought I had your number, but I don't. We have to catch up before the holiday Cotillion ball."

"Oh. Yeah, here." Maxmillian scrambles to get his phone—a perfect match for the one Colton gave me—and leers as she opens her peacoat to reveal a sheer black polka dot top with a sweetheart neckline. "Give me yours? I'll text you. We can grab dinner at Le Solstice. It just opened and the wait for a table is six months. I can get us in."

"Aren't you sweet."

Isla giggles and Levi's sharp jaw flexes. He takes out a butterfly knife, whipping it around with alarming speed and skill.

"She's good at that," I murmur.

Colton huffs in amusement. "Jude's conman tricks fascinate her. See the way she's touching his arm every time she smiles? Classic psychological reinforcement of the dopamine spike he gets when a pretty girl smiles at him." He angles his head to mutter against my ear. "Now pay close attention."

Levi's shoulder bumps into Maxmillian's when he turns to put his phone in his bag, deftly catching it before it slides in. Reaching back, he passes it off to Colton.

"You're up," Colton rasps. "Give me a good show. I'm timing you."

I roll my eyes and slouch in the seat while the lecture begins. "Couldn't you just do this yourself?"

He shrugs. "I could."

He traces the shell of my ear with the titanium stud piercing his tongue. My breath catches and I press my thighs together as an electric spark races through me. Shit. I never knew my ears were that sensitive. My past hookups have been quick and dirty, allowing little time for exploration because I didn't want to waste time getting close to someone who wasn't going to matter. It was about getting off as fast as possible and moving on.

I keep my gaze trained on the two phones in my lap, refusing to show him how much he affects me. The last thing I need is for him to use this against me.

His tone lowers to something shadowy and caustic. "But you're my asset and I want to make sure you're a team player when I need you to do something. If you don't..."

My heart stutters as a strong, inaudible vibration starts out of nowhere right against my pussy, then vanishes as fast as it started. Just enough to leave my clit tingling from the small dose of pleasure. What the—? I release a harsh breath and scan my surroundings. No one pays us any attention in the back row. Isla keeps up her murmured conversation with Maxmillian and Levi seems poised to deck him if his hands stray from the armrest.

Finally, I turn a *what the absolute fuck* look on Colton. The bastard seems pleased with himself, chin dipping and dark tousled hair falling into his face. His smirk is devious, thumb hovering over his phone with an app open. The app—that's how he triggered it. Oh god, he's been planning this moment.

"I'm testing your focus." He drags me back into his side by the arm around my neck to whisper. The graze of his lips on my skin makes my clit throb. "Be good and maybe I'll let you come."

"I'm going to kill you," I grit out. "We're not about to—Not here."

The look he gives me brims with challenge. He doesn't have to say it, but I hear the words in his devilish tone echoing in my head. *Let's play a game, Quinn.*

Stripping out of the quilted down jacket he gave me when we left, I lay it across my lap, feeling like everyone can sense the loud drum of my heart. He caught me by surprise, but I'm not about to let the other people around us hear if he pulls that again.

An ache thrums between my legs in response to that forbidden thought, my mind amplifying the idea into trying to stay quiet while he makes me fall apart again and again in a room full of people. My eyes slam shut. Damn it. Damn *him.*

I should've known a gift from him wasn't without strings. He lured me into a false sense of security by giving me that duffle bag waiting for my reaction. I shift experimentally, trying to work out how the hell he snuck a vibrator into the panties I threw on in a rush. When I tuck my hips I feel the brush of a small disk shape between the fabric lining. That clever bastard.

Oh yeah? Bring it, pretty boy. I'll handle whatever you throw at me.

Working my jaw, I focus on getting this cloning done. I can't get out of here and strip this underwear off until I do. Then I'm going to cram them up Colton's ass.

The weight of his gaze doesn't let up. In my periphery, he traces his smirk with his thumb. I keep my face a mask of concentration.

Focusing on redirecting Maxmillian's unique identifying IMEI number to the new phone feels like navigating a minefield, waiting for Colton to toy with me. Now that I'm aware of the wicked game, the anticipation is what makes my heart race. This hack is something I can do easy—I used to make quick money cloning phones to resell in high school—yet my attention frays, split between the task and his thumb dancing impishly over his phone.

There's no way I'm hoping he'll turn the hidden toy back on.

My core clenches. Nope. My thighs press together to alleviate the hot ache in my pussy. Nope. My lips press together in preparation to keep quiet. *Nope.*

Last night's games ramp up the heady fog teasing the edge of my awareness, the dirtiness of grinding against the vibrator Colton handed me while he fucked my face, using my mouth roughly until he came. A wave of heat crashes through me at the memory of showing him my tongue coated with his release before he grabbed my jaw and spat in my mouth, making me swallow all of him. I suppress a shudder, licking my lips.

This is not the time to think about a depraved fuckboy that gets me hot when I fight with him, and hotter when he makes me succumb to what he wants. It doesn't matter that he perfectly aligns with a deep seated desire to have someone to fight with that also knows when to take control, that revels in taming me when I don't obey right away to earn the moment I give in. I don't want to analyze why being with him shuts out the world and takes away all the stress that I carry, letting me just *be*.

Shoving it to the back of my mind, I shift my focus to the two phones tucked in the folds of my jacket. Once the clone is done, I type in a combination of symbols and numbers that overrides the lock screen with a master pin code I picked up on a Reddit forum when I learned how to do this. I poke through to check that everything transferred over, pausing on the nudes library of different girls to rival PornHub. Shaking my head, I go to erase them.

A pulsing vibration hits my clit and a strangled noise of surprise lodges in my throat. Everything I shoved aside comes flooding back. Oh god, the vibrations increase in speed, making my legs tremble. I kill the urge to roll my hips. When I move my finger away from the trash icon, it stops.

"We need it all," Colton murmurs. "I'll give you the honor of trashing it once I have a backup. It'll be therapeutic for you."

"Asshole," I hiss.

"Keep going."

"This would be easier if you just stole his phone," I retort.

He makes a noise of dissent. "I don't want to tip off Newmont senior that junior is a security risk. If he gets flighty about junior's derelict collection falling into the wrong hands, he'll ruin what I've got planned."

I get what he's focused on when I check the text messages. The back and forth with his dad mentions not knowing a girl he slept with was underage—and inebriated. I glare at the back of Maxmillian's head, curbing the desire to kick it. The text conversation goes on to talk about contacting Snyder & Associates to handle it so the girl's allegations don't stick.

Handle it. The universal phrase for a cover up. Daddy dearest promises his winner of a son won't face a statutory rape charge on his record. Acid burns in my stomach and my furious gaze slides to Colton.

"Don't look at me like that. You were the one working for his dad's private club," he says darkly.

"I didn't—"

"Know," he finishes for me. "Yeah. But you could've guessed. I hope the money was worth it."

"I wasn't even paid in full," I snap under my breath to distract myself from the slimy feeling of knowing I worked for the wrong people. "Bastard cut me loose and never made the final payment. I only got the transfer to TPU and ten percent upfront."

Colton smothers a snort. "Damn, you got played."

The pointed tips of my acrylic manicure prod my palm. Yeah. He's not wrong. Hindsight's a goddamn bitch and a half.

I twitch, half-jumping when he puts his hand in my lap. His mouth tilts in a shitty smile as he collects Maxmillian's phone and taps the back of Levi's seat with his toe. Levi barely makes his movements noticeable. It's only because I'm paying attention to them that I witness the smooth exchange when Colton gives him the phone. A beat later, he signals Isla.

"Oh my god." She snickers into her hand, whispering to Maxmillian. "I just realized this isn't my class."

"Huh?" Maxmillian reaches for her hand. She evades him with a smooth move, tightening the black velvet bow her wavy chestnut hair is secured in. "I thought we were going to grab lunch together?"

"Oh, no, sweetie. Sorry, my boyfriend and I should get out of here." She gestures with her head at Levi, smile stretching when Maxmillian pales. "Bye!"

Levi takes her hand and they slip out of the room through the side door. The lecturer doesn't bat an eye at their departure, droning on about...I don't even know, at the front of the tiered hall. Whatever the hell nasty rich white boys like Maxmillian Newmont VIII study to kill time until their trust funds kick in.

He glances around in bewilderment, then checks his phone, none the wiser to what we pulled off. Shaking his head, he gathers his things and leaves class twenty minutes early.

I make to get up, but Colton stops me with the arm he bands over my lap. "Did I say you could get up?"

Liquid fire floods my veins at his tone. It's mischievous and light, yet demanding in a way that sets me alight.

"We're done, right?" I try.

His smirk makes my heart race faster. "We're nowhere near done, little queen."

Then his thumb draws a circle on his screen and I have to bite my tongue to hold in the cry threatening to escape me at the burst of pleasure I get from the vibrator. Fuck. When I think I can manage, I look at him. Oh *fuck*. His expression is pure sin, full lips parted, sly green eyes locked on me.

I shake my head. He nods slowly, the corners of his mouth curling in a devious grin that spells my demise. He cocks his head to the side, the crow tattoo stretching as he takes my suppressed reactions in with fascination as he changes up the pattern on the vibrations with a flick of his thumb. Jesus, I'm trying to ride it out, but I'm not going to last, unable to withstand how good the seductive torture is against my pussy.

Colton leans in when I tip my head back against the seat in an effort to silence myself as I squirm. His hot breath fans across my face and he grasps my jaw, stopping me from turning away, from hiding from him.

"Does that feel good, baby?" he rasps in a smoky tone that caresses my lips. "Are you going to cream your panties for me, little queen? Mm, I wish you were soaking my cock instead. You can picture that's my tongue stroking your clit until it's unbearable."

"Shit," I choke.

There's nothing I can do to stop the tight coil of ecstasy ready to snap in my core. I'm going to come. He's going to make me shatter in public, forcing an orgasm whether I want it or not.

My breaths come in thick pants and my cheeks prickle as my hips roll with the vibrator in my panties. I'm so close. Tingling jolts spread through my pussy as I dance on the edge.

Then the vibrations disappear once again before I get there. A whine of dismay lodges in my throat and someone two rows ahead of us peeks back at us. Goddamn him.

Glaring at Colton, I shoot to my feet and rush out of the room. I don't get far. He chases after me and pulls me into an alcove behind a statue of one of the Thorne Point founders, pinning me to the wall with a hand around my throat. I'm still disoriented from almost reaching my orgasm before he denied it, and he breathes in my needy little sounds with a cocky grin I want to smack.

"You need more?" I shake my head, clamping my mouth shut. He chuckles, licking my cheek. "That's what I thought."

The vibrator turns on again, the intense pulsations walking a fine line of too much and not enough to my oversensitive, throbbing pussy.

"No," I moan. Then, in a mortifying, wrecked whisper, "Please."

"Tell me how badly you want to come. Beg me to let you, little liar," he says against my lips.

"No."

His grip on my throat flexes and he lowers the vibrations to barely there. "By all means, drag this out, brat."

I squirm to seek pressure, but it's useless. He keeps me pinned with little effort, his height and his muscle tone giving him the advantage over me. My knees buckle when he gradually increases the pulse pattern until my lips part.

"There?" He hums. "I know you want to come."

"I—yes." I'm hot all over, my chest and pussy both on fire—my chest in defeat and my clit because I'm about to erupt. "Please."

"Can't hear you," he croons. "Louder."

I swallow thickly. The idea of someone hearing and catching us only adds to the arousal drowning me. I take too long to answer and he cuts the toy off again. I can feel how damp my panties are from how turned on I am.

"Please, you fucking asshole," I push out, my voice getting louder. "I need to come."

Before I finish speaking, the vibrator is on again, the pulse strong and constant just how I like it. I melt against the wall and he supports me, nose grazing my jaw as I reach oblivion with a faint, ragged moan, the rippling pleasure rising up and rolling through my core. The orgasm stretches on, intense and bursting like an exploding star behind my eyes.

"Oh god," I whimper.

"Good?" He mouths at my neck.

I shudder. "So fucking good."

When I catch my breath, I crack my eyes open. My heart flutters at the intent look he gives me. My gaze dips to his mouth. With a rough noise he slams his mouth against mine in an angry kiss that consumes me. I let him in, moaning when the stud piercing his tongue collides with my tongue, stroking it. He bites at my lips and tightens his hold on my throat, making my thighs clench as I scrabble at him. When we part, we're both panting.

Colton's seductive air is gone. He serves me a hard look, green eyes glinting with ire. He adjusts his grip, moving up to grab my jaw. I go cold all over, awareness slamming back into me. It chases away the lingering arousal and my desire for another kiss.

"You wish you didn't fuck with me, Quinn. Because I would've been so good to you."

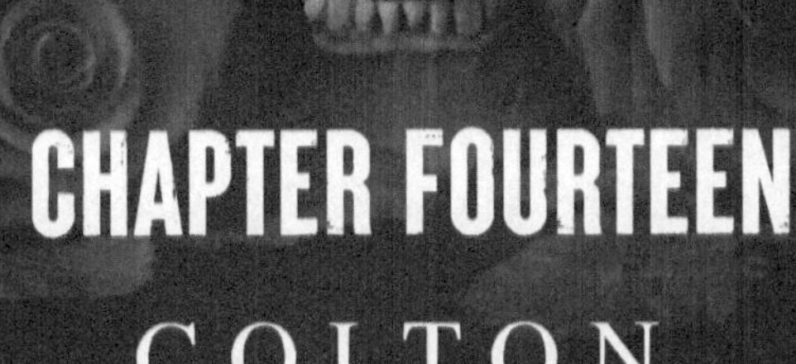

CHAPTER FOURTEEN

COLTON

Wʜᴇɴ I shift back from a kiss fueled by my fury and remind her of how badly she fucked up, Quinn's gaze is hazy. Same as it was when she sucked my cock. Shit, I like that look on her. It's more honest than the lies she's thrown in my face.

Despite my harsh words, she stares at me, plush lips parted, chest heaving with husky breaths. Enemy or not, she's stunning when she comes. No doubt. Jude's warning not to get attached to my asset echoes in my head, then quickly fades into background noise, overtaken by the desire for more of this. More of her.

Then her pretty brown eyes shutter. She thinks that will hide how much my games turn her on? Nah.

I'm a gambling man, and I'm all in with my bet that she's wet. My eyes rove the micro shifts in her expression as she does her best to recover from the orgasm I forced out of her, then land on the nearly healed blisters on my fingers gripping her jaw. Clenching my teeth, I drop my hand and shove my phone in my back pocket.

"Let's go," I mutter.

We emerge from the alcove. She shoulders past me and heads for the bathrooms instead of the exit. Scrubbing my jaw, I follow to make sure she doesn't try to bolt.

I wait outside with my arms crossed. Ten minutes later, she comes out with her jaw set. She won't look at me directly.

"Aren't we going?"

I scrutinize her until she squirms, then huff. Grabbing her arm, I march her right back into the bathroom.

"Where are we—Hey. Colton, hey!" She releases a frustrated noise and struggles, jerking against my grip on her elbow. "You can't just go into the women's—"

I pull a face. "Do I seem like a guy who gets along with rules?"

My gaze sweeps the room. The trash can by the marble sinks. Peeking at her from the corner of my eye I know I'm right. Her mouth tightens, giving her away.

I make a show of reaching inside and snagging the crumpled pair of underwear she ditched.

"Panties. How about that? It's my lucky day." I waggle my brows and run the damp material through my fingers. "These are soaked. Someone had a good time."

"You're an asshole," she bites out.

I hum with a malevolent smirk as I tuck the panties in my pocket and steer her out of the room. "Could be worse. I could force you to put them back on and feel the evidence of the pretty little mess you made. Could turn the vibrations back on and make you come over and over the whole ride back until you're dripping. Would you be quiet, or would Levi and Isla have to hear your broken moans?" With each suggestion, I walk into her until her back hits the wall. My chest presses against her. "They're pretty hot, baby. I might lose control if I hear them again. My friends could watch while I fuck you in the back seat."

An uneven breath hisses out of her and I grin. It doesn't matter which part of the hypothetical illicit fantasies turn her on the most, only that she can't hide from me how much she likes when I mouth off like this.

We meet back up with the others at the car. Quinn doesn't talk to me for the rest of the day. It suits me fine because we've got shit to do.

She still won't say a word when I collapse back on the bed later that night, folding my arms behind my head while she plays chicken with the edge.

"You're going to fall."

Nothing.

"There's no way you're asleep already. Not after such an exciting day on Team Awesome."

Nada.

Smirking, I roll over and drag her against me. Her body remains rigid until she gradually relaxes. I don't buy it. Even prepared for her to do something, I'm not expecting it when she kicks me. I grunt, trapping her legs between mine in a neat little twist hold Levi taught me.

She grumbles something under her breath that sounds like an insult.

"Keep playing, Quinn. You won't win against me."

* * *

We've been unraveling the web of secrets surrounding the Kings Society since the first moment Rowan came to us to find her missing brother, followed by

Isla's foiled kidnapping. With each new discovery of how deeply ingrained the Kings are with the city's history, dating back to the founding fathers of Thorne Point, we've pulled back on the bigger picture.

From the mysterious crossed keys symbol hidden repeatedly throughout the city to old secret passages. Underground meetings to cryptic messages from family with their tacky membership badge rings. Elaborate parties to cover up what really goes on to straight up murder. All of it has proven how much the poisonous roots are entangled with our city. I've always said nothing's random here, but the truth is still a bitter pill to swallow.

Old traditions. Legacy. They called it their oath to serve the city, guiding it on the correct path to their ultimate ideal at the meeting Wren attended, yet in reality it's their own twisted kingdom bred by greed from the start. There's no greater good here, only ensuring they're the ones who remain on top. Classic rich, dramatic as hell cliches.

They expected us to join them—Wren and Levi following in their father and uncle's footsteps, and invitations extended to me and Jude for the promise they see in us. Baron Astor's words from the masquerade last month filter through my head. *Let us show you what it truly means to be a King in Thorne Point.*

Utter fucking horse shit. Like Levi told Stone when he killed him, the Crows stand on our own legacy. Our morals might be skewed in shades of dark gray. We'll do what it takes to achieve our goals, yet we're not monsters who stoop to the vile things the Kings engage in.

They've been cocky and that leads to sloppiness. The hotel fire was a pot shot from someone seizing the opportunity to level up, but we learned first hand by taking out the Castle that the society doesn't run things with many guards, only a skeleton crew of ex-military private security. They think they're a well-oiled machine with an ironclad grip on their thrones.

They'll learn. Viciousness simmers in my veins. They'll all fucking learn.

Quinn's expression is set in concentration standing at the fold out table covered in tech beside me, her nimble fingers writing code without pause. She's been uncharacteristically quiet the last couple of days since I forced her to come after edging her with the hidden vibrator. The urge to do it again, to swallow her sweet as sin cries and push her until she begs me hasn't left me alone since that angry kiss in the alcove.

In retaliation, she's continued to sleep fitfully, pretending to kick in her dreams so I don't hold her like I did the first night. What can I say? I'm a man who likes to cuddle up to anyone I share a bed with. If it makes her uncomfortable, even better because it's one more thing I can use against her to rile her up. A reminder that she won't escape me.

Yesterday I was bored waiting for the video I cut for today's operation to render and tested the toy's control app on her. Nothing. A smirk twisted my lips when I realized that meant she wasn't wearing any of the panties I provided under the pastel purple star-patterned blanket hoodie I grabbed from my downtown apartment since she seemed to live in it whenever she was there. And those fucking fishnets that drive me crazy and get my cock rock fucking hard.

Note to self, get some fishnets delivered stat because I want to play with her through them and dig my fingers in the holes when I fuck my frustrations out by stretching her pussy with my dick.

"Stop staring at me," she snarks without taking her eyes off the tablet screen. "Eyes on your own work."

"But you're just so pretty to look at when you do your braids in space buns. It puts so many good ideas in my head. I'm definitely picturing you wearing them buck naked, those gorgeous tits bouncing while you ride my cock." I hum a laugh when she flips me off. "You good?"

"All set," she confirms, finishing off the last command lines with a jaunty keystroke.

There's an air of the girl I thought I knew in her demeanor today, a sly confidence that twines around my heart and squeezes. It constricts at the readiness brimming in her big brown eyes and the pleased curve of her mouth. Her obvious anticipation at the plan coming together messes with my head, making me want what I refuse to have. I rub at my chest, tearing my attention from my little temptress.

I cast a quick glance around the warehouse. Rowan and Jude talk to the girls Pippa brought from the safehouse, his gaze flicking to her more often than he realizes.

They're all looking better since we rescued them from the fate of being auctioned off to the highest bidder. A couple are girls we've tracked down that went through what Isla did when she was younger, carrying the brand on their skin that marks them as girls who have been violated by one of the Kings' no-limits entertainment.

Pippa keeps a watchful eye over them, while Jude and Wren scrutinize her with matching shrewd gazes. Our little Pipsqueak might be as much of a liar as Quinn, but I don't doubt her compassion for these girls that have been done dirty by the Kings. Pippa always did have a bleeding heart for those in need. She's the one that brought us our first job five years ago when her friend couldn't find anyone to help.

Serena, Penn's girlfriend, sits in a chair while Isla does her makeup. She's dressed in a bright red, attention grabbing dress while also looking the part of a hot newscaster. The idea is people won't think anything of the spoofed broadcast since I Photoshopped the branding to match the top local station. Not until it's too late. The damning headline will already be out there: Thorne Point's Politicians With Predatory Pastimes.

Levi taps Wren's shoulder with the back of his hand and gets his help putting the finishing touches on the greenscreen set I built with Quinn early this morning, dragging her from bed over my shoulder when she didn't want to get up. That's what she gets for trying to outwit me by putting up a fight at night.

The plan I worked out with Wren is coming together. After getting a clone of that idiot Maxmillian's phone on campus two days ago, we have our nail in the coffin to link Westley Snyder's law firm. We're set up in the warehouse for showtime to go public with the victims of the Castle.

It's a crapshoot that all of this will stick. Snyder's always been slimy. He made everything disappear five years ago with his law firm before he became a top judge in the city. Knowing what we do now, I'm sure he's a society member. I'd bet my entire investment account that he's a purple member with more pull. Given Snyder's age, a generation older than Wren's father, I've watched the video recording from after hours at the Founders Museum over and over trying to match him to the one that presided over the meeting.

We've always known he was bad news, but he's careful, hiding behind the law firm his family established. The best I've been able to salvage about that shitty night when Jude got arrested for arson and Elise Sheffield wound up dead is partially redacted records. She came to us for our help and we thought we could do something. Some help we were.

I scrub my face, checking the connection on my laptop. The multiplex data I need to override the local stations' receivers and trick the digital transmission so I can hijack the signal to broadcast our own feed is almost ready. It's been a long time since I've pulled off something like this. The digital evolution has made it way more complex than simply splicing in like I did as a joke in middle school.

Everyone's relying on me. I won't let them down. I'm the hacker and this is my goddamn job.

As for Senator Vonn and the other pigs that partake in the Kings' secret virginity buying men's club for their nauseating entertainment, we've got our smoking gun. No more hurting girls like Vonn's own fucking daughter, drugged and offered up for sacrifice to the psychotic asshole obsessed with her.

Isla's rapist, Silas Stone, met his end at Levi's knife when we took out the Castle—the human trafficking auction he ran for the Kings. Their operation was used to sweeten the fucking deal with powerful people to show that the Kings' are untouchable, above law and order because they create their own rules. Somewhere safe to invest their money because greed follows like-minded bastards.

My teeth clench hard enough to ache. Thorne Point dates back to the dawn of the country. That's how long the Kings have enjoyed the crowns they claimed for themselves in their whack ass kingdom of bullshit.

Not anymore. Not on our watch. My brothers and I haven't spent the last five years since our first failure cultivating our own reign to stand for this in our city. Fall in line with our parents' wishes because our futures were decided by our bloodlines before we were born? Nah, fuck that. Fuck that up the ass with a massive dildo and no lube, not even spit to prevent tearing.

We're coming for every single Kings Society member. Some needed to die, like that maniac Silas Stone. The rest will go down in public disgrace with nowhere to hide from their misdeeds.

"Dude, chill. I can't stand it when you grind your teeth like that." Quinn elbows me, knocking me out of my head. She reaches across me for a signal booster, peeking at me.

I grab her wrist before she can snatch my phone. "Nice try. Next time you've gotta be quicker than that. Gave yourself away without something to distract me." I pinch the bridge of my nose and sigh. "Just get through this, then you can call your brother."

She quiets at my serious tone, eyeing me like she's waiting for the other shoe to drop. "No joke?"

"No joke," I confirm. "So behave."

There's too much on my plate to deal with. I don't have extra brain power to prevent her trying to swipe my phone. The pressure of making sure we pull this off without a hitch rides me. The rest of our plans against the Kings depend on how this goes.

"I'm holding you to that," she sasses archly.

Wren walks up to the table, interrupting my response. He's in true form today, ruthlessness rolling off him in waves. "Ready?"

"And willing, big guy." I tongue my cheek to divert myself from the hundred and one tasks running through my head. I can't take his look of disappointment, so failure is not an option today. "You and Ro say the word, and I'm down to watch if you still don't want to share."

Quinn stiffens at my side, releasing a pissy little breath. Her typing gets louder, fingers pounding the keys much harder than necessary.

Wren growls impatiently. "You even think about touching her, and I'll break every bone in your body. You hear me?"

"Loud and clear. Come on, you know I'm joking. It's tense in here." I roll my shoulders, grunting when Quinn pinches me. I rub at the inflamed spot on my side, shooting her a questioning look. She avoids my eye. "Tough crowd."

"I'm not in the mood for games, Colt," Wren mutters.

"Only when they're kinky and involve feisty little redheads, I know. Oh shi—" I dodge the fist that grabs at me, hopping back behind Quinn. Wren's icy blue eyes flash menacingly. "Okay, chill the fuck out, man. We're ready to go here. Is Serena good?"

Wren stalks off without answering. I blow out a breath. Probably not the best idea to taunt him like that when he's in a brutal mood, but me and foresight aren't always on speaking terms. I doubt I'm out of the woods yet. Wren will probably deck me when I least expect it. Gotta love him for it, though. We keep each other in check when we can't hold back.

I slide my attention to Quinn, about to ask her to hand me the wireless keyboard at the end of the table. Her fiery expression gives me pause.

"What's wrong, little queen? Jealous?" She goes rigid at the accusation. Fascinated, I pry at the crack in her mask. "Oh shit. You are. How about that? I knew you loved me."

"I—no. I don't," she pushes out. "Idiot."

"Uh huh. It's too bad, baby." I trace her nape, grin stretching when she twitches her shoulder to get me off. "You can have my cock anytime you want it, but it will never really belong to you. I don't lock it down exclusively with liars who play me. A hate fuck's all you'll ever be to me."

Her shoulder's hunch and she presses her lips together. "I don't want anything to do with you."

The tetchy mutter drags a sharp laugh out of me. I tuck a hand around her hip, drawing her into my side. She resists until I croon in her ear.

"So good at lying, aren't you, babe?"

"Colt!" Jude calls, waving me over.

I plant a filthy, open-mouthed kiss on Quinn's neck, licking until she pushes out a strangled noise, struggling against me. "Hold that thought. And don't fuck this up. You want me so badly, I'll bend you over later and reward you."

"Fucking asshole," she barks at my back when I walk off with a case of wireless mics.

"Hello, ladies," I greet the group of girls Pippa brought. Most of them have the same expression, wary but determined. "I know this can't be easy for you all, but with your help, we'll make it so the people that wronged you won't be able to do it again."

"We're ready," one girl says.

Pippa puts a hand on her shoulder. I recognize her as the blonde with a strong fighting spirit that we rescued at the estate outside of the city where the Castle was being operated. I offer her a fist and she bumps hers against mine.

"If you'd like your identity masked by blurring your face, you're going to step over next to this handsome guy once I mic you up." I nod toward Jude and clutch my chest. "Hold onto your hearts. When he smiles, it's like *oof*."

"Shut up." He shoves at me without heat.

Once I get all the girls ready, I move back to my computer while everyone finishes setting up. "Ready to get this show on the road?"

"It's not like I have a choice." Quinn salutes me mockingly when I look up. "Yes, sir."

I press my tongue into the inside of my cheek. "I'd prefer yes, Daddy."

She scoffs. "Yeah. Never happening."

"You say that now, but all I'm hearing is a new challenge to accept."

She flips me off while typing code, and I have to admit, I find that sexy.

"Let mayhem reign," I mumble to myself since Levi is too focused on Isla to kick us off.

I narrow my eyes in concentration, flicking them back and forth between the connection and the livestream feed while I work. There. We're in. Snapping my fingers to get everyone's attention, I give a thumbs up.

"Here we go." Jude signals Serena to begin.

"Our top story this evening casts a dark shadow on the city and brings into question whether or not we need deeper investigations to vet elected officials we're supposed to be able to trust," Serena reads in a perfect hard-hitting journalist tone from the script Jude and I wrote. "I'm joined by Isla Vonn, daughter of Senator Artimus Vonn."

Isla gives the cameras I've set up to capture two different angles a bright, fearless smile. The corner of my mouth hitches. Nothing snuffs out her light.

Levi stands behind the camera directed at her, shoulders a rigid line. He nods to her and she returns it.

"There's a secret you've carried for a long time. Tell us about that."

Serena says her lines beautifully. I'm glad I didn't go the deep fake route. This is better than trying to make it look like a more seasoned reporter held the interview.

Isla rests her hand over her thigh where she keeps a knife strapped in a holster Levi gave her, gathering her thoughts. "I used to idolize my dad. I thought he hung the moon." She shakes her head. "I was disillusioned of that idea at age fourteen."

The warehouse goes completely silent as she continues recounting what she went through. Quinn holds her breath. I nudge her as a reminder to keep working. Her throat works with a strained swallow. The story ends with what happened at the Castle. Isla blinks back tears as she finishes.

"Thank you for your bravery and willingness to share," Serena says. "Is there anything else you'd like to say? Perhaps to your father if he's watching this?"

Isla shakes her head. "That man doesn't have the right to call himself my father anymore. I've said everything I needed to say to him. He dismissed my traumatic experiences and expected me to hold it in, as so many victims are forced to, for the sake of his political career. No one should have to live in fear, no matter what." She holds her head high. "The truth can't be buried."

Within minutes of Isla's story concluding, Twitter goes crazy. I have the feed open on the side of my screen, tracking mentions of Isla's dad. They're calling for Vonn's resignation in light of these allegations, spewing hatred and disgust. Photos of Vonn having lunch at the country club surface in the feed. He's red-faced and panicked while he talks on the phone, then shouting at whoever is taking photos, his blurred hand outstretched to cover the camera.

"Smile, fuck face," I mutter acidly. "Time for your close-up."

Posts pop up tagged #VixenVonnDaily—the hashtag I started for Levi's obsession with his girl back in high school. Supportive messages for her flood the internet. People commend her for speaking out about what she went through and share their own experiences. Several mention eerily similar details and post pictures of their brand scar. Shit, I didn't expect this.

Working my jaw, I grab several of the organic tweets corroborating Isla's story and the ones that posted Vonn's flustered, caught out photo from the country club and throw them up on the green screen so they'll show blown up in the background behind Serena and Isla. Serena has a tablet I set up at her desk showing what the set looks like for viewers.

"What you're seeing on screen is the social media response being sent to the studio. Supporters and others are coming forward with their own stories," she announces. "Senator Vonn's office couldn't be reached for comment, and it's clear to see why. He's enjoying a lavish lunch at the Thorne Point Country Club."

Quinn snorts disparagingly beside me. "What a piece of shit."

"Hard agree. They're all like this." I watch her reaction from the corner of my eye.

She braces against the fold out table and nods in understanding. "But they won't get away with it anymore."

"No," I confirm.

For the first time since she hacked me, since the fire, since Levi and Penn tracked her down, the hatred dwindles. It feels like she's on our side because I believe the remorse shining in her eyes. I'm not ready to trust her, far from willing to forgive her, but it's a step in the right direction.

After Isla, the survivors take turns telling their stories one by one. While they recount enduring kidnapping and the kidnapping ring, Serena points out that there are countless victims residing in the city, living in silence.

That's my cue. I throw up the text messages and photos we pulled from Maxmillian's phone, highlighting the one where his dad assures him Snyder's law firm will clean up his mess.

"Money and connections shouldn't mean the power to evade the law, to evade justice," Serena says gravely.

Pippa scoffs, leaning over my shoulder. "Did you have to drag Snyder into this?"

"Yes," I snap.

Jude grabs her elbow. "What, now you have cold feet? I thought you wanted to help."

"I do." She clamps her mouth shut, glancing at the girl being interviewed. "It's just—I don't think Judge Snyder is involved. Maybe his firm is since they take on high profile clientele, but he's the one who saw how important justice is to me after..."

She trails off. Jude's jaw clenches.

"Can't even say her name, can you?" He lowers his voice. They stand close enough for me to hear. "Synder was the lead prosecutor that got me sent to juvie, baby girl. He covered up what happened. He's as dirty as the rest of them."

"No, he made sure no one found out what you did, he—"

"Don't." Jude sighs. "Don't kid yourself. You're only clinging to that dumbass belief because you don't want to face the truth."

"I'm here, aren't I? Ignoring the illegal shit you're pulling." She shakes her head and moves to watch from behind the other camera.

"You good, man?"

Jude waves me off. That night is a sore spot for all of us, but while we suffered our first failure and lost a friendship, he lost so much more. I return my focus to maintaining the signal interruption.

With our live public broadcast circumventing people like Snyder & Associates and the corrupt police force, there's nothing they can do to shut us down. This time the evidence won't end up buried. It's hit the internet and that shit's forever no matter how much money they try to throw at it. Not when it's the domain where I rule, guarded by my network of underlings that will make sure this doesn't go away.

CHAPTER FIFTEEN

QUINN

ONCE the broadcast ends, I swipe away tears. Listening to what's been going on dredges up so many unpleasant memories I've buried and locked away.

These girls are each like me, surviving monstrous things we shouldn't have to face. We wouldn't have to if the world wasn't teeming with evil, always out to get you. As they shared their stories, all I felt was the phantom touch of foster guardians that took advantage of me, touching my body without my permission. It didn't go as far as what these poor girls faced, but it crossed a line that made me uncomfortable and was enough to leave a mark on my ability to trust because no one ever believed me.

I can't believe I blinded myself for the sake of money to work for the same fucking bastards that hurt these girls. A knot forms in my stomach.

"Aight, with that done, now I can smoke a bowl and kick this anxiety. As much as I love the digital age, interrupting a signal with your own is a real bitch." Colton disconnects everything, coiling wires around his arm.

Between the guilt and the bad memories this dredged up, I'm not okay.

When he begins to walk away, a weak part of me that fears being left alone reaches for his hoodie, gripping it. Damn it. I let go as soon as he turns, berating myself for showing any vulnerability he can use against me. Being around him all the time is messing with my head, making some subconscious part of me turn to him because he's familiar, breeding a false sense of security.

It's only been a few days. I shouldn't feel like this for the guy keeping me glued to his side. For the asshole who is basically holding me hostage. I ignore the voice in the back of my head reminding me it's been far longer than a few days, more like weeks spent living in his apartment.

Colton starts to say something that's probably crude, then pauses, studying me. His smirk falls and he steps into me, arms snaking around my waist. A shuddering breath escapes me and more tears threaten to fall.

"I'm fine." I don't sound it, my voice hoarse and broken.

"Yeah? That's why you look three seconds from falling apart? Because you're *fine*?"

His embrace tightens. I hate that it feels good. Safe. Like someone's watching out for me for once instead of it being my job to survive. I hate it more that I allow myself to curl my fingers in the material of his sweater.

He turns us, shielding me from everyone with his body. "Whatever demons you're battling in that clever little mind, they can't beat a girl as tough as you." His chin touches the top of my head. "Don't cry. It's okay."

I sniffle, swallowing past the lump in my throat. I give myself one more minute of being weak, of needing someone else to lean on when I'm not strong enough to stand on my own, before I get it together.

When I push against his firm chest, his arms drop. I wipe beneath my eyes, avoiding the weight of his penetrating gaze. Neither of us speak. He doesn't prod at my weaknesses and I don't beg him to forget he ever saw me cry, though my stomach burns with humiliation and a flicker of gratitude. He could've been a dick about it and he wasn't.

While I busy myself powering down the equipment, he turns to the others. "We'll monitor progress and coverage from up in the office. I'm going to publish articles on two other national news sites to drive it home and leak his shady financial records. People are already calling for Vonn's resignation from office."

"Good," Wren says callously. "Make this so big that the Kings understand their power and reach isn't what they believe it to be. There won't be any covering for him, or anyone else we come for."

Rowan steps away from his side and takes Isla's free hand when Levi guides her away from the group of girls with his palm at the small of her back. Rowan's pretty features shift into concern. "You okay, babe?"

"Yeah. Feels like a huge weight off my shoulders, honestly. Is that a little crazy? I kept it a secret for so long." Isla murmurs when Levi swipes a tear from the corner of her eye with his thumb and kisses her temple. For a guy so savage, he's gentle and protective when it comes to her. "The truth is out there now. He can't hide from what he's done anymore."

"Come on," Colton prompts.

He leads me upstairs to the office. It's a tight fit with the duplicate gamer chair he had waiting here when we got back from campus the other day. His has a strip of duct tape across the headrest of the original chair with his name on it. I perch in that one just to annoy him, lips twitching when he pauses and sighs.

Dropping into the newer chair, he grumbles under his breath. "Guess I'm starting over on the memory foam sculpting to my ass. Here." He slides me a thumb drive. "Post this to Reddit while I get the article up on the other sites."

We work in silence for a few minutes, the room full of the muted sounds of our typing. I jolt when he captures one of my wrists once I've uploaded damning financial leaks from Vonn's personal and professional accounts online.

"What are you—?" My words end in a strangled noise when he squints at the screen while brushing my fingers against his lips, then sucks two of them into his mouth and teases them with his tongue. My clit throbs. "What the fuck? *Why* the fuck?"

He doesn't answer, completely zoned out. His tongue piercing dragging against my skin makes me shiver and squeeze my thighs together. It's only when I yank hard on my hand that he blinks twice at his screen, then swings his gaze to me.

"I think better that way. I need something to occupy myself." He cocks his head. "If you won't let me do that, then you're going to have to offer up that mouth."

"What? No."

I scoot back, ignoring the burst of heat in my core, only for him to hook a foot on the base of my chair and wheel me back. My chest collapses with a forceful exhale as he leans into my space and traces my lips.

"Let me in."

I shake my head, nipples tightening at his smoky tone. He lifts a brow in challenge and it makes my pulse thrum. I can handle this. My lips part and he grins as he teases me for another minute before pushing inside. An ache echoes between my thighs when he pets my tongue.

"That's it. Doesn't that feel nice?" Colton brings his lips to my ear. "Can you still concentrate on the tasks I give you while I play with you?"

I swallow back a moan. Goddamn him. How can he get me so keyed up in a matter of seconds with one look, one suggestive game?

Sitting up straight, I pour my focus into the laptop in front of me, acutely aware of him watching. The air crackles in the office and I concentrate on breathing evenly to hide what this is doing to me. Each purposeful stroke of his finger along my tongue, each time he plunges deeper to test my gag reflex, each time he murmurs to keep working while he tries to distract me has me aching for him to touch me elsewhere.

"Bet if my fingers were buried inside your pussy instead of petting your tongue, you wouldn't be able to focus like this." He chuckles, the soft puff of breath fanning across my tingling neck. I fight not to squirm. "Next time. I like the look of these lips wrapped around me too much to stop."

Without stopping, he splits his concentration between toying with me and typing one handed to finish posting an article to the top national news site.

Once it's live, the game ends. Winking, he removes his fingers from my mouth, then pulls up live network feeds on YouTube. I clear my throat, swiping at the sides of my mouth, quelling the warm arousal coiling within me. I'm not disappointed he stopped instead of continuing. I'm *not*.

We watch other news stations pick up the story as breaking news to keep up with the news cycle now that it's been "reported" by two other reputable news sources in addition to the station we spoofed.

His expression turns lethal. "Cover this up, Judge Snyder. Information is power and it's out there before you could bury it."

"Are we going after Fitz Mortimer, too?" I roll my lips between my teeth as soon as the question is out.

Colton stops what he's doing and gives me a long look in consideration. When the silence stretches too long, it spurs me to say more.

"He's part of this. He said the words in the file. The Latin shit." It's unnerving to be the sole focus of his wily green gaze. "Mortimer's the one who made me spy on you guys. The one responsible for the fire at the hotel."

"Where do you stand on heist movies?"

I blink at the topic swerve. He lifts his brows, circling his wrist to encourage my answer.

"They're cool. Why?"

Colton's mouth curves into a wicked grin and does a raise the roof move with his hands while he speaks in the same beat as an old Vanilla Ice song. "Heist, heist, baby."

CHAPTER SIXTEEN
QUINN

I'VE got to give it to Colton, his mind works in mysterious ways I'm not sure anyone could ever top. He's someone who doesn't stop thinking. Who never stops period.

Maybe going for Fitz Mortimer was already on his mind. It's the only explanation for how he's got this insane plan put together in a matter of hours after my hedged suggestion. Two nights later, we pull in at the marina full of luxury boats while Levi and Isla are across town keeping an eye on Mortimer at some swanky dinner.

"Damn, I wish I could've been there in person." Jude shows the rest of us a text from Levi as we move through the shadows. Fitz Mortimer's face is pale, mouth slack as if he's seen a ghost. He looks like he can't believe the Crows survived his attack on their hotel. "We should frame this."

Wren grins savagely. "That's nothing. Just the first taste to get him sweating. Wondering what we'll do for coming for us." He passes a calculating look over the quiet marina that gives an air of impending danger, like a provoked predator about to strike back. "Publicly, he and the Kings can't touch us. To anyone outside of the society's exclusive membership and the rest of the city, our names and reputations still stand. Just like this party we'll infiltrate. I'm betting it'll be similar to the masquerade, where there'll be non-society guests on the invite list."

"And this time, we'll have a much better understanding of the tricks they like to pull," Jude says. "They won't take us by surprise anymore."

Before we left the warehouse, Colton presented the others with an invitation for Mortimer's annual holiday party hosted on his yacht that I extracted from a Trojan virus I left on Mortimer's wifi network for backdoor access before he cut me loose.

"I've always wanted to steal a yacht." Colton waggles his brows, impish expression lit by the blue glow of his tablet screen.

Excitement comes off him in waves. Tonight he seems more like he used to be and, despite the fact he's forcing me to stay with him as his asset, my unwanted attraction to him runs rampant, refusing to be curbed or controlled. Maybe I'm too fucked up by the crap hand of cards life dealt me. I can't go for nice boys, only the ones as messed up as I am.

Jude snorts. "Because you're a little psycho."

"Aren't we all," he says cheerfully.

My lips slide together as Colton, Jude, Wren, and Rowan huddle over his tablet screen. I'm the odd one out of their circle. I've seen some whacked shit in my life, forced to grow up too fast in order to survive. It's skewed my morals, and exposure to the corruption that infects the world has left me cynical toward the idea of right and wrong. Hacking is one thing. But this? This plan feels crazy.

I grapple with my need to keep my head down and not ask questions.

Look where that got me before. Maybe it's time I give up on that policy.

"We're seriously doing this?" I stiffen at the weight of their stares. Rolling my shoulders, I stare right back. "We're just a bunch of college students and post-grads. Hell, I'm supposed to be working on a paper and a ground-up program for my computer science class for the final next week. This isn't normal."

I haven't thought about the classes I'm missing since I did the assignments for all of them the first week I transferred from Castlebrook College. Truthfully, I know more than the professors in all of my computer programming degree classes. I could probably teach them. But earning the piece of paper that says I graduated from TPU is why Sammy and I needed to come here. A degree from the college is what opens doors that have been slammed shut in our faces.

The mocking curve of Wren's mouth is sharp. "Nothing's normal in Thorne Point." He doesn't speak to me much around the warehouse—not that I have much opportunity to be one-on-one with any of them because Colton doesn't leave me alone unless it's in our room—but since the broadcast he doesn't look at me like he's ready to murder me anymore. "Haven't you learned that by now? If not, then after tonight it should be clear. The Crows don't play by typical rules. We don't have a sense of right and wrong, only what we want and what we're willing to do to make it happen."

"Is it normal for a college student to accept a bribe from a pompous douchebag?" Colton doesn't lift his attention from his tablet. "Come on, it's not like things have ever been normal for you up until now."

"He's got a point." Rowan regards me and seems to come to some conclusion that chases off the last of the wariness she's directed at me. "I don't think any of us know what normal is. Even if being in with these guys is chaotic, it's not like my life was simple before this. I lived with the traumatic belief I killed my father for years, and then the fucking Kings kidnapped and murdered my brother. I think we're drawn to people who match our energy and darkness. If you wanted what society considers ordinary, you and your brother wouldn't be here, right?"

I press my lips together, unused to the idea of someone else knowing things about me I wouldn't normally share. The way she casually drops her own horrible experiences catches me off guard. Does she expect me to open up? What kind of twisted girl talk is that?

"What I'm trying to say is that I think I would've made the same choice as you did if they came to me," she elaborates. Wren rumbles something cold under his breath and she elbows him. "I'm serious. I would've done anything to save Ethan if they found me before I went to you. We go through hell for the people we love, and if I didn't know what I do now, I would've jumped at any chance to protect him."

I swallow, understanding arrowing through me. The thought of the Kings murdering Sammy sends ice into my veins. Maybe she's right. If I wasn't so determined to get back everything stolen from us, we could get by on my poker winnings at a public college and make new lives for ourselves starting fresh. But I refuse to accept that someone else can take from us without consequence.

Wren gets in her face. "If I didn't love you, I'd punish you for admitting that, kitten."

She lifts her chin, unbothered by his threatening stance. His anger bleeds away and he cups her face, kissing her forehead. She leans into the touch with a sad smile.

"Are we standing around talking or are we doing this?" Jude surveys the security feed on Colton's screen from over his shoulder. There aren't any guards, only an automated security system. "We don't have a long window to sneak aboard."

"We've dealt with tighter," Colton says. "Give me a minute to record a loop to overlay over the camera's live feed. That'll make this easy peasy."

I sigh, moving to Colton's side and pointing out what I see. "And the motion detectors?"

"Cake," he chirps.

"Are you going to—"

"Yes. Well, more like you are." He hands me the tablet to deal with disabling the motion sensors and smirks at me from the corner of his eye. "It's so nice to have someone around who thinks just like me."

I huff. "You wish."

Once the marina security is taken care of between the two of us, we find Mortimer's obnoxiously large yacht. We enter on the middle deck and the first thing we're met with is an enlarged blueprint of the boat serving as a map and an art piece. It says there's a main deck above us, then a panoramic observatory above it. Two more decks sit below us with god knows what sort of rich men bullshit.

"Thank you," Colton drawls, snapping a photo.

"Think he's compensating for his dick size?" Rowan suggests.

"More like his self worth. He's the type of overconfident asshole that believes his dick is a gift to the world no matter the size," I mutter.

Jude chuckles. "I love it when they're confident. It makes them so much more fun to break."

Wren flexes his hand into a fist, knuckles cracking. "Even more fun to punch. First we'll make this pissant taste our vengeance, and then my father."

"All in good time, big guy." Colton shoots us each finger guns as he fires off directions. "Quinn and I will take the main computer system. Wren and Ro, get the upper decks with the range extenders for our epic light show.

Jude, you're on the lower deck duty to map out the escape route. Place my network boosters as discreetly as you can. Cool? Cool."

We split up and my heartbeat picks up as the first surge of adrenaline courses through me. This is happening. I follow him to the control room.

"Over here." The ship has three widescreen computer monitors stationed near a wall of instruments. He sets a small dark bag on the counter and pulls out two fold up keyboards, handing me one. "Bingo. We'll splice my system over top of theirs to override the admin authority. It'll look like business as usual until we're ready to show our hand."

My lips twitch without permission. "How long have you been waiting to slip that in?"

The invitation described the holiday party as a black tie affair with a fifty grand buy in poker game as the highlight. Guests are invited to enjoy a luxurious night aboard the Gentleman's Ambition, Mortimer's stupidly named boat. It'll be a who's who of Thorne Point's biggest bank accounts patting each other on the back for making it to the end of another year at the top.

He shoots a crooked grin over his shoulder. "I've had it locked and loaded. Buckle up, because I've got plenty more."

I roll my eyes, fighting back a smile, then smack his hands off the keyboard to take over. He steps back, circling his wrist with a flourish to allow me to step in. His intent stare makes my nape tingle while I work. The two months I spent working with Mortimer's system gives me a better insight to how he likes things set up. I have the protocols disengaged and access the mainframe within minutes.

"There."

Colton whistles low, crossing his arms. "The things I could accomplish if you didn't evade my recruitment tests and slip through my grasp."

"I've already told you, I had no interest following some self-centered douchebag's orders." Chewing on the corner of my lip, I watch his long, tattooed fingers move on the keyboard. "That wasn't a lie."

He hums skeptically, though his good mood doesn't break. He pulls up a digital map of the boat, pointing out the different decks. Two dots represent our heat signatures in the control room while the others blip in different areas of the ship while they complete their tasks.

"For the first half of the party, we'll be blending in," Colton explains. "Mortimer will be shitting bricks, but to everyone else it won't seem that out of the ordinary that the city's favorite sons are in attendance."

"So we have some champagne and try not to freeze our nipples off." My nose wrinkles and my voice lowers to a mutter. "Who has a holiday party a week before Christmas on a yacht in Maine?"

It'll be my first time at one of the high class black tie events that fill the city's social calendar. If Astor Global Holdings hadn't destroyed everything my grandparents built, Sampson and I would be in this world. I would have grown up with Colton and the others. Our names would be amongst the prominent ones included on the guest lists. The thought causes a weird knot to form in my stomach.

"I'll keep your nipples nice and warm. And then play some poker." He traps his lip between his teeth and lifts his brows impishly. His elbow nudges me. "Cleaning them out will be an added bonus. I think between the two of us, we can do it in, oh, say the first forty-five minutes? You can keep the pot if you beat me."

I lift a brow. "You're on. I can beat you at cards with my eyes closed."

He chuckles and gives me a wry jerk of his head while he connects his tablet to the USB hub. "We'll see about that, little queen. I need your competitive spirit on this. It'll make the perfect distraction. We'll draw attention to the card game." He pauses what he's doing long enough to step into me, skimming a finger down my arm. "And give them a show before the main event. While we hold everyone's attention, Jude will get everything else in place when it's time for the drones to start up."

I suppress the shiver threatening to race down my spine at his touch, eyeing him when he returns to his task. "What about Mortimer's private security? Sosa and his guys are ex-special forces. They could be a serious problem. Plus, they'll be armed and we'll be in formal attire."

He doesn't look up from reprogramming the existing operations system to mask the upgrade with his own tweaks. "Leave them to Levi. He can handle them if they're stupid enough to make a move." Finishing off with a showy keystroke, he directs a languid grin my way. "And never underestimate the opportunity for a Bond moment. I have all sorts of toys to keep us protected."

"Bond, huh? Yeah, that tracks. Especially the overinflated ego."

He takes my hips and pins me to the table, grin stretching at my scoff. "Baby, you haven't lived until you've experienced me in a tux. You ain't ready, so watch yourself. I need you on your A-game."

I put on a starstruck act. "Wow, you really do believe you're god's gift to the world."

"Damn straight," he taunts with his mouth scant inches from mine.

Before he kisses me, Wren's deep voice sounds at the door. "You done?"

"Yeah." Colton winks and eases back to pack up his gear. "We're golden."

"Good. Let's go," Wren says.

We disconnect from the computer system and meet up with Jude and Rowan. Part of me can't believe this worked with minimal effort. The wealthy families who keep their toys here believe they're completely untouchable.

"You know I don't have anything to wear for this, right?" I point out to Colton.

"We'll go shopping with Isla this week," Rowan says. "She loves it. If it were up to me, I'd show up in leather and boots."

Wren rumbles in approval, placing a hand at the small of her back. The smirk she shoots him is the look of a woman who knows how to get under her man's skin.

Colton holds up a sleek black credit card. When I go to grab it, he folds it back into his fist with a skilled twist of his deft fingers. "Ah, ah. Say the magic words."

I squint. "Having a small penis doesn't make you less of a person."

Jude barks out a laugh and Wren buries an amused noise in the top of Rowan's head. Colton shakes his head and hands the card to Rowan. He strides to the front of the group, walking backward to the SUV while grabbing his junk.

"I have no problem whipping it out to show it off."

"Please." Jude holds up his hands. "I've seen your dick too many times."

"Maybe I want a look." The end of Rowan's teasing sentence chokes off as Wren lifts her over his shoulder with a growl. "Hey! It was just a joke. You know he's just my friend."

"The only cock you ever need is mine, kitten." He stalks past Colton to beat us to the Escalade and the echo of her laughter surrounds us in the alley near the marina.

A smile tugs at my mouth when the five of us pile into the car to head back to the warehouse downtown. Tonight's the first time I don't feel like their enemy. It goes against every instinct I've honed, yet I can't lie, I don't hate the feeling that I could fit in with them. It's better than being on their bad sides.

152

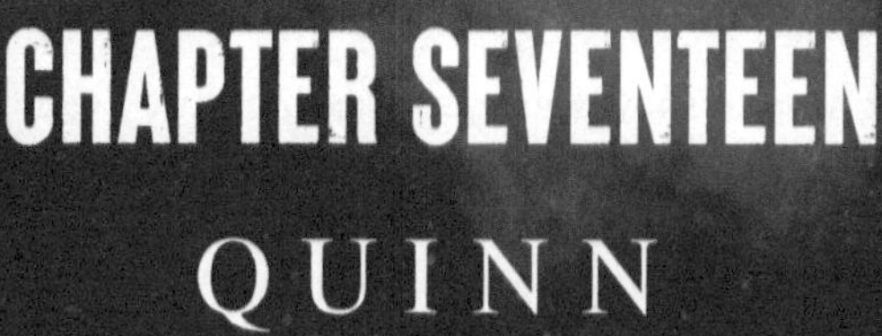

CHAPTER SEVENTEEN
QUINN

"Ooh, you have to try this one on." Isla bounces on the balls of her feet, waving a sleek poison ivy green gown at me. "And this one."

I take the dresses, a small smile curving my mouth. I don't bother checking the price tag, aware that everything in this boutique is expensive. Whatever. This is on Colton's dime.

Today's the first time I've left the warehouse without Colton breathing down my neck. If I pretend my life didn't fall apart because of Baron Astor's greed and if I didn't accept Fitz Mortimer's offer, this shopping trip could almost seem like I'm just hanging out with Isla and Rowan after class.

I've never really made time for girlfriends. It's kind of nice. Each time Isla picks out something for me to try on, an odd sensation tightens in my stomach.

I keep expecting them to remember what Colton refuses to forget— that I tricked them—yet they ask questions like they genuinely want to get to know me.

"Isla, I can't do this one. I don't have tits like yours." Rowan shakes her head with a grin and puts the dress back.

"What! Come on, just try it on." Isla waggles her brows and does a little shimmy. "Just send Wren a photo of you rocking it from the dressing room."

A husky laugh leaves me. "I mean, if the goal is to give your man a show, then yeah. That's the winner. But do you want to give every moldy sleazebag a look at your goods, too?"

"Point." Rowan selects another one and offers it to Isla, then takes the dress she refused off the rack again. "Here. If we're just going to tease the guys, then you have to show Levi you wearing this. Twenty bucks says he drives his new bike over here in less than ten minutes."

Isla finds one for me with a plunging neckline. "Here, you do this one. Colt won't know what hit him."

"Nah. Just you two do it." I rub my fingertips together. "Things aren't like that with Colton."

"We're not blind," Isla says. "He's got you staying in his room, doesn't he? It's okay, you don't have to be shy. And don't worry, whatever you want to vent about, we won't say anything to him or our guys."

"For real, though. He flirts, but he does that with everyone, right?" I clear my throat, ignoring the knot in my stomach protesting my insistence. "I'm just with you guys to get their help protecting my brother and to kick the Kings in their dicks."

Isla snorts. "For now. Things could change."

"Trust us. It takes these guys forever to sort out their feelings." Rowan smirks. "Wren kept warning me I couldn't handle him, but damn if he didn't snap when he thought I could want someone else other than him."

"Same for Levi." Isla grins. "But underneath all that brooding and danger, they have big hearts. They love intensely."

Love? Yeah, no. Far from it.

"It's definitely not like that between us. I—"

Well, shit. I can't say I don't want him, because it's a complete lie at this point. The games are heady and irresistible, and there's just something about him, about his brand of chaos, that I'm drawn to.

I run my thumb along the bearded strap of the dress. "I think he's too pissed to ever get past what happened."

They exchange a sympathetic look and shrug. Isla opens her mouth, but a familiar voice stops her.

"Show me what you've got, girls. I'm ready to be your hype man."

Whatever she was going to say, I'll never find out. Colton strolls through the boutique. So much for escaping his constant presence.

"What are you doing here?" Rowan squints at him suspiciously. "Did Wren send you?"

"Nah." He plops on the plush velvet seats arranged by the dressing rooms, arms spread across the back. "I came for the show."

Isla rolls her eyes affectionately. "Levi's going to kill you one of these days, and the only sympathy you'll get from me when he stabs you is an *I told you so*."

He grins, clapping a hand over his heart. "Babe! You mortally wound me." He shrugs. "It wouldn't be the first time he stabbed me. What's a little bit of stabbing between friends? It's just how we show our love."

"You guys are crazy," I mutter.

Rowan snickers. "So damn crazy. I'm going to try these on."

Isla browses the rack on the other side of the room, leaving me alone with him.

"I hope you weren't getting any ideas in that clever little head of yours," he warns in a soft, lilting tone. "Waiting for the right moment to slip out of here. I'd know how to find you. Just keep that in mind."

The suspicious way he studies me makes my stomach clench. Maybe he still doesn't trust me to be on my own around his friends.

I thought after sneaking onto the yacht the other night and helping with the broadcast that we were getting somewhere. It seems I was wrong. At least right now. His mood swings back and forth so often, from playful to flirting, seductive to cruel, as if he doesn't know where he stands with me at any given moment. I never know which he'll land on, leaving me unsure why some part of me wants to let my guard down around him.

"Why would I run when I need you to keep my brother guarded?" I fold my arms, lifting my chin. "I'm not going anywhere."

Colton narrows his eyes, stroking his chin. After a beat, he huffs and tears his gaze away.

"Oh, hell yes, Ro. That one," he calls when she emerges to see the gown in the tri-fold mirrors. "For sure. You'll drive the big guy crazy if you wear that."

"You think?" She glides her hands over her hips, checking herself out in the mirror.

"Totally, babe," Isla chimes in. "You look so good in that color."

I grit my teeth. His phone sits forgotten on the seat. While he's distracted by hyping Rowan up with Isla's help, I snatch it. Serves him right.

A smirk tugs at my lips as I go into a dressing room to try on my dresses. I like the gold one I try on first. It dips low in the back and the gold brings out the warm undertones in my dark complexion, creating a luminous effect. I feel every bit like the goddess Nyx in this. Smiling, I brush my fingertips over the hint of my tattoo of the night deity on my ribcage.

The tattoo reminds me of my grandmother. She's the one who encouraged all my interests. When I was obsessed with mythology as a little girl and begged her to let me be a goddess when I grew up, she bopped me on the nose and told me she already saw a little goddess running around her house. My mouth curves at the memory.

Taking Colton's phone, I snap a few photos and send one to my brother. He texts back with fire emojis and asks what the occasion is. I tell him it's for my new career as a sugar baby because being an adult is expensive and not it.

The door opens while I'm smirking at his unamused response. Didn't I lock it? I freeze, staring at Colton in the mirror. He leans against the door, one brow raised.

"Still taking things that don't belong to you." He nods with his chin to the phone.

I spin to face him, cocking my hip. "I think you left it out on purpose for me to take." I toss it to him and he catches it. "I only wanted to check in with Sammy. Don't leave it out in the open if it's off-limits for me to *borrow*."

The corner of his mouth twitches. He comes away from the door with a languid move and the spark of deviousness in his eyes stirs a thrum of heat between my legs.

"Why'd you show up?" I breathe.

"For this."

The press of his gaze is a sensual caress, sliding over my body. My nipples harden and I squeeze my thighs together as he closes the distance between us.

"Take this off," he commands quietly.

He hooks a finger beneath the strap and slips it off my shoulder. Then he does the other side. I fumble for the hidden zipper and he gets it for me.

When the dress falls away, I'm naked. I haven't trusted any of the underwear he provided in that duffle bag since that stunt with the vibrator on campus and none of these dresses work with a bra.

"Fuck," he mutters raggedly.

There's unrestrained want gleaming in his eyes. Our gazes lock in the reflection, then he steps around me, tracing random paths across my skin.

He comes to a stop beside me.

My eyes fall shut and I lick my lips. I don't expect the way I react to the brush of his fingers against my Nyx tattoo. I stifle a gasp, gaze flying open. He's watching me in the mirror, then drops his attention to my tattoo, touching it again.

"Next one," he rasps.

It takes me a moment to realize he means I should try on the next dress. I grab the green one with trembling hands. He helps, zipping me up, touch feathering over my erogenous zones that shouldn't make my clit throb, yet every slight caress leaves me hoping for more, my mind running away from me with fantasies about what he'll do next.

We continue like that, trapped in the entrancing silence and tension building between us. He helps me try on dresses, then directs me to take them off and strip myself bare for him again and again.

I don't know what this game is, but I'm playing it to the end.

"Off."

I swallow at the smoky demand. When it slips off my body, the whisper of fabric rustles against the floor.

He doesn't touch me the way I'm burning for him to. Both of us are teetering on the edge of snapping. He simply stares at me in the mirror, breath ghosting over my neck as he presses his erection against my back. If he wanted to fuck me right here, right now in this dressing room I'd welcome it.

"We'll take all of them." He traces my shoulder, tracking the rise and fall of my chest with my thick breaths. "Wear the gold dress to the party. That one was my favorite."

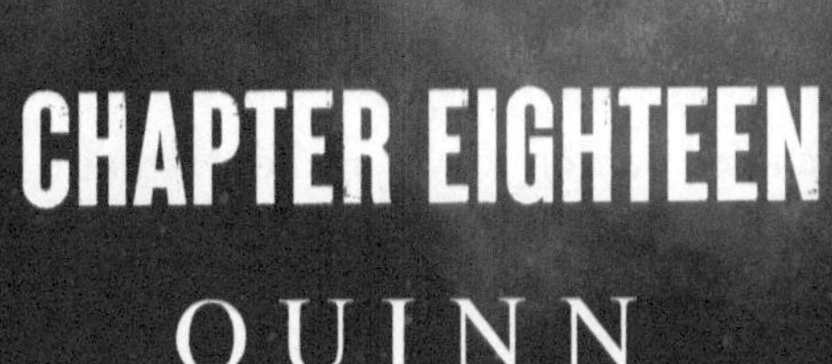

CHAPTER EIGHTEEN
QUINN

As a survivor, it's easy to accept major changes and ride the tide of a new normal compared to someone not used to the ingrained instinct to pivot on a dime just to keep living to see tomorrow.

That's what my life becomes at Colton's side in only two weeks—normal. Routine. Just a regular Tuesday waking up in the same bed as the guy who keeps me locked in his room without my own biometric access programmed in the high tech lock to come and go as I please.

I dropped fighting him about it within the first few days once I was sure they would keep their word to protect Sammy in exchange for me. He won't let me go, but he's eased up from breathing down my neck all the time. Like now, leaving me alone in the office in the middle of running a web crawling script while he steps out. He said something about a delivery of drone parts with a gleam in his eye I've learned not to question.

It's all for Sammy. The Crows are watching his back and I've gotten the chance to call him a few more times to check in with him in the last two weeks. Living in Colton's pocket, more closely than I did as Mortimer's puppet, isn't the worst sacrifice I've made to ensure my brother's safety.

My face heats and thoughts of the filthy games Colton plays with me flit through my mind.

The construction noises muted by the office's soundproof one-way glass windows pull me from zoning out to memories that make me hot and achy. I touch my soft natural curls self-consciously, glad he wasn't around to witness me thirsting over him. Willing the heated flush to leave my face, I gather my unbraided hair on top of my head, securing the pile of curls with a loose elastic band.

After taking down Isla's dad, we've exposed a Ponzi scheme to lure unsuspecting investors and bleed their accounts dry, a two generation old murder where a man bricked his sister into the literal wall of his estate to hide that he killed her, and a secret sex party club disguising itself as a charity event.

If I bide my time, Baron Astor will meet the downfall I've longed for, too. He's on their list of Kings to destroy, sitting right at the top priority along with Wren's father.

When Colton still hasn't returned almost fifteen minutes after he ducked out, my attention drifts to the window with a frown. Did he get sidetracked? I swear, he has zero impulse control when it comes to shiny syndrome dragging his focus in new directions.

Bored with watching the web crawler run, shift his insane to-do list out of the way and click around the open windows while toying with the band of the thigh highs I'm wearing under a comfortable sweaterdress that looks like a long hoodie. The warehouse is freezing with the resumed construction to get their new club finished, but a space heater appeared in the office by the end of the first week without me saying anything.

The script to search for proof to back up the dirty, deplorable, and depraved things the rich people of Thorne Point have done their best to bury runs on his computer. He's still logged in with the admin account. My gaze darts to the door and I lift a brow.

If he catches me, he'll be pissed. It's a risk, but I can't let the opportunity pass me up. He said he'd looked into me and I want to make sure it's not the truth I worked hard to bury. I've also been curious to find out what useful information he has on Levi's corrupt uncle. Something more incriminating than I've ever been able to get my hands on. With the secrets the Crows have stashed, he might even have proof of what Astor Global Holdings did to my family.

By nature, hackers are curious. We like to chase knowledge and live for the triumphant natural high of success when we access something restricted. Following the rabbit hole through Colton's files is no different. Some of the folders are encrypted and I have to do some work. Each time I crack the code, I get a thrill.

God, he's an information hoarder. Aerial maps of an estate outside of the city, some old and a duplicated version updated with arrows pointing to satellite images of what looks to be a small set of ruins on the mansion's property. Some of these files date back years. He has old news reports, stolen corporate internal briefings, a school photo of a girl from Thorne Point Academy.

A folder nested within a maze of others turns out to have reports from a fire five years ago just outside the city. Most of it's redacted, but my brows jump as I skim through. Jude was arrested and served seven months in juvie. There's a coroner's report for a girl who died, but most of the information is blacked out.

"What the fuck is this?" I whisper.

I suppress a startled jump when he comes in, heart pounding as I try to mask my caught out expression while he strides across the room. Oh shit.

Close the window, close the window. Don't be sus.

"This light show is going to be sick. I've got music to go with it—you know, play on emotional connection as we peel back the curtain to ramp it all up and—" He stops abruptly, intelligent eyes flicking between my blank mask and the computer monitor.

A sharp humorless laugh punches out of him and I realize why—I missed one of the reports when I was panic-closing everything. Fuck, that's such a rookie move. My lips press together to hold in an explanation. Explanations imply guilt. I blink innocently.

Colton's steps slow, then become prowling. Predatory. He comes to a stop behind me, braced against the high back of my chair. The tension rolling off his body makes it difficult to keep my breathing level.

"And here I thought we were making progress, little liar. Thanks for the reminder."

Oh, screw him. I'm sick of this high and mighty act he holds over me as if he and his friends aren't just as corrupted by their choices as I am. I could've done so much worse left alone with his computer system than look through old files that seem like they're connected to all this Kings shit.

"I'm just doing what you told me to," I reply in a tone dripping with saccharine sweetness. "Analyzing the data on hand."

"Come on, baby." He grazes my cheek with his knuckles, grasping my chin forcefully when I jerk my head away. He shifts to my side and wrenches my face up. My gaze collides with the fiery anger burning in his eyes. "You can do better than that. You were fucking snooping. Just sitting here biding your time until I think you'll behave. I walked away for *two minutes* and you're looking for leverage. Haven't learned not to fuck around with me yet, huh?"

"More like thirty minutes." I drop the act and switch tactics. "The dates on these files go back five years. Why have you sat on stuff like this for so long without doing anything?"

"Oh, yeah, of course. My bad. Let me tell you." He gets in my face, smirking when I don't shrink away. He snaps his fingers beside my head. "That's right. You're an untrustworthy, backstabbing liar and I don't owe you shit."

I narrow my eyes when he pushes away, shooting to my feet. I'm sick of him acting like I'm the bad guy because I worked for the Kings. It wasn't the right choice—I know that now—but I can't take it back. He won't let me move on without reminding me every five seconds that he hates me for it.

That shit isn't going to fly with me anymore.

"Don't turn your back on me. This isn't over. Believe whatever the hell you want, but I wasn't looking for leverage." Not against him or his friends, anyway. I'm done with him holding this over my head unless he decides he wants to toy with my body. My lips slide together before I push on. "I'm not your damn enemy, so just get that through your head already. You only seem to remember whenever you want to fuck me with your dirty games."

Colton moves fast when he's not putting on his languid air. His usual attitude of being a lazy fuckboy who only puts in an effort when he's chasing a hook up makes it easy to forget he's much stronger than he appears. I've seen him train with Levi and Wren in the gym they set up in the creepy ass basement, forced to sit down there with them while he was shirtless, muscles glistening temptingly.

Before I'm able to dodge him when he charges me, he pins me to the wall, one hand holding my throat. My eyes widen, then narrow. I swing a hand, anticipation simmering in my veins for the fierce slap he's had coming. He grabs my wrist to stop me, pinning it beside my head against the exposed brick with a glare.

"Are you about done? Behave."

I bare my teeth. "Make me."

His fingers tighten around my throat. "Goddamn, woman. Everything about you drives me fucking crazy. You get under my skin and make me want—"

"What?" I snap.

It's not smart to push him when he's like this, but I'm powerless to stop myself, driven by the thrill racing down my spine and the rush of my racing pulse. Those alluring green eyes spark with fury, bouncing between mine as we press closer, breathing each other in. The air around us crackles with tension.

"Fuck it," he growls. "*This.*"

Colton crashes his mouth against mine in a demanding, punishing kiss that steals my breath. His fingers dig into my wrist he has pinned to the wall as my free hand yanks on the neckline of his pullover—whether I want to push him away or pull him closer isn't clear. Then he bites my lip, forcing his tongue into my mouth and I'm a goner. My hand flies to his messy brown hair, sinking into it and tugging. An aroused pulse echoes through my body at the filthy groan he elicits while he devours my mouth.

Releasing my wrist and throat, he drags his hands down my sides and fists one hand in my hoodie dress while the other delves between my thighs. I freeze as it occurs to me belatedly I've been going bare under my clothes since that trick he pulled with the hidden vibrator in my panties when we went to campus. I figure if he did it to one pair, he probably did it to all of them, and I'd rather not be at the mercurial whims of his wicked urges to make me come in public no matter how much I liked it the first time.

It means there's nothing to stop him when he cups my pussy beneath the dress. He smirks into the kiss, chest vibrating with a cocky, pleased rumble as he torments me by sliding his fingers through my folds until my arousal coats them. He doesn't spend long teasing me, pressing on my clit with purpose.

I break away from the kiss with a garbled cry, riding his hand and clinging to him for support. His nimble fingers know exactly how to make my thighs quake and the irresistible coil of desire fill my core.

"Easy access." His sultry croon snakes around me while he rubs my throbbing clit with the same demanding fervor he kissed me with, intent on making me come. He brings his lips to my ear and rasps, "Damn, baby, you're already slick and dripping from that? I love that fighting gets you this wet and ready for my cock." His tone hardens, losing the sensual playfulness. "Come here. I'm going to fuck that attitude right out of you."

I bite back a needy protest when he stops touching my pussy just before I crest into oblivion. He tugs me away from the wall and bends me over his desk, not being gentle or sweet. Air gusts out of me at the sound of his zipper lowering. The need thrumming through me has me pushing back when he peels my dress up roughly to expose me.

"God, that's a sight. Your bratty, sexy little ass bent over, pussy shining and begging to get fucked." He smacks my ass and it makes my clit throb. "I'm going to wreck you so good, baby. You're going to feel my cock for days."

I hate him. But it's undeniable that I need this release. Irrefutable how much I want this with every breath I draw.

Inescapable that I want *him*.

He doesn't waste any time. There's nothing affectionate or loving going down. His fingers dig into my hip as he lines up. I throw my head back with a choked scream when his cock thrusts in with one long stroke that stretches me with a burn I crave, that makes me feel fucking alive.

"Fuck," Colton drags out, braced over me. "So goddamn tight."

"Shut up and fuck me." I clench around his dick, rolling my hips to encourage him to move, to make me forget everything wrong with the world for a while.

"Always with that mouth. Do I need to order you a special silicone replica of my cock to shove in your mouth to keep you quiet? Then I could always be in you. Make you choke on my cock while you sit on the fake dick.

Then make you lick the dildo clean while I fuck you."

I shudder at the mental image that suggestion puts in my head. He sets a pace that makes my snarky words come out strangled and husky.

"Are you always this talkative during sex? Someone might think you're obsessed with the sound of your own voice or something, pretty boy."

"Knew you thought I was pretty, brat."

I trap a whimper before it escapes when he clamps a hand on the back of my neck and fucks me hard enough the desk rattles. An all-consuming heat engulfs my body in the addictive, scorching burn of pleasure. My breasts ache with the force of my desire and my core tightens with an enticing throb of need. He stops right when I'm about to come and it takes all my willpower not to scream at him for denying my orgasm again.

Flipping me over, he tugs my sweaterdress higher, above my tits so I'm completely exposed to him. Fire burns in his darkened eyes as they move over me. Then he bends my knees back as he drives into me once more. His cock fills me deeper, the raw explosion between us growing more intense until all I can think about is him.

"Jesus," he grits out. "What the fuck is it about fighting with you that makes my dick hard enough to drill through steel?"

"More," I demand.

I moan when he picks up the pace, the obscene sound of his cock slamming inside my pussy filling the room. He hits a spot that lights me up with the rough way he squeezes my hips and rails me. It makes it difficult to catch my breath, each ragged gasp of air tinged with whimpers of pleasure.

"Oh my god." I arch, scrabbling over my head for something to hold on to. A wireless keyboard slips off the desk from my fumbling reach, clattering to the floor as my fingers curl around the edge.

Colton grabs my face, leaning close to speak against my lips. "I am your god." The dominance in his tone makes my entire body tighten and I release a strangled plea. His cruel grin stretches and he fucks me harder. "Fuck, your pussy is fluttering so good. You're close for me, aren't you? Come. Show me how much you love this. How much you love taking my cock, my pretty little slut."

A sharp cry tears from me at his dirty praise, making me splinter apart.

He groans in response, burying the sound in my neck as he slides his hands under my ass to grind into me. His cock throbs deep within me as he comes while I'm still riding the waves of oblivion. I drag my nails through his thick hair, tugging on it to keep his pierced tongue in place while he teases my sensitive skin with his mouth. Neither of us move for long minutes, lost in the rawness of what erupted between us.

Colton's shoulders stiffen when his open-mouthed kisses reach my tits and he lifts his head.

I gape, watching the lust drain from his gaze until anger is all that remains. He shoves away from me, leaving me splayed on the desk as he turns his attention to the computer, jaw locked while he closes out of the files he caught me snooping through.

"Did you finish downloading the output data from the crawler?"

I blink slowly. He's not going to say anything after that? While his come is dripping down my thighs?

"I'm not one of your mindless VR porn bots I found on your local drive." My words come out breathless and quaking. "You can't just fuck me every time you want to avoid talking. It's not like I'll drop it."

"Can't I?" Colton closes the distance he put between us to plaster his hard body against mine. I arch against him and he chuckles darkly, speaking in a filthy tone while he reaches down to cup between my legs. "See? Your body begs for me so much, all I hear when I'm around you is this pussy crying out for me."

Heat races through me, crashing against my indignation. I shouldn't find that so hot, and yet. *And. Fucking. Yet.* My swollen pussy throbs and I can't control the rock of my hips against his hand for more even though we just fucked. The movement earns me a wicked, satisfied smirk.

I bite my tongue to smother a faint whimper when his fingers glide through my sensitive folds, gathering his come and pushing it back inside. His gaze pierces into me. I fight not to turn away to hide my face or allow the pleasure he's bringing me by slowly fingering my pussy to flicker across my face, not about to back down from the challenge in his expression. This one's no different from every other one he's presented and I'm determined not to let him break me.

"Fuck." With the gruff curse, he dips his head to mouth at my neck, dragging his piercing along my pulse point. "I like this pussy used and loose with my come leaking out. Makes me want to have you sit on my cock and spend the rest of the afternoon fucking it back into your body while I go through the data."

I grip his forearm, gulping at the muscles flexing under my fingers. "But Snyder—"

"Leave it," he growls dangerously and pulls his fingers free. "Or I'll fuck your throat with my cock until it's so raw and swollen you won't be able to speak."

A hint of the guy who hates me resurfaces, overpowering his carefree cocky attitude. My head jerks back. I thought since he'd been more open and joking in the last two weeks, he finally understood it wasn't personal for me. I'm starting to sense it doesn't matter if it's personal or not, he sees all betrayals the same.

I don't know why I wanted to find a way to connect with him. To earn his forgiveness. The small pieces of my truth I offered him don't matter. He's not willing to give me the same without trust.

I shouldn't want any of that from him because I don't need anyone but myself. This is why I don't do boyfriends. Why I don't do love.

A hate fuck's all we'll ever be.

My throat is tight when I swallow. Fine. This is the reminder I needed. Colton isn't going to forgive me. Even if the others have moved past what I did, he's always going to see me as his enemy.

CHAPTER NINETEEN

COLTON

I WAS starting to think I could trust Quinn after she played nice during the interview we broadcast and with the preparations we've been working on for our next major targets during the yacht party.

Seeing her upset two weeks ago triggered my instinctive need to care for anyone who can't protect themselves. Then when we went to the marina to set up for the yacht, it was almost like she could fit in with us. It tempted me to want things I've never entertained for myself—things like what my boys have with Rowan and Isla. I've never pinned myself down like that, yet something about her still demands all my attention in a way no other girl has achieved.

Having Quinn's brilliant mind around the Nest 2.0 has eased my workload and given me the chance to breathe without feeling like I'm barely keeping my head above water because I refuse to fail my brothers when they're all relying on me. But when I came back up to the office after one of my minions delivered the rest of the parts I need to program the drone show that's the pièce de résistance to my plan for Mortimer's seafaring holiday party, the joke on the tip of my tongue died. She was snooping in my redacted files from five years ago.

Still spying. Still fucking lying.

I won't let her play me. Not again.

I can't allow my attraction to her cloud my judgment when it already almost cost me everything. She's a game I want to win. Nothing more. I won't give her a free pass to slide through my defenses.

Narrowing my eyes, I lick her divine taste from my fingers once I pull them free, shoving down the flare of enjoyment I get from her hazy gaze locked on my tongue curling around my knuckles. I turn my back on her and tuck myself away.

This is on you, a nasty little corner of my mind whispers. Fuck you, demons.

The overly self-critical side of my brain has a point. I left her alone without locking down that information. Stupid, trusting idiot.

What is it about this girl that makes me slip up? The answer is obvious. I pinch the bridge of my nose and try not to think of how good her pussy feels choking my dick when she comes.

Turning my attention to the computer when the web crawler script pings to alert me it's reached completion, my mouth sets in a grim line. I locate the scraps of information I have from the shitstorm five years ago, the only cobbled together proof of what happened other than the disappointing memory of that night, and store them in the encrypted database where Quinn won't be able to access them without my supervision. Shoving back from the desk, I crack my neck side to side.

"Stay here," I order flatly.

She scoffs, yanking her dress back into place. "Where are you going?"

"I need to concentrate. Can't do that with you around right now. I'll either fuck you again or kill you, and I've got important shit to do."

It's only half-true. I wouldn't really kill her. We've moved past that, yet I could go for strangling her pretty little neck. Just a bit. Just to see how she'd struggle, to see her question if I'd go that far. My tattooed fingers close into fists.

My brothers have found women who temper their psychotic tendencies unless it comes to protecting them, but Quinn? Quinn brings my fucking monsters out to play. Makes them thirst for chaos. Makes me want to push the line to see where the breaking point is, though I don't know which I want more—to know hers or to discover if mine's changed because of her influence.

Quinn doesn't match my darkness, she ignites it in an explosive, out of control inferno.

Without looking back, I stride from the office, slamming the door behind me. She can't follow, her biometric still not programmed. I've let her slide by leaving the door ajar, but that's done.

My dick is the only thing protesting the distance I put between us as I reach the ground level of the warehouse with my heart rate drumming fast and tumultuous. If fighting with her gets me hot, fucking her while riding the raw, explosive tension between us is on a whole new level. I already want to be inside her again.

The voice in my head that gives me shit for thinking with my dick sounds too much like Levi. Like he can talk. Well, he did have years worth of building his tolerance up to wanting to pin Isla down and fuck her.

My tolerance level and impulse control are sketchy at best when it comes to the feisty little queen who challenges me even when I threaten her.

"Hey." Rowan's greeting echoes as she hops off her perch on the bartop and crosses the newly lacquered dance floor. She surveys the fold out table I brought down here earlier, picking up drone parts. "What are you up to? Can I help? If I have to fill out more paperwork for the club right now, I'll scream."

I need the monotony of assembling the small parts on these drones to blow off steam. Fucking Quinn didn't stave off the agitation scraping my nerve endings.

"I guess you have a new assistant now, huh?" Rowan teases. "You don't need me anymore."

"I'd rather have your company," I grumble.

She rescues the precision screwdriver and battery from my brutal grip. "What's up, dude? Did you get in a fight with your girlfriend?"

"Quinn's not my girl and you know it." I frown, bracing my hands on the table. "She's not like us, babe. Not part of our chaos crew. A liar like her doesn't know the first thing about loyalty."

Rowan's brows jump up. "I think you should ease up on her." I shoot her a look of disbelief. She holds her hands up. "I get that you're reluctant to let your guard down around her again, but I doubt she's here to trick us this time. I think since she sacrificed herself to you guys for her brother's sake, she's more like us than you're willing to admit."

My jaw works. Damn it. I hate when I have nothing to refute sound logic.

"Whatever." I focus on the drone's body frame to avoid her stubborn green eyes because I have a specific weakness that folds to them every time.

She puts a hand over mine. "You know I'm right. Quinn's not like the Kings. She's just someone also caught up in this mess."

I grunt in response. Christ, I'm turning into Levi.

She cups my nape and drags me down to her level to kiss my head. "Just shout if you need help. You're not alone, Colt."

My throat constricts. I cough to clear it. "Aight. What are you doing?"

Rowan pulls a face, gathering her hair into a bun. "The rest of the paperwork hoops to get our permits and licenses so we can open this place on time."

"The Nest 2.0."

I look around at the warehouse's transformation. Soon enough it'll be poppin' with people who love the hedonistic experience of partying in our presence. None of them will know what secrets this place holds, just as it was in the hotel.

The real kings in this city will take our thrones once again. Bigger. Better. Un-fucking-challenged.

"It's not the place that makes it our home," she says with a soft smile. "It's because we've landed here that makes it the Nest."

Her words strike my heart, leaving my chest hollow. I nod slowly. "You're right."

Levi and Isla emerge from the basement's secret wall panel door, their workout clothes rumpled and eyes bright. It's not difficult to guess what they've been up to in the gym we set up downstairs. His hand rests on the small of her back as they head our way once he catches sight of me.

"Oh good," Rowan says. "I'm desperate for a break from all the legalese."

Isla laughs, moving from Levi's side to Rowan's and hooking their arms together. "Say no more, babe. What will we get up to instead?"

"Want to go to that cafe I like near campus?"

"Sounds like a plan. Oh! Is Quinn busy with anything? Can you spare her? We'll take her with us."

"No." The short, biting note of my response has all three of them giving me odd looks. Rowan frowns once more and I push out an agitated sigh, waving with one of my tools. "I've got her going through data that I need analyzed stat."

"We wouldn't be long," Isla says.

"Just—no."

"Okay." She sighs, then kisses Levi's cheek. "I'll see you later. Want us to bring you back anything?"

"Sure. Text Penn if you're going over there," Levi says. "Don't let your guard down."

"Always be prepared," Isla recites.

Levi stops her for one more kiss before he allows them to walk away. He doesn't follow, waiting until they're gone before I sense the moment his focus zeroes in on me.

"Look at that. Growth. You're not stalking your girlfriend." He doesn't answer. I motion to the steel column on the other side of the table. "If you're going to lurk there and brood, you could at least do it over there. You're standing in my light and these screws are a bitch when they don't thread right on the first try."

He prods at his lip ring with his tongue. "What's up?"

"Nada. Just have to build these and put the finishing touches on the grand finale, then we'll be good to go for Saturday night."

We both look up when Wren and Jude walk in. They're carrying enough suit bags for all of us. Our plan is to leave from here this weekend since we're closer to the marina. The suit bags make me think of Quinn in that dressing room. I tamp down on tempting thoughts of her.

"Where are the girls?" Wren asks.

"Isla and Rowan went to get coffee." Levi pauses and again I feel the press of his dark eyes. "Quinn's upstairs analyzing data."

I tune them out while I work. I have to get this done today. There's only this week left to prepare. My fingers won't obey, hands too tense to hold the delicate screws steady. They're so rigid the veins on the back of my hands are more prominent than usual.

"Colt." Jude prods me and I jolt back to reality, unsure how long the three of them have been staring at me. My lungs burn as I put effort into drawing a full breath. He raises a brow, studying me with keen eyes.

"What's going on with you?"

"What?" I wave a hand. "It's nothing. I'm fine. Totally. Fine, fine, fine."

Lie, lie, lie.

"Don't try to play us," Jude says. "We know something's up."

"You've pulled back from us." Wren's chin dips and his stare bores into me. "You only do that when you're hiding whatever it is you think you can fix yourself."

Fuck. I didn't want them to find out how much I struggled after the fire. I tried my best to bury this, to be the guy they need me to be, but it's bleeding out of me, overpowering my ability to control it. Playing games with Quinn was a bandaid to distract me from it, but it's poked its fucked up little head out.

"It's stupid," I mutter.

"Just spit it out. Jesus, and you call me dramatic." Levi shakes his head and moves closer, squeezing the back of my neck to soften the bite of his tone.

I huff. "No, I call you an edgelord. There's a difference. You're feral, not dramatic. The big guy's dramatic. Hell, Jude's dramatic. All lovesick and shit, for what?"

"Oh, fuck off." Jude grumbles at Wren's snort. "Either get it off your chest or take it to the ring downstairs to work it out."

"He's got a point." Wren scrutinizes me, stroking his jaw. "We can't let anything fester. Get it all out on the table, otherwise you risk carrying whatever it is over into the job."

My throat goes dry. That's the last thing I want because it brings my worst fear to life: putting any of them or the girls in danger because I screw up when I'm not focused. I gulp, grimacing.

Moment of truth. "I'm—worried. I don't want to be the reason we lose. This is the biggest thing we've faced."

The admission comes out in a gruff, jagged rasp. I pick a spot on the floor to focus on so I don't have to see the disappointment in my brothers' eyes, so I don't have to see the moment I lose their trust.

As the Crows, we've cultivated a reputation that precedes us. We're morally bankrupt. The fearsome thing that goes bump in the night. We're who people turn to for favors. My brothers are all strong, but I'm the weak link. I almost got us killed, and if I'm not good enough then it could happen again.

My heart beats hard and fast, my mind split between the present and the memories of my father's impossible expectations. Never good enough. Every inch of my body burns as I force the words out.

"You're my brothers. My goddamn family. If anything happened to you because of me, I'd—"

"Colt," Wren says.

His understanding tone makes my gaze snap up. It's not what I expected when my 4am anxiety thoughts played this conversation out. The three of them exchange a look. I don't know which of them grabs me first, but someone fists my pullover and drags me close. They give me a crushing embrace.

"How many times have we told you? You have to stop internalizing when your head gets all messed up like this." Jude rests his forehead against my temple. "You need to stop doubting yourself. What do I always say? Don't sell yourself short, sell for double so you come out on top with a profit."

A pained laugh catches in my throat and I scrabble to hold on to them to ground myself from the abyss of my mind that wants to drag me down into the shadowy depths. "Greedy bastard."

"I don't know where you got this idea. Without you we'd never have come so far. Your skills are the essential glue that binds us together. You made our legacy grow into our own empire." Wren's firm tone brooks no argument. He grabs me by the collar and gives me a shake to drive his point home. "We need you. And none of us blame you for the fire. You hear me? The only ones to blame are those Kings bastards. Not you. Not her—" He lifts his chin to indicate the office above us. "—not anyone but our true enemies."

"You forgot we know you, man. Enough to recognize when there's something you're not telling us." Levi's arm tightens around my shoulders and I close my eyes. "Stop trying to do everything yourself. We all bring something important to the table. You can't take on our enemies on your own when we're right here with you."

"We do this *together*." Wren's blue eyes flash and he pats my cheek. "As family."

Without me voicing everything, they dig to the root of what has me so off kilter because our bond goes deep, beyond flesh and blood.

Emotion wells up inside me. I love these assholes with everything in me. They crush the fears that reared up with the inescapable weight of their support.

They know me too well—know which of my tattoos cover up physical scars, and how deep the more sensitive emotional ones run—so when I reach my breaking point, they're always there to cushion my fall and remind me that I'm not that weak little kid who couldn't fight back. I'm not alone because I have them by my side.

Even a bunch of psychos with questionable morals can have heart to hearts. We bust each others' balls and we're there for each other when shit gets too hard to deal with on our own. That kind of support is what it means to be a family.

I can't speak. All I'm capable of is nodding. I scrub at my stinging eyes and blow out a shattered breath. With it, the tension in my muscles ease. The stress doesn't feel as overwhelming as it did when I stormed downstairs.

The guys don't release me for another moment. When they do, they each squeeze my shoulder or pat my back. Wren waits until I meet his eye, his brows lifting in silent communication. I nod again, taking his words to heart.

"I've, uh, got to get these built," I push out, scraping my fingers through my hair.

Wren lingers as the other two move off, crossing his arms over his broad chest. "Remember who we want to destroy so we can reclaim our city."

"Right."

This isn't small time. It's not about the rumors that follow us on campus or our fight nights to lure in the city's elite into our gritty world. We're not up against drug runners encroaching on our territory. It's the Kings' poisonous infection in Thorne Point we're fighting to take down so they can't spread, so they can't manipulate everyone in this city to fall to their knees before their false throne.

What they're doing to this city is a larger scale of what I learned to fight against growing up in my father's house. The Kings Society preys on the weakness of others for their own benefit.

My mind goes to Quinn when I pick up a motherboard for the custom drone I'm building. Shit, I left her up there, freshly fucked, like a complete dick. Maybe she doesn't deserve the brunt of my anger. If I was in her place, I'd be doing the same, utilizing every chance to collect information. But can I trust her?

Another harsh breath leaves me as I pass a hand over the parts to assemble the drones.

The story she fed me about her family's mob ties is bullshit. Everything about her is fabricated. My gaze rises to the mirrored glass blocking the view into the office. I want to know what her real deal is. I'm guessing she buried it since I already looked into her to vet her secret. What I found matched the information she paid with for my protection the first time.

It doesn't add up. She needs money. Plays poker like a goddess, though she tries to hide her true skill level around me. Hacks like a viper. All of that I've picked up on being around her all the time between my apartment and staying here.

There are little signs I've refused to acknowledge, but I recognize some of her behavior from growing up with foster siblings who had it rough before my parents brought them into the lap of luxury.

It's in the way she eats like she isn't sure when she'll see her next meal. The way she shrinks to her side of the bed, curled into a ball to take up less space like she's used to sharing.

I lace my fingers behind my head and exhale. Fuck, those habits aren't fake. I just haven't wanted to analyze them since I don't want to care about her. Was she in the system? Is that what she's hiding from me?

The old instinct to protect flickers to life in my chest.

One way or another, I'll get the truth out of Quinn. It's the only way I'll be able to move past the ingrained fear her betrayal tapped into. Except if she's erased herself from online, I'll need to go right to the source to get it out of her.

The question is whether or not I'll still want to punish her for tricking me once I find out who she really is.

CHAPTER TWENTY

QUINN

COLTON doesn't come back upstairs. I keep watching the door, waiting. The part of me that has always hated being left alone clambers to the surface. It's not like he's leaving me behind. Not like he's gone forever. My nails dig into my palms.

Then I grow annoyed with myself. Why should I hold my breath? The iciness in his tone when he snapped at me should make it clear where things stand between us.

"Ugh, why do I even care?" I mutter as I glare at the computer screen. "This is ridiculous."

It's the prolonged proximity. It has to be. I'm living in his pocket, sleeping in the same bed, around him constantly. All of it is tricking my mind and my heart into believing something's there that isn't. All those small gestures that make me think he's paying attention mean nothing. The space heater. The silk scarfs. The winter jacket. All meaningless.

It doesn't help we're both attracted to each other and the sex is... No. Not going there right now.

I don't need him. I don't want a connection with him.

This is why I learned to only rely on myself, so I don't have to face this.

An hour later, Rowan and Isla pop in to check on me. They bring me lunch and sit with me while I eat.

"This place is great," Rowan says. "I'm addicted to their coffee."

"Have you been to it?" Isla asks.

"No. It's good, though. Thanks." I hold up my sandwich. "You didn't have to come up to babysit me for him."

Rowan shakes her head and leans close to make sure I understand her. "Colt's our friend, but we're not doing anything for him. We're your friend, too."

I blink, a flutter rushing through me. It chases away the murkiness, leaving behind a bright light that glows within my chest. I think I'm happy. Friendship isn't something I've ever made time for, too reluctant to open myself up when I've faced so much rejection. It's easier to be on my own, but I'm finding it harder to back that up the more I spend time with them.

Isla giggles. "If any of these boys try to boss us around, they get a rude awakening every time."

"Exactly." Rowan grins slyly. "Next time we'll take you with us for lunch."

"We were going to, but—"

Rowan cuts Isla off with a look. I guess that means Colton had something to do with it after all. He gets fucking possessive over everything—his tech, his tinkering projects, and his friends.

Tough fucking shit. They want to be my friend. There's nothing he can do to stop me.

"It's okay. Next time," I say.

Their smiles set me at ease. They hang out with me while I go through data from the web crawler, telling me how they both fell for their Crows. By the time they leave, I don't feel as bad as I did when Colton left.

When he finally does show his face again, it's several hours after he stormed out. He stands in the doorway, studying me with an unreadable expression. Whatever demons he left to work out, he looks like he went five rounds and lost. The bags beneath his bloodshot eyes seem more prominent and the distrustful anger no longer rolls off him in waves.

He just seems exhausted, like he's carried the weight of the world on his shoulders for too long, on the verge of collapse. It makes me think of that night he came back to the apartment in the middle of the night and passed out on the floor.

I'm annoyed that the memory and seeing him like this now resonates with a part of me I keep locked up tight. I stamp out the sympathy he doesn't deserve.

Without a word, he motions me to follow. Sighing, I stand to stretch, working out the kinks from the position I sat in for too long.

I need a goddamn shower, still messy from earlier. The best I could do to clean up was use a random t-shirt I found laying around—definitely Colton's, I don't see any of the others wearing anything with anime boobs on it—to wipe between my legs.

"How long were you going to leave me in here?" He doesn't answer as we head for the bedroom. "What if I had to use the bathroom?" Still nothing. I narrow my eyes. "Fine. I'll make sure I take a piss on your pillow, then."

He's unable to stop an amused scoff, coughing to cover it. His fingers drag through his hair and he squeezes a handful of his longer fringe, releasing a sigh.

I shoulder past him and spend a long time in the shower.

When I come out forty-five minutes later, there's food waiting for me. I eye the steaming fries. He got two orders of them since I tend to steal his while he's distracted. I chew on the inside of my cheek and pick at the dinner he brought me.

Which is it? I want to demand. *Hate me or not? Want me or not?*

All these little things he does that come off like he cares throw me off. Then there's the way his moods flip without warning.

The weight of his eyes follows me as I go about my nightly routine. I ignore him as I apply lotion before changing. Let him look. He's already seen all of me.

He finally breaks the silence when I'm wrapping my hair for bed. "I shouldn't have snapped at you."

My head jerks up. "Is that an apology?"

He shrugs. "Not really. I don't do apologies."

"You're an asshole." I give him my back, working my jaw. "I hope you fall out of bed and smash your face on the ground tonight."

He snorts. "Probably will if you plan to go back to kicking me all night."

The resignation in his tone makes my lips twitch. I curl up in a ball to keep on my side of the bed, determined not to touch him.

CHAPTER TWENTY-ONE

COLTON

At the end of the week, me and Quinn are putting the final touches on the show the drones will play tomorrow night at the yacht party when we're ready. We've worked late into the night for the last three days to get everything done and it's left time for little else.

The rendering process is long and boring as fuck. All the technological advancement in the last two decades and there still isn't an innovative new way to export large videos quickly. It leaves my mind free to roam seeking other stimulation because it doesn't like the quiet.

I drum a rhythmic beat on the desk to the music I put on in the background while Quinn shakes her head. After another minute of my epic drum solo, she reaches over and snatches my hand to stop me.

"Cut that out," she grumbles. "You're not making it go any faster."

I raise a brow. "Oh? So now touching is back on the table?"

After we fucked the other day, she's been quieter, almost as if she retreated into herself the same way the guys called me out for doing. It's always easier to recognize your own shitty habits in others, like looking in a mirror honed in on the flaws you're most aware of. And yeah, the harsh way I snapped at her didn't help. When I tried to tell her that I shouldn't have done it, she wouldn't hear it and blocked me out.

We haven't touched since, other than the brush of our hands while we work and in the bed we share when she migrates to my side in her sleep. When she wakes, she gets tetchy about it and ignores me for at least an hour. If we touch in the office, she glares at me like it's my fault.

I'm not like Levi or Jude. I'll hold a grudge with the best of them, but I don't absorb it as my entire personality. I've always been someone who can bounce back and forth between the anger and my humor. It's a tactic I learned to do as a way to bear the brunt of my father's punishments.

I haven't pushed her like I want to, both of us too busy with all the last minute preparations we've been taking care of to steal control of Fitzy's party. But once this job is over, I'm determined to figure out who she really is. I've only broached the subject of her past briefly in the last few days, and every time she's shut me down. As much as I'm used to splitting my attention between more than one thing at a time, I'm too tapped out to make her tell me until we get this done.

"Shut up." She scoffs and lets go of my hand.

Smirking, I capture her wrist and bring her fingers to my lips, thinking of the last time I had them in my mouth and that tantalizing flare in her eyes. Now that I know what her pussy feels like clenched around my dick, it's been difficult not to want to splay her on the desk and sink into her every day this week. She wrenches her hand from my grasp with an irritated sigh.

I study her profile. The sides of her plush lips turn down and she stares too hard at the render progress bar on the screen.

"Instead of pretending I don't exist, you could answer my questions you've been evading while we wait." At her flat look, I chuckle and play with my tongue stud, the corner of my mouth curling up as I lean into her space. "Sooner or later you will. I can be very convincing. Plus, I'm told I have an irresistible face."

"That's what you think. Personally, I think it's a punchable face."

I move closer, eyes hooding at the alluring, sweet scent of the lotion she favors. "There's always the other option. I could fuck what I want to know out of you. Don't deny it. We both know you like playing my games."

At my suggestive tone, she swivels away in the matching chair I bought her, smacking me with the backrest. While she covers her laugh, I prop my elbow on the desk and rest my chin in my palm.

The twin chairs make us look like king and queen of my command center of the Nest. The thought snags my attention for a moment. It's always been just me as the computer guy, but surprisingly I don't hate the idea of having a hacking queen at my side. Maybe more specifically, it's her. I'm just drawn to her.

It's a shock to my system to think the girl who betrayed me could be the same one I picture as the only match for me. Part of the reason she pissed me off so much with her lies is because I want her—her brilliant mind, her knockout body, her sexy as hell sassy attitude. I'm still bothered that she tricked me, but since the guys cornered me downstairs while I built the drones, the hate I felt toward her has muted to a dull twinge from the full-blown fury it was when we first brought her here.

Wren's reminder has run through my head all week. The Kings are the ones responsible for everything. Quinn was only their pawn, only looking out for her own the way me and the guys look out for each other.

"Not happening," she bites out.

Snorting, I kick back in my chair, crossing one ankle over the other on the edge of the desk. Ideas filter through my head for how I'll get my bratty, stubborn little queen to break. I could bribe her. She certainly likes every chance to get money. Ordering her is another option, but I can already picture how well that would go over.

Another idea pops in my head. I bought a new vibrator when I was scrolling my phone in the middle of the night. I could hold her down and torture her pussy with it. Bet her that if I get her to beg for mercy, she'll need to offer up a truth. Tracing my lips with my fingertips, I rake my gaze over her, imagining the sounds she makes when she's close to coming.

I adjust in my seat so my half-hard dick isn't obvious. We don't have time, otherwise I'd pass the mind numbing wait for the render to complete with her luscious lips wrapped around my cock. Wren texted me once he and Rowan left our shooting range with the heads up we're meeting up here to go over the final details for tomorrow night. They should arrive any minute.

"I won't let it drop. I'm just biding time until I can focus on you again without everything else going on." My head tilts when she goes still. "Once that happens? Game over, baby."

She darts a narrow-eyed look at me. "Give me your phone."

"What?"

"You heard me." She holds out her hand. "I want to check in with my brother before tomorrow."

"You really love him." It's an observation, not a question. Understanding filters through me at her look of disbelief.

"Of course I do. He's my little brother." She sighs. "You wouldn't get what it's like to worry about someone else all the time."

I snort at how wrong she is. Worrying about others is the way I'm programmed. My brothers and Fox. Their girls. My other foster siblings. A whisper tugs at my mind that she might make that list, too.

"I do, though. Told you not to underestimate how much I get that, didn't I?" She peers at me through her lashes, a crease forming between her brows. I prod the inside of my cheek with my tongue and waggle my brows. "Nothing's free. What are you willing to do for it?"

Her lips slide together. "You want to keep hounding me for the truth? Here's a truth, asshole: I'm nervous about you dragging me along to this party. Mortimer knows my face. That dickweed Sosa will probably be on board as security for the event. Our presence will already piss them off and you're stranding us out at sea."

"We won't be stranded." I grin. "We have a getaway ride all planned out. How do I know whether or not you're lying to me?"

She opens and closes her mouth. Her hands drop into her lap, fingers twisting together. I track every tiny shift of her body language, reading her fear. This Sosa guy really gets under her skin. He's the one she worried about going after her brother.

"Kidding. Fine, here." I unlock my phone and slide it across the desk. Curiosity tugs at me. Mortimer was always going to be on the list once we found out he fucked with our Nest, but she's the one who brought him up as a potential target to seek her own retribution. "I thought you wanted to take Mortimer down? Don't you want the satisfaction of being there to watch his face when he realizes his number's up?"

She looks up from the text thread with Sampson, the lifeline to her brother helping some of the tension to bleed out of her posture. "I do." Her brows pinch as she hesitates, eyeing me warily like she isn't sure what I'll do with her admission. "It's just—"

Quinn cuts off when the door opens. Wren comes into the office, followed by the others. Dropping my feet off the desk, I slump back in my seat. The first real opportunity I've had all week to get in her head vanishes before my eyes.

"Just waiting for the render to export so I can program it on the drones," I say.

Levi props against the wall next to Jude, twirling one of his daggers through his fingers deftly. Isla comes around the desk and perches on the corner next to Quinn. Wren goes to the window and braces on the small lip, looking out at the club we created from nothing. Rowan stands at his side, brushing against him in silent companionship.

"Party starts at seven. According to the lovely ladies I followed to the gym and stood in as their personal trainer—" Jude winks at Isla's squeak of surprise. "—the ship will remain docked for the first hour for drinks and hors d'oeuvres. Once it sets sail, I'll follow outside the radar's range in the speedboat with the gear so I don't alert the crew until it's time for the drones to launch and our show to start. Then I'll move into position once the mayhem begins."

I swivel a tablet so they can see, pointing out the ship map covered in dots scurrying around the security system I'm connected to through the install we did the first time we snuck onto the Gentleman's Ambition.

"We'll blend in and act like we own the place until the time's right. Lure them into a false sense of security that, hey, no hard feelings for blowing us up. What's a little attempted murder between the wealthy?" Quinn smothers a snort of astonishment and I flash her a grin. "Most of our work is done, so we can kick back, play a little poker, and watch them squirm wondering what's coming. Maybe it's nothing. Maybe we've got a bomb on the boat."

"This is so much easier than infiltrating the Castle for a rescue mission." Isla pats her thigh and beams at Levi. "Still, always be prepared."

"Damn right." Rowan molds her fingers into a gun and blows imaginary smoke from her fingertip. "They won't have any creepy dungeons to take us to."

"They won't touch you at all this time," Wren growls. "Anyone that does is losing fingers."

"Fingers?" Levi catches his knife from midair, dark eyes glinting. "They touch our girls, they die. They won't see the end of the party."

"Okay, psycho," Quinn mutters.

My lips twitch. "I'd do the same for you, babe. Team Crow perks. Full service protective detail."

She gives me a look like I'm nuts. And, okay, yeah. I am a bit. No doubt. Doesn't change the fact that if one of those Kings bastards came at her, I'd ram the barrel of my gun into his groin and pull the trigger. My chest feels funny and I rub at it absently.

"It'll be our first time seeing my father and Lev's uncle since the masquerade." Wren shifts his focus from the club below to Levi. "It's inevitable they'll want to speak to us. Probably try to manipulate us some more if the Kings still see us as theirs to sponsor or whatever the fuck they called it. They'll want to corner us to do damage control."

Levi's lip curls. "Their arrogance will be their downfall."

Wren crosses his arms, his rolled up shirt sleeves straining against his inked muscles. "We have their attention after the broadcast pulled the curtain back on Vonn and the Castle for all to see. By tomorrow night, we'll prove their efforts to control us failed. Then they'll know: we're not their legacy, we're not their heirs. We're the Crowned fucking Crows."

Rowan shivers, eyes gleaming. "Is there anything else we need to talk about?"

Wren looks at her and he smirks. "Not tonight. Everyone meet here by three to load up."

The two of them leave first, Rowan's breathy sound of pleasure audible before the door closes all the way.

Isla hops off the desk and turns to me, wiggling her bright red manicure. "Make sure you finish up whatever with Quinn by noon. We're going to get our nails done. We deserve some pampering."

"Stealing my asset for girl time, Isles?" I mime a blow to the heart. "Do you love her more than me?"

Isla's nose crinkles and bats her lashes jokingly with a shrug. Jude snorts and nods to me on his way out. Levi pushes off the wall, waiting by the door for Isla.

I wave a hand. "Fine. Go if you must."

"Perfect." Isla lets Levi snag her around the waist and guide her out. "We'll pick you up, Quinn."

CHAPTER TWENTY-TWO
COLTON

It's chill. I'm not worried she'll try anything. We moved past that the moment she realized she wanted to crush the Kings as much as we do. And if she does, I've got backup trackers hidden in the lining of her shoes, plus some decoy AirTags she'd be clever enough to find.

"Really?" Quinn hedges.

"You want to, don't you?" She nods and I gesture. "Then go."

I wait until a few minutes after they all leave to speak again, studying her from the corner of my eye while she moves her lips together in uncertainty. "You don't have to be nervous about tomorrow night. It'll be fine. You're with us and you've got our protection. We don't leave anyone behind. Period."

"I believe that about your friends, but your *asset*?" She frowns. "I can watch my own back."

"And I believe that. You're tough as nails." I form a mock-lion's claw and

She huffs and lowers her voice. "Maybe I don't want to be tough all the time."

Something shifts and expands in my chest at the vulnerability breaking through the cracks in the fierce armor she shields herself with. She's always reactive, ready to fight, but underneath that she's hiding so much from the world. No one truly wants to be hardened all the time. Deep down, all of us hope for the chance to have someone else protect us when we're too beat down to protect ourselves.

My gaze remains on her while my tattoo-covered scars tingle with awareness. Those ones only run skin-deep. The others I can't see carved jagged paths straight to the depths of my being.

I run my thumb along my lower lip. "Is that another truth?"

The corner of her mouth kicks up, then falls. "That's the last free one you get."

There's that damn protective urge again, taking root in my chest, pushing me to step up and take on the burdens she carries. My gut instincts are all out of whack ever since she deceived me. I've never questioned whether or not I could trust my own intuitive read on people. She has me caught between what I want to be real about her and cautiously holding myself back because I hate being wrong.

It feels like something's changing between us. A storm about to break. I don't know whether it will leave devastation in its wake or be the catalyst we never saw coming that overwrites everything.

I gesture to the computer. "You keep an eye on the file render and check Mortimer's emails to see if he's in touch with any of his crusty brethren. I don't want any last minute surprises interrupting this bomb ass burn book I've got ready to go."

Quinn rolls her lips between her teeth to stop the smile she almost let free.

"What are you going to do?"

I lace my fingers together and stretch my palms outward to crack my knuckles. "I'm looking ahead to our next big fish."

As soon as her attention is off me, the cocky slant of my mouth drops. Our next goal is Wren's father. We're coming for the thing most precious to him. Not his lost daughter. Not his wife. Definitely not his son. We're going for his business empire and dismantling it after the club officially opens.

I grab one of the laptops from the shelf to work on while Quinn hacks Mortimer's inbox to comb through his messages for any Kings Society trigger words.

With Ethan's restored file, it's been much easier to decode emails masking the true messages they send each other. After we publicly destroyed Senator Vonn, he sent several thinking his secret society friends would save him. He was wrong.

While I'm looking into ways to buy out a business that isn't for sale, my hand wanders like it has a mind of its own. As I skim through the stock values of the various businesses that make up Thorne's conglomeration, I trace patterns on the peeks of rich brown skin showing through the cutouts in Quinn's leggings. She pauses her infiltration of Mortimer's inbox for a moment, giving me a sidelong glance like she's searching for my ulterior motive, then resumes her task. By now she's used to my tactile habits, though this is the first time she hasn't wrenched away at the slightest touch in the last few days.

My mouth curves in satisfaction when I picture Daddy Thorne's face—the pompous one, not our true BDE king—when he realizes we acquired ruling shares for every one of his companies.

Teasing beneath the holes in her leggings, I stroke her inner thigh, enjoying the shiver she attempts to suppress. She works her jaw, keeping her eyes glued to the screen. This is the furthest I've gotten with her after we clashed together in that raw, stress-fueled fuck. If she's not going to stop me...

Quinn clamps her legs around my hand to halt its path and angles an obstinate look at me. "If you want me to hack this, you need to stop trying to distract me. Which is it?"

I flex my hand, wriggling to brush her center with a light, teasing touch. "Shh. Keep working. I'm trying to think and playing with you gets me to focus. You can focus while I finger you a little, can't you, Q?"

An uneven breath rushes past her lips and her brows furrow. Her eyes bounce between mine. Whatever she sees in them, she swallows.

"I—you. Why are you so impossible?" She whips her attention back to the screen, mumbling, "Don't even know why I bother asking. You're crazy."

I hum in amusement. Once she relaxes, I stop holding my hand still and draw a slow circle with my fingertips.

"Damn it," she curses under her breath.

I read up on Thorne's current board members overseeing his umbrella company, but only make it through half before I'm more interested in riling her up. Playing with her goes straight to my cock and feeds my most impulsive tendencies.

I want to make her squirm. I want her biting those lips until she can't hold back. I want her trying to hold her focus until it breaks and she lets go of everything except the need to come.

Shit, I want her, period. It's not deep. I'm not someone who denies myself what I desire.

This time it's not about punishing her, or making her break for me. I'm not thinking about the truth I want from her, or the anger I can't seem to reignite toward her.

My hand continues moving between her legs, alternating between too-soft touches that get her chest rising and falling, and grinding the heel of my palm against her mound until she tilts her hips to get that pressure on her clit. I don't bother with the pretense of working on my laptop, shifting to face her, gaze burning into her profile with hunger for every tiny flicker in her expressions. The part of her lips is fucking erotic as I cup her pussy.

"What are you doing?" Her lashes flutter and her thighs open wider.

"This."

I haul her from her chair to sit on my lap, facing the dual monitors. The long sleeve sweater she's wearing drapes off her shoulder. My arms lock around her waist, palm dragging down her torso. When I reach the band of her leggings, I delve inside, pressing the curve of my mouth against her nape when I find her slick folds bare again.

"Always ready for me." I mouth at her skin, teeth grazing her shoulder. "That's so fucking sexy."

"Colton—"

"Pay attention to what you're doing or I won't let you come."

I grin when she shudders against me, rewarding her with my fingers gliding through her slit. Her rapid typing falters. She presses into my hand for more only to rock her hips back against the hard ridge of my cock nestled in her ass. The thin material rides up, molding against her curves as we move together.

I groan against her skin and hold her down on my lap while I buck against her. "Fuck yes. Do that again. Grind that ass on my dick."

The more I tease her, the harder I get. She's got my fingers coated and slippery before I sink the first one inside, grinning at the strangled noise of pleasure that escapes her. My cock throbs and my nerve endings feel so fucking alive, riding the addictive anticipation the night before a job brings. My pulse drums in exhilarated arousal and fire spreads through my veins.

"Can you take another finger while you work, baby?" I suck on a patch of skin that makes her legs open wider. "Can you take three? Think you could ride my cock and still hack that shithead's server while I make you come? Answer me."

"I, ah," she breathes when I add another finger. "Yes."

It's a gorgeous, shattered confession. A fantasy unfolding before our eyes.

My chest vibrates with a rough noise. "You dirty girl. Such a pretty little slut who needs my cock to fill your pussy when you're supposed to be working."

"Yes, shit. Okay. I'm—I'm in." Her words come out husky, sliding into a moan as I push deeper, wrist and forearm flexing to stroke her until she's shaking.

"So am I, baby," I rasp against her ear. "You feel me?"

"Fuck." She gasps, arching her back as I curl my fingers inside her.

"Check his emails."

My smoky, commanding tone makes her clench around the fingers I have buried in her pussy. Watching her struggle to stay on task while I finger her is the hottest damn sight I've ever seen.

"Anything suspicious?"

She forces out a shaky breath. "Nothing. Just—just the usual pretentious shit."

Rewarding her for keeping it together, I put all my focus into pushing her to the edge, fucking her harder with my fingers and squeezing one of her tits through her sweater. My tongue flicks at her sensitive pulse point and when she's close, I bite down.

"Oh fuck, oh fuck, yes," Quinn cries.

God, it sounds fucking stunning when she comes. She tilts her head back on my shoulder as her body trembles.

"How badly do you need to get fucked?" I pump my fingers until she whimpers and my voice lowers into a rough growl. "Tell me."

"*Nngh.* B-badly," she pleads hoarsely. "I need you to fuck me."

"You need it?"

I bite her neck again and she smothers a scream, nails digging into my forearms. Reaching back, she fists my hair and tugs, sending a pulse of molten arousal rocketing through my cock when she's not afraid to be rough back to me.

"Yes! Yes, goddamn it!"

Good. My need for her is just as intense.

Pulling my fingers free, I push to my feet, holding her against me, keeping her shorter legs half off the ground. I don't bother shutting anything down. I'll come back later to deal with it all. I need to fuck her too much to care about anything else right now.

"Let's go." She slides down my body when I release her and stumbles, knees buckling. I automatically tighten my loose hold on her to steady her. Once I'm sure she's good, I slap a hand on her ass, squeezing the delectable handful. "I'm fucking you in a damn bed this time so I can clap these cheeks right. You're never going to forget the feel of my cock imprinted on the inside of your pussy."

"Prove it," she says through her teeth.

"Oh, you know I'm a man of my word. Challenge accepted, little queen."

I grin, dragging her out of the office, through the upper bar level to our room. Huh. I pause with her pinned to the door, massaging her waist.

Our room. When did I start thinking of it like that?

"What is it?"

"Nothing. Can't decide if I want to fuck you so I can watch your face when you fall apart on my cock or if I want you on your hands and knees so I can grab this ass while I rail you."

She shivers, gripping my hair to keep my mouth on her warm skin. "Just—do it." Her leg hikes up on my hip as I grind against her through her thin leggings. "Come on, fuck me."

"Love the sound of your begging."

I peel her top off and she helps me remove her leggings, gripping my shoulder for balance. I pause, gaze dragging down her body, lingering on that sexy as fuck Nyx tattoo on her side. Reaching behind my head, I tug off my TPU thermal shirt. Her eyes hood as she takes in my tattoos.

Lifting her, I swing around for the bed and drop her on the mattress. "I will fuck you. But first I need to eat you. I missed out last time and dessert's my favorite meal."

She props on her elbows, opening her mouth. Whatever snarky comment she had ready dies when I press her knees apart and lower my head to swipe my tongue over her pussy. I peer up the length of her body, smirking at the lust clouding her gaze. I hold her attention while I circle her clit with my tongue piercing then suck on it.

The soft sigh she releases is music to my ears as I devour her. I've wanted to eat her pussy since the first night I saw her cleaning up at our card tables down at Castlebrook College. From the first moment she stood up to me and gave me all that attitude. Her taste is divine. I can't get enough of it, growling while I feast on her.

"Shit! Oh!" She threads her fingers in my hair and uses the leverage to get more pressure, practically suffocating me with her pussy.

With a high-pitched cry, her thighs clamp around my head. I grin against her, not stopping, even when my lungs burn. It's worth it to extend her orgasm, her legs quaking on either side of me, her breaths tinged with sounds of pleasure.

Prying her legs open, I catch my breath, speaking against her pussy while she's still sensitive from coming. "You good?"

She nods, then shakes her head, then nods again. "Fuck me right now, asshole."

I torment her clit with my tongue piercing for a little longer until she tears me away by her grip on my hair. "Hell, I've never been that into having my hair pulled." A chuckle falls from my lips as I trail open-mouthed kisses up her body, pausing to capture one of her nipples in my mouth. "But damn, when you do it, it makes me want to bend you over and fuck you so hard you scream yourself raw."

"That's what I'm sitting here waiting for you to do. You gonna keep running your mouth about it, or do I have to take care of myself without you?" She lifts her brows, imperious and bratty and fucking gorgeous with her eyes bright from coming.

Smirking, I get up to undo my jeans, kicking them off. I stand there a moment, stroking my cock while my gaze roves over every sensual inch of her beautiful body. She meets my eye, biting her lip as she teases her fingers between her legs to pet her pussy.

"Fucking hell, Quinn."

Kneeling on the bed, I cover her hand with mine while I draw her leg wider by my grip on her knee, settling between her thighs. Her eyes have turned molten with heat and I can't resist kissing her while I line up. We both sigh in relief as I push into her body.

Being inside her is pure fucking heaven. I deepen the kiss as I begin to move. Her tongue glides against mine, back arching. Ending the kiss, I nip at her lip.

"I don't hear any screaming."

She huffs and licks her lips slowly. "Guess you're not doing a good enough job then."

"Oh yeah?" I hike her leg higher to change the angle when I sink into her again.

"Like a four. Four and a half."

An amused breath punches out of me and my competitive side kicks in.

"That won't do."

I set a pace that makes her gasp and cling to me, hips undulating to meet each thrust. The LED lights I decorated the room with flicker with the slap of skin on skin. I don't stop.

"Jesus," she grits out while the lights flash from red to purple each time I slam into her.

I dig my fingers in and drive into her with sharper force, feral satisfaction hitting me when she throws her head back with a scream. Her body clenches tight around me, fluttering as she comes. It feels so damn good I have to brace over her, mouth dropping open. My balls tighten and I grab her by the nape to pull her close, lips colliding with hers in a scorching kiss.

Quinn moans into it when I bury my cock in her pussy as my orgasm crashes over me. She reaches down to dig her nails into my hip and ass to urge me deeper, and I break away from kissing her to hiss in ecstasy, the flash of pain heightening the intensity of my release.

"Oh fuck, that's good."

When I kiss her again, something expands in my chest. I still can't get enough of her. My hand drops between us to play with her pussy. She releases a faint whimper, wrapping her fingers around my wrist, shaking her head while her body continues to move against my teasing.

"One more," I rasp against her swollen lips. "Give me one more, baby. I need to feel you come again."

"I can't—ah!"

"That's it," I praise.

"Fuck you," she cries through her shuddering.

"If that's what you need. Just give me ten minutes, you really wrung me out. I'll eat your pussy until I bounce back. I think my balls turned into raisins from coming so hard." I stifle a groan as I shift to pull out, feeling how full of come she is. "Damn, feel that?"

"Oh my god." She covers her face with her hands. "I can't with you right now."

"Let me see."

Mischief fills my voice. I catch her shins when she curls up to hide herself, wrestling with her until I get my way. A smug laugh escapes me as I spread her legs, keeping them pinned. She squirms while I admire the view.

I like it. Maybe too much, the sight awakening a deep, primal side of me that wants to be the only one that gets to see this.

"Oh yeah. Look at this pussy leaking come." She presses the back of her hand to her forehead, biting her lip while I graze my knuckles up and down her swollen cunt. "That's how it should always look because you're such a good little slut for my cock, aren't you, my little queen?"

The look she gives me when she darts her eyes to mine steals my breath. I see the same feeling unfurling in my chest reflected back in her gaze— something more than lust.

Whatever this is between us, I don't want it to end.

CHAPTER TWENTY-THREE

COLTON

We arrive fashionably late, nearly an hour into the cocktail reception before the Gentleman's Ambition is due to set sail on the icy waters off the Maine coast. The seven of us draw attention as we climb aboard the luxurious yacht with the event in full swing, and not only because the girls look like knockouts. The four of us exude palpable confidence and power in our sharpest tuxes, a knowing smirk passing between all of us at the momentary hush that falls over the party.

Do all of us need to be here for this? No. It's a job that should only take Jude and myself since everything else is preprogrammed.

With all of us here, we send the message that we're not going anywhere to Mortimer and any other King hiding in plain sight tonight.

They all know who we are. Most of the guests were patrons of our fight nights, living for the thrill of the violent experience we served them. Moreover, they know we belong here by our names alone.

Heads turn our way and a waiter hustles over to offer us his tray of freshly poured champagne. Rowan and Isla accept glasses. I give Quinn a nudge at the small of her back to encourage her, caressing her skin. Her gown that seems made of liquid gold drapes low enough to expose a tempting amount of skin while still being elegantly tasteful.

She takes two glasses, her long, single-strand gold earrings grazing her shoulder as she turns to offer one to me.

"Cheers."

I clink the flute against hers, peering out at the old biddies nearby doing a piss poor job of making it seem like they're not gossiping about us. Jude flashes them one of his lethal charming smiles and chuckles at the way they scurry off, one glancing back with open interest. Quinn hides an amused noise behind a sip of champagne.

I watch the column of her neck as she swallows, revisiting the memory of peeling the gown off her in the dressing room. "By the way, you look fucking stunning tonight."

"Oh." She dips her chin, a surprised smile playing at the corner of her mouth. "Thanks."

Her hair is pulled back into a low, sleek bun and she created a beautiful flat curl design with shorter gelled strands along her hair line. The dark red, almost plum shade of her lipstick makes her plush mouth appear fuller and even more kissable. I know we're here to work, but the urge to find a place to sneak off with her is tempting.

I feel on top of the damn world walking into enemy territory knowing we're about to crush the sniveling man who thought he could kill us and get away with it. Even better, the girl he thought he could use as a pawn to play us is on our side to help us pull this off.

Everything is ready and tonight should go off without a hitch. Levi's the only one of us armed to the tits with his knives, but that's any day that ends in *y* with him. If things do get out of hand, he'll be on it. I have a concealed taser disguised as a pen and some of the self-igniting fireworks I used when we infiltrated the Castle in my pockets. They're tweaked to go off like crackers on their own, but I don't anticipate needing to use them.

Smirking, I trail my knuckles down the curve of Quinn's spine and lean into her, murmuring in her ear. "Remember. Mortimer can't touch you while you're with us. Ready to fuck his shit up?"

The determination that crosses her face sends a rush of heat through me. I love that expression on her. There's something more genuine about her tonight when she looks at me, like she's gradually dropped her guard around me. I didn't notice it as much at the Nest, but it's evident to me here in the way she angles herself towards me unconsciously, like she's relying on me, and holds herself with closed off, proud poise around the other guests who flash her curious glances.

It makes me want to trust her no matter what her real truth is.

"Yes. I want him to get what he deserves." She searches the crowd mingling on the deck, wariness flashing in her eyes.

"Hey. You don't have to be tough all the time." Ever since she confessed that last night, it's stuck in my head, echoing in my heart and solidifying my desire to protect her the same way I do for everyone I care about. I duck to catch her attention. "I'm here. You're my partner tonight."

She slides her lips together and nods. The girls step away from Levi and Wren to sandwich her between them, Isla's beaming smile helping chase away the tension in her posture.

"Seriously, you look amazing in this. I'm so glad we picked it," Isla says.

"Son."

All of us turn. Wren covers the rigid line of his shoulders with skill, but we know him well enough to recognize the subtle difference in his stance when he faces his father. I wrap an arm around Quinn and set my jaw. Rowan moves to Wren's side and stands tall with her man.

When none of us follow etiquette instilled in highbred society, Mr. Thorne grits his teeth. "I've been trying to get a hold of you since the masquerade." A dark expression crosses his face. "Then I heard news of the hotel fire. To be plain, I'm surprised to see you here of all places."

I swallow back a snort. Yeah, he seems really torn up about it. Based on the way Wren clenches his jaw, Levi's restless shifting, and the curse Jude utters under his breath, they're all thinking the same.

"We were invited." Wren holds out his hands, the double meaning of his words hanging between them. "Why wouldn't we be here?"

Here, at a party hosted for the wealthy social circle of the city. Here, with the Kings Society that wanted us to join their rank, jizz-stained fold.

My parents are on board somewhere, invited as part of the rich families who aren't members of the society padding the guest list.

"Right," Thorne says.

"Enjoy the party," Rowan says with perfect delivery of polite words dripping with disdain.

Wren smirks, rubbing his girl's back. "Say hi to mom for me, won't you?"

He leaves his father standing there and we join him.

"If we run into my uncle, I can't promise I won't stab him," Levi mutters at my side.

"Control yourself," Jude says. "At least until everyone's distracted. And for god's sake, make it look like an accident."

Levi scoffs. "Like I'm some amateur?"

Quinn's grip digs into the crook of my elbow as I escort her, waving to guests. "Don't mind them," I say from the side of my mouth. "Just act like you belong. We're blending."

Wren halts and turns to face us. "Stick to the plan." He meets Levi's scowl. "They're next."

Levi nods. "Fine."

Isla slips her hand into his and smiles when he gives her all his attention. "Let's do a lap. We'll find a good spot to watch from."

"Looks like they're about to push out." Jude checks his smartwatch. "See you in about an hour."

"Watch yourself out there," Rowan says.

"Always, firecracker." Jude winks and loosens his bowtie. "Don't think you've got the easy part because you're staying on the boat."

Levi's smirk is vicious. "Let mayhem reign."

Jude waggles his brows, backing away. He makes his way through the crowd, a master in his element striking up brief but memorable conversations as he meanders toward the exit to the dock. With each person he talks to, he deftly plants the idea of a rumored surprise at tonight's party. It's backed up by the line we added to the invitations by hacking the printing company Mortimer's assistant used to have the invites made, uploading my own version with a hint about an unforgettable night. Once he's off the ship, it's all most people are talking about.

"That's freaky to watch in action," Quinn comments.

"You get used to it. No matter how much I practice, I can't nail it the way he can with his natural charisma, and I'm charming as fuck."

Her lips twitch. "That's what you think."

I grasp her chin, lifting it. Her attention drops to my mouth, which tugs into a smile. I lean in, hovering over her lips. "You know you can't resist me."

She clicks her tongue and twists away before I kiss her. "I thought we were here to play poker."

Rowan's watching us when I look up. She smiles knowingly and tucks into Wren's side against the mid-December chill. The opulent yacht has its discreet space heaters cranking, but it doesn't help against the winter breeze coming off the ocean. I scratch the bridge of my nose self-consciously.

"We're heading up a deck to see if they've opened the poker tournament," I say.

"We'll hang down here until we're out in open water," Wren decides. "Don't let your guard down."

"Let's make them sweat," Rowan says with a hint of savageness in her tone that first made me believe she fit in with us.

Quinn's smile matches that savage vibe and an odd burning sensation settles in my chest. "Payback's a motherfucking bitch."

I check my phone on our way to the upper deck. Jude texted to say he's in position. We went without comms tonight since they won't work without me building a cell tower on board. Not even the signal boosters we planted around the ship for the drones are enough to support both frequencies, so we'll have to make do. We all know the plan.

Making a mental note to design a multi-frequency signal booster that can handle it if we need to pull off something like this again, I absently trace Quinn's back on our way up the grand staircase leading up to the panoramic observation deck where the poker game is happening. She hesitates at the top of the stairs when Fitzy's sniveling voice booms over the holiday music playing in the background.

"I told him, Charles, there's no money to be made in horses. It's all in real estate with the recession breathing down the middle-class' necks." Mortimer laughs with the others around him, Petra and Sebastian Yates. "Buy it all up and inflate the selling value. That's where the real profit's at."

Quinn's lip curls. "Fucking pig."

I hold her hip and step into her back, brushing my lips against her temple. "Still worried about him seeing you?"

"No," she says fiercely.

"That's the spirit, babe. Walk by him, look him in the eye, and make him shit his goddamn pants knowing we're here."

She lifts her chin and walks like the enticing badass she is, embodying Nyx, the goddess of the night she dressed as for our Halloween party. The moment Mortimer spots us is priceless. His eyes bug out, bouncing between us. Color drains from his face and he backs into the path of another guest walking behind him, yelping as his drink sloshes all over his tuxedo. I cock my head, smirking.

"Mr. Mortimer, right? Killer party." The tip of my tongue traces my lower lip. "So glad we could make it out."

He breathes heavily. "Yes, well. You, that is, I should—I'm being called away. Excuse me."

We watch as he scuttles off. The Yates give us tight, pompous smiles and move along to another group of high profile guests.

"I was hoping to whoop his ass in poker," Quinn murmurs.

"He'll be back. We shocked him good, but he's the type of man that still thinks he's coming out on top no matter what. A slimy, mucus-coated turd who squeezes through even the tightest sphincters."

She grimaces. "Gross."

"On that note, let's go play. I've got our buy-ins."

"You're really dropping a hundred large, just like that?" She squints at me. "Like it's nothing?"

"Babe, a hundred g's is peanuts to me. Welcome to my world." I grin. "That also tells me you haven't gotten past my security protocols and seen my investment accounts. So you're good, but you're not *that* good."

She frowns and hugs herself. I rub her arms to fight the chill and she shrugs me off.

"What's wrong?"

"It's whatever. We need to focus." She flaps a hand and heads for the oval table set up for poker with a dealer shuffling cards. "Buy us in."

Trying to work out what I said to piss her off, I follow her and get our chips. We choose seats beside each other. She sends her sharp gaze across the others already seated, waiting for the game to begin, probably already reading them for potential tells she can use to her advantage.

People always think cards is about number strategies and the luck of the draw. The real strategy is in knowing how to play the people you're against so you can win every time no matter what hand you're dealt.

My fingers stroke her nape. "You look hot when you're sizing up the competition. I didn't get to appreciate it the last time I saw you play in person."

"Watch closely." She ducks her head to hide a smirk, toying with her chips. "Maybe you'll learn something."

Heat barrels through me at her confident, sexy as fuck tone and my focus drops to the high slit in her dress when she crosses her leg over her knee.

Just as I predicted, Fitzy makes his way back to the table, chest pushed out proudly. "We're setting sail. Shall we begin tonight's game?"

He looks around the table, stopping on me and Quinn. The corner of my mouth lifts and I twirl a thousand dollar chip between my fingers. Let the game begin.

"Do you understand the rules, girl?" Mortimer sneers at Quinn.

I clench my teeth at his condescending tone, ready to forget the plan in favor of punching him, but she lays a hand on my wrist. "I do." She narrows her eyes slightly and waves a hand. "Unless you need a refresher."

A slow grin curves my mouth and I drape an arm across the back of her chair, proud that she can handle her own against these assholes. Mortimer scoffs, muttering to himself. She's already doing a perfect job at drawing just the right amount of attention to us. As long as she keeps it up, we'll distract everyone from the real reason we're here until the drones are in position.

The dealer starts the game and I check my watch to set a countdown timer to alert me two minutes before showtime when the program's automation will trigger. Slouching in my chair, I check my cards, keeping my expression blank. Not the best hand, but not a bad one either. My gaze moves to Quinn. Her true emotions are hard to read, masked by the exaggerated show she puts on to fool the others at the table when she peeks at the hand she's dealt.

She's a phase player. First she lures her opponents in, making them believe she's got dumb luck and doesn't have a clue what she's doing. It gets them betting, not taking her seriously until she changes tactics and reveals she knows exactly what the fuck she's doing while she shakes them down for all their chips and takes the pot from under their noses.

Just like my online card nemesis, Queen_Q.

The poker game moves quickly in the first half hour while we sail away from shore until downtown Thorne Point is a small glitter of lights along the coast. Quinn's playing ruthlessly enough to draw an audience gathered around the table. Even better, she has Mortimer sweating, checking his cards every two minutes when she stares him down. Seeing her in her element, bringing these self-important, greedy men and women down several pegs has my dick hard.

Wren and Rowan stand directly in Mortimer's line of sight, adding pressure to his increasingly precarious state of mind. Levi and Isla join them, encouraging the bulging vein of concentration in Mortimer's temple. Others stand out in the audience, too. Wren's father watches briefly, and I swear I spot that piece of shit Judge Snyder's fake as fuck white toupee—seriously, with all that money and he goes for a wig instead of implants—floating around at the edges before he slips away.

"Raise," Mortimer finally decides haughtily, tossing chips worth eight grand into the center of the table.

The game continues and my hand caresses Quinn's thigh, teasing inside the slit of her dress. "Still on for our wager?"

"If you like losing." The edge of her mouth quirks with confidence. "I told you, pretty boy. You can't beat me."

"We'll see."

Sliding my hand higher, her gasp is music to my ears when I slip between her legs to stroke her bare pussy. She still refuses to wear underwear. The idea that maybe she's grown used to being ready for me to play with her all the time fills me with devious satisfaction.

She tilts her head, flashing me a fierce look that definitely means *are you kidding me right now*. I'm addicted to the way her sassy tone fills my head as I think it.

"Call." Smirking, I keep my touch light. "You have a good hand, little queen?"

"You're playing dirty." Her whisper is shaky and her hips shift against my hand. "I don't need unfair tactics to beat you, otherwise I'd be playing naked."

"Mm, as good as that sounds, I'm not trying to beat you. I'm playing them." I tip my head to the dusty old men salivating over her. They want what I'll never let them have. Licking my lower lip with the tip of my tongue, I press against her clit, indulging in my favorite way to multitask. "What's wrong, baby? Can't handle it?"

Her lips purse and she stifles a faint sound, eyes darkening. Fuck, I love the thrill of a job, but I love this more. I can't wait to get back to the Nest 2.0 for victory sex because I need to fill her with my cock and kiss that tantalizing Nyx tattoo on her ribcage.

"I thought you understood the rules—young Mr. DuPont, is it?" Mortimer's dismissive, smug smirk is extra fucking punchable. "You'll need to keep yourself in check if you wish to remain here."

I lean back, reluctantly extracting my fingers from between Quinn's thighs and give him a carefree shrug with my hands that might still be glistening. "Maybe it's you who doesn't know the rules, Fitzy." He chokes, eyes bulging in astonishment at my balls to talk back to him. Clearly he doesn't know me very well. I talk over him before he can speak. "See, maybe you don't play the game enough, but pretty much nothing's off-limits when it comes to chatting during cards. I wasn't talking about the hand. Just flirting with the lovely goddess to my left. I mean, can you blame me?" I whistle. "Total fucking knockout. Honestly, man, I'm ready to punch my simp card."

The dealer chews on his lips to hold back a smile and murmurs drift around the table. Quinn gives a small shake of her head, looking anywhere but at me.

"Let the hand ride, Fitz," someone says at the opposite end of the table. "They're just kids."

I grin, nodding to the guy with my chin. Hamilton Danford's about to change his mind once we spill his secrets.

"Can we resume the game now?" Petra Yates lifts her nose primly.

My watch vibrates. Ah, damn. Now I'll never know if Quinn won or I did because it's time. A rematch will be in order, maybe some strip poker to up the ante—fuck yes. I'm a genius.

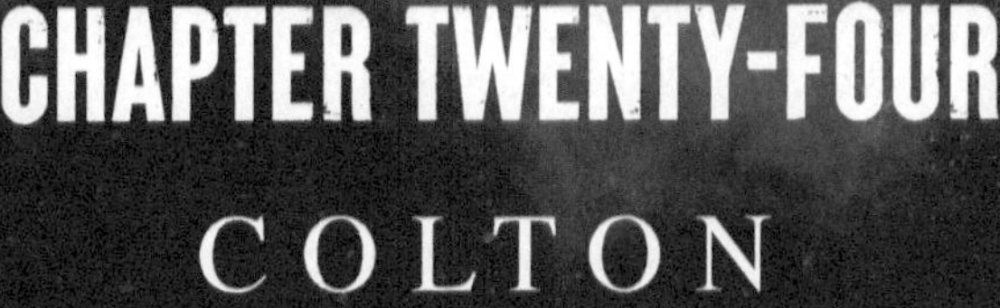

CHAPTER TWENTY-FOUR
COLTON

EXCHANGING a glance with her once I check my drone flight app to see if they're in position, I pass her my phone under the table to handle our livestream controls tapped into the ship's computer system. The custom drones I built favor silence, and with their dark color they're difficult to spot against the night sky and the ocean.

The holiday music playing over the ship's state of the art speaker system fades away. At first no one notices.

Then our show begins with a sick electric guitar riff. People startle, their noses wrinkled as though they've caught a whiff of fresh, steaming shit. Goddamn, they have no taste. The sky lights up with projections from the drone formation to create a huge screen. They work like a theme park show, displaying whatever I want in the sky while being able to create a dynamic effect because the drones can move.

I suppress a laugh at the people who jump. Mortimer's expression morphs into confusion, his gaze searching around. One of the drone's zooms in on him, projecting his image above the yacht's observation deck before switching to the reactions of several others at random. They're programmed with facial recognition to go for big expressions between random people in the crowd and the predefined stars of our little show.

"Oh, how wonderful," an older woman says from somewhere in the crowd gathered around the poker table. "This must be the surprise."

"Surprise?" Mortimer mutters. "There's no—"

He clears his throat, seeking me out. I wiggle my fingers at him in a cocky wave, lifting my champagne flute in a toast.

"Hell of a party." I allow some of my anger about the loss of our original Nest, the rage at what my boys and I went through to bleed into my expression, overtaking my mischievous humor. His throat bobs with a heavy swallow. "You could say it's *lit*. Oh, my bad. Not sure if you catch my meaning. This party is really on fire."

Mortimer clenches his jaw, a vein popping in his temple. He raises his eyes to the sky, watching the opening finish out, drawing the attention of everyone on board.

"Twenty," Quinn murmurs at my side. "And climbing."

I nod. Twenty thousand plus viewers tuned in thanks to my minions tweeting about the livestream, getting the link out. There's not much for us to do now other than sit back and enjoy the chaos about to unfold while we monitor everything and use my control over the ship's system to ensure no one can shut us down.

The intro closes out with clips the drones recorded of the party, showing the ship sailing out of the marina, of people mingling on the main deck, of the poker match, projecting a badass panning shot while I tossed my raised bet into the pot.

Then it switches gears, the music growing more intense and epic to tug on people's interest and get their hearts pumping while the images shift. The drones create a new formation, transitioning from the recorded clips to the black feathers of a crow. When the feathers clear, snooty Petra and her husband Sebastian Yates' names are blazoned across the sky with a set of crossed keys and a silhouette of a bride and groom kissing.

A titter of laughter filters through the guests as Mortimer shakes his head. Petra makes an irritated noise and glares at her husband like it's somehow his fault.

"Who is... PETRA YATES?"

The voiceover I recorded is edited, much like the modifiers the Kings Society used in their meeting to hide behind their masks and games.

"Philanthropist. Two-time Forbes recognition for a rapidly growing business in exports."

As the show flashes through images of her glamorous life with her husband, enjoying the Thorne Point high life, the edges of the photos catch fire and curl inward, stopping on a final black and white photo of her hand up.

"Married her stepbrother Sebastian."

"What! Who's doing this? Fitz?" Sebastian puts an arm around his wife's shoulders and glares at the host.

Photos from their wedding appear, followed by birth certificates, genetic tests, and a grainy video clip of them from one of Wren's family's founders galas where I caught them fucking in the rose garden while I was out smoking a joint.

"Who is really her blood relation. Her half brother, hidden by the family to keep the father's dalliance a secret. His children carried on his legacy by remaining married after discovering the proof early on while trying to get pregnant, burying the evidence of the blood tests."

The amusement from the crowd shifts with the tone of the music growing darker, heavier as the Yates' taboo secrets are splashed across the sky. People stare at them in a new light. It's not like they're any different—most of the city's elite are far from innocent, but they love to judge others for it. Many of the guests flick wary glances around, worried if their hidden sins are next.

The audience gathered around the poker table rearranges in their restlessness and I catch sight of my father amongst them. He looks at the images in the sky, then finds me, his expression stony.

Petra's moans from the video clip fade out while feathers rain down on the projection to switch to the next story. This animation might be my favorite and I snort at the depiction of the next target digging up a grave. There's a shocked cry when the animation pulls a goat from its resting place and sticks his cartoon dick in its carcass.

"*Who is... HAMILTON DANFORD?*" A heavy beat for suspense follows before the story continues. "*An upstanding head of household continuing the founding family name, Hamilton needs no introduction amongst his friends tonight.*"

People laugh, but it's more nervous this time, all of them antsy with anticipation for what bomb will drop next. I whistle low when the drone captures a live image of him, his face twitchy with nerves.

"*Hamilton's secret pastime is an inclination his family tried to hide, but sending him away didn't work. Neither did keeping him locked away in their estate for five years. Perhaps he seems in control, but when the urge strikes...*"

The damning proof Quinn helped me dig up splashes across the sky— Hamilton Danford gets his kicks with dead animals.

"Oh my god," someone utters.

The cherry on top is the audio I found of a screaming goat to overlay with the final sickening images to really drive the point home. Quinn makes a disgusted noise, ducking her head over the phone to pay attention to the livestream and keep the ship's crew from interrupting. I don't blame her; seeing this shit once was enough.

Hamilton backs away, his slow steps breaking into a run. People are shouting now, though they're not louder than the show. I gesture to Quinn and she increases the volume on the sound system while the projection transitions with crow feathers blotting out the images of Danford.

My dad's gaze bores into me from across the observation deck. He knows better than anyone how good I am at collecting secrets and using them as leverage. Every line of tension in his expression broadcasts his dread that he'll be splashed across the sky next. He might not be a member of the Kings, but his secrets and skeletons are just as heinous.

As I meet his eyes with a hard stare, I give nothing away. I thought about it when I saw his name on the guest list. This would be the perfect opportunity.

As the feathers blow away again, it's not my father's name. Instead, Mortimer's name is blazoned across the sky with a set of crossed keys and a fat, stumpy animated likeness wearing a crown.

Mortimer pales, grabbing at the person closest to him. That's it, shithead. By now he realizes this is just like when we came for Vonn and went public with the Castle.

Wren was right. Killing them would've been easy, but destroying their reputations and shattering their pride in the presence of their peers, broadcasting their secrets for everyone to see is so much more satisfying because there's no way to come back from this, no way to save face and brush this under the rug. Their precious business opportunities will evaporate because they won't want to get caught in the crossfire of the disgraced members of a society that's not as untouchable as it believes.

One by one the Kings will fall at our feet as we wrench their power from them.

"Turn this off. Now!"

Mortimer snaps his gaze to me and takes a threatening step. Levi is there to trip him, sending him toppling over the stationary chairs. He scrambles to his feet just in time for his feature to begin.

"Who is... FITZWILLIAM MORTIMER?"

"No! Don't listen to any of these slanderous lies. I haven't authorized this!" Mortimer waves his hands uselessly.

Shouldn't have fucked around with us, Fitzy, because we always make sure our enemies burn to the ground.

The drones reorganize to create a miniature version of his company's corporate office building downtown with his face overlaid on the skyscraper.

"Social climber and relative newcomer in terms of Thorne Point's illustrious history of founders, his father was a distant cousin to a founding family line. They took the title for themselves." Some guests scream at the loud bang of a gunshot I added in for effect. *"Like father like son, Fitz ensured his father met an early end, and his older brother mysteriously disappeared on the day of the transfer for the family company. Later, Jeffrey Mortimer was declared dead. As the sole survivor of both, Fitz has enjoyed the life insurance payout on top of his position as CEO."*

Pandemonium ensues as the drone show continues playing, revealing more secrets we've collected over the years. It's madness. Hysteria.

Absolute fucking chaos.

People converge on Mortimer, their shouts like music to my ears.

"You invited us out here for this embarrassment!"

"How could you let this happen?!"

"You!" Mortimer spots me through the people standing between us and bellows unintelligibly. "You will pay for this!"

Smirking victoriously, I reach for Quinn. "That's our cue."

CHAPTER TWENTY-FIVE

QUINN

Colton snatches my hand, and even though I've never relied on anyone but myself to survive, I hold on tight, unwilling to let go. He pulls me through the people crowding around the poker table on the observation deck, some standing still, gaping at the drone show in the sky while others converge on Fitz Mortimer, blaming him for the madness we caused.

"What do you mean you can't shut it down?" Mortimer's face is an ugly shade of red and he won't release the waiter he grabbed, splitting his tirade between ordering him around and reassuring his guests everything's fine. "No—No of course not, it's not true, I—Find out how to stop it or shoot those fucking drones down."

Colton chuckles wickedly. "Sorry, Fitz. I programmed them with targeting evasion."

I look back at the pot of chips, lamenting the epic win that would've been mine. People bump into us, their necks craned to look up. Some asshole steps on my foot and I grit my teeth when he doesn't even realize.

The crowd bottlenecks with people pointlessly searching for an escape from the spectacle. Colton frowns, sweeping the area with a calculating look.

He nods to the stairs. "It'll be faster if we cut down through the lower decks. Less people."

We descend to the next deck, then decide to go down another when it seems other guests had the same idea in their frenzy to search for the staff. I snort. As if they'd do anything about this. They're probably sneaking their way up to the main deck to watch their rich boss' downfall.

"Guests aren't allowed down here. Please return to the party."

I freeze at that voice coming from further down the deserted hall. Shit. Tanner Sosa is on board. My gaze snaps to Colton's. If he recognizes me, we're screwed.

Levi's not here to take care of the muscle, like Colton said would be the case. He has a small taser concealed in a pen that's not even close to the voltage of the one I use for self-defense.

"Time for those toys. Can you do anything with the security system you tapped into?" I don't know what kind of miracle I'm hoping for when I know damn well from all the prep work we've done this week that there's no command we could give the ship's computer system to help us with this.

"They're all more ideal for a close quarters situation, so I need him to come within range."

"What?" I smack his chest. "No."

Colton's green eyes light up with impish delight. "Come here. I've always wanted to do this."

He herds me back against a wall where we're partially hidden by a staircase and kisses me. We're in danger of getting caught by the guy who hunted me through the city the night Mortimer cut me loose and he's *kissing* me.

I push against his chest, ready to tell him off for thinking this is the right time, but he massages my waist, keeping me pinned in place at the mercy of his searing kiss. My lips part for him and his chest vibrates with a rumble of approval as he makes my head swim.

Someone bangs on the metal railing, startling me. We separate, but he doesn't move, shielding me from the guard. I peer past Colton's shoulder with wide eyes. Sosa stares us down, recognition gleaming in his gaze.

"You," he snarls.

Colton hangs his head and there's an evident smile in his tone. "I wanted that to work. Oh well, it was worth it." He flashes me a confident look at odds with the danger we're in and mouths *go* before shoving back to distract Sosa with a punch to his gut. Sosa grunts in pain, hunching over. "Oh, kidney shot. Smarts like a bitch, doesn't it? Night night!"

While Sosa's down, Colton snatches the concealed taser from inside his jacket and shocks his bulging neck.

We run down the hall. Except the thing about big boats is that it's difficult to hide from someone who's going to chase your ass down. There aren't a lot of options on this deck for escape routes other than to keep sprinting ahead to the end of the hall for another set of stairs.

"Stop!" Sosa bellows.

We're almost there. Two shots fire that make me stop breathing, pushing myself to go faster. My arm burns, but so do my lungs and the muscles in my legs from running with these damn heels. Colton ducks against a small cubby-like part of the hall with a fire extinguisher, hauling me against him. He cradles my head, using his own body as a shield when Sosa shoots again.

"What are you doing? We don't have time." I push against him. "You didn't have enough voltage to knock him out."

He stops me, cupping my face. "We're good, but not invincible against bullets. Are you hurt?"

I freeze as he checks me over, thinking of last night when I admitted I didn't want to be the tough girl all the time. He pauses on my arm with a glare. It stings when he touches it, his fingers coming away bloody. What the—?

I click my tongue at the graze wound I didn't feel with the amount of adrenaline coursing through me. It oozes a trickle of blood down my arm. Returning my attention to Colton, I gape at the worried expression that crosses his hardened features.

It's always been up to me to keep myself and Sammy safe. There was never anyone to do the same for me and it makes my throat close over to see Colton guarding me like I'm someone he wants to protect.

Sosa only slows down for a few moments before the echo of his boots stomping after us fills the hall. We have to get out of here.

"I'm fine. Move," I hiss.

"Wait." Colton grabs the fire extinguisher and points the nozzle around the edge of our hiding spot, spraying the powdery foam cloud until it fills the hall. Reaching into his pocket, he tosses a handful of something that looks like circuit board chips into the fog. "Okay. Go."

Sharp crackles make me smother a scream until I realize it's coming from whatever he threw. Another gunshot cuts through our cover, the awful bang echoing off the walls.

"Fuck! Who's dumb enough to shoot in close quarters?" Colton growls, reaching the stairs first and grabbing at me to urge me up them in front of him.

We don't go up to the main deck, weaving through the one above us. Staff and shouting guests are in our way, but they create a buffer between us and the Kings Society's private security tracking us down.

The strategy works until we circle around to the other side of the ship to an open-air stretch of cabins where there's no one to stop him from shooting at us again.

I pull up short, yanking on Colton's hand. "Wait! I have an idea."

The trust in his eyes knocks the breath from my lungs for a moment as he gives me his focus. Gulping, I plant my foot on his thigh, the slit in my dress riding all the way to my hip. I ignore the burst of warmth in my chest when he automatically shifts his stance to provide balance while I undo the strap around my ankle, sparing a glance over my shoulder to watch for Sosa.

Thank god for button closures on the thick velvet band. If I'd gone with the platform heels that first caught my eye at the store, there wouldn't be enough time to undo the intricate straps. Once I have one off, I switch and he undoes the other for me. Clutching my shoes, I peer up at him, bare feet scrunching on the cold, damp deck.

"I'll distract him, then we charge him together," I say in a rush. "Tase him again."

Colton nods. "Good thinking. We'll try to knock him overboard. Even if he manages to hold on to his gun, he won't be able to shoot at us while we get away. Hey." The corner of his mouth lifts and he steals a quick kiss that tugs on my heart. "Don't sweat it. We've got this. Once we deal with that limp dick roid-head, we're getting out of this—alive."

I lick my lips, words crowding my throat. Words I've never given to anyone except for Sammy.

"I trust you."

"Good." His crooked smile stretches into a full one. "Same. Oh, shit!"

My eyes widen. "What?"

He smacks his head. "We totally just blew our chance to reenact Titanic. I was supposed to ask do you trust me first."

I slump against him, pressing my forehead against his chest, inhaling his sweet and spicy scent with my exasperated laugh. "Why do I even like you,

you goddamn idiot?"

My eyes grow wide again when I register what I said. What the hell is wrong with my mouth? Liking Colton is...no. Hell no. After everything in the last couple of months? Hell to the fucking no, this isn't happening.

The feelings I've fought against and buried deep down because I don't need anyone, especially not someone like him, rise up without permission, expanding wildly in my chest. Those flirty remarks that somehow stir my heart and fill me with warmth. The way it feels when we end up close enough in our shared bed for him to hold me. That wicked smile he gives me when we're hacking together.

Most of all it's the way he's really good at taking care of the people around him. Even when he swore up and down he hated me and wanted to punish me for betraying his trust. He has a knack for anticipating people's needs. He comes off cocky, yet he would give the shirt off his back for someone who needs him.

I don't need him. I *can't* need him.

My world has always been me and my brother. Colton and his friends won't change that just because they're not actively hating on me now that I'm on their side. This isn't permanent. I have a lifetime of lessons to remind me that everything good is temporary.

"I knew you liked me. It's because I'm so handsome." He kisses the top of my head and I ignore the way it makes my heart flutter, just like earlier. "I hear him coming, get ready. When I say so, throw those shoes."

We nestle into a small alcove for the cabin doors to hide us from Sosa's view. His heavy steps pound toward us. Closer. My heart pounds. Closer.

"You can't hide forever," Sosa barks. "You're not escaping."

"You think he's got a list of response programming, like some figurine?" Colton murmurs.

I press a finger against my lips to mime shushing, glaring at him.

"Now," he orders in a firm tone against my ear when it sounds like Sosa's right on top of us.

Gathering my courage and my survival instinct, I step out and hurl the first shoe, then ready the second with a running start. Colton's right by my side. I smother a cry of success when it clocks Sosa in the back of the head. He starts to whirl in our direction, face blotchy and enraged—and in the perfect position to throw him off balance.

Launching the second shoe before he aims his gun at us while he's still turning, I release a fierce yell, watching it smack into Sosa's forehead hard enough to jerk his head back. Colton runs faster on his longer legs, crashing against Sosa's large frame first, taser jamming against Sosa's throat. With his balance compromised while electricity jolts his system, Colton's able to push him against the railing. He pulls some kind of cage fighter-esque move I didn't even know he was capable of to lock his knee behind Sosa's, driving it up to further topple his balance.

I slam into them, helping push. Colton has Sosa's wrist, smashing it against the railing twice to make him drop the gun over the side of the boat. Heart drumming, I shove with all my might.

Everything feels like it's happening in slow motion, when in reality it only takes a matter of seconds.

Sosa releases a garbled bellow when his weight shifts and he flips over the railing, falling overboard into the frigid ocean. The choppy waves swallow him in a plunging splash. We don't wait for him to surface.

"Good job, babe. We make an excellent team." Colton takes my hand and pulls me behind him. "Let's get the fuck out of here. And, seriously, next time remind me why I hate jobs like this without comms."

Next time. We make an excellent team. I swallow, ignoring the tiny, flickering glow the sentiment sparks in me. I've survived for so long on my own so I wouldn't need someone else.

My grip tightens on Colton's hand.

We're the last to reach the getaway boat idling near the back of the yacht. Jude and the others relax when they spot us. Colton keeps a strong hold on my hand while Wren reaches up to help me down from the ladder leading off the back. He follows behind me, jumping the last few feet.

"Your arm's bleeding. Are you okay?" Isla rubs my back.

I nod, focusing on calming the dizzying beat of my heart now that we're safe.

"Their damn guard dog," Colton grumbles, undoing his bowtie. "He found us while we were on our way here."

"I was about to come back for you," Levi says. "I knew I heard gunshots. Remind me who's terrible idea it was to come to this unarmed?"

"Mine—I know, so you can stop giving me that look. My op, my ideas. Next time you can be in charge and we'll all stab first." Colton rakes a hand through his hair. "It's fine. We were able to push the guy overboard after he caught a shoe to the face. Great aim, babe."

Shooting me a finger gun, he drops to a seat, popping the top button of his shirt. The wind blows his tousled brown hair as Jude disconnects our speedboat from the yacht. A funny feeling moves through my stomach, something that makes me reluctant to sit as far from him as I can to reorient myself.

Even if I did like him, I doubt he feels the same. We have great sex and the irresistible games we play take the edge off. This is temporary, not forever.

"I don't like when we don't have comms," Wren mutters, scrubbing his face. "Makes it feel like we're operating blind."

"That's what I said." He huffs. "Can you believe that guy didn't fall for a fake out make out? The movies lied to me, man."

Snorting, Rowan points to the seat next to him. "Come over here, Quinn.

We'll look when we get back to see if you need stitches, but let me clean it and put a bandage on it for now."

I twist to examine the graze wound. It's not bad, nor is it the worst I've ever had. "It's nothing. I'll be fine."

"Sit." Wren glances at Colton with a curious, yet understanding expression that throws me off from his normal callous attitude. "We take care of our own."

Colton grins at me and pats the open space. Rubbing my fingertips together, I join him, trying not to acknowledge how good it feels when he tugs me closer into his side and brushes a quick kiss on my temple. It's the first time he's done something like that in front of his friends and it makes my heart thump hard. It surprises me, but the rest of them don't seem that shocked.

Oh god, have they heard us? I thought the office and the room we're using were both soundproof. Heat pricks my cheeks despite the wintry air.

"I'll kiss it better."

The wind steals his teasing whisper as Jude picks up speed to take us away from the chaos still reigning over the yacht party. While Rowan tends to the shallow cut I got from the bullet, I work up the courage to look at him. His gaze is on me and my breath catches at the intensity burning in it. He shifts his attention to the minor injury and his expression turns more serious, almost angry.

The answering thrum in my heart is impossible to quell. He saved my life tonight. He's kept his word about guarding my brother from danger.

Maybe it's not the end of the world to rely on others. To rely on him. It doesn't make me weak to need someone, and it's growing harder to deny that despite everything, I want to trust him.

CHAPTER TWENTY-SIX
COLTON

When I make a promise, it means something to me. I told Quinn she'd be safe, but that meathead Sosa could've killed her last night. I don't like that she got hurt, even a little. It was still on my watch.

There's no point resisting that I'm into her. More than into her, I'm willing to trust her. Last night pushed me over the line. My gut instinct wasn't wrong about her after all. By now she's proven she's on our side.

I've dropped the pretense that she's here under my watch. When we got back last night, I added her to the biometric scanners with access to the bedroom and the office. She stared, but didn't say a word, her expression heartbreakingly open—the same one I recognize from my foster siblings when they first realized they had me looking out for them, me to lean on—then shuttered like it does when she attempts to hide how she's feeling. She was still in my bed when we woke up this morning and it stirred a pleased feeling within me that she didn't slip out in the middle of the night like I half-expected.

While she's downstairs with the others, I sit up in the office with the door open. I can hear her laughter every so often and it makes warmth spread through my chest, tempting me to drop everything to go seek her out.

Once again I'm looking to find her records—the real ones, not the false ones I first used to vet her that she planted to cover up who she really is—but for once I don't have the urge to steal the truth. It's a first for me. When it comes to all the other girls I've hooked up with, I have a need to dig for information. I drag a hand through my hair for the third time, straining my ears to hear her voice echoing through the warehouse. Isla says something that makes her laugh again and I rub at my sternum.

Instead of finding what she's hidden, I'd rather have Quinn decide to tell me herself. Since I'm inclined to put my trust in her again…maybe I can live without knowing the truth until she's ready to tell me.

A huff flies out of me and I shake my head. "Losing my damn edge."

Going soft. Like Levi. Like Wren. But only for that one person we want to let in.

My pulse thunders and my stare becomes unfocused. Is that what I want from her? To let her into my world completely? Not as an asset, not as a fuck buddy, but more.

Maybe. Shit, that's crazy. And since it snuck up on me, concealed behind my obsession with her, maybe what I should be doing is getting her out instead of pulling her in deeper.

My heart tightens in protest, but I tell that twisted little freak to simmer down. It's already causing me enough trouble.

Frowning, I follow my impulses. They don't do me dirty. Well. They do. But no one's here to keep me in check.

Colton: Before you say anything, I'm aware what you have with your flower girl is a unique, epic childhood love soulmates and shit sort of thing, but bear with me because I'm not asking Wren or Lev about this.

Colton: What sealed the deal that you were serious? Sticking your dick in her with all the pent up hate? Stalking her all over town? When she snuck in your car? Trying to gauge a comparable matrix here and I need data.

Fox: Next time I see you, I will hurt you.

Fox: And shut the fuck up.

I groan, substituting strangling my foster brother by squeezing my phone in a chokehold. Whatever. I'll deal with this later, filed under problems for future Colt in the complicated maze of my mind that never quiets.

Except, when Quinn's around, she hones my focus better. Her intelligence challenges my own, demanding my absolute best. And when I have her beneath me, on top of me, in my arms...it just feels so damn right.

Fox: When you know, you just know. Actually, you don't until it flies out of the dark to knock you on your ass, then it's all you think about. Love is weird. If you're in it, good fucking luck. All I can tell you is fighting it is fucking pointless.

Fox: What's going on there? You haven't updated me since we left.

Colton: Everything's under control here. We'd call you back in if we needed you.

Fox: Okay. And Maisy says to say hi to everyone, she sends her love and hopes you're kicking ass.

My lips curve wryly. It still boggles my mind a broody little shit like Fox found his perfect match in an adventurous, wild-hearted girl he met when they were kids, before his parents' accident, before my parents pulled him out of the foster system and gave me someone else to protect. It's better that they're home in California. I'm not dragging them back into this.

Sighing, I resume my work, skimming the database of secrets. They're all marked if they're tied to a favor owed. One of them catches my eye, sparking an idea.

I'm not the apologizing type. None of my brothers are. I'm someone that takes action, and often the result pisses someone off. What's done is done. There's only moving forward.

I don't understand what this growing feeling is when I'm around Quinn, yet I know I want to protect her now. As soon as that instinct kicks in, it doesn't turn off. Once I give someone my all like that, it's for life. I still look in on my other foster siblings and make sure they have good lives. Everyone I've helped as a Crow, I keep tabs on.

Whether she wants this or not, Quinn has me to watch out for her. My lips twitch at the irony that I once demanded she pledge her loyalty to me, and here I am pledging mine to her.

This feels like the right call, the path onwards lit up in my mind. Cashing in this favor will help me do that.

I trace my chin with my fingertips. Usually I use my own resources. I've only ever cashed in one other favor I'm owed from the flush bank we've built in the last five years, and it was for Fox.

The fact I'm willing to call a favor in to help Quinn without any strings attached is a glowing neon sign that things have shifted between us irreversibly. I don't know what that means yet, but I know there's no going back.

I promised to protect her, so I'm going to do it up right. Opening a new window, I get down to business.

Jude comes in shortly after while I'm bidding on stocks. I'm working gradually so Thorne won't notice until it's too late for him to recover from the power we're siphoning away from him.

Mortimer's company stock value plummeted overnight after the livestream. He's hemorrhaging money trying to bury the spectacle we turned his holiday yacht party into, but the IT team he's paying has nothing on the network I've recruited over the years. They flood the internet with a constant replay—his company website, social media, the works.

No one's coming to his rescue. It's just like Vonn, the Kings members' self-preservation directed at armoring themselves instead of helping their brothers and sisters of the hideous non-denominational cloth (unless you count the Church of Greed).

"What's up?"

"Are you staying up here all day? We're celebrating. We've earned it. Come have a drink." He waves encouragingly. "Come on, man. Take a break."

My attention returns to my dual monitors with ten different windows spread open between both screens with stuff I need to do for the club's grand opening and setting my Dolos minions up with new tasks for our next targets. "In a minute. There was just some stuff I wanted to bang out."

Jude shakes his head and ambles closer to the desk, bracing his hands on it. "How many times do we have to tell you, Colt? You're not a one man army." He freezes, the easy smile dropping off his face, golden eyes hardening when they lock on the messy pile of papers with my endless lists written in an attempt to remember everything crammed in my head at the moment. "Where did you get that?"

Brows furrowed, I search for what he's talking about, stiffening when I spot the teal vibrator I stole from Pippa's peeking out from beneath the pile. Ah, shit. I knew I was forgetting something. Must've gotten sidetracked from finally ditching that thing when I started thinking about Quinn.

He swats the papers aside carelessly and grabs the toy, fixated on it. Goddamn it. I know that look. It's his trip to Pippa memory land face.

"This perfectly generic model of sex toy?" I'm being cute to buy time before my boy knocks me out.

Jude's lips press together and he drags a hand through his thick dark hair. There's no evading the recognition in his clever gaze.

"Oh, yeah, hah," I say, offhanded. "I stole that from Pipsqueak's."

Dead silence follows.

"Come again?"

Jude's left memory land and slid into anger. Murder mode activated. I scrunch my face, shrugging.

"I was in a really shitty mood after the fire. I was going to burn it. Don't worry, I ran it under the tap first before I took it. Hygiene is important."

Jude growls. "You're an asshole."

He goes to pocket it and I cough, thinking how dead I am if he finds out I used it in a pinch on Quinn that first night I had her in here. "Uh, maybe you should—well. Okay. You do you."

"Damn right I will."

I push out of my chair to follow him from the office, circling around the top tier of the club's rafter balcony. "Are we cool, though?"

His brow raises dangerously. "Are you going to stand still and let me punch you?"

I flip my hand back and forth, searching for an honest answer. "In my heart, yes. In practice, fuck no."

He snorts, pocketing the toy. "Whatever. Go downstairs. You can't be left to your own devices."

"Stop, you're playing. You are." Quinn's amusement snags my attention.

She's seated cross-legged on top of the main bar in a pair of tight leather leggings and my TPU hoodie while Rowan perches on a stool across from her, leaning back into Wren's chest.

The enticing sound of her laugh drifts up to me, snaking around me, hooking into my chest. My feet move of their own accord to take me to her, something aligning with every step until I'm at her side.

CHAPTER TWENTY-SEVEN

QUINN

FALLING into intimacy with Colton is easier than it should be after I've closed myself off from making connections with people for so long. Maybe it's some whack form of Stockholm Syndrome, seduced by his proximity. Living in his pocket at the Nest for a month, it doesn't shock me when I wake up to find myself nestled against his side.

He's awake, massaging my neck while he scrolls through something on his phone. I roll my lips between my teeth. I'm not shocked I gravitated toward him in my sleep—I've done it even when we were fighting each other—but it surprises me he didn't get up right away when he woke up first, choosing to let me sleep longer while he held me.

A soft sigh slips out of me as he works my muscles. It feels nice.

"What do we need to do today?" My voice is scratchy with sleep. "I think I've cracked the firewall for the main Thorne corporation to see the private shares they don't have on the open market, but I need to work on it more."

"Actually, that's all on hold today. I've got something else to take care of."

His fingertips graze the bandage Rowan wrapped my shallow wound with. It's only been a couple of days, but it's on the mend.

Neither of us move from our position tangled together in bed. A warm flutter fills my chest when his palm skates down my back, pulling me closer.

"Stuff for the club opening?"

He hums without elaborating. His phone vibrates and a new text banner shows at the top of the screen. "Nice. Let's get going. We've got a meeting to get to."

It still takes him another minute of caressing my body before he sighs and gets up. I pick through the clothes in the duffle bag he gave me, unsure what sort of meeting we're going out for. I decide on a pair of dark wash skinny jeans over the boyfriend cut pair with rips that I prefer.

My gaze strays to Colton while he stretches, his shoulders rippling with the movement. He scratches at his stomach, smothering a yawn. I'm tempted to go up behind him and hug him.

When we're both dressed, he snags my hand on our way downstairs, threading his fingers with mine. When we reach his Mustang, he seems reluctant to let go.

"What's the plan?" I ask when we get in.

He winks. "We're going on an adventure."

I lift a brow at how tight lipped he's being. His inked fingers bounce on the wheel as we drive downtown. I watch curiously. He does that when he's on edge.

Surprise hits me when we pull up at a sleek building. For a moment, I'm distracted by Colton's driving, heat swirling low in my stomach at the expert way he maneuvers his Mustang into a spot, spinning the wheel one-handed while he grasps my headrest to twist. I tear my attention away. He doesn't need to inflate his ego by catching me thirsting for him.

The skyscraper is near the heart of downtown in the corporate district. We're not far from the building I escaped from when Mortimer cut me loose. I wonder if my Vespa is still in the parking garage or if it's long gone by now.

Then my gaze snags on something—some*one*—that makes my heartbeat falter.

"Sammy."

My lookalike in every way except his height, defined jawline, and cropped hair, his broad smile makes my vision blur. We've texted and talked on the phone, and Colton's shown me security images from campus, but it's not the same as seeing him in person.

He's standing outside with Penn, both of them talking and chuckling like friends. His laughter is muted, yet I picture the warm, lively sound perfectly. Shock and excitement rise within me, and before Colton finishes parallel parking, I dart from the car, consumed by the need to hug him after surviving the last month on viewing him through a computer screen or over the phone.

"Hey." My brother turns, grunting as I crash into him. "Okay, hi. What's up? You talked to me the other day."

"I know," I mumble.

When I pull back, Colton's walking up to us. He bumps his fist against Penn's.

"What are we doing here?" I ask.

Sammy's the one who shrugs and answers when I stop hugging him. "P said we were supposed to meet up here."

"P?" I've never heard anyone call him that, not even Colton or the guys.

He snorts at my gaping expression. "Don't listen to the rumors. He's chill."

It's Penn's turn to huff in amusement. "You only say that when you beat me in Mario Kart. When I win, you bitch about it like a little girl."

Sammy rolls his eyes and flips him off. "Only because you cheat. Where's your honor?"

"Dead," Penn jokes.

"Psh, whatever, man." Sammy's mouth tugs into a wide, lopsided smirk.

My mouth opens and closes. "You don't seem shocked."

"Nah. I figured something was up when I noticed the TPU Reaper was stalking me right after you went radio silent for a few days." He taps his temple. "You think you got all the brains, but I'm not blind or stupid. I get how things in this city work."

"Come on," Colton says.

He leads us inside. The lobby is modern compared to Mortimer's company. *Vitale, Associates of Law* is emblazoned above the front desk in chrome lettering.

"Don't get up on our account." Colton waves to the security guard with a flourish. "We're expected."

We bypass security without signing in. I exchange a curious glance with my brother and shrug. At the bank of elevators, a man in an expensive tailored suit jolts when we come into view.

"Mr. DuPont, sir. Hello. Welcome." He speaks at a quick clip, his nerves evident. He offers his hand for Sammy to shake. "And Mr. Walker. So pleased to have you with us. I'm Terry Vitale."

"As in Vitale, Associates of Law," I clarify.

"Precisely." He smooths a hand down his suit and gestures to the elevator. "Shall we?"

Again, I shoot Colton a glance, wondering what he's up to. The corners of his mouth lift and he brushes a hand against the small of my back to guide me into the elevator. We stop on a few floors as we ascend the building. Terry gives a tour of the offices, pointing out perks like an in-house full-service gym and spa center, a reference library, and a gourmet dining hall. He directs most of his attention to Sammy, engaging with him as my brother swipes his mouth, nodding along, eyes gleaming with interest while the rest of us follow them.

"Seriously, what's up?" I whisper to Colton.

He slips an arm around my waist and plays with the material of my top. "You'll see. We're not at the grand finale yet."

"As you can see, we're dedicated to providing a fully rounded, quality life at Vitale," Terry says.

"It's tight," Sammy agrees.

"Fantastic." Terry seems relieved and gestures for us to precede him into a big conference room overlooking the city. Penn goes to the windows while Colton and I sit down across from Sammy at the large glass table. "All that's left is to sign the paperwork."

"Sorry?" Sammy's brows furrow.

"Standard employment contract, a letter of mentorship acceptance for your professors at the university, admission to Sayercrest Law School with tuition and expenses fully covered by the company, a lease for your apartment accommodations with private entry." Terry flips through several papers in a leather folio, laying them out side by side in front of him.

My stomach bottoms out. Holy shit.

"Come again?" Sammy blurts.

Terry catches Sammy's stunned expression. He hands over the paperwork, and Sammy's brows creep higher and higher on his forehead.

"This isn't just an internship. You're offering me a job when I haven't passed the bar. Hell, I haven't even finished my undergrad, man." Sammy swipes a hand over his head as he examines the fine print. "Why?"

Terry pales, darting a look at Colton. "Sorry, I thought you knew why we were meeting today. We see great potential in you from your transcripts and academic history," he explains haltingly. "I want to foster that and help you achieve your dreams. You do want to be a lawyer?"

"Yes," Sammy says. "Still, this is—sudden."

Terry gives him a puzzled look. "Do you not want what I'm offering?"

"Are you kidding?" Sammy shakes his head and grabs the fancy fountain pen. "I'd be crazy to pass this up. I just wanted to make sure I wasn't dreaming or that there wasn't a hidden clause to sell my soul."

Colton chuckles, stretching an arm across the back of my chair. "Smart man."

This is crazy. My brother put it lightly, but I'm having an internal freak out. The Crows are rumored to have connections everywhere. I've seen how they work first hand, yet this is different. This doesn't benefit Colton or their efforts to take on the Kings Society in any way.

The only explanation is that he did this because of me. *For* me, maybe.

My heart sits in my throat as I turn to him. His gaze is locked on me and it steals my breath away.

* * *

After Sammy signed the contract to accept, the four of us return to the warehouse.

I asked Colton how—*why* he pulled strings to get Sammy this amazing opportunity for his future, but all he would say is he cashed in a favor he was owed like it wasn't a big deal. Maybe it's not to him, but to me it's everything I've been fighting for.

Shock filters through me again when Penn follows us all the way to The Crowned Crow. I glance at him on our way inside, but he says nothing. He's been uncharacteristically quiet, and as much as I'm glad to have my brother here, worry creeps in.

"You've been here?" Sammy's gaze moves around the warehouse and he snorts. "Damn, I've had it way better with his bomb ass apartment to myself."

I punch his arm lightly. "Shut up."

He waggles his brows and flashes me a wry look. "Now I have my own pad to chill at, too. Even better."

With a wide grin, I hug him.

"What's this for?"

"Nothing." I hide my face in his shirt. "Just missed you."

"Sappy," he teases. "Didn't you always used to say it didn't matter if we were apart for a minute or a year, we'd still always have each other? You're acting like I died and came back to life."

"Shut up." I huff in exasperation. "God, I hate you sometimes."

Chuckling, he squeezes me in his embrace and drops a kiss on top of my head. "Nah, you love me."

While we hang out, Penn and Colton talk, heading upstairs. When Penn comes down without Colton, I look up at the one-way glass of the office, frowning.

"I'll be back in a minute."

Sammy nods with his chin and ambles over to sit on the barstools with Penn.

I find Colton in the office with the look he always gets when he's absorbed in something, following his rapidly working mind down rabbit holes.

"Hey." I lean against the door when he glances at me. "What are you doing?"

"Nothing. I was giving you and Sampson your space." He motions me over. "Come here, though. I've got something important to show you."

He stands as I circle the desk, pointing to the screen. I blink at the financial account, unsure what I'm looking for.

"Is it another shell company?" I furrow my brows, trying to see what he sees.

"No." He sighs and scrolls up.

My name fills the account holder field. It takes a moment to register, then my stomach clenches as I take in the account balance again. That's a lot of fucking money.

"What the hell?"

"It's for you. An investment account I opened in your name."

"This is for me?" My voice sounds funny and my head swims.

He licks his lips and slides his fingers through his hair. "Yeah. I've done the same for Rowan and Isla. It's what I do for the guys, managing the growth of our investments. It's just the initial capital to get it going, but I'm very good at what I do. In no time at all, it'll begin to accrue a safety net that will always be there for you and your brother. We watch out for our own, and I consider you one of us now."

One of them. The others have made comments like that. This is the first time he's said it. My heart thumps.

When he talks about the others as his family, I wasn't included in that. Even though I've gotten to know them, I wasn't sure if I was welcome in their close knit chosen family.

"Just like that?"

His stare is inescapable. "Just like that. I told you, I promise to protect you. This is how I do that."

It becomes hard to breathe for a moment. First he surprises me with helping my brother, now this. This doesn't feel temporary anymore. This feels more like everything I've ever denied myself because it was easier to survive on my own without needing anyone to rely on.

"Here." Colton pulls me from my thoughts when he places a phone in my hands.

My fingers close around it and my eyes bounce between his. He dips his chin, darting his gaze away.

"What, you trust me with a phone now?" The humor in my tone is strained.

"You can go. If you want, you have the option to leave." He ruffles his dark messy hair and offers up a crooked grin that doesn't light up his eyes with their usual brightness. "Both of you. Penn and our other guys have continued to keep an eye out for any threats from team douchebag so you don't have to worry. We'll make sure you get out of the city safely and the Kings will never be able to find you."

My heart stutters to a stop.

Colton's letting me go?

My throat tightens, a lump forming. This is what I wanted, isn't it? My brother safe. No longer indebted to the Crowned Crows.

It's what I should want. I've made it through losing everything, losing my grandmother, and fought my way out of the foster system. I've been the one providing for me and my brother. I'm a survivor who takes care of myself.

The thought of leaving Colton makes my heart revolt in refusal. I don't want to keep fighting on my own. More than that, I don't want to let him go.

"I'm staying."

Colton draws in a sharp breath, gaze snapping to me with burning intensity. He grasps my shoulders like he doesn't want to let me go. "You're staying? This isn't your fight."

"Yes. I'm right where I want to be." My lips twitch. "You need me. Admit it, pretty boy. You're a whole ass disaster without me."

He huffs raggedly, nodding. His tattooed fingers flex on my shoulders. "Those are dangerous words, little queen."

My chest swells with how right this choice feels. I don't stop at my admission that I want to stay.

"The truth is, I can't go. Thorne Point is where my brother and I belong." I weather the thump in my heart telling me it's even more specific—that I want to belong here, with the Crows. With Colton. "This was our home."

A crease forms between his brows and he slides his hands down my arms, capturing mine to stop me from twisting my fingers as I let him in.

"You and I probably would've met a lot sooner if things didn't go the way they did, because the Walker family had money and success. My grandparents were highly respected members of the community for the company they built. They raised me and Sammy after we lost our parents, and showered us with fierce love. Granny was never too busy to make time to play with us." My fond smile falls. "Then Baron Astor destroyed my life eight years ago. His company took everything from us. He didn't stop at buying out my family's company, he came for their estate. Through some damn loophole that gave him the ability to steal my whole life. Granny couldn't take it. She died of a heart attack not long after."

His expression goes slack. "Shit."

"I made a vow that I would get back everything we've lost. No matter what it takes. Without any other family left to take us in, the state placed us in the system—"

"The foster system?" he interrupts. At my nod, his jaw clenches and something haunted clouds his eyes, stealing their light. He cups my face and brushes my cheek with his thumb, voice hoarse. "Tell me."

I swallow against the memories crashing into me. "What's there to tell?" A bitter, humorless laugh punches out of me. "Maybe in some states it's bearable, but for the most part it sucks and it doesn't give a shit if it separates siblings. Once I started learning my skills, I did everything to find Sammy and get us the fuck out of that life."

"Did..." He stops, a muscle in his cheek jumping. Blowing out a harsh breath, his . "Did any of the homes hurt you?"

I close my eyes. No one ever believed me the few times a foster parent's hands wandered to grope me. What's awful is I know I'm lucky it was only ever that. It could've been so much worse. "Yes. The times I was separated from Sammy. Even though he's younger, I've always been...petite."

A growl tears from him and he drags me into his arms. "I'm sorry. I'm so sorry, Quinn."

Life can be harsh and the turn mine took directed me down a dark path out of desperation. I faced difficult decisions. Made mistakes. Even after all that, it brought me here, to him.

"I just had to make it through. That's all I ever thought about. For Sammy's sake. I could take anything—bad decision or not, shitty hand or not—as long as I got us to the other side. Maybe I was wrong to think I could do it all on my own without friends, without—without someone standing by my side when I don't want to be the tough one." He emits a jagged noise and his embrace tightens, as if he's attempting to heal my old wounds by keeping me safe inside his heart. Clutching his shirt, I rest my cheek against his chest. My voice cracks. "The world isn't sunshine and rainbows."

"Don't I fucking know it." He strokes my back as though he wants to reach my past self and let me know it'll be okay, like he wants to take away all my bad memories and protect me. "I suspected, but I didn't know for sure. I wish—My parents used to pick out foster children to host. Fucking assholes loved to use them to make themselves look good. My father is a very particular bastard and if his little gold stars didn't live up to his expectations he got angry. I kept them safe. If you were with me, I would've kept you safe."

My mouth curves into a sad smile and I imagine it for a moment, meeting him when we were young, picturing him standing between me and anything out to hurt me. In another life, where I learned it was okay to rely on others to help you.

"We can't change the past," I whisper.

"No." His tone hardens. "But we can put a goddamn end to this. You're staying right here with me, baby. I'm at your side now and I don't want to let you go."

Quiet falls over us. We don't move for a long time, simply standing there holding each other. For the first time since I lost my grandmother, I feel like I can breathe.

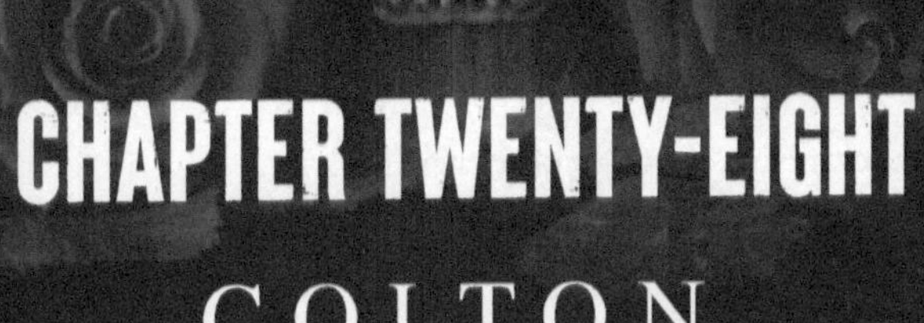

CHAPTER TWENTY-EIGHT

COLTON

On opening night of The Crowned Crow, me and the guys stand on the top level outside of the office, leaning on the iron railings to look over our Nest 2.0. After the fire nearly devastated our world several weeks ago, the sight has me gripping the metal tight, my tattooed hands flexing and the veins prominent.

The rundown industrial warehouse we added to our collection of properties has transformed into the club envisioned when we first started our party nights at the Crow's Nest Hotel. It's maintained the gritty edge we cultivated at our original Nest, the atmosphere forbidden, seductive, and a little bit illicit like rules don't apply here.

Secluded booths surround the perimeter of the main floor beneath the lowest tiered rafter balcony, providing a space for people to test their limits in the shadows or watch the wild show on the dance floor. The space has transformed for the grand opening, playing up the speakeasy vibe as a nod to the building's history and the way we operate our parties. It's a reflection of us in every way.

Tonight we show this city we haven't gone anywhere. Prove that we're the true kings of the shadows after dark in Thorne Point.

The girls emerge from the hall that has another secret entrance to the lower level looking smoking hot all done up for tonight's grand opening. Quinn captivates me the moment she lifts her gaze to the balcony to find me. Her natural curls are tied up in the space buns that drive me crazy. My gaze rakes over her wrapped miniskirt and thigh high boots hugging her curves and the tight camisole showing off her midriff.

"Everything's ready," Rowan calls. "Penn will let those who figure out the password in."

Instead of a VIP area upstairs above everyone who parties at The Crowned Crow, it's down below, inspired by the origins of the warehouse. We have plans for this club to become the new hub of all of our operations— fight nights, our card games, and the place where people will come to seek an audience with us to pay us with their secrets to earn our help.

Wren's mouth curves, cool blue eyes glinting. He looks at the three of us. Without a word, we understand what he's feeling, the same gratifying sense of triumph coursing through me and my boys going by the glances we pass between the four of us.

"Mayhem's found its new home." Jude tilts his head and flashes us a wry grin. "Like abue likes to say, *el que es gallo en cualquier gallinero canta.*"

A good rooster can crow anywhere, meaning that in any circumstance, a great skill will be the same. His abuela used to say it when he bought her the house she lives in now, insisting she didn't need such finery as long as she had him. He's taken it on as a reminder that regardless of what we go through, we go through it together and we make each other better because of it.

This. This is what we're good at, and it doesn't matter if we're in the decrepit remains of a hotel or if we build up enough to sit atop the city—we'll be good either way because our brotherhood only strengthens.

Loyalty above all else. The creed the four of us inked into our skin when we decided we were family.

"Come down, boys!" Isla twirls, the bottom of her off the shoulder high-low dress fanning out. "I want to do something before we pop the champagne and open the doors! Tonight's important."

"Don't make us come up there to get you," Rowan challenges with a lopsided smirk. She plays with the end of her red hair pulled into a high ponytail, her focus honed on Wren. "You know we will."

"The question is whether or not we'll listen," Wren answers, the corners of his mouth curling in sensual amusement. He loves playing games with Rowan as much as I enjoy them with Quinn. "Care to put your skills of persuasion to the test?"

Quinn looks between them and laughs, folding her arms. "My money's on her. You cave to her more often than you win."

That miniskirt is fucking enticing, making me trace my lower lip with the tip of my tongue when she cants her hips to underline the sass she gives the big guy. Pride rises up and I do nothing to stop my grin at her fearlessly mouthing off to him.

Jude snorts and claps Wren on the shoulder to get him moving. "It's true. Our little firecracker's got you by the balls, man."

I nod to Levi, drumming out an energetic beat on the railing before we follow them to go get our girls. I can't shake the sense our family's grown again, watching Quinn hanging with Isla and Rowan, smirking when Wren hauls Rowan into his arms and marches her to a dark corner growling low words in her ear that make her laugh, then moan before she can stifle it. Her wily hands fly out to smack him wherever she reaches first and both of their laughter twines together, echoing through the empty club. Levi shakes his head, wrapping himself around his little sunbeam, Isla. She winks at my girl.

Quinn fits, finding her space amongst our little chaos crew. And it feels fucking good.

This is what the Kings Society tried to stamp out. We'll always fight for this. Every time we'll claw our way out of any fire that tries to destroy us because we have each other.

Isla taps her fingertips together, bouncing with a wide grin once Rowan and Wren return hand in hand. "Okay, everyone wait here. Quinn?"

"I've got you."

Her thumbs tap her phone screen. She smirks, hiding it against her chest when I lean in to peek.

"So nosy," she chides.

My arm drapes across her shoulder and the edge of my mouth quirks up. "Can't help it."

"It's incurable. We've had him checked." Jude grins when I flip him off.

The lights dim and Levi stiffens, hand dropping to his concealed knife. Quinn holds out a hand.

"Down boy. I lowered the lights."

Levi mutters under his breath, scrubbing his jaw. He calls out for Isla. "Princess."

"Coming," she sing-songs. She reappears from the door to the bar's back room holding her hand around a glowing flame. "You assholes better sing."

The date clicks in my head and I smother a laugh.

Levi pulls a face. "Isla, no. I don't—"

"Tough, edgelord supreme. It's your birthday." I reach out to grab his shoulder, giving him a shake. "Happy birthday to you."

Wren and Jude smirk, chiming in together. "Happy birthday to you."

The others squeeze closer, forming a circle around our friend as Isla reveals a gourmet cupcake decorated with candy skulls and a small toy knife. The sight of it makes us all fight to control our laughter while singing. She presents it to him as we finish the last of the song.

Silence follows until Isla purses her lips at her man. "What are you waiting for? Blow out the candle."

Levi heaves a sigh, lips twitching at the effort she put in for him. His hands find her hips and tug her closer.

"You know the kind of dessert I'd rather be eating," he mutters.

Even in the dark, her flush is evident. She beams as he blows out the candle and allows her to feed him the icing she swiped off with her finger.

"Now we can pop champagne," she announces.

Quinn brings the lights back up. Rowan gets two bottles from ice buckets behind the bar. The staff we've brought on to bartend, run security, and our DJ for the night are all waiting to be let back in after Wren told them to clear out for an hour. She hands one bottle to him and her lips tilt slyly.

"Here's to a night we'll never forget," Wren says before sending the cork flying.

Quinn whoops as Rowan's bottle pops. Our king and queen of chaos clink the bottles and swig directly from the foaming overflow, passing them along. I snag it after Jude takes a sip and bring the bottle to Quinn's lips.

She holds my gaze as I let champagne pour into her mouth, then take a swig. I lean in close, my lips brushing hers in the barest kiss.

"Embrace your wildest thoughts and fantasies tonight, little queen."

She lifts a brow, the corners of her eyes crinkling. "Challenge accepted, pretty boy."

My cock throbs. Oh shit. I love the sound of her throwing my own words back in my face. Grasping her throat in a light grip, I steal a kiss that leaves both of us short of breath. Then I back away to give the staff the all-clear.

When the doors open to let in the line that formed around the block, the place becomes a hotbed of gritty decadence, of sensual hedonistic abandon. The four of us greeted the crowd pulsating to the music with a visual projection of crow feathers falling from the industrial ceiling and arched windows, much like the drone technology I used on the yacht.

We usually start our themed parties with epic theatrics, like Halloween, but tonight we simply stand on the DJ platform, basking in the crowd's energy and awe. The DJ hands Wren a microphone and fades the music.

"Welcome back," Wren announces in a crisp tone. "May your sins tonight be your salvation tomorrow."

The cheer that erupts from the people filling the tiered levels is wild and deafening. I grin at the guys and salute them with two fingers, jumping off the platform into the crush.

I make my way to Quinn and the girls at the end of the bar, stealing Quinn's barstool and boosting her to sit on my lap. The bartender brings me a drink before I have to ask.

"I've gotta admit, this is pretty badass." She peers around. "Does it feel good?"

I give her a slow grin, playing with my tongue ring. "Funny you should ask—"

She pushes at my chest, clicking her tongue in amused exasperation. "For real."

"For real." I nudge my nose against her cheek in a nod. "Yeah. Really fucking good."

Isla jumps up when the song changes and takes Quinn's hands. "Come dance with me!"

Quinn knocks back the rest of her drink and winks at me before she allows Isla to lead her to an open spot. I watch them, something unfurling in my chest.

Rowan covers my wrist with a hand while I spin my glass back and forth between my thumb and fingers. She gives me a warm look.

I cock my head. "What's that for, babe?"

"I'm glad you found someone like her that fits you." She squeezes my wrist, glancing at the dance floor. "Even if things started rough because we didn't see it coming, I'm happy it ended up like this."

I rub at my sternum, dragging my teeth over my lip. "Yeah. I am, too."

There's no going back. I only move forward.

Levi melts out of the shadows on the dance floor while we talk, leading Isla away after he kisses her through an entire song. Instead of returning to the bar, Quinn keeps dancing, and I keep watching.

"I'm going to find Wren."

"Give him hell." I wink at her. "Be extra wicked for me."

Rowan laughs and moves off. My focus returns to Quinn. A guy dances up on her and she allows it, rolling her hips and undulating her upper body to the beat. She's a fucking sexy as sin sight.

Then he puts his hands on her and the heated enjoyment of watching my girl evaporates, overtaken by a buzz in my chest.

I've never had a problem sharing a girl before. I sure as fuck have a problem with it now.

Stalking through the dance floor like a predator on the prowl, I move in behind her and tug her hips back into me. She angles her head, melting back without hesitation. I move my body against hers for a minute, watching the guy over her shoulder while she gives herself over to the music. He follows the roll of her body, shifting closer. When he reaches for her hips and I plant a hand in his chest, shoving him away.

He clenches his jaw, but holds his hands up, not willing to challenge a Crow. Making sure he's watching, I grasp her jaw, drawing her head to the side. Holding his gaze, I lower my lips to her skin and torture her neck with an open-mouthed kiss that makes her writhe, biting back one of those pretty sounds I fucking love. She snakes her arms behind my neck, holding on while I suck on her pulse point, her pointed nails scraping my neck to leave her mark on me.

The guy's eyes flare and satisfaction arrows through me when he moves away knowing he can't have her.

"Pissing on your territory?" Quinn taunts. "Maybe I wanted to fuck him. He was cute."

I growl in her ear. "Try it, baby. Just fucking try it." My hands move over her stomach, caressing beneath her top. "You're mine."

"Yeah?" There's a sassy smile in her tone that gets me keyed up in all the right ways.

"Hell yeah. Need me to prove it?" A devious grin twists my lips and my hand lowers to splay against her pelvis, applying pressure until she shivers for me. "I know we enjoy playing with toys, but we both know I don't need them to make you come right here in the middle of all these people dancing. What do you say, little queen? Let's play a game to see whether or not you're mine."

"Right here?" She's breathless, eyes gleaming with interest when she peeks back at me.

Smirking, I bring my lips to the corner of her mouth as I trace the exposed skin above the waistband of her skirt.

"Right fucking here."

"What if someone sees?" Her hooded gaze roams the dancers surrounding us.

"Let them." My fingers dip beneath her skirt to tease her, petting her mound underneath. She backs that luscious ass into my hard length. "Show them all, baby."

"Fuck," she mutters breathlessly, only loud enough for me to hear her with the heavy beat the DJ's rocking the house with. "This is insane."

"That's why you love it when I play with you like this," I counter. "I've got your number."

She spreads her legs wider to give me better access, arching against me when I touch her clit. Her lips part and her head falls against my shoulder.

"Any of them could look at you right now." Between each thick croon, I kiss a path up her throat while I caress her. "It's not hard to see I'm touching what's mine every time the strobes flash on us to light up the shadows. They can all watch you get your pussy fucked with my fingers, baby."

"Colton." She gasps and I hold her tighter around the waist, moving us to the music as my fingers push inside her. "Oh my god."

"Such a dirty little slut for me, riding my fingers in the middle of the dance floor," I rasp against her ear. "I want everyone to see your face when you come just so they understand you're mine."

She whimpers as I thrust deeper, stroking her as her pussy flutters. I scrape her skin with my teeth as the song builds to a high point, covering the sound of pleasure that slips out of her as her thighs tighten around my flexing hand.

"Do you wish I was filling your pussy with my cock right now? Do you wish they could all see how pretty you are when you come on it?"

"Ah!" Quinn bites her lip as she shatters, her hips falling out of time with the music, slowly riding my hand to her own oblivion in the middle of a packed dance floor.

"That was so fucking hot," I rasp. "Come on. I need to be inside you, and if we don't move I really will fuck you right here."

She gasps. "You're such a maniac. But I like it."

Spinning in my arms when I pull my fingers free, she tugs on my neck to draw me into a kiss. I grab the back of her thighs, digging my fingers in as one thought repeats in my mind on a loop: *mine.*

CHAPTER TWENTY-NINE
QUINN

Colton wanting to claim me as his hits me in a tender, buried part of my heart that I've built my walls around. Piece by piece, he's found a way to tear them down to grant him access. He's hacked my heart.

After we lost our grandmother, Sammy's the only one who felt permanent, even when we were apart. But outside of my brother, I've never gotten close to people, not willing to give anyone the chance to reject me. I learned early on in the system how much it stings when no one picks me.

Except Colton. He keeps picking me.

I click my tongue when the online poker game dings with the notification that someone else won. Shit. I'm letting this affect my game.

I started looking for a card game while he's talking to the guys downstairs.

It's the first time I've logged into my Queen_Q account in a month. There's no point in sneaking around now. I don't have to hide this from him, not after I told him about my real past. I think back to the night he came back to his apartment in a delirious state when I let him sleep in my bed. My lips tilt at his raspy suggestion to ante up while he watched me play, hugging my pillow and faking being asleep. I should've known back then when I managed to fall asleep in the same bed as him that he wasn't temporary like everything else in my life.

Online poker was my first way to build a new safety net to get Sammy and myself out of the foster system. It helped us make our way in the world. Helped us survive.

It's strange to think I don't have to win to earn quick cash now that Colton's set up an account with more money than I've managed to scrape together in the eight years since we lost everything at the hands of Baron Astor's insatiable greed. For the first time, I feel like my goal of getting it all back isn't an impossible dream, but something within my reach. Colton called it a safety net, too. It's not the money that makes my throat tight with emotion, but his promise to protect us—both me and the only family member I have left—that means more to me than the money does.

I text Sammy, sure he's still up. We're both night owls.

Quinn: Olives and juice.

When we were kids, he got a kick out of different words you could mouth that looked like you were saying something else. Except he couldn't figure out olive juice for I love you. He kept saying olives and juice, so it stuck as one of the ways we let each other know we're thinking of them. It feels so good to know he's safe and free from the influence of the Kings.

Sammy: Same. Can't sleep?
Quinn: Not yet. Up playing poker.

Sampson: Don't do that thing you always do.

Quinn: What thing?

Sampson: Don't mess with me. You know what I mean. You love pushing yourself as if you're solely responsible for everything. We're grown, so you don't have to be the one watching out for me always. It's my turn.

Quinn: Tell me where you got all that damn audacity [eye rolling emoji]

Sampson: From you [laughing emoji]

I lick my lips, my brows jumping up at his nagging. Telling him I love him again, I promise to get some rest. Right after I win back what I just lost in the last round of poker. I've got a rep to defend.

All my focus is on winning this hand. Playing online, it's difficult to read people without seeing their faces. In the early days, I had to doxx people mid-game to figure them out. I smirk, thinking how much it would piss off GrandAce100 if he learned a punk sixteen year old in Maine was kicking his ass because I understood the desperation of a low balance bank account. I learned to read their tells through their betting strategies, through the time it takes them to make their play, even their usernames gives me something to work with. Everything is information, and information is a powerful tool.

I'm so absorbed in the game, I don't notice Colton come in until his voice sounds behind me.

"That's a damn good hand, little queen. You've got them on the run."

My heart leaps into my throat, startled out of the zone. "Jesus."

He drops into the seat next to me, wheeling closer and propping his chin in his hand. It impresses me how quickly he assesses the game with only a brief glance. I know the moment he registers the different username from the one I used to use at his place because he inhales sharply through his nose.

"I'll be damned."

I lift my chin, fighting the urge to squirm self-consciously. This is fine. It's okay for him to know.

He gives me a crooked smirk that ties an unbreakable knot around my heart. "It's been you all along." Wonder colors his words, making my stomach flutter. An amused sound leaves him and he looks between the card game on the screen and me. "I can't believe I didn't see it."

"I didn't want you to see it before." This account is one of the few places I feel like my true self.

Colton cradles my face, drawing me in, hovering his mouth over mine. "One of these days I will beat you, nemesis."

My lips quirk into a grin. "Yeah, you think that, pretty boy. We'll see."

"Shit, little queen."

The smoky rasp is all he gets out before his lips connect with mine in a kiss that heats up to an inferno that has me burning up within seconds. I forget all about my poker game in favor of this. He swallows the faint sound I make, then pulls back, taking me in with a reverent, smoldering gaze.

"You look good in my shirt."

I look at the graphic tee hanging off my smaller frame, sucking my bottom lip between my teeth. "Rowan came in earlier. Said it was laundry day. This was all that was left."

He smirks and dips his head for another kiss. The flame he stokes in me builds, spreading through me in a rush.

Breaking away from the kiss, he lifts me onto the desk with a sinful rough noise that sends a pulse of heat in my clit. I yelp, trying to watch for the electronics he doesn't seem to care about. He's more intent on spreading my knees wide, shoving the shirt I stole from him up to expose me. Those wicked green eyes gleam.

"I'm fucking starving for you."

He drags me to the edge before spitting on my sensitive folds, the raunchy, sinful act making my core throb with need. Then his mouth descends on my pussy. My head tips back with a cry and I sink my fingers in his hair, fisting it because it always drives him wild until he makes me come so hard I wonder if I'll pass out. A moan falls from my lips when he torments my clit with the titanium stud piercing his tongue.

I stop caring about knocking the computer off the desk when I'm close, only able to focus on grinding against his face, core thrumming with the tightening coil of arousal. A scream catches in my throat when he pauses to look up from between my thighs, chin glistening.

"Goddamn, I love the way your thighs tremble when you're about to come."

"So make me come," I demand. "Make me come so fucking hard, Colton."

His lips curl. Fuck. That devious look only means one thing: he wants to play a game. Fire sears through my veins and air rushes out of me.

"Flip over," he growls, massaging my thighs. I hesitate, balancing on the edge. I just want his mouth back on me because I'm so close. A deep, rough chuckle drops from his lips. "What, you think I'm afraid to eat ass? You're the whole meal, baby, and I'm going to enjoy tasting every fucking inch of you."

Warmth spreads through my cheeks and across my chest. "I-I've never had someone do that."

His eyes darken and his gaze drags over me with a possessive, almost feral edge. "Good." His fingers dig into my thighs and his eyes pierce into me. "No one ever will. Only me because you're *mine*."

I nod, swallowing thickly as my heart thumps harder, my nipples erect and aching with the heady arousal flooding my system. "Yes."

"Now turn over so I can serve my pretty little queen."

My lashes flutter and my lips part. He helps me reposition myself, moving the keyboard and wireless mouse out of the way. I drop my head to my folded arms, feeling more exposed than I ever have. It's odd that I was fine a second ago on my back with my thighs wrapped around his head, riding his face without shame to take my pleasure, but when his nose traces a path across one of my cheeks and he spreads me with his long, dexterous fingers, my core tightens and I hide my face in the crook of my arm.

"No hiding. I want you to look up."

I squirm. "Why?"

"Just do it."

Huffing, I raise my head and my thighs clench when I stare back at myself in the monitor. He turned the webcam on.

Colton smirks at the camera. "I didn't want to stop. This works in a pinch as a mirror." He kisses my ass cheek, flicking his tongue against my skin teasingly. "Now. Eyes on me, baby."

At first he teases me, ghosting a hot breath over my exposed hole. I shiver, shifting my hips, eager to come. The more I urge him on, the more he toys with me, giving me light kisses and grazing touches.

"Come on." I send a fierce look at the screen when he stops, pulling back to watch the sight of us on the monitor. "Colt."

His eyes gleam, but all he does is squeeze my ass, fingertips grazing the edges of my tight hole. The sensation makes my clit thrum and my stomach tighten.

"Please," I try.

"I love it when you beg."

Leaning back in, he swipes his tongue over my hole while kneading my ass. A strained noise slips out of me and he chuckles.

"Like that?"

"It feels—I like it." My cheeks bloom with heat.

"Good, because I fucking love to eat you. Your pussy, your ass. Every inch of you."

When he covers me with his mouth and swirls his tongue, I moan, back arching. His fingers tease my clit, then glide through my wet folds to press against my entrance. I rock against them, eyes hooding when he allows the tip of his finger to push into the first knuckle.

"Your pussy's dripping for me, my pretty little slut." His praise makes my skin tingle while he plays, the pressure too light to get me there yet enough to leave me breathless.

I bite my lip at the filthy words said with such warm affection, core clenching. "I need—"

"I know exactly what you need," he promises. "Don't stop watching. Don't take your eyes off us, baby."

Then he stops messing around and buries his face in my ass. It's as good as it is with his mouth on my pussy. Better because the new sensations make me gasp and arch. He eats me with the abandon of a man who loves to use his mouth to bring pleasure, dragging his tongue down my crack to lap at my pussy before going back for more.

Fuck, the sight of me spread for him while he takes me apart is captivating. My lips are parted with each gasp, gaze clouded with desire as I watch his head move against me, feeling every sinful movement of his mouth two-fold from watching it on the screen.

Colton lifts his head, catching his breath, but he doesn't stop focusing on my pleasure. He plunges a finger inside my pussy and teases two fingers at the spit-slick bud of my ass. Biting my lip, I press back until he works a finger inside, the stretch new and overwhelming while he's filling my pussy with a second. A wrecked moan slips out of me.

"That's it, baby. It feels so good to have your ass played with and eaten, doesn't it?" he croons. "Are you watching?"

"Y-yes," I choke. "Close."

"I know. I can feel you about to shake apart. You're going to make such a gorgeous mess all over this desk when you come, aren't you, my little slut?"

I whimper, only able to nod with my hazy focus locked on the camera feed in the monitor. Colton hums, devouring every inch of me as he sinks another third finger inside my pussy. The sight of us heightens my pleasure until it's too much.

"Fuck!" I cry out, clutching the edge of the desk for support as I shatter.

And I do mean *shatter*. The orgasm crashes over me, unlike any I've had before, even with him. I roll my hips with it, still riding his fingers as it goes on. He mutters a curse behind me and pulls free.

Before the intense shockwaves fade from my system, he yanks me back by my hips and sits me on his cock. Another whimper escapes me as I sink down the rigid length, losing my breath.

"Fuck," he groans into my neck. "Best goddamn feeling in the world when my cock is inside you. Especially when you're wet and soft from coming."

I think I nod. I'm not sure, too keyed up from my orgasm to be aware of what I'm doing. All I know is pleasure and the fiery burn of arousal. Of the way my heart needs this man who knows how to unlock every fantasy I didn't know I had.

"Ride me," he commands against my ear, sending a flood of ecstasy pouring through me.

He helps me move, holding my hips to guide my pace. My head falls back in ecstasy as he kisses my shoulder where his t-shirt hangs off.

He takes over, lifting my legs over the armrests of his gamer chair. His arm bands around my waist to hold me in place while he fucks me harder. I pant in pleasure, each breath tinged with a moan as his cock lights me up.

We're still visible on the screen, the pair of us a debauched, erotic sight as we fuck. It's going to be imprinted on my memories, both of us wild and untethered.

"I'm going to come again," I whimper.

His growl vibrates against me and he reaches down to stroke my clit, meeting my gaze on the webcam feed. "Come on my cock. Soak me."

His hold on me tightens when I clench around him, his length throbbing inside me. I want to feel him come. I want him filling me.

The desire unfurls in my chest, spreading through me as I let go, tipping off the edge into oblivion again. Colton's thrusts grow sharper, then he stiffens, burying his cock deep, his head resting against mine as he comes with a ragged sound.

We fall back together, both of us panting. His arm remains around my waist, caressing my stomach beneath the t-shirt.

"Holy shit," I breathe.

"Yeah." His body shakes with a laugh and he hugs me, kissing my cheek. "That was unreal. Let's download it and watch it back. I want to fuck you while it plays. Our first spicy home video."

I gape at the screen, registering the recording symbol. "You recorded it?"

I smack him, but I'm too worn out to do much more than flap my hand against whichever part of him I can reach. I'm not mad—in fact, it gets me hot. I like the idea of watching us.

"Yeah, you really hate the idea." He thrusts, making me gasp. "That why your pussy fluttered around my dick, little queen?"

"Shut up." There's no bite in my tone, my amusement too strong to hide.

Colton grasps my hips as I get up, trailing his touch between my legs because he's obsessed with feeling me up after we fuck, my folds swollen and sensitive, dripping with the evidence. I peer over my shoulder and meet his leer. He smacks my ass with a crooked grin.

"Come on."

He tucks himself away, downloads the webcam recording, then snags my hand to lead me through the upper level of the club to our room. Once inside, he strips me out of his borrowed shirt and ditches his clothes, pulling me to bed.

"You're more than my little queen," he rasps after a few minutes of comfortable quiet. "You're my goddess."

My heart lights up with an incandescent glow as he traces the Nyx tattoo on my ribcage.

"Do you know why I like the goddess of the night?" I whisper.

He hums in interest, splaying his hand over my ink.

"My granny had this big book of mythology. I got into it when I was little and loved flipping through the stories." My heart pangs with the old sorrowful ache of missing her. "She encouraged my love of mythology and bought me all these books. There were these illustrations and the one of Nyx captivated me. There was just something about the way she was depicted that hit right. It resonated with me. I didn't get why until I was older, but I feel like I shine at night like her. Under the cover of darkness, anything I want becomes possible."

"I was right." His lips find my forehead and he tugs me closer.

"About what?"

"You're a goddess. My Nyx. And you're mine, baby. All mine."

I bite my lip. "That make you mine?"

"Damn right."

A pleased flutter fills my chest. I imitate his tone from earlier. "Good."

"Mm, I like the sound of you possessive, baby. Makes me all tingly right here." He places my hand over his heart, then lowers it to his dick. "And here. Nice tingles all in my balls."

I snort. "Oh my god."

"I'm serious."

"I can't with you."

"You love it," he challenges in a cocky tone that makes my stomach dip.

And yeah. I just might.

Colton brushes light kisses across my face, drawing a soft smile from me. I turn to my side and he pulls me into him. There's not an inch of space between us and he wraps me in him—in his arms, his scent, his palpable affection.

This is what it's like to have my heart in the care of someone else. It's scary, something I've resisted for so long, but I like it. I know all good things are temporary. I don't care if they never last because I want to hold on to this. I don't want to let this go. Don't want to let him go when he's quickly become someone my heart recognizes as vital to my survival.

My heart is Colton's, and his is mine. I'll fight to keep this until my dying breath.

CHAPTER THIRTY

COLTON

Tʜᴇ recorded footage from Wren's button camera the night of the meeting at the Founders Museum is paused on my tablet screen while all of us sit in the basement for a strategy meeting. It's almost like old times at our first Nest. Almost, but not quite.

I'm seated on the end of a weight bench while Quinn straddles a chair next to me, Isla and Rowan not far off, sharing another workout bench. Jude leans back on the ropes of the boxing ring, and Wren strides back and forth between us. Levi leans against one of the support pillars, twirling a knife through his fingers.

This damn clown presiding over the subtle hierarchy of the Kings Society is fucking bugging me. Quinn and I have matched everyone in the room to prominent players amongst Thorne Point's wealthiest families, yet we can't confirm if he's Westley Snyder. We're only guessing by process of elimination.

We've created chaos for the Kings members in the last month and a half, coming for them one by one. We're winning left and right, dismantling their business empires, challenging their self-proclaimed crowns to rule over the city, and airing out their hidden crimes and darkest secrets.

It feels awesome. What bothers me, though, is that from everything we've learned of the Kings Society, they fucking love dramatics. The masquerade ball hiding the Castle with that carnival maze to separate out society members from non-members, the theatrics for the meeting beneath the Founders Museum, the damn symbols and clues nodding to their existence planted all over campus, all over the entire city, hiding in plain sight.

So why are they waiting to clap back at us?

Are they truly so arrogant in their belief that they hold all the cards that they don't see us as a threat to tame? They practically welcomed us in after inviting us to see who's in the shadows messing with our interests. After we spat on that invitation, why have they toppled so easily?

I know I'm good at what I do—hell, even better with Quinn at my side— but I expected more of a challenge to stand in our way.

The sight of the masked King on my tablet screen makes me frown. It has to be Snyder.

We're sure he's the one who usually covers up the Kings' messes, and other than the files I've scraped together from five years ago, I can't find shit to pin on him. It's safe to assume if he's so good at erasing these messes, he's done the same for his own secrets. He's like a goddamn ghost.

I don't like waiting for shoes to drop out of the sky to bludgeon us when we least expect it, but the acid buildup worrying about when the inevitable is coming is also likely to give me an ulcer.

Wren turns to me. "Where are we at with preparing to take on my father?"

"Just about ready. We already have a good chunk of his conglomerate acquired. Anything that was available for public trade, I've snatched up."

Wren smirks coldly. "He hasn't noticed his precious empire slipping from his grasp?"

I shake my head, gesturing to the stock report. We're close to 50% control with the shares I've been siphoning away. Quinn cracked the firewalls of the main umbrella corporation's security protocol, allowing us to infiltrate the system and cover our tracks.

"I have it so he won't see how much he's losing on his end until it's too late." I wiggle my fingers with dramatic flair. "The finale will be all you, big guy."

"Good." Wren lowers his head, glaring at the numbers. "I want to make this as painful for him as possible."

"And what about my uncle?" Levi prompts, opening and closing one of his knives with a vicious *snick*.

"We want to create the illusion that we have him right where we want him," Wren says. "He's aware of the rumors about us, and what Levi is capable of."

Levi nods. "He's always implying he's the one covering up Pippa's effort to charge me as the suspect for the Leviathan case."

"Wait," Quinn says. "That's you?"

Isla covers her mouth to hide her dainty laugh. "I still can't believe I was reading that article to you in the student union while we had lunch on campus and you just scowled at me while I speculated about sea creatures."

Levi mutters something too low for us to hear, dipping his chin to hide the twitch of his lips. He huffs exasperatedly. "It doesn't matter. Wren's right. We have to make him believe he's got no way out. It's our only hope of tricking him. If he's feeling the pressure we apply, he's more likely to snap. We have to use every advantage to win against him."

"Our best bet is to let him do the talking," Jude proposes. "With his arrogance, he'll tie his own noose as long as he believes he'll come out on top.

He has for this many years, so he won't think we'll succeed."

"He's always boastful," Wren says. "This goes beyond bugging his office in the hope he'll say something. I think we can help him along if we slip something into his system without him noticing. It could loosen his tongue and encourage his need to brag."

"We could dose him with pure caffeine and create a threat of failure scenario," I suggest, twirling a pen. "Get his heart pumping so hard he feels like he has to tell us everything before the perceived heart attack kicks in. Or there's always whatever new designer drugs people cook up for raves. I can source that easily enough. Actually, let's drop some MDMA in his drink, that'll do the trick to lower his inhibitions. In fact, it'll help him believe the illusion we want him to see with the hallucinogenic side effects. Question is, how should we pull it off?"

"He would be suspicious if I went to his estate now after I've made it clear I don't want a damn thing to do with him," Levi says.

"We need to catch him somewhere he's comfortable," Jude says.

Wren nods in agreement. "Where he won't suspect a thing."

"It shouldn't even be us," Rowan says. "If he sees any of us, he'll know."

"We've definitely caused a fuss every time we're around them," Isla adds. "Can we be sneaky about it?"

"Definitely, babe. I have an idea for how to get him." I squint at my screen. "It should be Christmas Eve. Two days is enough time to get this together. We'll hit Daddy Thorne and Baron on the same day."

"Never," Wren growls, whirling on me, "say the words *Daddy Thorne* again, you little psycho."

Rowan snorts. "I mean..."

"No."

He points at her with a warning look. She holds up her hands, a gleam in her eyes.

Smirking, I cut back in. "Does he still go to that gentleman's club?"

"The cigar lounge?" Levi nods. "As often as he can. He always preferred it over the country club."

"Probably because those snakes feel even more guarded, free to make their deals there with the exclusive membership. I bet you it's got Kings origins—their little home base in the heart of the city. It's gotta be." Making a mental note to circle back to the private club, I skim through our database, tapping the entry when I find it to highlight it. I show them the tablet with the staff member's name. "I've got our in right here. Takes care of how we'll loosen him up."

"Good. You and I will go pay him a visit." Wren tucks a hand in his pocket and strokes his jaw as he paces sedately. "Jude, call Pippa. We'll meet up with her tomorrow night."

Jude sighs, then nods. "Fine. Not here, though."

"We'll grab Baron when he leaves the club and transport him." Wren's attention pauses on Rowan for a long beat. "The girls should be on lookout rather than inside."

Rowan scoffs. "Lookout?"

"Excuse me?" Quinn's head jerks. "Fuck that. I want to be there. I'm not missing a second of this."

"Same. You know what I'll say," Isla chimes in. "We're doing this together. This isn't any riskier than what we did to get into the Castle, and it'll only be against one old man rather than the guys who overpowered me and Rowan."

Levi frowns at the three of them. "It might not be safe, princess. I won't take that risk with you." He closes the distance between him and Isla, taking her hand. "My uncle's a deranged man who will always protect his self interest when he senses a threat. It's why I haven't come at him directly."

My chest tightens with an echo of his sentiment and my gaze shifts to Quinn. I already know from her fierce expression she'll be down to kick my ass if I even voice the protective urge to keep her away from this. She deserves to be there as much as Levi does.

"I don't give a shit about safe," Quinn insists. "He ruined my life."

I haven't told the others. I also haven't told Quinn of Baron's other sins, namely what he's done to Levi and his family.

Levi furrows his brows, sweeping his dark, surly gaze over her. I fight the instinct to yank her behind me and stand between my brother and my girl. The momentary worry is unfounded. Understanding passes between them when he nods.

"I didn't know," Levi mutters

"No one did." She crosses her arms. "But I want to be there to see his downfall in person."

"It's better if there are two of us to run tech," I say. "If we want him to think he's in one of our safe house locations for the Leviathan to take his pound of flesh, I'll need her managing everything else while I control the sound design and lighting to give the right atmosphere so he believes we've dragged him out of the city. I'll need to influence his senses just enough to trigger him over the edge."

Wren nods stiffly. "Okay. But we're going in prepared for anything."

"We've got this, King Crow," Rowan says.

Our strategy session breaks up, Jude slipping away to call Pippa, and the others coupling up on their way out. It leaves me and Quinn in the basement by ourselves.

She folds her arms over the back of the chair she straddles, resting her chin on them. "Where are we getting our hands on E?"

"One of my minions. He's a part-time pharmacist, part-time DJ at pop up raves."

I switch windows to log in as Dolos. I'm halfway through drafting a message to the guy when I realize I opened up my network in full view without stopping to hide it from her. Trust barriers are a wild thing. Lifting my brows, I finish contacting him for what I'll need and set a drop point for delivery.

"So this could've been me, huh?" She's studying the Discord-adjacent build of my hacker network. Aesthetic and organized. "One of your little worker bees, ready to hack on command."

"Nah." I flash her a smirk. "You're too good to be a minion. You're my queen, baby. You'll rule at my side. Hell, maybe I'll be the one getting on my knees for you."

"Damn right. That's exactly why I gave you the slip every time you caught up to me with those little tests for recruitment." The corners of her mouth curl. "What do you need me to do?"

I wave a hand, typing as fast as I think on the tablet's touchscreen. "Uh, check on the Trojan hiding on Thorne's system. We can't let his IT team detect it yet. I'll handle the rest."

We should move upstairs, but I'm absorbed in my tasks, stuck in my own digital world that makes reality become murky around me. Everything I have to do in two days to pull this off runs on a loop.

Sound design to make it seem like we're in the middle of the woods. Lighting effects. How else can I tease the senses? I get sucked into a rabbit hole researching which artificial scents I can use with portable battery-powered diffusers.

Whatever. I just have to get it done. They're all counting on me.

I scrub my jaw, fighting back the whispers in my head that sound too much like my father. Too much like his disappointment. Too much like his tirades while he used me as his punching bag so I could stop him from hurting my temporary siblings.

Not good enough. A disappointment. The bastard son I should've buried.

The last one is a favorite phrase he picked up as his only way to reach me since I discovered his secrets about my real mother and found leverage to keep him from breaking my body as an outlet.

Why does this shit always have to rear up at the worst times when I do everything in my power to shove it back down where it can't get at me?

Fuck, I need to do something about what I have on him. Maybe I should've used it on the yacht after all. He clearly expected me to reveal it. Am I a pussy if I can't bring myself to reveal it?

I don't realize how harsh my breathing's grown until I slam a fist on the canvas mat of the boxing ring we installed in the basement. I don't remember moving over here from my seat on the weight bench.

"Hey."

Quinn stands beside me. Her touch melts away the tension in my body and quiets the torrent of thoughts racing through my mind. I release a strained breath and lean into her, reality coming back to me with her as the tether to guide me. My neck and shoulders are cramped from hunching over the tablet propped on the edge of the boxing ring instead of going upstairs to work in the office.

I swallow. "Sorry. I was in my head."

"I thought you were doing that thing where you hear only half of what I say. We had a whole conversation."

"We did?" I press my fingers into my eye sockets. "Shit."

"It wasn't deep." She tilts her head. "Where'd you go?"

"It's dark and twisted in here." I tap my temple. "I don't recommend looking inside."

She rolls her eyes, not with her usual snark, but with fondness that tugs on my heartstrings. "I usually ignore warning labels. Life's more interesting that way."

"Fearless. I like it." I try for a smile, but it doesn't form right. It's more of a grimace.

She hums and covers my clenched fist with her hand. "Talk to me."

Pulling free, I rub my forehead, then scratch at the tattoos on my knuckles covering old scars. "You know how we've been sacking these guys in the balls—or the clam, in the case of that snooty bitch running that Ponzi scheme to get investors—left and right? Well, they're not the only skeletons I have stored in the database. It started right in my home."

Drawing a fortifying breath, I pull up the bank of secrets and scroll to the first entry, allowing her to read my father's sins.

"Holy shit," she murmurs. "The date on this—you—"

"Yeah. I caught the bug for hoarding people's secrets a long time ago." My nail scrapes against my inked skin until she takes my hands to stop me. I clear my throat. "My dad didn't just have this in his closet. Lying about my bio mom is only the tip of the iceberg of the things he did to me."

Her beautiful features shift, dread creeping in. "What else did he do?"

I'm quiet for a few moments. Once I start explaining my past, it comes pouring out.

"Most of my tattoos cover up a scar." My lips twist as I point them out. "Belt. Cane. Back handed while he had a ring on. The time he almost severed a finger. Plastic surgery fixed most of it, but he would just tear into me again. I covered up the memories with the marks I'd rather bear on my skin than reminders of him."

With each one I tap, her grip on me tightens. I like the pressure of her holding me so fiercely. It helps keep me anchored while I tell her the darkest part of my life. She keeps me here, rooted in reality with an exit point so I don't get lost in my head.

"Fuck. That's terrible." She tugs, bringing my hands against her chest, cradled between her grasp. She searches my eyes. "What about your mom? She didn't try to stop him?"

My lip curls. "She wasn't really a mother. She did feel guilty. When the foster coordinator called her when I was older and she brought Fox home, he was her second chance at motherhood. Not the shit she pulled bringing home young, helpless children as trophies of how generous they were. By then, I wasn't interested in her new leaf. I don't consider her or my dad family. What's the point? Neither of them give a fuck about what he did. I'm not looking to reconcile or have the satisfaction of throwing this in their face now."

"Why did he do this to you?" Her voice shakes. "You were just a kid."

My forehead rests against hers, trying to set her at ease. "I couldn't let him touch them," I push out. "If I wasn't enough of a son for them, I needed to be a good brother to protect them. See? I told you, if you'd been with me, I would've kept you safe."

"Colt," she whispers tightly.

"Then I learned something he didn't want me to know. That secret. It was the first one I ever collected and snowballed into this." I gesture around us. "The first time I learned what kind of power a secret can hold. He never touched me again whether or not I failed to respect his high standards. Having that edge over him made me feel so fucking alive."

"He doesn't get to define your worth," she says fiercely. "Not then. Not now. Fuck him."

I give her a jerky nod. She's right. I know she's right. The guys have all said the same thing. I just need to let this go. Holding on to the secret isn't doing me any favors.

"I think... I've been holding back from putting him on blast because in a way, that lanky little computer nerd is still me. I'm afraid to let go of the only leverage that ever gave me power over him. If I use what I've got, then what do I have to stop him? Logically, I know he can't touch me. That I'm not his punching bag anymore. But the part of me that remembers? I don't know."

"Colt. Look at me." She guides my face up to meet my eye. "I will never let someone come at you."

My lips twitch and I force the humor out to cover up the buzzing filling my ribcage. "You make a sexy knight in shining armor, babe."

She frowns. "I'm serious. Who takes care of you?"

My head jerks. "What?"

"You heard me. You give a hundred and ten percent of yourself to everyone you care about. Even those you don't know." Her brows pinch and understanding compassion shines in her eyes. "But who takes care of you, Colt?"

Goddamn, why does my chest hurt? I can't draw a full breath. It feels like a fucking semi parked on my ribs and the driver pissed off to fuck knows where.

"The guys," I answer tightly. "Rowan. Isla. My brother Fox. We're all a family. We watch out for each other. We always have."

"I know," she says softly as she cards her fingers through my thick, tousled fringe to sweep it out of my face. "But that's not what I'm asking. You and me, we're survivors who put those we care about first above all else. God, it's scary how similar we are. I see your pain. It's mine, too. All my life since we lost our grandmother, I've fought to make sure Sammy and I would make it through after everything was taken from us. It was my choice to do that and I never asked him to put himself out for me. I didn't want him to, because I saw it as my responsibility."

I swallow, pulling her into my arms. She comes willingly, picking up on my need to have her close.

"See? Even now you're doing it." I stiffen and she hushes me. "It's hard to turn it off, isn't it? But you're the first one who's taken care of me. Who let me have a break from being tough enough to withstand the world all the time and it's opened my eyes to how much I push myself down for the sake of others."

I hold her closer. "Caring for people is how I'm wired. If I don't do that, then they won't want me around."

"That's not true. This isn't about equal exchange. You aren't loved less one day because you don't provide as much as the last. You're enough just being you and your big damn weirdo heart, pretty boy." Her lips press against mine hard and it eases the weight constricting my chest. "So let me take care of you, too. Okay?"

Something cracks open within me and I drop my head against hers with a harsh exhale. "Yeah. Deal, baby."

The way I need her slams into me. It's been all these little signs pointing to the one thing I can't deny any longer: I'm all in with her.

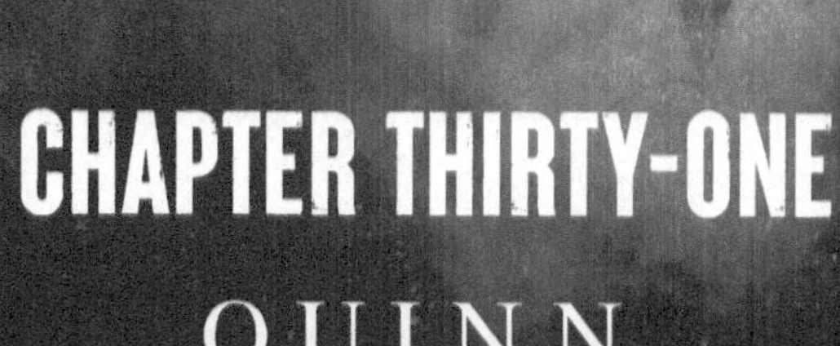

CHAPTER THIRTY-ONE

QUINN

When we pull up to an oceanside cliff to meet with Pippa, I don't recognize it at first. Not until we're picking our way across the scorched rubble and demolished remains where the Crow's Nest Hotel once stood. My throat closes over at the sight and I freeze, thoughts swirling with the awful fire I watched helplessly from a laptop screen.

My voice is scratchy, skin prickling as if I can feel how hot the flames were. "This is—"

"Yeah." Colton's expression is shuttered. "It was here or a bar downtown where the owner owes us a favor. This is better."

"No one to listen in," Levi clarifies.

They all have an air of sorrow around them, like they lost a piece of themselves here. It pierces my chest, making it difficult to breathe. Seeing the aftermath of this place in person is so much worse than watching it all play out on a computer screen.

"I'm sorry," I say.

"It's not your fault," Rowan says.

"Not entirely." Colton holds up his hands at the fierce look she flashes him. "Relax, I don't blame my girl, either."

"Just shut up and let me apologize, you jerk." I rest my head against his shoulder. "I didn't want this. If I'd known… I would've told him to go fuck himself."

"I know, babe." His nose touches my head and he pulls me closer, blocking me from the chill in the air. "Can't change it now. And we've built something new. Something better."

Wren checks his watch. "She's late."

Jude looks at his phone. "I don't have any messages. She'll be here."

It's only a few minutes later when headlights come up the winding drive that leads to the top of the hill. Pippa parks and crosses her arms against the biting winter wind, making her way to us. She frowns at what's left of the hotel.

"Couldn't we have done this over the phone? It's cold as shit out tonight."

"This won't take long." Wren gestures to Jude.

He explains the plan to come at Baron Astor tomorrow night.

"So you come in as back up." He tilts his head. "Think you can handle that job this time?"

Pippa hesitates, gazing at Jude resolutely like she's trying to convey something without words. "I can't."

Jude's brows furrow. "What the hell do you mean you can't?"

She reaches into her pocket and shows us her badge. Wren mutters a bitter curse and Levi growls under his breath. Colton goes rigid at my side and Jude stares at her in oppressive silence.

"You didn't," he finally says, low and rough. She flinches. "Tell me you fucking didn't, Pip."

She releases a shuddering breath, taking a step. He backs up, keeping distance between them. She works her jaw, pressing her mouth into a thin line.

"I didn't know it would happen," she explains. "Warner called me out of the blue tonight and reinstated me."

"I don't get it," I cut in. "What's the big deal? I know the TP police suck balls at their job, but doesn't this benefit us with her on the inside?"

A dark laugh leaves Jude. "You'd think, but no." He turns his back on her, scraping a hand through his thick hair. He spins back and takes her by the shoulders. "Come on, baby girl. You're smarter than that. How could you roll over so easily and go back like nothing happened?"

"Don't waste your goddamn breath, Jude," Wren says. "Let's just go."

Colton wraps an arm around my waist, holding on firmly while shaking his head. Levi hesitates for a long beat, then makes to leave.

Isla tugs on his leather jacket. "Hang on. We should listen."

"It's not what you think." Pippa releases a harsh breath and clutches Jude's arms. He drops her shoulders, stepping out of reach. "You know I've been looking into everything suspicious."

"And doing fuck all about it," Colton points out.

Jude pinches the bridge of his nose. "What about the Castle? You get it, don't you? It's all tainted by their poisonous influence."

"I know." She sighs, hanging her head with her hands propped on her hips. "But that's what I'm saying. I couldn't do much from outside. This is my opportunity to access information and investigate from the inside."

"Don't expect us to get you out when this lands you in hot water," Levi mutters. "We're not coming."

Jude's hands ball into fists, shoulders tense.

"I wouldn't expect you to," Pippa says. "I don't need saving."

"What's the catch?" Wren demands. At Pippa's sharp glance, he smirks and cocks his head. "Come on. There has to be one."

"Just a warning," she admits. "Warner told me to stay away from you all. So if we want to find out more, I need to keep my head down for now. I can't do what you're asking."

Colton whistles, the piercing sound making her grimace. "Just like old times, Pipsqueak. History just loves to repeat itself."

I rest my hand against his back and he squeezes my waist.

"Remember this choice," Wren cautions. "You keep making it, then wonder how you lost your place with us."

Jude shakes his head. "Thanks for nothing."

"Believe what you want. You always do anyway," she accuses.

"Whatever. Let's go."

Jude stalks away first. As he passes us, I catch the flash of anguish that passes over his somber expression. The others follow him. We remain for a moment longer.

Colton sighs. "Watch yourself, Pip. There are all kinds of monsters lurking in the dark."

"I'll be careful." Pippa's gaze moves beyond us to Jude's retreating back. "Watch out for him."

"Always, girl." Colton gives her a humorless smile. "Because that's what family does. Come on, Quinn."

* * *

I expected to go back to the Nest, but Colton takes us to his apartment. I haven't been back here in weeks.

"What are we doing here?" I ask when he drops his keys on the kitchen island counter in the open layout space.

I listen carefully for Sammy. The place is silent. He did tell me he was moving into the apartment Vitale provided.

"As much as I like our bed at the Nest 2.0, it doesn't feel like home quite yet." He cups my nape, squeezing lightly. The sadness from earlier at the hotel grounds is gone, adoration brimming in his eyes. "I want you in my bed here."

"What about everything we still have left to do?"

"We can worry about everything happening tomorrow in the morning. Come on. We're going to climb into bed. Make out a little. And then I'm going to watch you play poker. Probably while I finger you, just to see how long your concentration lasts. Think you can win a hand of cards while I tease your clit with a vibrator?"

"Colton." His name comes out as an amused, affectionate, breathless exhale as warmth spreads through me.

He waggles his brows. "Sounds good, doesn't it?"

I trail after him as he saunters through the apartment. My gaze snags on the door to the room I claimed for myself.

His expression at the cliffside where the Crow's Nest Hotel once stood returns to pick at my mood. The haunted look is something I never want to see on his handsome face again, yet I can't stop thinking that I did have a hand in putting it there.

Even if he's forgiven me, he could decide he's done with me at any moment. I swallow, clenching my hands in front of my stomach.

"Colton."

He pauses, angling to glance back at me. "Yeah?"

My pulse rushes in my ears. I stare back at him, fighting past my instincts to clam up, to just get through life on my own.

I've grown too used to this life. To being with Colton.

"I—" My throat stings.

The vulnerable note in my voice annoys me because I hate the uncertainty. Between the safety net he gave me and me deciding to stay, things have been implied without saying out loud where this is heading. I need to know.

"What about after? When this is over? You and me, I mean. Are we..."

"Hey. Shh, come here." He holds my face in both hands. "Nothing changes when we finish this. You're not going anywhere. You're staying, like you said, right? You belong with us, little queen. Right at my side. I should've seen it before. I should've listened to my gut because it's never wrong—you've belonged with us from the start. And when you're in with us, that makes you family. You have us. You have *me*." He searches my gaze. "Do I have you?"

Some part of me was still afraid this wasn't going to last. That at some point, he'd decide he didn't want me anymore and my world would shrink back to me fighting against everything coming at me.

I nod, fighting the tight lump in my throat. "Yes." It comes out hoarse. "You have me, too."

"Good." He kisses me, speaking against my lips. "You still going to be the one who takes care of me? We made a deal. Because I'm a disaster without you, remember?"

A wobbly laugh escapes me. "That's the damn truth."

"I need you. Not because of your sexy big brain—although, I've gotta say, I love that about you." I laugh and he cups the back of my neck, squeezing it as he brings our foreheads together. "I just need you."

My throat closes and it's difficult to speak for a moment. "I need you, too. I think it's incurable."

He snorts and kisses me. "Fuck, how are you so perfect? My waifus ain't got nothin' on you, baby."

"Stop." I swat at his chest, sniffling.

I rarely let others see me cry, but it's okay with Colton. He's the one who gives me the safe space to put being tough on hold. Somehow this cocky fuckboy hiding a heart under all that chaotic mischief is exactly who I've always needed.

He holds my waist and grins. "Now quit stalling, woman. I want to watch you crush it at poker while I play with your pussy. Just the thought of it's getting me hard."

Colton guides me backwards down the hall. He has me gasping before we reach the bedroom. I don't spare a glance at the room I used to stay in, my focus solely on the man who stole my heart for himself.

CHAPTER THIRTY-TWO
COLTON

IT works out nicely that I complete the transfer of the biggest share of private stock Quinn and I accessed from inside the company's system early the morning before Christmas, giving us complete control over Thorne's business empire. Time to give him an early present just in time for the holiday.

The seven of us stride into the main offices downtown shortly before ten ready to fuck his shit up. I wink at Quinn, holding her hand.

"Mr. Thorne," the middle-aged woman at the front desk says in surprise.

Wren straightens the cuffs of his sharp suit. "Call my father. Make sure he knows I'm waiting for him upstairs."

"Of course." She reaches for the phone. "He should be on his way in."

"I know." Wren checks his watch. "I'll wait in his office."

"Your guests will need to sign in."

Wren lifts a brow, drawing Rowan into his side, sending their power couple vibes off the charts with both of their confident expressions. "No. They won't."

"Come on. Let's not make her job difficult." Jude leans on the counter next to them and gives the secretary a charming smile that makes her perk up. He reaches for her hand and she places it in his palm, blushing when he pets it. "We won't be long, and we're only here for the boss."

I smirk at his wordplay. It's true, we're only here for Wren.

"Oh. Well, I suppose it's fine." She pats her hair.

Jude's hazel eyes gleam. "That's the holiday spirit." He raps his knuckles on the counter. "Do me a favor? Check your email in about half an hour. Happy holidays."

We leave the confused woman behind. I tug on Quinn's hand, following Wren's lead to the elevators. She checks her phone.

"Emails are queued to go out with the codes to claim their share from the account we set up," she says.

"Good." Rowan tosses a relieved smile over her shoulder at us.

"Your bleeding hearts are expensive," Wren mutters. "These people aren't my concern."

Rowan elbows him. "You're the boss, so yeah, King Crow, they are. A good leader takes care of his own, doesn't he?"

He sighs, kissing the top of her head. "Yes."

While we're here to topple the Thorne business empire, Rowan and Quinn both argued that we'd need to do something for the people put out of a job by the dissolution of these companies while we were strategizing. None of the girls were down to leave people high and dry, especially since it's not their fault they work for a dick like Thorne. Once this goes down, there's a severance notice that will go out to all employees with a generous bonus that most will be able to retire with.

"He still won't know what he's lost from under his nose?" Wren clarifies on the way up.

"Not until we kill the bug we've been using to keep things looking copacetic on their end." I wiggle my phone.

When we reach Thorne's office, Wren unbuttons his suit jacket and claims his seat at his father's desk. The rest of us take up posts around the room, subtly creating a unified front for Thorne to face when he arrives. I plop in the chair across from Wren and pat my knee. Quinn snorts and takes the other chair, flashing me a look that says *nice try*. The edge of my mouth quirks up and heat spreads through me, emanating from my heart.

Rowan moves to Wren's side and cards her fingers through his blond hair. He tilts his face up to her, reverence filling his gaze. They don't need words and she bends to kiss him.

"Ready?" she murmurs.

He nods. "More than. I want to see the pretentious light dim in his eyes when I crush him."

It only takes another ten minutes for him to arrive. We all turn as he opens the glass door. He pauses on the threshold to his own office.

"Son." Thorne flicks a wary gaze from Wren seated at his desk to the rest of us. "This is unexpected. Have you finally realized your place is here? I'm glad to see you stepping up to accept your responsibilities."

Wren steeples his fingers. "How's mom?"

His father doesn't respond.

"You never change. The morning of Christmas Eve and you're here instead of home with her. What would Charlotte think? Oh wait," Wren growls coldly. "You were never there for her when she was alive, either."

Thorne's mouth presses into a thin line. "Must you always do that?"

Wren's brows shoot up, then flatten dangerously. His hand flexes instinctively toward his inside jacket pocket, as if he's reaching for the locket he no longer carries with him. Rowan takes his hand, her own throat working and eyes shining because she understands the pain of having her sibling ripped away from her. The two of them hold on to each other.

Wren's been better since meeting Rowan, less angry, less reckless, but faced with his father's callous dismissiveness, his cold blue eyes are right back to where he was for the last two years since we tracked Coleman out to Ridgeview, Colorado to stop him, to make him pay for what he did to Charlotte Thorne and countless other young girls teaching gave him access to.

"Must I always remind you of how you failed my little sister? Failed to keep her safe from her predator? Failed to see how it destroyed her until she couldn't take it anymore?" Wren slams a fist on the desk. "Since you're so insistent on forgetting she ever existed, fuck yes I do."

Quinn stiffens and I bump my foot against hers. She relaxes and presses back against me.

Thorne tears his gaze away, striding into the room. "I take it you haven't come to discuss what you'll be doing at the company since you've brought your friends."

"Look at that, you're a smart man after all." Wren gets control over himself. His cutting tone makes his father clench his jaw. "Is this not where you've always pictured me? You've only gone on for years about me taking over."

"Taking over—now, hold on a moment." Thorne narrows his eyes. "You're far from ready for something as great as that. You'll work your way up from the position I provide. That's how my father brought me in, and his father before him, and so on."

"Yes." Wren smirks. "Our rich family history. Generations of one self-important asshole after another. Well, until your grandmother shook things up with her hotel."

Thorne's head jerks with a scoff. "A wasteful endeavor. Look how it turned out. What you did—or should I say failed to do with it. And now it's nothing more than rotten ash."

All of us go rigid at his dig at our Nest. Wren's eyes narrow and he holds out a hand. I pull my tablet out of my bag and pass it across the desk.

"This is why I'm here."

Wren turns the screen so his father can see. Quinn's thumbs move across her phone screen to tap into the company's network remotely and remove the virus we planted that gave us access.

Thorne's brows furrow as his eyes bounce back and forth the faster he takes in the information before him.

"That's not possible," he says hoarsely.

I snort, wiggling my fingers at him in a mischievous wave. "I think you mean not probable." I pull a sarcastically sympathetic face. "Oof. Really shouldn't underestimate us. Especially not when you piss us the fuck off."

Thorne shakes his head, pulling a phone from his pocket. I grin when he realizes it's not just Photoshop and a dummy site replicating the information. He has nothing left. We've stolen his power away from him.

Wren stares at his father's increasing dismay in satisfaction. "Everything you're proud of, everything you think makes you a king with a right to control the city because a long time ago our family line found a rocky seaside cliff and pissed on it to stake a claim. I'm taking all of it from you. The Thorne name won't be so lauded in this city now."

He stands, squaring off with his father, making sure he's watching as he presses the button on the tablet, opening the sale of company shares on the open market priced at a pittance. Notification bells ping immediately, chiming with hardly a second between sales as his family's business empire is broken up and sold off. Quinn and I might have spent the last few days hyping up the possibility of a private corporation going public on finance and broker forums to prime the machine.

Thorne slashes a hand through the air furiously. "How could you spit on our family legacy like this?" he demands, getting in Wren's face. "Your grandfather and great grandfather—"

Wren challenges the advance with his bigger size, smirking when his dad falters, falling back a step from his son's broad, muscular frame.

"This is what you wanted," Wren says sardonically with a wave of his arm. "You've pushed me to step up and take my place in the family business for years. Well, now I have. By taking it over by force. It's mine to do with as I see fit. The Thornes as you know them are finished."

"You can't," Thorne snarls. "You'll regret this."

Wren's lips tilt in victory. "No, I really won't."

"Son. Son, come on now." Thorne resorts to begging rather than commanding. "Just listen to me. Hugo, you can't do this!"

Levi holds Thorne back as Wren smiles caustically. Jude comes up on his other side.

"I've told you not to call me that." Wren's chin dips with a stony expression. "My name is Wren."

Thorne gapes, then jerks against the hold the guys have on him.

"Apologies, but we'll have to ask you to leave the premises," Jude says smoothly. "Authorized personnel only on this floor, I'm afraid."

"I know you wouldn't, but don't worry. I've taken care of mom. She'll be moved to a facility where she can get some goddamn help and the care she needs since you don't give a shit about doing it yourself," Wren sneers. "There's nothing left for you. Get him the hell out of my sight."

I cover a laugh with a cough, taking in the apoplectic look contorting Thorne's face. He struggles as Levi and Jude take him to the hall, his shouts audible as we follow out. People start receiving emails with their severance bonuses and the commotion explodes all around Thorne as he's dragged off by our boys.

Not such a proud King now, is he? His beloved legacy is in shambles. Obliterated. Wiped out from the city's history.

Without their business empires and their wealth, the Kings are worthless to the people they seek to partner with outside of the city's circle of money. I doubt they're a giving bunch who will help each other out. They don't know the true meaning of pledging loyalty when their values are based in their hungry greed for power.

Hugo Nicholas Thorne is on his own now.

One by one, they'll all fall down. One by one, we'll burn these bastards to the ground.

CHAPTER THIRTY-THREE
COLTON

Rɪᴅɪɴɢ the successful high of sticking it to Wren's dad earlier in the day, I've waited eagerly for this moment to arrive.

Baron Astor is glassy-eyed and swaying slightly when he exits The Royal Crown, the favored gentleman's club with a cigar lounge that has the patronage of most wealthy men in town. It's somewhere he's comfortable. Somewhere he feels untouchable because we've never stepped foot inside.

But we never needed to. Not when we had someone who owed us a favor on the wait staff. The guy almost shit himself when Wren and I stepped out of the shadows in the alley behind the discreet staff exit two nights ago to call in the favor we've held on to for close to three years.

It doesn't matter how long, the Crows always come to collect.

Baron never saw us coming with this plan, not because it's our best ever, but because it hinges on using his own arrogance and his belief that we'll never beat him. He's a shrewd, intelligent man whose downfall is relaxing when he's in a space where he feels in control.

"Right this way sir. We hope you enjoyed your evening." I direct him with a white-gloved hand to the town car idling at the curb at the end of the red awning protruding from the club.

Levi stole it from his uncle's estate so we wouldn't cause alarm to anyone who could be watching. He's waiting inside to incapacitate him for a little nap while we ditch the car and meet up with the others where we stashed our rides for phase two of this epic takedown. Or phase three, if we're counting smashing Thorne's world to dust earlier today.

Baron pauses, peering at me. His pupils are blown. There's no recognition. I smirk, tugging the driver's cap down to keep it that way.

"Merry Christmas, sir," I say.

Baron waves a hand—well, he attempts to, points for effort—and stumbles his way to the car. I open the door for him and flash Levi a smug look of triumph. His dark gaze shifts to his inebriated uncle and hatred contorts his brooding features.

Shutting the door, I circle around the car at a quick clip and slide behind the wheel. Baron's out, mouth slack and head lolling to the side. Still breathing. Good. I was a little worried Levi might decide to screw the plan and seek his own retribution—which I'd stand by one hundred percent. What we have planned for this bastard is better than a quick death, something that will twist the knife in a far more satisfying way.

I adjust the mirror to meet my brother's eye. "Look at you, not stabbing first, asking questions later. That's growth, my friend. Isles does you so much good."

"He deserves to die," Levi grits out while bringing his blade closer to his uncle's bulging neck. He halts, touching the razor sharp knife to the skin without piercing it, exercising impressive control when he has the man he hates most in this world at his mercy. "But I want everyone to know what he's done."

My grip tightens on the wheel. After learning that Quinn's family was another victim of Baron's unstoppable greed, I want the same. Every member of the Kings Society is going down until we dismantle them entirely.

The drive through downtown to the secluded street we selected as our rendezvous point isn't far. It's a route I picked because it utilizes CCTV blindspots so it'll be harder to track if anyone alerts the authorities. Within ten minutes of winding through the streets, I park behind Levi's replacement for the SUV that got trashed when the hotel burned down.

Wren and Jude come around to Levi's side to help move Baron while I strip off the driver's gloves, jacket, and hat, rustling my hair. Quinn stands next to the girls with her arms folded around herself and her lip curled in disgust when the guys cart his unconscious body from the ditched town car to Levi's Escalade. Rowan and Isla keep watch until they finish.

"Stay close, but don't make it look like we're a caravan," Wren directs. "We don't need any unwanted attention. I don't want to alert any Thorne Point police with suspicious activity. It's Christmas Eve and they'll be antsy. We'll ride out first, then Levi's car."

"We've got the caboose." I mime pulling a train whistle and Quinn claps a hand over my mouth before I get the sound out. I smirk against her palm, kissing it. She drops it away, hiding a small smile. "The hard part's over."

Levi cocks his head. "We'll see. Don't relax just yet."

"See you there." Swinging my keys around my finger, I reach for Quinn automatically as the others split up between the three cars.

"I can't believe that worked," she says when we get into my ride. "He doesn't have any security?"

"Too proud for it." I shift the Mustang in gear and pull out to follow the others. "As far as we know, only guys like Fitzy keep those ex-military clowns around. We encountered one of their private security teams at the Castle but it was more like a skeleton crew. They all think they're untouchable because of the society."

"Probably Snyder, too." She sighs. "I just don't want any surprises."

"We'll be fine."

I trail behind Wren's new Bugatti and Levi, not worried about how many cars enter traffic between us. We pre-planned the path to wind our way to our destination, so I don't have to stay close.

The streets at the busy heart of the city are packed with last minute shoppers hitting the holiday market in central downtown, people going out for a holiday dinner, and visiting loved ones. A light snow flurry makes the road glisten.

Drumming my fingers absently on the wheel, my focus moves to the mirror. An SUV catches my eye. Something makes me look again. An instinct I've honed from the work my boys and I do after dark.

It changes lanes to pass a car. A block later, it moves into the lane I take for our turn. I narrow my eyes, playing with my tongue piercing. Every few moments, I watch what the car does. It could be nothing. Or it could be what the pit in my stomach is telling me. Damn it.

The SUV moves again, passing another car to slowly gain on us. Only three cars away now. My gut clenches and an ominous feeling passes over me. We're being followed.

"Colton."

I tear my suspicious squint from the rearview mirror to glance at Quinn. She's spotted the guy too, her eyes wide.

"I know." My jaw works and I watch the car moving through traffic, following every move we make. "I see it."

"It has to be them, right? They've let us go after people without trying to stop us, other than Tanner Sosa going for us on Mortimer's boat." She runs a hand over her head. "Shit. We have to lose them."

"Yeah."

She's right. If we don't lure them away, this could make the whole plan fall apart. This is our shot. If we mess this up, we'll never get close to Baron again. I'm not risking it and I don't have time to warn the others. They'll know the plan comes first.

Turning at the next light instead of following the others ahead, I watch behind me, waiting until the moment the SUV follows. Game fucking on, bastard.

At first I keep my speed the same, long enough to ensure the others have reached their destination. When the tail is only one car away, I floor it to make it through a light just as it turns red.

Quinn curses. "He ran the light."

"Don't hold your breath for TP police to nab him for it." The road is slick from the fresh snow and my Mustang skids around the next corner.

"Can you lose him?" She twists to peer through the rear windshield.

"No sweat," I say lightly.

She stares at me. "Don't even play."

"I turn to humor as a coping mechanism." I flash her a wild grin. "Weren't we saying everything's been easy street? I could do with a car chase. It's good for the constitution."

"Oh my god." Quinn's head hits the headrest as she looks up. "Granny, do you see this fool? Why couldn't you send me a nice boy?"

"Admit it, babe. You don't want nice. No one wants nice." I rev the engine with a smirk, pulse kicking up in a way I'm addicted to. "Bad boys do it all better. Fucking. Loving. It's the intensity."

She scoffs. "I'm not having this conversation in the middle of losing a tail."

I shrug. "You started it."

We go around in circles, creating a confusing game of cat and mouse to keep the SUV on us long enough for the others to be in the clear. I make turns at random, splitting my attention between gauging the best route to take and doing the opposite of that when it's feasible to trick the driver.

It's when I start to put effort into losing the tail that things get hairy. The SUV speeds up, not messing around anymore. Shit.

I take the next turn and it cuts right across the curb, knocking a trashcan off the pavement to make up the distance. We weave between cars as I head for the outer streets of the city where there won't be as much traffic. It allows me to accelerate, but it gives the SUV the same advantage and it's gaining on us.

"We should get married."

"What?" Quinn darts a wide-eyed look from me to our tail. "You're spewing crazy shit."

"What's crazy about wanting to spend my life with the most beautiful girl I've ever known? I'm just trying to lighten the mood. This douchebag's killing my vibe and I'd rather see my baby smiling."

The idea of marrying her isn't technically new, not after finding out she's the elusive Queen_Q who had me under her spell. I was half in love with her brilliant mind without even knowing her, and the fact that it was her all along?

Yeah. Whether it's an impulsive act that happens like this or in another ten years, I'm all in for her. She's it for me.

"Really? You're joking about this now?"

"Seems appropriate." I hitch a shoulder, knuckles turning white from my grip on the wheel when the dick chasing us down rams my Mustang from behind. She yelps and I hate the terror in it when all I want right now is to make her smile and hear her gorgeous laugh. "High-tension. Not sure if we'll live or die."

"Forget that. Focus on losing Sosa!"

This is helping me focus. It's drawing my thoughts away from the death knell beating in my chest.

"What, you don't want to marry me, babe? I'd be excellent hubby material. Actually, wait, scratch that because I'm new to the whole one person that's my entire goddamn world thing, but—"

She smacks her palm on the dash. "Are you seriously trying to propose to me while we're in a car chase?"

"Propose? Nah. I'm trying to wifey your ass right here, right now. I can do it." I waggle my brows while speeding down a clear straight away. "I'm ordained."

She's stunned speechless for a moment, then shakes her head as she blurts, "Why?"

"Idle minds."

The Mustang outmatches the blacked out SUV in speed and handling the whipping turns around city corners. Just when I think it will be fine, we'll get out of this, Sosa rams into us a second time.

"Fuck!" Instinct and the panging ache in my chest drives me when I reach for her, grasping her hand. She holds on tight like she always does. "If we don't make it out of this—"

"Don't say that!"

I don't have time. My heart is racing, blood rushing in my ears, every screech of tires and the speedometer dial ticking higher and higher sending my nervous system into overdrive. There's so much I want to say. To my brothers. To her.

"Shh, I'm serious, baby. This is important. I just want you to know, I'm in love with you." I risk a glance at her because if we're going to die here, I want her face to be the last thing I see. "Never expected to find love, and I don't think there will ever be anyone else I could ever feel the same about. You're my queen, Q."

"Fuck," she chokes out. "I love you too, asshole. I need you. That wasn't supposed to happen. I don't do needing people, but you're my vital piece."

Her voice breaks and it slices into my heart. "Without you, it's game over. I wouldn't survive it. But we're surviving this, goddamn it. Now get us the fuck out of this so I can kiss you!"

We both duck at the sharp squeal of tires and a deafening bang followed by a crunch, but I have control of the car. Confusion tugs at my brain. I'm unable to focus on anything except driving us the hell away. Quinn twists, eyes wide. In my periphery, I make out orange light flickering across her features. My gaze snaps to the rearview mirror and my heart stumbles in relief and shock.

The SUV lost control. That was the noise we heard. It keeps rolling, flames from the smoking, crushed engine and sparks from the metal scraping across the road flying out.

I slow the Mustang and throw the car in park, not caring that we're still in the middle of the road. This street's empty except for the burning hunk of metal several hundred feet back.

"Shit." My throat is hoarse. "That was way too damn close for comfort."

She angles an *are you serious* look at me, brows lifted, mouth parted. "You think?"

I lean my head back against the seat, a strained laugh escaping me. I don't feel much like laughing, but it comes out anyway, the mind's odd defensive response against a traumatic event. She breathes raggedly, rubbing her forehead. When my hands stop shaking from adrenaline after a few seconds, I unbuckle my belt, my need for her flooding my senses. A small, desperate sound catches in her throat as I move my hands over her in a flurry, then cradle the back of her neck to tug her to me across the center console.

"Come here, beautiful."

"Colt—" Quinn gasps in a strained tone, twisting her grip in my hoodie.

We crash together in a wild kiss, breathing each other in, each frenzied slide of our lips and tongues tinged with the intensity of our passion, of what we made it through, of being fucking alive.

My phone vibrates in my pocket. It's been going off nonstop, but awareness filters back in now that my focus isn't solely on survival and saving my girl.

Wrenching away, I dig my phone out and answer it. "You're interrupting a we-just-survived-kiss."

"Survived—what? Jesus fucking christ, where the hell are you? We've been calling for fifteen minutes. What happened?" Jude demands. "You were following and then we lost you."

"Someone tailed us after we left. We think those ex-special forces guys the society uses as their guard dogs. I didn't want them to stop what we have planned." Blowing out a breath, I scrub my face. "I lured them away and they took the bait. Minor detour. We're still downtown, near the outskirts."

"Shit. Did you lose them?"

"Ehh." I glance back at the smoke rising into the flurries of snow. "Yes?"

Quinn snorts and raises her voice loud enough for Jude to hear. "They rolled and crashed."

There's muffled chatter in the background as Jude relays my explanation to the others.

"Give me that." Wren's voice grows louder when he takes the phone. "Are you both okay?"

"Debatable." I pull a face. "On most days I'm okay. I'm known to lash out when I'm moody, but you love me for it anyway."

"Goddamn it, Colt—"

"We're alive." I reach for Quinn's hand, lips quirking into a smile when she laces her fingers with mine. "We're on our way to you now. It's time to end this."

CHAPTER THIRTY-FOUR

QUINN

I'M still on edge after the car chase. We didn't hang around long enough to see if Tanner Sosa survived the crash that totaled his SUV or not. The dark room isn't helping calm my rapid heartbeat.

Or maybe it's because the man who imploded my life for his own greed sits across from me lit by two studio lights Colton set up.

Retribution is within reach at last. I've waited a long fucking time to see this man brought down.

Colton nods to me after he finishes placing portable mini diffusers around the room along with small speakers. I start the sound recording he mixed, the room blanketed by white noise that creates the vibe we're in the woods with rustling trees. Then I check the video stream is ready to go with the settings picking up a decent view of where we really are, shooting him a thumbs up. He taps Levi on the shoulder, handing him a Santa mask.

"Really?" Levi pulls a face. "Get that shit away from me."

"What?" Colton shakes it. "You knew we'd make you wear something. We're streaming this."

"I don't need that. I've waited too damn long for this. He should look me in the eyes when he ties his own noose."

"Just do it," Jude says. "He's a smart man. High or not, he'll figure it out."

Levi grumbles, snatching the cheerful mask from Colton. Wren snorts at him once he pulls it on and tugs the hood of his black sweatshirt over his head.

"I'm taking a picture," Colton wheezes through laughter.

Levi pulls a knife and points it at him. "You do, and you're dead."

Colton smirks, holding his hands up, one of them clutching his phone. He edges behind Jude as Levi stalks him around the room. Rowan laughs under her breath, hovering behind me, and mumbles what idiots they all are. The affection in her tone is evident.

"But they're our idiots," Isla murmurs from her seat beside me.

Wren sobers and turns his attention to Baron. "Wake him up. Let's do this."

"Can I tase him?" I reach for my backpack.

"Stay back there," Levi grumbles. "Be ready to turn that shit on."

I exhale, nostrils flaring. Crossing my arms, I lean back in my chair. Isla pats my leg.

"Ask him again after. Then you can give that prick a good jolt."

Colton snorts, glancing between the controls on his tablet and the two Astor men. Shaking my head, I start the livestream.

Levi pounds his fist on the desk between them. Baron jerks into consciousness, casting a wild-eyed look around, landing first on Levi, then squinting against the bright studio lights. The plan to disorient him is working.

"What is this?" He narrows his glassy eyes. "What have you done?"

"You've been wicked, Baron," Colton says into a small microphone attached to his tablet. It comes out of Levi's mask in a modulated voice as he stands ominously before Baron. "So many reasons to be on Santa's naughty list."

Baron scoffs, his glare rankling me. His pupils are blown from the ecstasy they dosed him with at the gentleman's club and his mood is irritable. There's still enough of it in his system to dampen his inhibitions, making him more prone to reacting.

"Levi," Baron says. "That's you, isn't it, my boy?"

He doesn't respond.

I'm a bit surprised he worked it out so quickly, even with his brain addled by a night of indulgence plus the drugs the waiter slipped into his drink.

"It's gauche of you to kidnap your uncle and take him to one of your torture rooms. Tied me up."

He's not tied up. We only draped some nylon climbing rope over his arms. His mind did the rest under the influence of the drug.

Baron's mouth curves in a sickening, proud smile. "After all I've done for you to cover up your violent tendencies? Though you do have what it takes to carry on my legacy. My worthy son."

Levi rips off the Santa mask, forgoing the plan. "I am not your son."

Wren's hand curls into a fist, the crack of his knuckles audible. He holds out an arm to stop me as I hover my finger over the button to end the livestream early.

"Not yet," he says quietly. "Not until we have what we need."

Baron laughs. "Oh, but don't you see? You are. You are Leviathan Astor, crafted by my hand in every way. You walk the path I laid out before you to lead you to greatness. To lead you to the day you accept what you cannot deny: this—" He holds up a hand, displaying a gilded ring on his pudgy pinkie finger with a pair of crossed keys. "—is where you belong. There is no alternative."

"No," Levi snarls. "You don't get it, old man. You're done."

"Go on, then." Baron's amusement grows. "You dragged me all the way out of the city. Get on with what you prepared before I walk out the door unscathed."

"You're a man on top of the world," Levi mutters.

Baron shrugs arrogantly. "I climbed my way to the top."

I hold back a snort. Sure. By detonating everything in his path to conquer it.

"On the backs of others." Levi leans into Baron's face. "A climb stained in blood."

"There's no success without a little bloodshed. It's how the world works. This is how the Astors have built our empire for generations. We seek out the weak and take what they do not deserve. The world rewards those who are strong enough to take what they desire. *Carpe regnum*. That's what I strive for."

Baron's proud grin is nauseating, his words turning my stomach.

"You and your friends know how true that is, don't you? Are they here, too?"

He searches the darkness at the edges of the lights trained on him, releasing a chilling laugh out of nowhere. Wren mutters angrily under his breath and Jude crosses his arms.

Colton's jaw clenches. "He's even fucking creepier high on Molly."

Levi regains his attention. "You have no honor. All you care about is your power. I won't rest until I strip it from you."

Baron snorts. "Please. You sound like Nathan. So goddamn noble with that bleeding heart of his. How funny how that works out, given that I'm the one who raised you after he died. He hardly influenced you at all, yet still you think similarly. A pity. At any rate, do what you must. You can't stop me, and it's not as though you have the balls to kill me. He certainly didn't before I got to him first."

"He was your business partner. Your best friend. Why orchestrate the kidnapping of his wife and son? Me," Levi snaps. "I was only seven, you goddamn monster. Just a fucking kid, but I was disposable. My mom was disposable as long as you achieved your means. Is that what you intend for me to inherit as your named heir?"

Baron grows annoyed, his mood swiftly changing with his inhibitors at the mercy of the MDMA's effects. He grips the armrests of the high back leather chair, sending the nylon rope to the floor with a soft rustle and releases an irritable noise.

"Your father was a visionless coward. That was why he had to go." Baron's angry spittle catches in the light. "I had to take control. He was too spineless to take our company where it could really go. Buying him out was too simple." He jerks his head. "True, the kidnapping didn't go according to plan. But I got my end goal once your father was out of the picture. I always get my end goal, boy. You should know that very well by now. I've acquired countless fortunes of others too stupid to hold on to their assets by force and dealt with numerous others like your father who tried to stand in my way. No matter what, I will rise to the top."

Just like Mortimer's downfall after the yacht party, the public stock value for Astor Global Holdings drops at a rapid rate before my eyes when the numbers update in the window I have open beside the livestream as he boasts about all he's done.

Victory burns within me, a strong, brightly glowing flame that will never snuff out. He can't hide behind his money or his name anymore. His sinister greed is out in the open. The world will see him for what he truly is, a parasite that needs to be eradicated.

Levi's shoulders form a rigid line. "And your sister?"

Baron's features twist with a merciless bark of laughter. "Weak. A pitiful whore. Your mother was as weak as your father. She couldn't overcome a simple kidnapping and succumbed to her pathetic mind. If she hadn't, I would've taken her life myself sooner or later."

With a jagged, lethal roar, Levi stabs his blade into the table between him and his uncle. "They raped her." His growl is deadly. "And that's your great legacy? Those are the standards for *carpe regnum*? Fucking bullshit."

Isla releases a faint, pained sound, holding a hand over her heart. I reach over and squeeze her knee in support.

"Now," Wren commands in a quiet, brutal tone.

Narrowing my stinging eyes in horrified disgust, I type with harsh keystrokes to bring the lights up in the room, showing Baron he's in his own office, seated at his desk and not some remote location like he believed. He peers around in confusion until he registers what's past the studio lights that blinded him—us. The cameras.

"No." His eyes bulge and his red face pales. "No, tell me you haven't— that you didn't, you stupid boy."

"I didn't," Levi says flatly. "You did. All I did was ask questions. The truth came from your own mouth, you son of a bitch."

"No," he repeats, angrier this time.

A greed-fueled man who believes he was untouchable at the top with his power stripped away.

For a moment he's frozen, then in a flurry of action, he rummages through a drawer and pulls out a gun with a garbled yell, his mind snapping. We all freeze as he waves the weapon while shouting in delirious rage. Wren, Jude, and Rowan draw their guns, training them on him. Colton curses, reaching across me to cut the livestream. He keeps me behind him, grip tight on my wrist as he backs us further away.

"Stay down," he orders. "I won't let anything happen to you."

"You will not ruin me!" Baron yells, unhinged. "No one will take this from me!"

Taking aim at the large floor-to-ceiling glass windows, he fires three shots. The glass cracks, splinters running out from the center in ominous webs, then the window shatters. He doesn't look back before he flings himself through the window and plummets from the high rise office.

"What the fu—no!" Levi rushes over, slamming his hand against the steel frame with a curse. "God fucking damn it!"

My fingers clench the back of Colton's jacket, eyes wide at what just happened.

Isla recovers from the shock blanketing all of us first, rushing to his side. Colton and I follow a beat later, crowding next to them. Cold air whips into the room as we take in Baron's gruesome demise splattered across the ground far below.

Did he hallucinate that he was escaping? Or did he truly understand he was taking his life instead of facing the fallout?

"Pride goeth before the fall." Colton swipes a hand over his mouth. "Literally."

"I hope that bastard rots in hell," Levi growls. "He got what he deserved in the end, even if I didn't have the satisfaction of finishing him myself."

"Amen," I say in a tight voice.

He tears his gaze from the horrible sight below and nods to me. I return it, the knot of tension in my stomach loosening. Isla murmurs to Levi and slips her hand into his. His gruff reply is too low for me to hear, but he rests his forehead against hers.

Turning my back on the broken body of the man who destroyed my family and took everything from us, I silently send a prayer to my grandmother. It's over now.

Colton's arm winds around me and we step over broken glass to get back to Wren, Rowan, and Jude.

"We should get out of here," Rowan says. "Before the cops get here. Someone's bound to come across his body soon and report it."

Jude pulls a face. "Yeah. There's one in particular I don't want to see."

As they pack up the equipment, my gaze drifts to the window Baron shot out and jumped from. I hug myself as my granny's husky laughter fills my head. He's the catalyst that took her from me and I miss her every day.

"You good?" Colton buffs my arms, stepping close. His lips connect with my forehead. "Talk to me."

"I'm good." I turn into him, because I don't have to survive on my own anymore. "Let's get the hell out of here."

CHAPTER THIRTY-FIVE

QUINN

A FEW days later, we're enjoying our own bubble in Colton's apartment. We've been here since Christmas Eve and spent Christmas here.

Sammy stopped by to hang out with us in the afternoon. Before he left, Levi came over and handed us both paperwork and financial statements. We gaped at each other once we finished reading them. With Baron dead, Levi's the sole heir to the Astor estate and his business. He repaid every cent his uncle stole from our family, as well as others who faced the same by dissolving the business. On top of the investment account Colton set up for me and the opportunity he acquired for Sampson, we're set for life.

Colton interrupts me while I'm laying in bed playing a round of online poker. It's no longer about the money, just the enjoyment of the game and playing the players to win.

"Come here." He sets the laptop aside with barely contained excitement. He's been out in the main room for most of the night, telling me I wasn't allowed to come out to see what he was doing.

"I was about to win." I squint, getting up. "What's that look on your face for?"

"What look? This is just my handsome face. A face you love, might I remind you." I huff, rolling my eyes fondly and he kisses my cheek. "Now close your eyes. I have a surprise."

"What? Christmas is over. What are you up to?"

"Woman, you're killing me. Stop peeking." He covers my eyes with his hands and murmurs in my ears. "I'm trying to be sweet here."

"Oh yeah?" I don't fight the affectionate smile that breaks free.

He kisses my neck. "Because queens need to be worshiped."

I hum, reaching back to slide my fingers through his hair. "Your tongue is good at worshiping. Are you getting on your knees?"

He bites back a rough sound, the hard line of his body shuddering against me. "Shit. In a minute, I will be. You know how much I love to eat you, baby. I'm always hungry for your taste."

Colton drags a hand down to my hip and guides me from his bedroom. Since we've been staying at his apartment instead of the Nest now that the club is open, I haven't thought about venturing back into the haven I carved out for myself when I lived here before under false pretenses.

Everywhere he is—that's my haven now.

"Okay. Open your eyes."

When I do, my brows jump up. The desk used to only hold Colton's dual monitor custom build. I always admired it. Okay, maybe I envied it, because that system is a sexy piece of hardware and specs.

Now there are two desks. Two custom-built computer systems. Side by side, facing out to the huge windows that overlook the magnificent view of the city.

"You built me a computer?" I turn to him, heart climbing into my throat.

"Yes. Now you won't steal mine." He chuckles. "It's got the latest processor, a fifteen terabyte SSD, and maxed out memory. All built with high performance in mind, just like mine."

Other than my Vespa, my refurbished laptop was the only other prized possession I ever purchased for myself. I got by on the limitations of the only hardware I could afford to have a semi-decent device. All of my previous computers have been cobbled together and used. This is the first time I've had something brand new.

I coast my hand over the colorful backlit keyboard, eyes shining. "I love it."

"I want you to move in with me. Kind of backwards since I asked you to marry me first, but yeah." He rustles his hair, flicking his gaze between the his and hers computer setup and me. "Say yes?"

My heart clenches at the uncertainty in his tone. As if I'd say no. I need him. "Duh."

He pushes out a relieved breath and wraps me in his arms. "Good. That's good."

I bite my lip around a smile. "Can we break it in? First to access a restricted government branch gets victory head."

"Mm, baby. I love playing hacker versus hacker with you." He draws me into a kiss. "I'll definitely take you up on that challenge in a minute."

He herds me over to the floor-to-ceiling windows and makes me face out to the city, fitting himself behind me. I lean against him, enjoying the way he slips his hand beneath my shirt to caress my stomach while he tucks his face into my throat and breathes me in.

"You're my everything, Quinn. I'm all in with you."

My love for him crashes over me. I twist to kiss him when he lifts his head, pouring everything I feel into it. His embrace tightens and my heart thumps.

He rests his forehead against mine and I smile softly. "I'm all in, too."

We don't need anything more than this at the moment. The connection of touching each other while we look out at Thorne Point. This is where I'm meant to be, right here in his arms.

* * *

Our first club night at The Crowned Crow since we took on Wren's dad and Levi's uncle coincides with New Year's Eve. The gritty speakeasy converted from the old warehouse is packed tonight, each balcony tier decorated with black, silver, and gold streamers.

We hang out at the main bar, people watching.

"You'll kiss me at midnight, won't you?" Colton gives me one of his cocky grins he believes is so charming. "It's almost time."

I smirk, planting a hand over his face and shoving playfully. "Maybe I'm keeping my options open. That guy over there is cute. Or maybe her."

He scoffs, locking his arms around my waist to haul me against him. "Don't think you'll kiss anyone else." His lips graze my ear and I shiver at the intensity in his murmured words. "I might seem like a very charming, lovable jokester, but you'd better believe if I catch anyone touching you, they're dead. You're mine, baby."

"No, pretty boy. You're *mine*."

My safety net. My heart. My permanent home I've been searching for.

I serve him a sly look that matches the mischief-tinged reverence in his gaze, holding up a balled fist, each of my stacked gold rings catching the light. "And if anyone tries anything with you, they'll learn what happens when they fuck around with me."

"Goddamn, I love you. My fierce, brave little fighter." He captures my mouth in a kiss that pierces my heart.

"Back at you," I murmur against his lips.

A whoop from Isla distracts us. She beams at us as her and Levi come off the dance floor, his hands glued to her hips. He motions to the bartender and lifts Isla to sit on the bar stool, pressing against her back.

Wren and Rowan slipped off to the shadows, and Jude is with Penn and the pretty girl with him on the first balcony level.

"Isn't that your brother?" Isla points Sampson out at the other end of the bar with a blonde girl.

I'll still always be protective of my brother, though I no longer feel like I need to fight so hard to do it. I'm not surviving on my own anymore. We're both grown. We made it through, and things have turned around for us, bringing us back to the life we were always supposed to have.

"Oh shit, look." Colton taps Levi's arm with the back of his hand. "That's one of the Castle girls, isn't it?"

"Looks like it," he confirms.

"She was here for the broadcast," I say as I recognize her.

"I'm glad." Isla leans against Levi's chest. "Life goes on. We all find our way to survive."

His arms circle her waist in a fierce embrace and he kisses her cheek. Her words arrow through my heart and I nod as Colton rubs my lower back.

"When do you want to do it?" he asks.

"What?" I squint at him, a smile breaking free.

He does this so often, chasing thoughts in his head and picking up a conversation as if I'm aware of what's on his mind. Sometimes I figure it out, because we're wired the same, more similar than either of us realized. This is one of the times I'm not sure where his mischievous impulses will take us. It sends a thrill through me to entertain the possibilities.

"Lock it down, baby." He flashes me his left hand, wiggling his ring finger. "We can get Lev to be our ring bearer—except he'd probably bring the rings on the end of one of his knives."

"Shut up," Levi grunts while Isla laughs.

Colton cracks up, burying his amusement in my shoulder. His laughter dies off and he trails kisses up my neck.

The DJ makes an announcement that we're a minute away from the new year.

"Come on, we have to be out there for this!" Isla tugs on Levi's hand and waves for us to follow.

Colton doesn't let me go as we weave through the dance floor, making our way to the center. The crowd starts the countdown to the New Year. As they reach one, they erupt in cheers around us, but I have eyes only for my man.

"Midnight."

The crooked tilt of Colton's mouth sends a flutter through my stomach. He bats away gold confetti and tugs me against him, arms snaking around my waist.

He kisses me with a smile that makes happiness rise within me. It's a feeling I never thought I could claim for myself again.

Confetti streams down around us and we don't stop kissing.

CHAPTER THIRTY-SIX
COLTON

New Year's Day is quiet the morning after an epic club night. Quinn's not fully awake when I drag her downstairs, half carrying her until I pause to haul her up in a piggy back. She sleepily loops her arms around my neck and plants soft kisses on the Crow tattoo covering my throat.

"Should I turn right back around and fuck you awake, little queen?" I rasp.

She hums. "Coffee."

Chuckling, I readjust her on my back and continue downstairs.

Wren and Rowan are up, murmuring to each other at the middle of the dance floor while they sway in a circle to a tune only they can hear. He dips his head to capture her mouth in a languid kiss and her arms wrap around him.

Passing by them, I deposit Quinn at a seat in the booths lining the edge of the ground level. She stretches, my stolen Lord of the Rings shirt draping off her shoulder tempting me to take her right back up to our room.

"Morning," she mumbles to Rowan and Wren when they come over.

"Hey," Rowan greets.

Jude stumbles in from the room he picked off the secret passage leading to the basement. His thick hair sticks up on end at the back as he blinks at us blearily.

"Morning, handsome," I tease as I take a seat across from Quinn. "Looks like you had a good night."

He makes a semi-intelligible noise, pushing his shirt up to scratch at his tawny, trim stomach while he yawns.

Levi and Isla are the only two that look alert as they come down from their room on the second balcony tier freshly showered. The brightness in Isla's eyes and the looseness of Levi's limbs tells me they've been up for a while.

"Last night was amazing," Isla says.

Wren's lips twitch and he looks around us. "It was."

I pull a card deck out of my pocket and Quinn perks up. "Play me?"

"You know it, babe." I shuffle the deck, pulling a few flashy tricks that make her grin.

Isla scoots in next to me. "Are you going to play poker? I want to watch."

"I'll do you one better. We'll teach you to play." I wink and her eyes light up.

"Which target will we hit next?" Levi asks. "We can't take a break for too long. The list isn't done."

"I've got some potentials cooking," I confirm.

"We'll go pick up coffee and donuts first," Wren says. "Then we can decide together."

Rowan leans into his side, faceplanting against his chest. Her words come out muffled. "God, yes. I need the biggest coffee."

Wren huffs in amusement, circling her in his embrace. "When don't you, my little monster?"

"Exactly." Rowan grins. When he lets her go, she snags Levi's sleeve and pulls. "We'll need help carrying enough for everyone."

"Fine." He kisses Isla's temple, rubbing her back. "You coming, princess?"

"I want to learn how to play. Love you." She gets up from the booth and presses on her toes to kiss him. "Bring me a strawberry frosted donut, please."

"Later." I nod to them with my chin as I deal cards. "Now, Isles, pay close attention. The first thing every good player has to learn is how to cheat."

Quinn kicks at me from across the table, clicking her tongue. "Psh, don't even listen to him." I grin at her, blowing a kiss. She smirks, dipping her chin, her brightly patterned silk head wrap catching the light. "Come sit with me. I'll show you the skill you need to win."

"Those are fighting words, baby." I throw down the first card. "I'm gonna kick your ass."

She grins. "Yeah, you wish though. You haven't beat me yet, and I'm keeping it that way."

During our second round, the door opens and Pippa hurries in. "Jude?" She spots us in the booth and heads our way. "I'm glad you're here."

Jude's hard stare bores into her. "The fuck are you doing here? Don't tell me you're hoping to raid fight night." He checks his bare wrist. "You're early. They haven't started back up yet."

She glances at the rest of us, then lowers her voice. "No, I came to see you. I have to talk to you."

He shakes his head, getting up to herd her away from the table. "Not interested after that shit you pulled."

"Jude, come on. Please." She grabs the sleeve of his hoodie, tugging. "Just give me ten minutes."

A bitter laugh falls from his lips and he doesn't bother to keep his voice from carrying. "We both know it was always far more than ten minutes, baby girl. The way you'd scream for me..."

Quinn clears her throat, shooting me a disapproving glance at my obvious eavesdropping. I hold my hands up with an unapologetic lopsided smile.

"Don't look at me like that, babe. They're the ones interrupting our card game."

Isla pinches my bicep. "We should let them talk. Maybe they'll work things out between them. I hope so, anyway." She leans in to whisper to the two of us, glancing at Jude and Pippa. "That look he gets on his face when she's around seriously breaks my heart."

"Isles, you sweet summer child." I chuck her under the chin. "Don't hold your breath."

Just because Jude and Pippa are soulmates doesn't mean they're right for each other. All they do is cause destruction when they're close enough to set each other off.

The door opens again, drawing our attention. My playful smirk drops off my face. Goddamn it. I should've reengaged the security system.

"Judge Snyder?" Pippa frowns. "What are you doing here?"

Judge Westley Fucking Snyder walks into our club like he owns the place, casting a dismissive look around at the reclaimed warehouse converted into our Nest 2.0. His shock of artificial white hair is combed back, amplifying his widow's peak hairline, and he carries his tall, thin frame with importance. His dark winter coat sweeps the floor and he comes to a stop several feet away.

"How quaint." His eerie gray eyes lock on me, then move to Jude before finding Pippa. "You were warned not to come here, no? Not very good at taking orders from your sergeant."

"Why are you here?" I stand, moving away from the table, putting the girls behind me. Jude moves with me.

"Come now, you didn't think I'd let you keep having your fun, did you?" Snyder clicks his tongue in disappointment. "I let you weed out the weak for me, but we're done with that now."

"What the fuck are you talking about?" Jude grits out.

"For the sake of appearances, I led them to believe you'd be offered positions as legacies and new blood for our kingdom." Snyder waves a hand. "I had hoped that by planting the idea in Mortimer's head, I'd be rid of you, but alas. His incompetence has reached new lows."

Shit. Fucking *shit*. It wasn't Fitz Mortimer's idea to climb the ranks within the secret society by burning down the hotel. It was Snyder pulling strings.

I knew we'd be waiting for a shoe to drop and this is it. Weed out the weak? We ruined most of who we believed to be high-ranking members in the secret society.

"You'll come with me now, Miss Bassett," Snyder says.

All of us stiffen and Jude edges in front of Pippa. I don't think he thought about it before he put himself between her and the perceived threat.

She lays a hand on Jude's arm, moving around him. "Why?"

Snyder hums. "Do you not know to do something simply because I ask? You used to be so obedient for me. Warner will need to inform you better. Tell me, who do you think allowed you back on my police force? Warner? No. It was my order."

Obedient? My gaze snaps to her. Is that why she betrayed us that night? Why she wasn't where she was supposed to be?

Her brows pinch. She seems as shocked by this as we are. I know this asshole likes to move pieces across the board without getting directly involved. Maybe she never realized. The alternative is that she's secretly been a lapdog to the Kings all along, and that's just—fuck. I can't think about it. My head is too full of questions and this needs all my focus.

"You? Your force?" Pippa reaches for the holster at her hip with measured movements.

"I wouldn't," he says, unbothered. "Yes, my force. My everything. Thorne Point is under my reign. We have controlled everything that goes on in this city since its founding. Which businesses rise up that align with our goals." He smirks at Isla. "Who gets elected to positions of power. We molded this city into our ideal image—our perfect kingdom."

Hell nah. I think the fuck not.

My fists ball. I've had enough of this bastard manipulating our lives from the shadows. It started five years ago and it hasn't stopped.

"You think you get to walk in here and control us? Screw that. This isn't like back then, you piece of shit. We're not kids you can push around anymore. We've grown the fuck up."

Gritting my teeth, I stalk to the bar and get one of the guns stashed there, taking aim at the bastard's head. The threat doesn't faze him and that pisses me off more. I stride closer, Quinn following in my wake. Reaching back, I keep her behind me when I stop at point-blank range, close enough there's no chance I'd miss when I pull the trigger and splatter Westley Snyder's brains all over our Nest.

He spares a benign glance at the gun, then lifts his gaze to mine, tilting his head like he's giving friendly advice. "If you shoot me now, you'll never see your friends alive again."

What?

I lose my breath as my mind turns, producing ten plausible scenarios, each more terrible than the last.

Fuck. *Fuck.* A tremor runs down my arm and the barrel lowers an inch. My throat burns with my thick swallow.

Isla whips out her phone and presses it to her ear, bouncing a frantic look between me and Snyder. "Pick up, pick up," she breathes. "Come on, answer your phone."

"Princess, don't—" Levi's gruff tone is interrupted by the distinct sound of gunshots, a garbled yell, and the screech of tires through the phone's speaker before it cuts out in deafening silence.

Isla releases a strangled sound, meeting my wide eyes with tears shining in hers. "The call dropped."

No. My heart drums so hard it hurts. This isn't happening again. My brothers' lives are at risk again at the hands of the Kings.

"Colt," Quinn whispers tightly. Her fingers twist in my hoodie and she presses closer, burying a pained noise against my shoulder. "We don't know what else he'll do. What if he has this place rigged? I can't lose you."

Snyder's smug grin enrages me. This isn't over. He won't fucking win.

He holds out his hand in invitation, the gilded ring on his finger unmistakable. It's the Kings Society's calling card. The crossed keys symbol found all over the city, planted there by generations of the secret society's members.

"Come along, Miss Bassett."

TO BE CONTINUED...

A THREAT TO ONE
IS A THREAT TO ALL

THANK YOU + WHAT'S NEXT

Thank you for reading A Fractured Reign! If you enjoyed it, please leave a review on your favorite retailer or book community! Your support means so much to me!

Need more Crowned Crows series right now? Have theories about which characters will feature next? Want exclusive previews of the next book? Join other readers in Veronica Eden's Reader Garden on Facebook!

Reader group: bit.ly/veronicafbgroup

Are you a newsletter subscriber? By subscribing, you can download a special bonus deleted scene for the Crowned Crows world.

Sign up to download it here: veronicaedenauthor.com/bonus-content

ACKNOWLEDGEMENTS

Reader, we've done it! We've made it to the final cliffhanger of the series. I'm sending you all my hugs for surviving them! Things have been dire and our Crows haven't had it easy, but the end is in sight. They'll survive the madness and at the end of it all, they'll each earn their HEA!

As always, I'm endlessly grateful for you! Thanks for reading this book. It means the world to me that you supported my work. I wouldn't be here at all without you! I love all of the comments and messages you send and live for your excitement for my characters! I hope you enjoyed your read!

Thanks to my husband for being you! He doesn't read these, but he's my biggest supporter. He keeps me fed and watered while I'm in the writer cave, and doesn't complain when I fling myself out of bed at odd hours with an idea to frantically scribble down.

These chaotic characters don't make my life easy to tell their saga. Thank you to Sarah, Becca, Ramzi, Sara, Kat, Jade, Mia, Erica, Bre, Heather, Katie, Jennifer, and everyone who cheered me on for keeping me arguably sane and on track until the end! With every book I write my little tribe grows and I'm so thankful to have each of you as friends to lean on and share my book creation process with!

To my lovely PA Heather, thank you for taking things off my plate and allowing me to disappear into the writing cave without having to worry. And for letting me infodump at you, because that's my love language hahaha! You rock and I'm so glad to have you on my team!

To my beta queens and sensitivity reader Mia, Katie, Erica, Bre, Jennifer, y'all I could never put books out there without you! Y'all are always amazing, but this book is what it is because of you! Thank you for reading my raw, sometimes messy words, for letting me roll into your DMs, and helping me see the forest instead of the tree. Thank you for offering your time, attention to detail, and consideration of the characters and storyline in my books!

Special shout out to @lunas_book_riot for the quote suggestion used for the epigraph!

To my street team and reader group, y'all are the best babes around! Huge thanks to my street team for being the best hype girls! To see you guys get as excited as I do seriously makes my day. I'm endlessly grateful you love my characters and words! Thank you for your help in sharing my books and for your support of my work!

Thank you to Ashlee of Ashes & Vellichor for the amazing book trailer for this series! I love the way you can look at something (or in this case, barely anything) and get it so perfectly, and I've been in awe of what you've come up with to bring my books to life!

To Shauna and Wildfire Marketing Solutions, thank you so much for all your hard work and being so awesome! I appreciate everything that you do!

To the bloggers and bookstagrammers, thank you for being the most wonderful community! Your creativity and beautiful edits are something I come back to visit again and again to brighten my day. Thank you for trying out my books. You guys are incredible and blow me away with your passion for romance!

ABOUT THE AUTHOR

STAY UP ALL NIGHT FALLING IN LOVE

Veronica Eden is a USA Today & international bestselling author of addictive romances that keep you up all night falling in love with spitfire heroines, irresistible heroes, and edgy twists.

She loves exploring complicated feelings, magical worlds, epic adventures, and the bond of characters that embrace *us against the world*. She has always been drawn to gruff bad boys, clever villains, and the twisty-turns of a morally gray character. She is a sucker for a deliciously swoony hero with a devastating smirk. When not writing, she can be found soaking up sunshine at the beach, snuggling in a pile with her untamed pack of animals (her husband, dog and cats), and surrounding herself with as many plants as she can get her hands on.

* * *

CONTACT + FOLLOW

Email: veronicaedenauthor@gmail.com

Website: veronicaedenauthor.com

FB Reader Group: bit.ly/veronicafbgroup

Amazon: amazon.com/author/veronicaeden

REVERSE HAREM ROMANCE

Standalone

Hell Gate

CONTEMPORARY ROMANCE

Standalone

The Devil You Know

Jingle Wars

www.ingramcontent.com/pod-product-compliance
Lightning Source LLC
Chambersburg PA
CBHW030707190726
48286CB00001B/211